Parker Gillmore, Lucien Biart

Adventures of a Young Naturalist

Parker Gillmore, Lucien Biart

Adventures of a Young Naturalist

ISBN/EAN: 9783337025359

Printed in Europe, USA, Canada, Australia, Japan

Cover: Foto ©Andreas Hilbeck / pixelio.de

More available books at **www.hansebooks.com**

FRONTISPIECE.

ADVENTURES

OF

A YOUNG NATURALIST.

BY

LUCIEN BIART.

EDITED AND ADAPTED BY

PARKER GILLMORE,

AUTHOR OF "ALL ROUND THE WORLD," "GUN, ROD, AND SADDLE," "ACCESSIBLE
FIELD SPORTS," ETC.

WITH ONE HUNDRED AND SEVENTEEN ILLUSTRATIONS.

NEW YORK:

HARPER & BROTHERS, PUBLISHERS,

FRANKLIN SQUARE.

1871.

PREFACE.

THERE is no country on the face of the earth that possesses greater interest in the eyes of the scientific or travelled than Mexico, the scene where the adventures so graphically and clearly narrated in this volume transpired: nor is this partiality to be wondered at when we recall to memory what a lavish hand Nature has subtended to her.

Although several of our most celebrated naturalists have climbed its lofty volcanic mountains, explored its lagoons and giant rivers, and traversed its immense forests, still, from the vast extent of that country and variety of climate —caused by difference of elevation—much yet remains to be done ere the public become thoroughly conversant with its arboreal and zoological productions.

The elephant, hippopotamus, lion, and tiger, the largest and most formidable of the terrestrial mammals of the Old World, are not here to be found; but their places are well supplied by the swamp-loving tapir, the voracious alligator, the stealthy puma, and the blood-thirsty jaguar, all well worthy of the sportsman's rifle, or of the snake-visioned native warrior's weapons—for the power of destruction in these animals during life is great, while after death they either furnish valuable skins or wholesome food. Moreover, here the wolf awakes the reverberating echoes of the forest with its dismal howl; the raccoon, opossum, and squirrel pass their lives in sportive gambols; the wild and the ocellated turkeys strut about, pompous in manner, as if conscious of their handsome plumage, while the timid deer and shaggy-coated bison roam over prairies or through woodland glades, as yet unacquainted with the report of the white man's destructive fire-arms.

Can it, therefore, be surprising that our little hero should have craved to be permitted to have a sight of this new land, so rich in the prospect of adventure. How he behaved himself throughout the numerous ordeals to which he was submitted, suffice it for me to say that his conduct was worthy of the representative of any nationality, and such as was calculated to make all parents proud off their offspring; for whether suffering from thirst or hunger, being persecuted by noxious insects, straying in the woods, even when within reach of the fiercest carnivora or in the presence of the deadliest reptiles, he never for a moment hesitated in performing his seniors' instructions, lost his courage, or, better still, an opportunity of improving his mind.

That the young English reader may benefit as much by the perusal of this work as Master Lucien, otherwise "Sunbeam," did by his journey through the Cordilleras of Mexico, and that they may enjoy the information herein imparted upon the wonderful works of the Creator, is the sincere wish of

THE EDITOR.

CONTENTS.

LIST OF ILLUSTRATIONS.

Also numerous Woodcuts embodied in, and illustrative of, the text.

INTRODUCTION.

THE evening before leaving for one of my periodical excursions, I was putting in order my guns, my insect-cases, and all my travelling necessaries, when my eldest son, a lad nine years old, came running to me in that wheedling manner — using that irresistible diplomacy of childhood which imposes on fathers and mothers so many troublesome treaties, and which children so well know how to assume when they desire to obtain a favor.

"Are you going to make as long a journey as you did last month?" he asked.

"Longer, I think; for, as we are so soon leaving for Europe, I want to complete my collection as rapidly as possible. I know you will be a good boy during my absence, and obedient to your mother. You will think of me sometimes, will you not?"

"I should much prefer *not* to think of you," he responded.

"You would rather, then, that I staid at Orizava?"

"Oh no; I should like you to go, and—to go with you."

"What can you be thinking of? Before we were a mile on the road you would be knocked up, complaining of heat, thirst, fatigue—"

"That's quite a mistake, dear father. I know I should be very useful to you, if you would only take me. I could pick up wood, light the fire, and look after the cooking, besides catching butterflies and insects, both for your collection and mine."

"That's all very well; but the first time you were scratched by a thorn you would cry."

"Oh father! I promise you I will never cry, except when—I can't help it."

I could not resist smiling at this answer.

"Then it is a settled thing, and I am to go with you," exclaimed Lucien.

"We must consult your mother, and if she sees no objection, I—"

The child ran off without allowing me to finish my sentence.

While I went on cleaning my guns, I found that I was pleading with myself in favor of the little would-be traveller. I also remembered that when I was only seven years old I had travelled long distances on foot in company with my father, and to this early habit owed much of the power of accomplishing dangerous and fatiguing journeys, which would have frightened stronger men. I even persuaded myself that it would be useful, before leaving Mexico, to impress the memory of my son with a sight of some of the grand scenes of tropical nature, so that he should retain correct ideas of the wonderful country in which his infancy had been spent. I moreover knew that l'Encuerado, the gallant Indian who had been my servant for so many years, perfectly adored his young master, and would watch over him just as I should, and thus ward off any possible mishaps. On the other hand, I risked inspiring my son with that love of travel and adventure which had contributed materially to my scientific collection, but very little to my fortune. Nevertheless, what a wholesome influence is exercised over the mind by an almost unceasing struggle with the difficulties that beset one's course through an unknown country. Both the mind and body of my son must surely benefit by such an excursion, which might be curtailed if desirable. Soon after the boy returned, accompanied by his mother.

" What is all this about a journey, for which my consent is the only requisite ?" asked my wife.

" Mine is needed too," I answered.

" Why not take him, dear ? L'Encuerado has promised me that he will not lose sight of him for an instant."

" What ! do *you* take his part ?"

" He does long so much to go with you," she said.

" Be it so," I replied. " Get your clothes ready, for we must be off the day after to-morrow at daybreak."

Lucien was almost beside himself with joy. He rushed about the house from one end to the other ; gave the servants much unnecessary trouble ; leggings, boots, and a gamebag, he wanted ; also a sword, a knife, insect-cases—in fact, a whole multitude of requirements. L'Encuerado, who was almost as rejoiced as the lad, cut him a travelling-staff, as strong and light as was requisite, and made him other auxiliaries necessary on such excursions. From this moment forward, Lucien was constantly running and climbing about all the rooms and the yards round the house, to accustom himself, as he said, to the fatigue of a long journey. At dinner-time he would take nothing but bread and water, in order to prepare his system for the meagre fare of the bivouac. In fact, I had to quiet him down by recommending more coolness to his excited little brain.

The eve of our departure arrived, and several friends came to bid me farewell. My son told them of all the great things he had determined to achieve—how he would crush the heads of scorpions, and with his sword cut down trees or kill serpents.   •

" If I tumble over the rocks," said he, " I shall only laugh at my bruises ; and if we meet with any tigers—"*

An extremely warlike attitude terminated this sentence.

Ceasing at length from want of further words, he would very willingly have reduced to silence, with his sword, those who disapproved of my project of taking into the forests and savannahs my child of nine years old, and exposing him to all the unknown dangers of savage life—to fatigue, rain, and all kinds of maladies ! Why, it appeared like tempting Providence, and risking, for mere amusement, the life, or at least the health, of my child. The unanimity of these reflections began to shake my resolution, and I expressed myself to that effect.

" Oh father !" cried Lucien, " are you going to break your word to me ?"

" No," I replied ; " neither now nor ever. I want you to become a man, so you shall go. But be off to bed, for you must be ready to start by four o'clock in the morning."

I had given notice of my intended tour to my friend

---

* The jaguar (*Leopardus onca*, Linn.) is frequently called a tiger in America. The tiger (*Tigris regalis*) is not found on that continent.—Ed.

François Sumichrast, a Swiss *savant*, well known for his dis-coveries in natural history, in whose company I had under-taken several journeys. About ten o'clock at night, I be-gan to fancy my letter of information had miscarried, when a knock at the door startled me, and I soon recognized the happy voice of my friend. He had come expressly from Cordova, in order to make one in our little expedition. I told him all my doubts and fears about my boy, but he quite took the part of the young traveller; almost what I might have expected from a companion of Töpffer.

"Come here," he cried to Lucien, who, half-undressed, had just peeped in at the door.

The boy ran to him, and my friend, whose stature much exceeded the average, lifted him up and embraced him as an ally.

"At your age," said Sumichrast, "I had made the tour of Switzerland, my bag on my back, and had tried my teeth on bears'-steaks. I predict that you will behave like a man. Shall I be wrong?"

"Oh no, M. Sumichrast."

"Can you live without eating and drinking?"

"I will do all you do."

"That's well; now go to bed. If you keep your word, when we return in a month's time you'll be a prodigy."

Next morning Lucien was up and ready long before day-break, and complained of our tardiness. He was dressed in a jacket and breeches of blue cloth, with his Mexican cloak over them; he carried in his belt a sword ready sharp-ened, to cut his way through the creeping plants; while over his shoulder was passed the strap of a game-pouch, containing a knife, a cup, and a change of under-clothing. The broad-brimmed hat, or *sombrero*, on his head, gave him a most determined air. I had almost forgotten the famous travelling-staff which for the last two days had been resounding against all the floors in the house. L'Encuerado, a Mistec Indian, and an old tiger-hunter, who, through a thousand dangers faced in common, had become much attached to my person, at last made his appearance, clad in a leathern jacket and breeches, which had given him his name of "*Encuerado.*"* The brave and adventurous Indian was almost beside himself with joy at the idea of conducting into the forest the child whom he had known from his cradle. On his back he fastened a basket containing our main stock of provisions—such as coffee, salt, pepper, dried maize, cakes, etc. Lucien's younger brother and sister had jumped out of bed, and were dancing all round us: the latter seemed somewhat sad and uneasy, but the former was dissatisfied, manfully asserting that he, too, was quite big enough to go with us.

At the last moment my poor wife lost all her courage, and regretted she had ever given her consent; but when Lucien saw the tears which his departure had called forth, he became heroic in his self-denial, throwing aside his hat and stick.

"Mother," he cried, embracing her in his arms, "I will not go away if it makes you cry."

"All right, then; I will go instead," said his brother Emile, who ran and picked up the stick and hat, and then walked towards the outer door, utterly disregarding his bedroom costume.

"No, no," said my wife; "I will not be the means of depriving you of so much pleasure."

The kind mother again kissed her child, and commended him anew to our joint care.

I led off my little companion; but when we got into the court-yard, I had to exercise all my authority to make his

---

* *Encuerado*, in Spanish, means both *naked* and *clad in leather.*

younger brother give up the stick and hat he had taken possession of. When restitution was effected, the two children kissed each other, and parted friends.

At last the outer gate was passed, and our footsteps rang through the quiet streets of Orizava. We were commencing the first stage of our journey in pursuit of scientific discoveries.

CHAPTER I.

WHO WE ARE.—GRINGALET.—SUNRISE.—THE SUGAR-CANE. —A HALT.

IT was the 20th April, 1864. The clock of the church of the convent of Saint Joseph de Grace chimed 4 A.M. just as we turned into the main street that leads out of the town.

Sumichrast took the lead. Tall in stature, noble in mien, and broad-shouldered, he was, in spite of his blue eyes and fair hair, the perfect representative of moral and bodily strength. I was always in the habit of permitting him to lead the way, when, in any of our excursions, it was necessary to favorably impress the imagination of the Indians. He was distinguished as an ornithologist, and was never so much at home as in the midst of the forests; in fact, he oft-

en regretted that he had not been born an Indian. His
gravity entirely devoid of sadness, his skill in shooting, and
his silent laugh, often led me to compare him to Cooper's
"Leather-Stocking;" but it was "Leather-Stocking" become a man of the world and of science.

Next let me describe my son. Like all children, he was
imitative, so had commenced very early to make a collection
of insects, and this was sufficient to give him a precocious
taste for natural history; but in his character he was ear-
nest and reflective, and very eager for knowledge. Sumichrast took pleasure in the boy's intelligence, and often
amused himself by arguing with him. From the flashes of

childish humor which he would display on such occasions, my friend sometimes gave him the nickname of "Sunbeam."

Next to the child came l'Encuerado, an Indian of the Mistec race—a strange mixture of delicacy, simplicity, kindness, candor, and obstinacy. In the interval that had elapsed since I first met him, twelve years before, in the Terre-Chaude, he had become my friend as much as my

servant. But he was never happy in a town, and was always praising wild life, even the inconveniences of the solitudes in which he had been born.

"What a pity that it is so dark," said Lucien, whom Sumichrast was leading by the hand.

" For what reason do you wish for daylight?" I asked.

" Why? Because every one is asleep now, and none of my friends will see me pass with my sword, my gourd, and my game-pouch."

" So you think that your travelling-costume would make your companions envious?—that's not a kind feeling."

" No, father; I should like them to see me, certainly; but I don't want to give pain to any one."

We passed along the foot of Borrego, the mountain which has become so famous, owing to the conflict which took place there between sixty French soldiers and two thousand Mexicans, and had just reached the gateway of Angostura when a dog ran past, but soon returned, barking and fawning upon us in every way. It was Gringalet, an elegantly although strongly made greyhound, which had been a companion of my boy's from infancy, l'Encuerado having brought him up " by hand " for his young master. Gringalet was an orphan from the time of his birth, and had found in the Indian a most attentive foster-parent. Three times a day he gave his adopted child milk through a piece of rag tied over the neck of a bottle. The dog had grown up by the side of his young master; many a time, doubtless, he had snatched from his hands the half-eaten cake, but such casualties were only a temporary check upon their mutual attachment. He manifested, therefore, a decided preference for three objects—Lucien, his nurse, and bottles in general. I was at first rather vexed that the poor beast should have taken upon himself the liberty of joining our expedition, so I tried to drive him back. Gringalet ran to take refuge by the side of Lucien, with ears laid back, and one paw raised; and looked at me with such mild eyes, so full of supplication, that I could not find it in my heart to carry out my intention. Sumichrast and l'Encuerado both interceded for the animal, which, crouching and wagging his tail, came and lay down humbly at my feet. Lucien, who was afraid I should behave harshly to his favorite, hid his face in his hands. I was vanquished.

"Come along, then, and let us take Gringalet!" I said.

So I caressed the dog, which, clearly seeing that he had gained his cause, bounded along the road in the most extravagant leaps, clearly indicative of his emotions of pleasure. In spite of all his efforts to keep them back, tears escaped from Lucien's eyes, and I had to turn my head away to avoid having to recall the promise he made to refrain from crying. But, nevertheless, although I wished him to learn how to bear stoically any physical suffering, I had no desire to quench in him the evidences of a feeling heart— that potent source of our sweetest pleasure and our bitterest sorrow.

The gates of the town were still closed. On arriving in front of the guard-house, I rapped at the window to awake the old man, the guardian of the keys of the town.

"Won't he open the gate for us? Shall we be obliged to go home again? Can't we start to-day, M. Sumichrast?" eagerly asked Lucien.

"Keep quiet," replied Sumichrast; "the porter is an old man, and we are disturbing him earlier than we ought, which always puts him a little out of temper. However active we may be, it is a good thing to know 'how to wait.'"

At last the door-keeper made his appearance, the chains dropped one by one, the heavy gate turned on its hinges, and Lucien was the first to spring out into the open road. The sky was starless, the morning dew chilled our blood, and we felt that uncomfortable feeling which, in the tropics, affects the traveller just at the period when night gives place to day. I led Lucien by the hand, lest, in the dim light, he might fall. He shivered with cold, but was unwilling to complain; I stepped on quickly in order that he might get warm. Perhaps, just at this moment, he regretted his little bed, and thought of the cup of warm chocolate which his mother often used to bring him as soon as he awoke; but, unmurmuring, he retained his place by my side.

Beyond the village of Ingenio, a brisk south wind blew the dust in our faces and retarded our speed. All round the trees bent before the squall, and the large plantain leaves flew about, torn into ribbons. We now turned to the right, and crossed a prairie. L'Encuerado required breath, for his load weighed at least eighty pounds, although, like Æsop's burden, it would surely get lighter at every meal. An enormous rock, which had tumbled down from one of the surrounding mountains centuries past, offered us a retreat sheltered from the wind. At this moment a line of purple edging the eastern horizon announced the dawn of day.

" Come here," I called to Lucien.

And taking the lad between my knees, I said,

" You see that bright band of light which looks almost as if the horizon was on fire? Well, from the middle of it the sun is just going to rise. At this very moment, in Europe, it is almost noonday; but, as recompense, they will have dark night when it is three o'clock in the afternoon here, and we shall be pushing along, overwhelmed with the heat of an almost vertical sun. The red line is now getting wider and paler; it is more like a golden mist. But turn round and look at the mountain tops."

The child uttered a half-surprised cry; although we were in comparative obscurity, the ridges of the Cordilleras seemed all on fire.

" Do you understand that phenomenon?" asked Sumichrast.

" Yes; for I know the earth is round, and these mountains,

2

which are higher than we are, of course first catch the rays
of the sun."

The day broke, and a burning glow suffused the horizon;
in a few minutes the sun rose and inundated us with light.
The birds began to chant their morning song, and the eagles, careering from every mountain top, soared above our
heads. The sunbeams twinkled through the dew-drops,
and the grass of the prairie seemed decked with diamonds.
Black vultures, which soared even higher than the eagles
and the kites, traced out in the blue sky the immense curves
of their majestic flight. On every bush insects spread their
gauzy wings; perhaps they felt that not a minute should
be lost by beings whose birth, life, and death are all com-
prised in one single day.

"Oh!" cried Lucien, "as soon as we get home I shall
tell mamma how beautiful is sunrise ! Is it not a shame
that so many of us sleep through the hour when this lovely prospect can only be enjoyed?"

I was obliged to cut short the little fellow's admiration—
an admiration I also shared. Each resumed his load; and
now, in spite of the wind, we all felt eager to advance.
Gringalet, as glad as we were at the return of day, frisked
round Lucien, barking, jumping over ditches, and rolling
in the dust in his wild gambols. Our young companion
began imitating his frolics; but I soon called him to order,
for our day's journey was to be as much as six to seven
leagues, and it was necessary to prevent Lucien fatiguing
himself unnecessarily.

"You always go either too quickly or too slowly," said
Sumichrast to the boy; " travellers, like soldiers, must walk
at a regular pace, so as to reach their halting-place without more than necessary fatigue. Come—form in line!
That's well; now, on we go!"

Lucien measured his steps by those of his instructor. It

"We were just then passing through a plantation."

was most amusing to see him trying to keep a pace quite at variance with the length of his short legs.

"Halt!" cried Sumichrast; "you can hardly imagine your legs are as long as mine. Perhaps in about ten years' time you may enjoy that privilege; but, in the mean time, walk naturally—without either effort or hurry. One, two, three!—now you are perfect. Keep on without noticing me; you can't walk at my pace, so I must take to yours."

As our journey was to extend to the distance of three hundred leagues, it was quite requisite that the boy should accustom himself to a regular step. After several attempts this was accomplished, and all progressed together.

We now directed our course towards the heights. Our intention was to make our way into the Cordillera, and, passing round the volcano of Orizava, to descend into the savannahs beyond, slanting off to the left so as ultimately to reach the sea. Then we thought of traversing the prairies and forests of the Terre-Chaude, so as again to come to our starting-point through the mountains of Songolica. This circuit would represent a journey of a hundred and fifty leagues as the crow flies, or at least three hundred leagues, reckoning all the circuits and bends we should be obliged to make. During this long expedition, we had made up our minds to seek, when opportunity offered, the hospitality of any Indian villages that might come in our road, and only when absolutely necessary to camp in the open air.

About eleven, the heat became overpowering, and Lucien began to inquire about breakfast. We were just then passing through a plantation, I might almost say a forest of sugar-canes. The stems of the plants were either of a yellowish hue or veined with blue, and were more than six feet high. The latter kind will ultimately supersede its rival; for the cultivators assert that, although not so large, it affords a much more certain crop. L'Encuerado, seizing his *machete* (a straight and a short cutlass, indispensable to the inhabitants of the Terre-Chaude), cut down a magnificent stem, and, peeling it, offered each of us a piece. The sugar-cane is extremely hard, and it is necessary to cut it up in order to break the cellules in which the sweet juice is contained. My companions set to work to chew the pith of the valuable plant; and even Gringalet seemed to be just as fond of it as they were.

Not far from the cane-field, some Indians were working on a new plantation. The ground was covered with ashes. The foreman explained to us that when the canes are cut down, the first thing is to pull off the long leaves, which are left on the ground. In eight days this rubbish is dried by the tropical sun; they then set them on fire, and the ashes which result serve as manure. Five or six Aztecs were cultivating this apparently sterile ground by means of a primitive kind of plough, made of a mere stake attached to circular discs of wood forming spokeless wheels; it was drawn by two oxen yoked together.

Sumichrast took Lucien by the hand.

"In future," said he, "when you crunch a lump of sugar, you shall know something of the manufacture of what you are eating. The sugar-cane is called, in Latin, *Saccharum officinale*, that is, 'druggist's sugar,' because the product of this plant was so rare that it was sold only at the druggists' shops. The plant itself is said to be a native of India, and is, as you see, a tuft of vegetation, from which spring six to twenty tall stalks, with joints varying, both in number and in distance, from each other. The most esteemed variety, the Tahiti cane, is striped with violet. The specimen you are looking at is one of the most remarkable as regards size, for it must be nearly thirteen feet high."

"It is like a stalk of maize," said the boy.

"That's true, except that maize has **only** one stem. Look, there's an Indian about to cut down **the very** plant I **was showing you;** he has severed it through obliquely at a single blow, as near the ground as possible. **Now he is stripping off the leaves, and** with another blow of **his weapon lops away the green top,** which is used for fodder. Next, he cuts it in lengths, taking care to **sever** it between the knots, as they are required for planting **new** ground."

" Planting !" repeated Lucien ; " the knots are not seed ?"

" No, Master 'Sunbeam;' the seed of the sugar - cane comes to maturity too slowly. It takes four years to produce a plant from it which **is profitable.** Now, as young fellows of your kind are rather numerous, and consume a good many preserves and **sugar-plums, it** is highly necessary to devise some **rapid method** of supplying the **sugar you devour. This** method has been found out. Each **of these pieces of cane** will be stuck into the earth, and the knot, **from which** in the open air the leaves spring, will send **down** roots into the soil. Small as it is, it will grow vigorously ; and in **a year, or** eighteen months at most, it will **have** produced a dozen stalks quite as fine as the one you have been looking at."

During this long explanation l'Encuerado, who, on account of his load, disliked standing still, had kept moving, so we had to increase our pace to catch him up. As we were passing on, Lucien saw the Indian planting the very pieces of cane he had just observed cut up. Ere long we came **upon** a fresh plantation, in which the tender shoots, almost **like grass,** appeared over the ground. Sumichrast dug a little hole round one of the plants, and showed to his wondering pupil that the fragment of the stem **was already** provided with small **rootlets.**

Suddenly, at the turn of a path, I was saluted by a man

on horseback.   It was the steward of the estate that we
were crossing.

"Hallo! Don Luciano, where are you off to with all that
train?" cried the new-comer.

"To visit the forest of the Cordillera," I replied.

"May you travel safely! but is the young gentleman going with you?"

"Yes, to be sure.   Good-bye, Antonio, till we meet
again!"

"Till we meet again?   By my word, you shall not say
that just yet.   The goodwife has some eggs and fried beans
ready for breakfast; and I ought to have some bottles of
Spanish wine, in which we'll drink to your pleasant journey, unless you're too proud to accept the hospitality of a
poor man."

Being very hungry, with pleasure we accepted this cordial
invitation.   The steward further insisted upon taking our
little traveller up in front of him.   The child was only too
pleased.

"Oh dear!" said Sumichrast; "why, it's spoiling the boy
at the outset."

"It will be half a league the less for his poor legs," said
Antonio; and, spurring his horse, he galloped off with Lucien to get our breakfast ready.

Gringalet was in consternation at his young master's departure.   Raising his intelligent face, he seemed as if he
wished to question us, and pricked up his ears as if to list-
en to the sound of the horse's feet dying away in the distance.   At last he raised a plaintive howl, and started off
in pursuit.

Surprised at not seeing l'Encuerado, I turned back, fancying he had remained behind.   I was expecting to see him
appear, when Sumichrast burst out laughing.   At a turn of
the road he had caught a sight of the horseman, with the

dog on one side and the Indian on the other, who, in spite of his load, kept up without difficulty.

This feat on the part of my servant did not much surprise me, for I do not think that in the whole world there are any more indefatigable runners than the Mistec Indians.

At twelve o'clock, just as the bell was calling home the laborers, I entered the court-yard of the sugar-mill, where I caught sight of my youngster sitting on the ground, with his dog at his feet, looking with rapture at some ducks that were enjoying themselves in a muddy pool.

CHAPTER II.

SUGAR.—GRINGALET IN THE MOLASSES TANK.—L'ENCUERA-
DO'S OBSTINATE IDEA.—AN INDIAN SUPPER.

THE breakfast was a cheerful one, thanks to the Spanish
wine spoken of by our host. The Indian laborers, with
their wives and children, assembled in inquisitive groups
round the windows of the dwelling. Lucien certainly carried the day, for he it was that they chiefly sought to see.
As for Gringalet, he was much less cordially received by
his brother-dogs belonging to the place; consequently, he
scarcely left his young master's side, and showed his teeth
incessantly.

Sumichrast wishing, before we set out again, to explain
to his pupil how sugar was made, took him to the mill, sit-

nated in a wide rotunda. Here two upright wooden cylinders, fitting close to one another, revolved on a pivot, set in action by means of two oxen yoked together, crushing the canes which an Aztec* was introducing between them. The machine groaned, and seemed almost ready to fall to pieces under the impetus of the powerful animals, which were urged on both by voice and gesture. Lucien remarked that the canes were cut in lengths of about a yard, and bevelled off at the ends, so as to be more readily caught between the two cylinders. After having been subjected to this heavy pressure, they came out squeezed almost dry, and the sweet juice, or *sirup*, flowed down into a large trough hollowed out of the trunk of a tree.

As soon as this receptacle was full of juice, an enormous valve was opened, and the turbid, muddy-looking liquid flowed along a trench, and emptied into a brick reservoir. On its way it passed through the meshes of a coarse bag, and was thus roughly filtered; it was then conveyed into immense coppers placed over a hot furnace. The fragments of crushed cane, having been rapidly dried in the sun, were used to feed the fire which boiled the juice so lately squeezed out of them.

Near the aloe-fibre filtering-bag, in front of which the morsels of cane and rubbish constantly accumulated, stood a little boy about twelve years old, whose duty it was to keep the passage clear. Lucien pulled my coat, to call my attention to the fact that the lad had only one arm.

---

* Two grotesque little phenomena were once shown in London and Paris as specimens of the Aztec race. When I speak of Aztecs, my young readers may perhaps think I allude to these dwarfs. I will therefore state, once for all, that this name is intended to apply only to the Indians, the descendants of the fine race over whom Montezuma was emperor when Cortez conquered them. By Mexicans, or Creoles, we mean the descendants of the Spanish race.

"How did you lose your left arm, pobricito?" I asked.

"Between the crushers, señor."

"Was it your own fault?"

"Alas! yes. My father looked after the machine, and I helped him to drive the oxen; and he had forbidden my going near the cylinders. One day he went away for a few minutes, and I tried to put a piece of cane between the rollers; but my finger caught, and my arm was drawn in and crushed."

"It was a terrible punishment for your disobedience," I said.

"More terrible than you think, señor. My father died six months ago, and I have several little brothers. If I had both my arms, I could earn a quarter of a piastre a day, and also help my mother."

"How much do they give you for watching this filtering-bag from morning till night?"

"Only a medio," * he answered.

I looked hard at Lucien, who threw himself into my arms.

"Oh! I will always obey you," he cried, with emotion; "but do allow me to give all the money in my purse to this little boy."

"Give him a piastre, my boy; we shall meet with others in want, and you must reserve something for them."

"Oh! young gentleman," said the poor mutilated lad, looking with wonder at the coin which represented sixteen days' work, "we will all pray for you!"

And he hurried to clear out the bag, which was already too full.

The process adopted in the sugar-mill we speak of was of most primitive simplicity. The European manufacturers

---

* About threepence.

employ iron cylinders turned by steam or water power; also lift and force pumps, which quickly convey the sap into the basins in which it is to be clarified by fermentation.

But for comprehending easily all the operations required in the extraction of sugar, Antonio's *hacienda*, in which every thing was done before our eyes, was much preferable to any of the modern mills provided with all kinds of improved apparatus.

When our young traveller saw the thick, muddy, and turbid liquid, which was being stirred up by a gigantic "agitator," he could hardly believe that it could ever produce the beautiful white crystal with which he was so well acquainted.

"But where's the sugar?" he eagerly asked.

"There, in front of you," replied Sumichrast. "The sugar-cane, like all other vegetables, contains a certain quantity of liquid, in which the sugar is held in a state of solution; if this is removed, prismatic crystals immediately form. Look now! the contents of the copper are just beginning to boil, and are covered with a blackish scum, which is carefully skimmed off; for in three or four days, when it has fermented, it will produce, by means of distillation, the ardent spirit which l'Encuerado is so fond of. The cloud of steam which is rising above the copper shows that the juice is evaporating; in a few minutes more it will be converted into sirup, and will ultimately form crystals. Come and see the result of the last operation."

We entered a large gallery, in which a number of moulds —made of baked earth and shaped like reversed sugar-loaves —were ranged in lines under the beams, like bottles in a bottle-rack. Into these, which had been previously moistened, some laborers were pouring the boiling sirup. A little farther on we were shown what had been boiled the day before, and was crystallizing, assisted in the process by an Indian, who stirred it slowly. From a trough, open at the lower end, a thick liquid was flowing, called "molasses," or treacle, which is used for making rum, gingerbread, and for other purposes. The lowest part of the sugar-loaf seemed, also, to be yellow and sticky.

Passing through a dark passage, Lucien noticed two half-naked laborers, who were moistening clay and converting it into a kind of dough.

"What a nasty mess!" he cried, with a self-satisfied tone. "What would mamma say, if she was here? It was only the other day she gave my brother and sister a good scolding."

"What was it for?" I asked.

"For mixing up mud to build a town and reservoir in the long passage in our house."

"What part did you take in it?"

"Oh, I was architect; but I was scolded as much as the others."

"That I can readily believe," replied Sumichrast, who could hardly keep his gravity; "but come, let us follow these laborers, and you will soon see that they are not mixing up this mud for mere pleasure."

To his great surprise, our little traveller saw them filling up, with a dark-colored liquid, the empty part of the moulds, from which the molasses had drained away.

"They are spoiling the sugar-loaves!" he cried.

"Quite the contrary; they are going to whiten it. The water that is contained in the clay will filter gradually through the sugar, and will drive before it the molasses that is left round the crystals; and this operation, several times repeated, will produce that spongy kind of sugar which is well known to retain a flavor of the cane, rather disliked by Europeans accustomed to the finer products of their refineries."

The only department we now had to visit was the "dry

ing-room," where the sugar-loaves are piled up to dry, and wait for a purchaser.

In our way thither we nearly fell into an immense reservoir, level with the surface of the ground, and full of molasses; the scum floating on the top so exactly resembled the rough and sticky floor of the sugar-mill that it was easy to make a mistake. Gringalet was unfortunate enough to be the cause of our avoiding this accident. Restless, like all his kind, he ran smelling about in every direction, just as if he was trying to find some lost object: forcing his way between our legs, to get in front of us, he suddenly disappeared in the thick liquid. I pulled him out directly; but as soon as he was on his feet, he rolled over and over on the ground, so that when he stood up his coat was bristling with pieces of straw and wood; in fact, he scarcely looked like a dog at all. I called him towards the pond outside, but the poor brute was quite blind and confused, and did not seem to hear. As a matter of course, all the laborers raised shouts of laughter; but poor Lucien, fancying that his dog was going to die, followed him in despair. Gringalet, no doubt wishing to comfort his young master, leaped upon him and covered him with caresses, and of course with saccharine matter, in which he so lately had a bath. As it was too late for any other course, I made up my mind to laugh, like every one else. While l'Encuerado was washing the dog, our hostess cleaned the boy's clothes, soon after which we resumed our journey.

Don Antonio, like a real Mexican, pitied us for having to travel on foot like Indians; he especially commiserated our young companion, and thought, indeed, that we were very cruel.

"He must learn to use his legs; that's the reason why God gave them to him," said Sumichrast, who delighted in an argument with the steward.

" What good are horses, then ?"

" To break your neck. Besides, there are plenty of infirmities in life without making one out of the horse."

" The horse an infirmity !" cried the Mexican.

" Yes, certainly—among your caste at least; for you could no more do without a horse than a cripple without his crutch."

Don Antonio whistled without making any reply, and, untying his horse, took Lucien up in front, and accompanied us for more than a league. At last, as his duties called him home, he shook us by the hand and turned back. Even after we had lost sight of him, we could still hear him wishing us a pleasant journey.

We had to cross a wide prairie; the heat was suffocating, and we marched on side by side in dead silence. Lucien's walking was much hindered by his game-pouch and gourd, which, in spite of all his efforts, would work round in front of him. I soon noticed that he had got rid of the troublesome gear.

" Hallo !" I cried, " what have you done with your provisions ?"

" L'Encuerado wished to carry them for me."

" L'Encuerado's load is quite heavy enough now, and you must get accustomed to your own. In a few days you won't feel it. Habit makes many things easy which at first seem impossible."

" Señor," said l'Encuerado, " Chanito (this was the name he gave to Lucien) is tired, and this is his first journey; I'll give him back all his things to-morrow."

" It will be much better for him to get accustomed to them now. Give him back his baggage, it is not too heavy for him; if you don't, you will be the one to be scolded."

The Indian grumbled before he obeyed; then, taking the boy by the hand, dropped behind, muttering to him:

"When you don't want to walk any more, Chanito, you must tell me, and you shall ride on the top of my pack."

"No," said I, turning round; "if you do any thing of the kind, I will send both of you home."

"My shoulders are my own," replied the Indian, earnestly; "surely I have a right to employ them as I choose."

Sumichrast burst out laughing at this logic, and I was obliged to go on in front, or I should have done the same. Nevertheless, I feared lest Lucien should learn, on the very first day of his journey, to depend too much on l'Encuerado's kindness. I was, therefore, pleased to hear him refuse several times the Indian's offer of putting him up on his pack, an idea which the faithful fellow persisted in with an obstinacy which I had long known him to possess. A little time after—thinking, doubtless, that his dignity compelled him to prove that he was easily able to increase the weight of his load—he seized Gringalet, who was walking close behind lolling out his tongue, and throwing the dog up on his back, and commencing an Indian trot, ran by us with a triumphant look. Gringalet was at first taken by surprise, and, raising a cry of distress, wanted to jump down; but he soon sat quiet enough, without displaying any uneasiness, to the great joy of my son, who was much amused at the incident.

The plain which we were crossing seemed absolutely interminable.

"It's no use our walking," said Lucien; "we don't appear to make any advance."

"Fortunately, you are mistaken," replied Sumichrast. "Look in front of you, and you will see that the trees on ahead, which a short time ago looked like one uninterrupted mass of foliage, can now be discerned separately."

"You mean the forest which we can see from here?"

"What you take for a forest is nothing but a few trees scattered about the plain."

" Isn't M. Sumichrast wrong in that, father ?"

" No, my boy; but those who have more experience than you might well be mistaken, for when objects are seen at a distance they always seem to blend together in a group. This morning, for instance, when we were walking along the main road, you were always exclaiming that it ended in a point; but you were convinced that your eyes deceived you. It is just the same now: these trees appear to be farther apart in proportion as we approach them; and you will be quite surprised presently when you see how distant they are from each other. The same illusion is produced by the stars, which are millions of miles apart, and yet appear so thick in the sky, that your brother Emile was regretting, the other night, that he was not tall enough to grasp a handful of them."

" And don't forget," added Sumichrast, " that light and imagination often combine to deceive us."

" Just as in the fable of the ' Camels and the floating sticks.' "

" Bravo! my young scholar; you've heard that fable ?"

" Yes. One evening I was going into a dimly-lighted room, and I fancied I saw a great gray man seated in a chair; I cried out, and ran away, afraid. Then papa took me by the hand and led me into the dark room again, and I found that the giant which had frightened me so much was nothing but a pair of trowsers, thrown over the back of an armchair. The next day mamma made me learn the fable of the ' Camels.' "

On our road I called Lucien's attention to a small thorny shrub, a kind of mimosa, called *huizachi* by the Indians, who use its pods for dyeing black cloth, and for making a tolerably useful ink. The plain assumed by degrees a less monotonous aspect. Butterflies began to hover round us, and our young naturalist wanted to commence insect-hunting.

"At last, lagging a little, our party reached the foot of the mountains."

I restrained his ardor, as I wished to keep our boxes and needles free for the rarer species which we might expect to find as soon as we had reached more uninhabited districts. At last, lagging a little, our party reached the foot of the mountains.

It was now five o'clock; night was coming on, so it was highly necessary to look out for shelter. We came in view of a bamboo-hut in the nick of time. An old Indian was reclining in front of it, warming his meagre limbs in the rays of the setting sun, clad in nothing but a pair of drawers and a hat with a torn brim. He rose as we came near, and proffered us hospitality. His wife, whose costume consisted of a cotton shirt edged with red thread, came running in answer to his call, and was quite in raptures at the prettiness of the "little white traveller," who completely ingratiated himself by saluting her in her own language. We had accomplished a journey of seven leagues, although Lucien, thanks to Don Antonio's horse, had not walked quite so far.

The aborigines set before us rice and beans. After this frugal repast, washed down with cold water, I wanted Lucien to lie down on a large mat; but the restless little being took advantage of his elders being comfortably stretched out to sleep, and ran off to see our hostess's fowls roosting for the night on a dead tree, and then to prowl up and down in company with l'Encuerado. The latter had ferreted out a three-corded guitar which was in the hut, and strummed away at the same tune for hours together—no doubt to the great pleasure of the boy, although to us it was quite the reverse.

At last our bedding was unrolled, and I enjoined repose on all. Gringalet couched down in the hut, at the feet of his young master. L'Encuerado, however, preferred sleeping in the open air, only too happy, as he said, to see the sky above, and to feel the wind blow straight into his face without having to be filtered through walls and windows.

CHAPTER III.

I ROSE long before day and woke my companion. Lucien rubbed his eyes two or three times, trying in vain to make out where he was. After some moments, drawing the coverlet over him, he turned round to go to sleep again.

"Now, then, young Lazybones!" I cried, "don't you hear the cock crowing, telling us we ought to be on our road? Jump up and look round, and you will see the birds and the insects are already busy."

The child got up, appearing half stupefied, and stretched himself with a long yawn.

"Oh, papa!" he said, "I ache all over; I'm sure I shall never be able to walk."

"You are quite mistaken," I replied, half supporting him. "You only feel a little tired and stiff; your limbs will very soon work as freely as ever. Go and warm yourself by the fire, where our kind hostess is preparing coffee."

The little fellow did as he was told; but he limped sadly.

"Do your legs feel like mine?" he asked of l'Encuerado.

"No, Chanito; we did not walk far enough yesterday for that."

"You can't mean that we haven't walked far? Papa says that we are now seven leagues from Orizava."

"Yes; that may seem a great deal to you, and perhaps too much; that is why I wanted to put you up on the top of my pack. Now, come, let me see where you suffer."

"All over my limbs, but particularly inside my knees."

"Wait a minute, and I'll soon cure you."

L'Encuerado then laid Lucien down in front of the fire, and began to rub him after the Indian method, vigorously shampooing the whole of his body. Next he made him walk and run with the longest strides he could take; and, after repeating this process, brought him a cup of boiling coffee. Having been revived and strengthened in this way, the lad quite recovered his sprightliness, and soon asked when we were going to start.

I gave a small present to the old couple who had so kindly accommodated us, and our little party began its second day's work; Gringalet sniffing the breeze, and evidently enjoying the excursion as much as any of the party.

When the sun rose, the sky was covered with grayish clouds, driven along quickly by a north wind; but the weather was cool, and well adapted to walking. A limestone mountain rose right in front of us, the slope of which we had to climb; but ere we reached the top, we halted at least twenty times to take breath. Our little companion, with his head bent down towards the ground, struggled to retain his place by our side. At last we reached the summit, and felt at liberty to rest.

Casting a glance on the plain beneath us, the boy surveyed a vast prairie, dotted over with clumps of bushes. He silently contemplated the panorama which was spread out beneath, although he failed to completely comprehend all that he saw.

"Look at those black spots moving about over the plain," said he.

"They are oxen," I replied.

"Oxen! Why they are scarcely as big as Gringalet."

"Don't you know that you must not trust to appearances? Recollect the trees you saw yesterday, which you thought were a forest."

"But if, from this height, the oxen appear no larger than sheep, the sheep ought not to look greater than flies."

"You can easily judge; there is a flock of goats down below."

"A flock of goats! It is like a swarm of ants."

"Exactly; but look at them through the telescope."

Availing himself of the glass, which he used rather unskillfully, Lucien raised a sudden cry.

"I see them! I see them!" he exclaimed. "How pretty they are! They are running about and crowding together, in front of a little boy who is driving them."

"It is most likely a man, who is diminished by the distance."

"The idea of men of that size!"

"Well, look at the foot of that wooded hill; the thin line which you might easily take for a mere pathway is the main road. Perhaps you may see an Indian family travelling along it."

"The basket and its bearer chased one another down the hill."

Lucien kept shifting his telescope about for some minutes without descrying any thing; but at last he broke out in a fresh exclamation.

"Have you discovered any men?" I asked.

"Oh yes!—men, horses, and mules; but they are regular Lilliputians."

"You are quite right," said Sumichrast; "how do we know that Dr. Swift did not first form his idea of 'Gulliver's Travels' from looking at the world from the top of a high mountain?"

After a time, I was obliged to take the young observer away from this point for contemplation to proceed on our journey. The ridge of the mountain was soon crossed, and we began to descend the other side. I took Lucien by the hand, for the slope was so steep that it needed the utmost care to avoid rolling down over the naked rocks. Several times I slipped, and scratched my legs among the bushes. Sumichrast, who had taken his turn in looking after the boy, was no better off than myself. The descent was so steep that we were often forced to run, and sometimes the only thing possible to retard our impetus was to fall down, and run the risk of being hurt. Therefore, in spite of Lucien's promise to walk prudently and with measured step, I declined to allow him to go alone. We at last, to our great satisfaction, got over about two-thirds without any accident, when l'Encuerado, losing his equilibrium, fell, turning head over heels several times; the basket and its bearer chasing one another down the hill, finally disappearing into a thicket.

"Look after Lucien," I said to my companion, who was a few paces in front. And I dashed forward anxiously to assist l'Encuerado.

I feared that I should find the unfortunate Indian with some of his bones broken, even if not killed; so I called to

him, when he replied almost immediately; but his voice
sounded not from below, but from a spot a little to my
left. I could not stay my rapid course except by grasping
a tuft of brush-wood, to which I hung. Then, turning towards the left, I soon encountered the Mistec, who had already begun to collect his burden.

"Nothing broken?" I asked.

"No, Tatita; all the bottles are safe."

"It's your limbs that I mean, my poor fellow!"

"Oh! my nose and arms are a little scratched, and my
body is rather knocked about; but there's not a single rent
either in my jacket or breeches," added he, looking with
complacency at the leathern garments which had given him
the name of l'Encuerado.

"Well, you have had a narrow escape."

"Oh! señor, God is good! In spite of the basket-work
case, the bottles might have been broken, and they are not
the least hurt."

For my part, I was more inclined to recognize God's
goodness in l'Encuerado's almost miraculous preservation.
As to the basket, the Indian had tied it up so strongly, that
I was not at all surprised to find that our provisions were
uninjured.

"Give a call-cry," said I to the Indian; "Sumichrast can
not see us, and may think that you are killed."

"Chanito, hiou, hiou, hiou, Chanito!"

"Ohe! ohe!" replied Lucien.

And the boy, looking pale and alarmed, almost immediately made his appearance. He rushed up to his friend,
threw his arms round his neck, and embraced him. The
brave Mistec, who had been but little injured by his terrible descent, could not help weeping at this proof of Lucien's
attachment.

"It was nothing but a joke," he said. "You'll see me
perform many a feat like that."

" Your face is all over with blood !"

" That's a mere joke, too. Would you like me to do it again ?"

" No, no !" cried the child, catching the Indian by the jacket.

I dressed l'Encuerado's hurts, and we were about to continue our journey.

" I say," said Lucien, archly, just as the Indian was hoisting his basket on to his back; " how would it have been if I had been perched on it ?"

" Then I should not have fallen," replied l'Encuerado, with the utmost gravity.

In a minute or two more we were at the foot of the mountain, when Lucien, overjoyed that the descent was accomplished, gave a leap which showed me that the back of his trowsers had suffered in the late struggle.

" There's a pretty beginning !" I cried; " how did you manage to get your trowsers in that state ?"

" It is my fault," said Sumichrast, with consternation ; " wishing to descend more rapidly, and fearing another tumble, I advised him to sit down and slide carefully. I did not foresee the very natural results of such a plan."

" Well, papa ! it does not matter in the country."

" If my advice had been taken," broke in l'Encuerado, " he would have had a pair of leathern pantaloons, which wouldn't suffer from such contingencies. Never mind, Chanito, we'll mend them with the skin of the first squirrel which comes within reach of my gun."

We were now passing through a dark gorge full of thick brush-wood. In front of us rose a wooded mountain, which we had to climb. The shrubs were succeeded by gigantic thistles, which compelled us to advance with extreme care. These troublesome plants grew so thickly that we were obliged to use our knives to clear a passage. L'Encuerado, putting down his load, taught Lucien how to handle his; showing him that a downward cut, if the weapon slipped or met with but little resistance, might be dangerous. Enchanted with his lesson, and cutting down several stalks at a blow, our young pioneer soon opened for us an avenue rather than a path. The thistles gradually became fewer. Sumichrast walked in front, destroying the last obstacles that severed us from the under-wood.

It was now breakfast-time, and as we continued our course we looked out for a favorable spot to halt at, when the measured strokes of an axe fell upon our ears. This noise told of the presence of wood-cutters, who were certain to be provided with maize-cakes and beans; so we resolved to make our way up to them, and thus economize our own resources. After an hour's difficult ascent, just as we were despairing of reaching the Indian, whose axe had ceased to sound, Lucien cried out:

"Look, papa, there's a fire!"

At the same moment Gringalet began barking furiously, and a few paces more brought us to a burning charcoal-oven. The charcoal-burner, who was surprised at our visit, seized his long-handled axe. But the presence of the child appeared to reassure him.

"Good-morning, Don José," said I, using the common name which is applied in Mexico to all the Indians.

"God preserve you," replied he, speaking in broken Spanish.

"Are you all alone?"

"No. I have six companions."

"Well, will one of you sell us some maize-cakes, and give us some water?"

"We have neither water nor cakes."

"I'm quite sure you will be able to find some," I replied, placing a half-piastre in his hand.

"Almost immediately the foliage was pushed aside."

The Indian took off his straw hat, scratched his forehead, and then, placing two fingers in his mouth, whistled a prolonged note. Almost immediately the foliage was pushed aside, and a boy about fifteen years old, wearing nothing but a pair of drawers, made his appearance, and halted, as if terrified at the sight of us.

" Run to the hut, and ask for cakes and some capsicums, and bring them here," said the wood-cutter, in the Aztec language.

" It's quite needless," I replied, in the same idiom ; " we can breakfast much more comfortably in the hut."

The wood-cutter looked at me in artless admiration, then taking my hand, placed it on his breast. I spoke his language, and I was therefore his friend. This is a feeling common to all men, whatever may be their nationality or social position.

Following the young Indian, in five minutes we reached a very primitive dwelling ; being but four stakes supporting a roof made of branches with their leaves on. The woodmen in Mexico construct such temporary places of shelter, for at the commencement of the rainy season they cease to dwell in the forests.

An Indian girl warmed us a dozen of those maize-flour fritters, which are called *tortillas*, and are eaten by the natives instead of bread. She also brought us a calabash full of cooked beans, which hunger rendered delicious.

" Why don't they serve the meat first ?" asked Lucien.

" Because they have none," replied Sumichrast.

"Haven't these Indians any meat ? Poor fellows ! How will they dine, then ?"

"Don't you know that the Indians never eat meat more than three or four times a year; and that their usual food is composed of nothing but black beans, rice, capsicums, and maize flour? Have you forgotten our dinner yesterday ?"

" I fancied that we had arrived too late for the first course, and that all the meat had been used. But shall we live on beans the whole of our journey ?"

" No ; our meals will not be quite so regular as you seem to think. Yet we shall have plenty of meat when we have been lucky in shooting, a little rice when we have been unfortunate, and fried beans whenever chance throws in our way any inhabited hut."

" And we shall have to go without dessert ?" said the child, making up his face into a comical pout.

" Oh no, Chanito, there will be dessert to-day," replied l'Encuerado. " Perhaps as good as the cook would provide at home; but, at any rate, it is sweet enough. Look at it !"

The Indian girl brought a calabash full of water, and a cone of black sugar, weighing about half a pound.

" What is that ?" cried Lucien.

" *Panela*," answered the Indian girl.

" Poor man's sugar," interposed Sumichrast. " The manufacture of white sugar, which you saw yesterday, costs a good deal, for the laborers employed to make it have to work night and day, and thus it becomes expensive. Now, some sugar-makers avoid all this outlay, and they merely boil the juice, so that it will harden in cooling. This dark-colored sugar costs about one-half as much in making as the other."

" I can well believe it," said the child ; " but it contains all that nasty scum which we saw."

" That makes it the nicer," said l'Encuerado ; " it has a richer flavor."

And taking a morsel of the *panela*, he soaked it in the water in the calabash and sucked it.

When Lucien saw that we, too, imitated the Indian, he soon made up his mind to do likewise, the sweet taste overcoming his repugnance.

When we had finished, our young companion was anxious to know how charcoal was made. Sumichrast led him close to a recently-felled oak, the small branches of which an Indian was cutting into pieces two or three inches long, by means of an instrument something like an enormous pruning-knife. A little farther, on the open ground, two men were collecting these pieces of wood in circular rows. This pile was already seven feet in circumference, and about the same in height, although it was not half finished. Lucien could easily see this when he approached the Indian who was looking after the lighted furnace, in which the wood, completely covered with earth, formed a kind of dome, from the summit of which a blue flame was hovering, proving that the mass inside was in a red-hot state. The Indian kept walking round and round the furnace, plastering damp earth on any holes through which the flame started. For, as Sumichrast properly observed, a charcoal of good quality must be smothered while it is being burned.

"Suppose the fire went out?" said Lucien.

"Then all the work must be begun over again."

"But the fire might burn only one side."

"They would then have badly-burned charcoal, nearly half wood, which would cause a bad smell when it was used. The wood in the oven we are looking at will be entirely charred to-night; for the fire, which was lighted at the centre, is trying to break through all round the outside. Before long the Indians will cover up the opening at the top, over which the blue flame is hovering. The fire will then be quite deprived of air, and soon afterwards go out. In about eight days your mamma may perhaps buy this very charcoal which you have seen burned."

"Suppose the charcoal went on burning?"

"Then the Indian, to his great vexation, would find noth-

ing left but ashes. But he will take good care not to lose
the fruit of his labor. He will use as many precautions to
prevent the fire burning up again as he does now to hinder
it going out."

A little farther on a man was filling up his rush bags
with charcoal which had cooled. As it would take him
more than one day to reach the town, he was lining his
sacks with a kind of balm, the penetrating odor of which
always announces, in Mexico, the approach of a charcoal-
carrier. This plan is adopted to preserve the charcoal
from damp.

"When I used to see the Indians carrying on their backs
their four little sacks of charcoal," said Lucien, "I had no
idea that they were obliged to live in the woods, and cut
down great trees to procure it; and that they had to pass
several nights in watching the oven."

"No more idea, perhaps," I replied, "than the little boys
in Europe have of the sugar-cane plantations; and that
without the plant all those beautiful *bon-bons*, which delight the sight as much as the taste, could not be made."

"But, papa, haven't I heard you tell the Mexicans that
in France they make sugar with beet-root?"

"Yes, certainly you have; and, in case of need, it might
be extracted from many other roots, plants, or fruit; but
beet-root alone yields enough sugar to repay the trouble of
extraction."

It was quite time for us to be off; so I put an end to
the ceaseless questions of the young traveller.

Our host told me that if we went on along the same path
which had led us to their place, we should come, in less
than two hours, to a hut situated on the plateau of the
mountain. The Indians certainly seemed to forget that
Lucien's short legs might delay our progress.

CHAPTER IV.

A DIFFICULT ASCENT.—THE GOAT.—THE INDIAN GIRLS.—
THE TOBACCO-PLANT. — THE BULL-FIGHT. — GAME. — LU-
CIEN'S GUN.—OUR ENTRY INTO THE WILDERNESS.

OUR way led through nothing but scrub oaks, for all the
larger trees had gradually disappeared from the mountain-side, which had for some time been cultivated by the
Indians. The path was steep, rugged, and stony; and
seemed, at first, to defy any attempt to scale it. Notwithstanding the measured pace at which we were walking, we
were obliged to stop every minute to recover our breath.
Lucien followed us so eagerly that I was obliged to check
him several times. He was surprised at not seeing any living creature, not even those beautiful golden flies which, in

Mexico, flutter round every bush.   But the north wind was
blowing, and the sun was hidden behind the clouds, so that
both the insects and birds kept in the deepest recesses of
their hiding-places.   As we advanced, our road became
much steeper, and we were obliged to cling to the shrubs
for support.   L'Encuerado, who was impeded by the weight
of his load, pulled himself up with his hands, so had hard
work to keep his balance.   Soon it became impossible for
him to go farther ; but, fortunately, we had foreseen ascents
of this kind.   So I gave the child into Sumichrast's charge, .
for if he had been left to climb by himself, he would most
likely have rolled over and hurt himself against the stumps
or sharp rocks.

I made my way into a copse, and with my *machete* I cut
down a moderately-sized branch, the end of which I sharp-
ened to a point.   Then, going forward and unrolling a
leathern thong, thirty feet in length, and commonly called
by us a *lasso*, I fastened it to the stake, which I drove firmly into the ground.   By means of this support, which served
as a sort of hand-rail, l'Encuerado could clamber up to me,
thanks to the strength of his wrists.   Ten times this awk-
ward job had to be repeated, and the path, instead of getting better, became worse.   We then shifted our work, and
I took charge of the load, while the tired Indian fixed the
lasso.   I was just making my third ascent, when Sumichrast, who had gone on before us to reconnoitre the ground,
made his appearance above.   When he saw me stumbling
and twisting about, falling now on my side, and now on my
knees, toiling to advance a single step, my companion burst
into a fit of laughter.   I had then neither time nor will to
do as he did, and his ill-timed mirth vexed me.   At last I
caught hold of the stake, bruised and exhausted, and ready
to wish there was no such thing as travelling.   Sumichrast
told us that we had scarcely three hundred feet more to as-

cend, and shouldered the basket himself. Now that I was a mere spectator, I could readily forgive him his fit of merriment. Nothing, in fact, could be more grotesque than the contortions he went through trying to keep his balance. L'Encuerado was the only one who retained his countenance. As for Lucien, he seemed to feel the efforts of Sumichrast as much as if they were his own.

"You see," I said to my son, "that in countries where there are no beaten roads a walk is not always an easy matter."

At last, we got out of this difficult locality. While all this was going on, Gringalet, gravely squatting down upon his haunches, seemed perfectly amazed at our efforts. Pricking up his ears and winking his eyes, he quietly surveyed us; no doubt secretly congratulating himself upon being able to run and gambol easily in places where we, less-suitably-constructed bipeds, found it difficult even to walk.

Here there were no trees to be seen. As on the evening before, we traversed a granite surface soil which formed the ridge of the mountain; but a sudden turn in the path led us to a plateau, on which stood a rudely-built hut.

Three children ran away as we came near, and two lean dogs began to prowl round Gringalet with any thing but friendly intentions. A goat, which was quietly cropping the scanty grass, suddenly raised its head, and, cutting several capers, ran with its head bent down, as if to butt our little companion. I could not reach the spot in time to prevent this unforeseen attack, nevertheless I shouted, in hopes of intimidating the animal; but Gringalet, who was far more nimble than I, boldly faced the enemy, and soon forced him to retreat.

"Weren't you afraid of him?" asked Sumichrast.

"Rather," answered Lucien, hanging down his head.

"Well, it did not prevent you facing the foe."

"If I had run away, the goat, who runs a great deal faster than I can, would soon have overtaken me. I waited for him, so as to frighten him with my stick, and, if possible, avoid his horns."

"You could not have acted more sensibly. At all events you've plenty of coolness, and that is about the best quality a traveller can show."

"All right now, but in future I shall keep clear of goats. But I thought they were afraid of men."

"Not always, as you were very near finding out to your cost. Perhaps, however," continued Sumichrast, smiling, "your enemy did not look upon you quite as a man; and, after all, I fancy he thought more of playing with you than of hurting you, for he must be thoroughly accustomed to the sight of children."

At this moment Gringalet came running up with his tail between his legs, and with a most doleful look; he was closely pursued by all the dogs of the plateau, who, instead of barking, were making a kind of howling noise, common to those that are but half domesticated.

On hearing all this uproar, two Indian women came running towards us, but stopped, abashed at our appearance.

The youngest of them, rather a pretty girl, wore nothing but a short linen chemise, and a piece of blue woollen stuff fastened round her hips by a wide band, ornamented with red threads. Her hair, which was plaited and brought over her forehead, formed a sort of coronet. Her companion, who was dressed in a similar way, wore, in addition, a long scarf, which was fixed to her head, and fell round her like a nun's cloak.

"God bless you, Maria!" I said to the eldest. "Can you take us in for one night?"

"On hearing the uproar, two Indian women came running towards us."

" I have nothing to offer you to eat, I am afraid."

" Perhaps you can sell us a fowl and some eggs."

" Well, I must see if my husband objects to guests."

" Surely your husband will not refuse the shelter of his roof to weary travellers ?"

She reflected for a moment, and then answered,

" No, he is a Christian! Come in and rest yourselves."

The Indian woman called to her children, who one after the other showed their wild-looking heads peeping out from some hiding-place, and ordered them to drive away the dogs.

It was not without some degree of pleasure we got rid of our travelling gear, as we felt no ordinary amount of weariness, which was easily accounted for by the exertion of our recent ascent. L'Encnerado, always brisk, began to assist the housewife; he stirred up the fire, arranged the plates, and looked to their being clean. The Indian woman then asked him to go and draw some water from a spring about a hundred yards from the hut; and off he went, led by the children of our hostess. His young guides, completely naked, and their heads shaved, rode on bamboo-canes as make-believe horses, and pranced along in front of him.

Except on the side we had just ascended, the plateau was entirely surrounded by high mountains. The hut, which was built of planks and covered with thatch, appeared very cleanly kept. Behind it extended a small kitchen garden, in which fennel, the indispensable condiment in Aztec cookery, grew in great abundance; in front, there was a large tobacco plantation, and an inclosure where both goats and pigs lived on good terms with each other. The situation appeared somewhat dull to us; but in the tropics the absence of sunshine is sufficient to give a sombre look to the most beautiful landscape.

Lucien wanted to pay a visit to the tobacco-field. The stems of this plant are more than three feet high, covered with wide leaves of a dark-green color. The flowers, some of which were pink and others a yellowish hue, indicated two different species; their acrid smell was any thing but pleasant. Lucien was not a little surprised to learn that this beautiful *vegetable* belonged to the same botanical family as the potato, the tomato, the egg-plant, and the pimento.

"Among the ancient Aztecs," said Sumichrast, "tobacco was called *pycietl;* it was the emblem of the goddess Cihua-cohuatl, or woman-serpent.* In Mexican mythology, this divinity was supposed to be the first mother of children; and, in the legend about her, the European missionaries fancied that they recognized some features resembling the sacred history of Eve. Up to the present time, the Indians, who have renounced the errors of paganism and profess the Christian religion, continue to make use of the plant consecrated to their ancient goddess, as a remedy for the sting of venomous reptiles."

"Then that is why they cultivate tobacco," said Lucien, "for I know that they seldom smoke."

"No, but they sell their crops of it to the Creoles, among whom smoking is a universal habit. It is said that the word *tobacco* comes from the name of the island of Tabago, where the Spaniards first discovered it. About the year 1560, it was introduced into France by Jean Nicot, who gave it his own name; for *savants* call this plant *nicotian*. It is a certain fact that the modern Mexican Indians smoke hardly any thing but cigars or cigarettes. As for pipes, they have not long known of the existence of such things; and the works of certain romancers, who so often describe the Aztecs as having the pipe of peace, war, or council constantly in their mouths, are simply ridiculous. You may recollect

---

* In the Aztec language, *cihuatl* signifies "woman," and *cohuatl* signifies "serpent."

how astonished the French were, on their arrival here, to find they could not procure any cut tobacco; while on the other hand the Indians crowded to see the foreigners inhale the smoke of the plant from instruments made of clay, wood, or porcelain."*

"I remember," cried Lucien, "that one day l'Encuerado took a pipe belonging to an officer who was staying with papa and began to smoke it. You should have seen what horrible faces he made."

"Well, what happened to him?" asked Sumichrast.

"The pipe made him sick, and then papa, who knew nothing about his smoking, gave him some medicine; but l'Encuerado told me that the medicine was not nearly so nasty as the pipe."

The culprit, who had just joined us, cast down his eyes at this tale about him, and murmured in a sententious tone of voice, "Pipes are an invention of the devil."†

Followed by my companions, I again drew near to the hut, and the master came out to bid us welcome. Our hostess placed upon a mat an earthen dish containing a fowl cooked with rice, and the Indian, his wife, and his sister-in-law, offered to wait on us. Lucien invited the children to partake of our repast; but they refused to sit down beside us. Towards the conclusion of our dinner, one of them brought us half a dozen bananas, which were most welcome; while we were drinking our coffee, the little troop made up a game of hide-and-seek. To my great satisfaction, I saw that, in spite of the long day's journey, Lucien joined in, and

---

* The Indians that inhabit the vast plains to the north of Mexico all smoke; from this, doubtless, arises the usual supposition that all American Indians smoke.—ED.

† In giving utterance to this anathema, l'Encuerado was unknowingly agreeing with James I., king of England, who published a work against smokers.

ran and jumped about with as much energy as his play-mates.

At last the children got tired of this game, and, bringing a kid, had a mock bull-fight. The animal, wonderfully well trained to the sport, ran after the youngsters, and more than once succeeded in knocking them down. When Lucien met this fate, Gringalet became furious and sprang upon the pretty little creature; but the dog's young master got up in a moment and soon quieted his protector's energy. We had noticed, ever since we set out, that Gringalet always preferred to follow close to the boy, and seemed to have taken upon himself the task of watching over his safety.

Our host told us that he was born and also married in the village of Tenejapa; but being enlisted for a soldier by force, he deserted and took up his abode on this plateau. We were the first white men who had paid him a visit for six years. His fields produced maize, beans, and tobacco, which his wife and sister-in-law took twice a year to Oriza-va to exchange for necessaries for housekeeping. He was as happy as possible, and was never tired of praising the charms of forest and plain. But his raptures were not re-quired to convert us to his opinions.

Nightfall was accompanied by cold, to which we were but little accustomed. The Indians lent us some mats; then we all wrapped ourselves up, and were soon asleep, notwithstanding the primitiveness of our couch.

About two in the morning I woke up numbed from the lowness of the temperature; Lucien also was nearly frozen. I hastened to cover him up with my *sarapé,* for on these heights we were exposed to the north wind blowing from the volcano of Citlatepetl, and the atmosphere would not get warm again until sunrise. Sumichrast soon joined me; he had also given up his covering to the child. I then set to work to look for some small branches to light the fire;

but our movements ultimately roused up our host, and, thanks to him, we were soon able to sit down in front of a powerful blaze. Still l'Encuerado, from force of habit, who was hardly sheltered at all, was sleeping like a top. At last, aided by the heat, sleep resumed its influence, and I dropped off again in slumber.

When I awoke, the sun was shining in a cloudless sky, and every body was up. Sumichrast was inspecting the arms and ammunition, for from this day forward we should have to provide our own subsistence. I was quite surprised at the time I had been asleep; but a slight touch of lumbago reminded me of yesterday's difficult ascent, which fully accounted for my drowsiness. I must confess I felt much more inclined to go to bed again than to continue our journey; but, as I was obliged to set a good example, I began to help my companions in their preparations for departure. I have already described the dress of Lucien and l'Encuerado; Sumichrast's costume and mine also consisted of strong cloth trowsers, and a blouse made of the same stuff. The weapons of each were a revolver, a *machete*, a double-barrelled gun, and a game-bag filled with necessaries. We duly examined the contents of the basket, which l'Encuerado carried on his back by a strap fixed across his breast or forehead. Sumichrast then took out a long parcel he had put into the basket when we started, and unrolled the cloth which formed its first covering. His smile and mysterious look quite puzzled us; at last he drew from the paper a light fowling-piece, which he placed in Lucien's hands.

The boy blushed and trembled with joy, and became quite pale with anxiety. He hardly dared to believe that his fondest dream was thus realized. He could not speak for pleasure, but threw himself into my friend's arms. I was as much surprised as he was. I had often thought of giving Lucien a gun; but I was so afraid of an accident that I had decided not to do so.

"Oh, Chanito! I pity the poor tigers; what a number of them you will kill!" exclaimed the old hunter. "What beautiful skins you will be able to take home to mamma! Come, let me handle your gun; it looks as if it was made on purpose for you. Oh! how I pity the poor tigers!"

And he began to dance about with the energy of delight.

It was decided that the gun should always be loaded by us, and that Lucien should only shoot under our directions. I also added that, at the least infringement of these rules, the gun would be taken away, and the little fellow well knew I would keep my word. In vain I advised him to put back his gun into the basket; but this was almost too much to expect, so I allowed him to carry it, which he did with great pride.

After a good breakfast, we regulated our compasses.

" Behind us opened a dark, narrow ravine, with perpendicular sides."

Lucien said good-bye to his little companions, and I thanked the Indian women for all their attention to us. Our host, however, accompanied us to the summit of the mountain.

There we found ourselves in a vast amphitheatre, commanded on all sides by wooded ridges; at our feet stretched the plateau we had just crossed, and far beneath us we caught indistinct glimpses of the plain below. Behind us opened a dark, narrow ravine, with perpendicular sides, almost like an immense wall. Above us was the pale blue sky, dotted over with vultures.

On the verge of the forest our guide parted from us with regret, and wished us a successful journey. Sumichrast loaded Lucien's gun, and told him to fire it off as a salute on our entering the wilderness. The shot was fired, the echoes reverberating in succession, each louder than the last; then all was once more silent. After casting a last look over the valley, I was the first to make my way into the forest. From this moment we had only God's providence and our own exertions to trust to; for every step we advanced only took us farther from the haunts of men.

CHAPTER V.

THE GREAT FOREST.—CROWS.—THE FIRST BIVOUAC.—THE
SQUIRREL-HUNT.—OUR YOUNG GUIDE.—THE CHANT IN
THE DESERT.

W E were now more than 5000 feet above the level of
the sea, and the coldness of the breeze quite surprised my son, who, being accustomed to the climate of the
Terre-Tempérée, had never before felt any thing like the
atmosphere we were now in. As if by instinct, he held his
fingers in his mouth, to prevent their getting numbed. But
when the sun had reached a certain height, there was no
longer any need to complain of the cold.

As we advanced, the trees grew closer and closer together. Lucien, who now for the first time saw these enormous
trees, to whom centuries were no more than years are to us,

seemed strongly impressed at the sight of their gigantic proportions. He almost doubted the reality of the scene which met his eyes. Having previously seen the pigmy world of Lilliput from the top of a mountain, he was now ready to inquire if this was not another illusion, exhibiting to him the empire of one of those giants whose marvellous histories his mamma had related to him. An oak-tree which had fallen across our path gave him a good opportunity of measuring its size, the limbs of which seemed to touch the sky. The ancient trunk was black, wrinkled, and partly buried in the earth by the weight of its fall; even as it lay prostrate, it was several feet higher than ourselves, while the large branches, scattered and broken, were equal in diameter to the biggest chestnut-trees. A flapping of wings suddenly attracted our attention, and we saw two couples of enormous crows take flight, saluting us as they went with a prolonged croaking.

"Be off with you, children of the evil one!" cried l'Encuerado; "you've no chance of frightening us, we are too good Christians for that!"

"Whom are you calling to?" asked Lucien, who looked round him with surprise.

"To the crows, of course."

"Do you believe that they can understand you?"

"Not the least doubt about it, Chanito. These scoundrels are harder in their flesh than they are in their bearing; and just because they are dressed up in a beautiful black coat, like that your papa wears on festival days, they think to have every thing their own way. But if one of them dares to come to-night and prowl round our fire, I'll kill and roast him, as sure as my name is l'Encuerado!"

The boy opened his eyes very wide at this, for he was always astonished at the whims of the Indian, who never failed to interpret the cries and gestures of animals according to his own fancy, and to give a sharp rejoinder to the imaginary provocations which, as he considered, were offered to him. Sometimes, even, he laid the blame on inanimate things, and then his conversations with them were most amusing. The old hunter had no doubt contracted this habit at a time when, living alone in the woods and feeling the need of talking, he conversed with himself, having no one else to address. However this might be, he kept up conversation with either a leaf or a bird in perfectly artless sincerity.

For four hours we proceeded through the forest, feeling almost overcome with the heat. Pines and oaks appeared, one after another, in almost monotonous regularity. Gradually the ground began to slope, and the altered pace we had to adopt both rested us and also increased the speed of our march. At length we emerged into a valley. The vegetation was now of an altered character, the ceibas, lignum-vitæ trees, and creepers were here and there to be seen.

"Halt!" I cried out.

I soon got rid of my travelling gear, an example my companions were not slow in following. L'Encuerado and Lucien immediately set to work to find some dry branches, while Sumichrast and I began to cut down the grass over a space of several square yards.

"Have we finished our day's journey, then?" asked Lucien.

"Yes," I replied; "don't you feel tired?"

"Not very; I could easily go farther. Have we walked very far?"

"About four leagues."

"And are we really going to rest after a trifle like that? I always thought travellers went on walking until night."

"Nonsense!" said I, taking hold of his ear. "What an

undaunted young pedestrian! Four leagues a day are no
such trifle when you have to begin again next morning.
'Slow and steady wins the race,' says an old proverb,
which I intend to carry out to the letter; for forced
marches would soon injure our health, and then good-bye
to the success of our expedition. As to walking until
night, it is perfectly impossible, except when one is certain
to meet with an inn. Under these large trees, no one will
ever think of getting ready a meal for us; and, I suppose,
you haven't much wish to die of hunger. We may very
likely have to tramp one or two leagues more before we
are able to kill the game which will form the mainstay of
our dinner."

"I never thought of all that," said Lucien, shaking his
head, and looking convinced; "but what shall we have to
eat this evening?"

"At present, I haven't the least idea; perhaps a hare or
a bird, or even a rat."

"A rat! I certainly will never touch one."

"Ah! my boy, wait till you are really hungry—you
don't know as yet what it is to be so—and then you'll see
how greedily you will make a dinner off whatever Providence provides."

"Do you think we shall often have to go a whole day
without eating?"

"I hope not," I answered, smiling at Lucien's anxious
and somewhat pensive tone.

During this conversation, l'Encuerado, as active as a
monkey, had clambered up a pine, and his *machete* was
strewing the ground with slender boughs. We also set
to work at shaping the stakes, which I drove into the
ground by means of a stone, which served as a hammer.
Some branches, interwoven and tied together by creepers,
formed a kind of hurdle, which, fixed on the top of the

posts, did for a roof. The Indian, assisted by his little companion, who was much interested in all the preparations, filled the hut with leaves, and covered the branches with a layer of dry grass. Under this shelter, we could set the rain at defiance, if not the cold.

It is impossible to describe Lucien's enchantment. This *house* (for this was the name he chose to give to the shapeless hut, in which our party could scarcely stand upright) appeared to him a perfect masterpiece of architecture, and he was astonished at the rapidity with which it had been built. He helped l'Encuerado to make up the fire, so that all that was requisite on our return was to set a light to it. Then, armed with our guns, we set off to seek for our dinners.

Seeing that we left behind us all our baggage, Lucien exclaimed,

"Suppose any one came and stole our provisions?"

"Upon my word," cried Sumichrast, "you're the boy to think of every thing. But there's no need to fear this misfortune; most likely, we are the only persons in the forest; or if any one else should be here, it would be an almost miraculous chance if they discovered our bivouac."

"Then we are not on any road?"

"You may call it a road if you like, but we are the only people who have trod it; no one could discover our encampment unless they had followed us step by step."

The child shook his head with a rather doubtful air; the idea of the desert is not readily nor suddenly comprehended. I well recollect that, during my first excursions in the wilderness, I was constantly expecting to catch sight of some human face, either just when I was emerging from a wood or in following the paths made in the savannah by wild cattle. At night, especially when I was troubled by sleeplessness, I was always fancying that I recognized, in the

" We now entered one of those glades."

distant sounds, either the crow of a cock, the barking of a dog, or the burden of some familiar song.

"But if no one can discover our bivouac," remarked Lucien, casting a glance behind him, "how shall we manage to find it again?"

"In a way that is simple, but rather laborious; we shall walk one after the other, and the last man's duty will be to notch the trees and shrubs."

"Shall I walk first?" asked Lucien.

"No; that place belongs by right to the best shot; for if we put up any game, we mustn't let it escape. In the mean time, until you know how to use your gun, you shall form the rear-guard."

This duty did not seem to displease Lucien, who immediately seized his sword and followed us, at a little distance, inflicting on the trunks of the trees the gashes which were to guide us on our return. He performed his work with so much ardor that his strength was soon exhausted. L'Encuerado afterwards taught him how to handle his weapon in a more skillful manner, and to notch the trees without stopping in his walk. A path marked in this manner is called, in Canada and the United States, a blaze road.

We now entered one of those glades which are so often met with in the midst of a virgin forest, although it is impossible to explain the cause why the trees do not grow just in these spots. As there was no living creature to be seen, I agreed with Sumichrast to leave Lucien and l'Encuerado on the watch, and that we should walk round, each on our own side, so as to meet again at the other extremity of the open space. Gringalet, seeing us separate, could not at first make up his mind which party he should go with; but bounded from one to the other, and caressed each of us, raising plaintive whines. At last he seemed determined to follow me, but scarcely had I progressed a hundred yards before he stopped, as if to reflect.   He probably thought he had left something behind, for he quickly disappeared.

I walked for half an hour through the brake, with eye and ear both on the watch, and my finger on the trigger, without discovering the least evidence of game.   My companion did not appear more fortunate than I was, when suddenly a gun went off.   At the same time, I saw Sumichrast pointing to a number of squirrels crossing the glade.

" Have you killed one ?" I asked.

" Yes ; but it is sticking fast between two branches, sixty feet above the ground ; it is a shot thrown away."

We watched anxiously the rapid bounds of the graceful little animals which we had just disturbed, as they were fast making their way into the wood.

" Is l'Encuerado asleep ?" I cried, with vexation.

My question was answered by two shot-reports in succession, and almost immediately Gringalet, l'Encuerado, and Lucien emerged from the forest.   After searching about for a few minutes, the boy raised up his arm and showed us two squirrels he was holding.   We now hastened our steps ; the Indian had taken possession of the game, and was moving on towards our bivouac, while Lucien ran to meet us.

" Papa, papa !" he cried, all out of breath, " my gun killed one of the squirrels.   Oh ! M. Sumichrast, you shall see it ; it is gray, with a tail like a plume."

" But was it really you that shot ?" I asked.

" Oh yes ! I shot, but l'Encuerado held my gun ; we aimed into the middle of them, for there were a great many. If you could only have seen how they jumped !   The one I hit climbed up on the tree close by ; but it soon fell as dead as a stone.   L'Encuerado says that it hadn't time to suffer much pain."

The poor child was making his *début* as a sportsman, and

his heart seemed rather full, although he was very proud
of this first proof of his skill. Sumichrast was the first to
congratulate him. As for me, although I was well aware
of the Indian's prudence, I made up my mind, if only for the
sake of economizing our powder, both to blame him and also
to caution him against his desire of letting the boy shoot.

"Come," said I to Lucien, who was hugging his gun
against his chest, "you must be our leader in finding our
way back to our encampment. You marked out the road,
so mind you don't mislead us."

Our young guide led us back to our starting-point with
far more self-possession than I expected.

"A child's attention is always being drawn away," observed Sumichrast to me. "How do you explain Lucien's
having followed the trail so readily?"

"Perhaps because it was partly his own work," I replied.

"It is, too, because I am so short," replied the child, with
an arch smile; "I am much closer to the ground than you
are, almost as close as Gringalet, who is so very clever in
finding a trail. You see, papa, that it's some benefit in being little, and that I have some chance of being useful."

I need hardly say how much we were diverted at this
novel argument against a lofty stature.

"At this rate," I replied, "I ought to have brought your
brother Emile; for he is so short that he would have followed a trail even better than you."

"Of course you ought. Don't you recollect that when
we were walking over the mountain of Borrego, he often
spied out insects that you had missed seeing."

I was evidently regularly beaten.

We sat down in front of the fire, before which the two
squirrels were roasting. L'Encuerado caught in a dish the
fat which trickled down from the animals, and every now
and then basted the meat with it.

The flesh of the squirrel, both in flavor and color, much resembles that of the hare; so our little mess-mate ate it with evident enjoyment. Dried maize-cakes, called *toto-po*, took the place of bread, and each one had his allowance of it.

We couldn't help feeling uneasy about Gringalet: we had given him about half a squirrel, but instead of eating it, he thought fit to roll himself upon it frantically. The poor beast had consequently only some scraps of *totopo*. It was, however, highly necessary to accustom him to feed on game, as our maize-cakes were far too valuable to be doled out thus. Each of us poured a little water from his gourd into a calabash, which served for a drinking-vessel. The poor dog, thus allowanced, must have been sorry that he ever joined us.

The sun was perceptibly sinking.

"Well, Lucien," asked Sumichrast, "what do you think now of rat's flesh?"

"I'll tell you when I have eaten some of it."

"What! don't you know that the squirrel and the rat are very near relations, and that they both belong to the Rodent family?"

"They certainly are a little alike," said the child, making a comical face.

"Especially the species which we had for our dinner; which, by-the-by, is not yet classed by naturalists. Look! its coat is black on the back, gray on the flanks, and white under the belly. The ears, too, are bare, instead of having those long points of hair which give such a knowing look to the European squirrels."

"Do squirrels feed on flesh?"

"No; acorns, buds, nuts, grain, and sometimes grasses, constitute their principal food."

"Then," replied Lucien, triumphantly, "the flesh of the

squirrel can not resemble that of the rat, for I know that the rat will eat flesh."

The assured and self-satisfied tone of the little *savant* made us smile; but I almost immediately desired him to be silent, for a noise of branches rustling, which had excited our attention, became every moment more distinct. Gringalet was about to bark, but l'Encuerado caught him by the muzzle, and covered him with his *sarapé*. A whole troop of squirrels, no doubt those we had hunted two hours before, made their appearance, uttering sharp cries. They sprang from branch to branch with the most extraordinary disregard to distance. We noticed them running after one another, sometimes along the top, and sometimes along the bottom of the most flexible boughs. They moved forward as if in jerks, sometimes stopping suddenly and climbing a tree, only to descend it again. When on the ground, they sat up on their hind legs, using their front paws like hands, and rubbed their noses with such a comical air that Lucien could not help speaking loud to express his admiration of them.

Hearing so strange a sound as the human voice, the graceful animals took flight, but not quick enough to prevent Sumichrast's gun from wounding one of them. The squirrel remained at first clinging to the tree on which it was when the shot struck it; but, after a pause, it relaxed its hold and rolled over and fell to the ground. Nevertheless, it had strength enough left to turn round and bite the sportsman, who carelessly laid hold of him. L'Encuerado skinned it immediately, keeping the meat for our breakfast next morning.

The sun went down; the cries of the birds resounded, and night at last shut us in, bringing with it the solemn silence of the wilderness. L'Encuerado struck up a prolonged chant, and Lucien's fresh young voice blended with

that of the hunter. The tune was simple and monotonous
in its character; but there was something touching in hearing the Indian and the child, both equally artless in mind,
uniting together to sing the praises of God. The chant
was ended by a prayer, which Sumichrast and I listened
to, standing up, with our heads bared; and it was with
earnestness that my friend repeated l'Encuerado's solemn
"Amen," expressed in the words, "God is great."

Having fed the fire with sufficient to keep it up all night,
we lay down, side by side, under the hut. The wind
moaned softly through the foliage, and, under the influence
of the gentle breeze, the pine-trees produced that melancholy sound which so exactly calls to mind the noise of the
surf breaking on the shore. By means of thinking of it, I
felt it even in my sleep, for I dreamt that I was at sea, and
that the vessel that bore me was sailing over silvery waters.

CHAPTER VI.

COFFEE.— TURPENTINE.— COUROUCOUS.— PINE-NEEDLES.—
THREE VOLCANOES IN SIGHT AT ONCE.—THE CARABUS
FAMILY.—SCORPIONS.—SALAMANDERS.—A MIDNIGHT DIS-
TURBANCE..

THE first thing I saw on opening my eyes was l'Encuerado, who was getting ready our coffee, and Lucien
crouching close to the fire, piling up a quantity of dry
branches round the kettle, at some risk, however, of upset-
ting it.

"Why, Lucien," I cried, "it is not light yet, and you are
up already! Didn't you sleep well?"

"Oh yes, papa," he answered, kissing me; "but l'Encuerado disturbed Gringalet, so he thought proper to come and
lie down on *me*, and that woke me, for Gringalet is very.

heavy. So, as I couldn't go to sleep again, I got up to look after the fire."

"And you are doing your work capitally. The kettle is singing loudly, and l'Encuerado will find it difficult to take it off without burning his fingers."

But the Indian had provided himself with two green branches, which he used to lift off the make-shift coffee-pot, into which he emptied both the sugar and the coffee.

"Where is the filter?" asked Lucien.

"Do you think you are still in the town?" I replied. "Why don't you ask for a cup and saucer as well?"

"But we can never drink this black muddy stuff!" cried Lucien.

"Never mind, Chanito," said the Indian; "I'll soon make it all right."

Then, taking his gourd, he poured from it some cold water into the mixture, and it immediately became cleared.

I told Lucien to go and wake up Sumichrast.

The child approached our companion, who was scarcely visible under the leaves, which served him both for coverlet and pillow.

"Hallo! hallo! M. Sumichrast; the soup is on the table."

"Soup!" repeated Sumichrast, rubbing his eyes. "Ah! you little monkey, you have disturbed me in such a pleasant dream. I fancied that I was no older than you, and that I was once more wandering over the mountains of my native land."

It is considered wholesome to take a cup of Mocha after a hearty meal; but, with all due deference to Grimod de la Reynière and Brillat Savarin, coffee seems still sweeter to the taste when taken at five o'clock in the morning, after passing the night in the open air.

The day broke; it was a magnificent sight to see the

forest gradually lighted up, and the trunks of the trees
gilded by slanting sunbeams. Before starting again, one of
our party carefully examined the ground on which we had
camped, so as not to forget any of our effects, which, if lost,
would have been irreparable. I also noticed that l'Encuerado's basket was decked with the three squirrels' skins,
which would thus gradually dry.

We had walked on for nearly an hour, the only incident
being our meeting with various kinds of birds, when the
melancholy cry of the *couroucou* struck on our ears. The
call of this bird is very much like that uttered by the Mexican ox-drivers when they herd together the animals under
their care; hence its Spanish name of *vaquero*. We gave
chase to them, and in less than half an hour we had obtained a male and female. Lucien was never tired of admiring
these beautiful creatures, with their yellow beaks, hooked
like those of birds of prey. The male bird, in particular,
was magnificent; the feathers on the head and back seemed
to be "shot" with a golden green, while the edges of the
wings and the belly were tinted with the purest crimson,
shaded off into two black lines, which extended as far as
the tail.

"Shall we find many of these birds in the forest, M.
Sumichrast?" asked Lucien.

"No, Master 'Sunbeam;' they are rather rare; so we
must take great care of the skins of these we have shot."

"Is their flesh good to eat?" he asked.

"Excellent; and many a gourmand would be glad to make
a meal of it. However, at dinner-time, you shall try for
yourself; and you will meet with very few people who, like
you, have partaken of the *trogon massena*."

"At all events, it isn't another relation of the rat—is it?"
asked the boy, archly.

"No; it belongs to the family of climbers—that is to

say, to that order of birds which have two toes in front of their claws and two behind, like your great friends the parrots."

After we had dressed the skins of the couroucous, and carefully wrapped up the game, we again moved on. The ground became stony, and the descent steeper. At one time I had hoped to find a spring at the bottom of the ravine; but we very soon discovered, to our great disappointment, that we should have to begin climbing again, leaving behind us the oaks and the *ceibas*, and meeting with nothing but gigantic pine-trees. The *pine-needles*,* which literally carpeted the ground, made it so slippery, that for every step forward we frequently took two backward. We fell time after time, but our falls were not in the least degree dangerous. Sometimes, as if at a signal, we all four rolled down together, and each laughed at his neighbor's misfortune, thus cheering one another. Lucien had an idea of hanging on to Gringalet's tail, who was the only one that could avoid these mishaps. This plan answered very well at first; but the dog soon after broke away by a sudden jerk, and the boy rolled backward like a ball, losing all the ground he had gained, but he at once got up again, quite in a pet with the dog, for whom he predicted a fall as a punishment for his treacherous behavior.

The troublesome pine-needles obliged us again to resort to the stake and lasso plan; l'Encuerado, with his load, strove in vain to keep up with us.

"Can any one understand the use of these horrible trees?" grumbled the Indian. "Why can't they keep their leaves to themselves? Why don't they grow in the plains, instead of making honest folks wear the flesh off their bones in a place which is quite difficult enough to traverse as it is?"

---

* The small tapering leaves of the pine are thus called.

" God makes them grow here," said the child.

" Not at all, Chanito ; God created them, but the devil has sown them on these mountains. I have travelled on the large plateau, where there are whole forests of pines, which proves that it was only for spite that they grow on this ascent."

Fortunately Lucien only half believed what the Indian said, and very soon asked me all about it.

" The pines," I replied, " are trees of the North, which never grow well except in cold climates and dry soils. If l'Encuerado had been acquainted with the history of his ancestors, he would have been able to give you some better information about them ; he would have known that, in the Aztec mythology, they were sacred to the mother of the gods, the goddess Matlacueye, who, curiously enough, fills the part of Cybele among the Greek goddesses, whose favorite tree was also the pine."

Just at this moment we were passing close to a giant of the forest, which had been broken by a squall of wind ; from three or four cracks in its trunk a transparent resin ran trickling out. Lucien, thinking these globules were solid, wished to take hold of one of them ; but his fingers stuck to it.

" I fancied," said he, " that turpentine was obtained by crushing the branches of the pine-tree, just as they crush the stems of the sugar-cane."

" You were wrong, then," I answered. " The Indians, in the forests where they manufacture it, content themselves with cutting down the tree within a foot of the ground ; the resin at once begins to ooze out, and gradually fills the leathern bottles placed to receive it. As soon as the resin ceases to flow, they cut the tree up into fagots for the use of the inhabitants of the towns, or the Indians living on plains, whose poor dwellings often possess no other light than the smoky glimmer from a branch of fir."

I was obliged to cut short my explanations, in order to help Sumichrast and l'Encuerado, who, in spite of the lasso, seemed as if they were trying who could slip fastest. The only way we could get on at all was by describing zigzags, and thus we were two hours in climbing a quarter of a league. At last we arrived on the verge of the forest. The rocky ground seemed quite pleasant to walk upon: we could now advance in a straight line, and were able, with very little trouble, to reach another summit.

From the crest a marvellous panoramic view was in sight, for we overlooked all the surrounding country. On our left rose the gigantic and majestic peak of Orizava or Citla-tepetl—that is, the "mountain of the star"—which rises to 17,372 feet above the sea-level. Lucien thought that this could not really be the same mountain the summit of which he was in the habit of seeing every morning.

"It is quite a different shape," he said.

"It is not the mountain, but the point from which you look at it, that has changed its appearance," replied Sumichrast.

"But it looks much higher," said Lucien.

"That is because we are nearer to it. From here we can discern the beautiful forest which surrounds its base as you ascend, the pines growing farther and farther apart, and gradually disappearing altogether. Higher still may be seen the glaciers glittering in the sun; and, last of all, the perpetual snow surrounding the crater, which was visited for the first time in 1847, by M. Doignon, a Frenchman."

"Popocatepetl, Istaccihuatl," said l'Encuerado gravely, pointing out the mountains.

The two mountains mentioned by the Indian were towering up behind us—a sight that alone repaid for our difficult ascent; we could admire in turn the three loftiest volca-noes in Mexico.

" Where is Popocatepetl?" asked Lucien.

" There; that enormous cone which rises to our right," I answered, pointing in that direction.

" Is it the smallest of the three?"

" No; on the contrary, it does not measure less than 18,000 feet in height. Dias Ordas, one of the captains of Fernando Cortez, made its first ascent. Its name signifies ' smoking mountain.' "

" Yes; and I know that Istaccihuatl means ' white wom-an;' but I do not know the height of it."

" It is 15,700 feet above the level of the sea."

" How can mountains like these be measured?" asked Lucien.

" In the first place, by geometrical calculations, and then, by the aid of a barometer, when an ascent has been made. The column of mercury in the instrument falls in pro-portion as the barometer is carried up the mountain, be-cause the air which presses upon the mercury reservoir be-comes less and less dense."

I quite forgot the lapse of time while contemplating the glorious panorama spread beneath. Just around us the ground was rocky and volcanic, and covered with mosses of various colors; rather lower down the ground was hid-den by the fallen leaves of giant trees; beyond was a suc-cession of smaller crests, frequently quite barren, sometimes covered with sun-scorched verdure. On the horizon, which was hidden by a transparent mist, the two volcanoes of the plateau stood out in bold relief against the blue sky, facing the other colossus, which seemed to protect us with its shadow. The peaks of these mountains, clad with their perpetual snow, can be seen by sailors forty leagues at sea.

I was really sorry to give the signal for departure. We

again met with the pine-needles, and though our ascent was
difficult and slow, our descent was proportionably rapid.
Thus we fell forward instead of falling backward. Gringalet, who seemed amused at our ridiculous postures, and was
too confident in his own powers, shared our mishaps, much
to the amusement of his young master, who had predicted
that such would happen. L'Encuerado, utterly tired out,
bethought himself of dragging his basket along the ground,
which was so thickly covered with leaves that he managed
it without damaging his load or breaking the bottles.

At last we came upon oak vegetation; and, still farther
down, tropical plants. Various birds enlivened our journey
by their song, while numbers of brilliant-colored insects
hummed cheerfully round us. In less than an hour we had
passed from autumn to spring, after having had a glimpse
of winter. The creepers very soon obliged us to cut a passage with our *machetes;* but what was our joy upon perceiving, at the bottom of the ravine, a stream bordered with
angelica and water-cress!

Thanks to the abundance of materials, our hut was quickly constructed. While l'Encuerado was getting dinner
ready, I went to examine the half-rotten trunk of a tree
which was lying on the ground. A multitude of insects,
of an elegant shape and of a metallic-blue color, fled at my
approach; they belonged to the numerous *Carabus* family,
the flesh-eating *Coleopteræ*, which are found both in Europe
and in America.

"Why don't they fly away, instead of running or tumbling over on the ground?" asked Lucien.

"Because they are but little used to flying, and are very
quick at walking," I answered.

"Oh papa! the one I have caught has wetted my fingers,
and it feels as if it had burned me."

"You are right; but you needn't be afraid; it will not

hurt you. Many of the *Carabus* family, when they are caught, try to defend themselves by throwing out a corrosive liquid; others make a report, accompanied by smoke, which has given them their name of *bombardier*."

" What do they find to eat under the bark, in which they must lead a very gloomy life?"

" Larvæ and caterpillars; they are, therefore, more useful than injurious."

" To what order of insects do they belong?"

" To the Coleoptera order, because they have four wings, the largest of which, called *elytra*, are more or less hard, and justify their name* by encasing the two other wings, which are membranous and folded crosswise. The cockchafer, you know, is one of this order."

A fresh piece of bark revealed to us two scorpions with enormous bellies, and heads so small as to be almost imperceptible; all they did was to stiffen out their tails, which are composed of six divisions, the last terminating in an extremely slender barb.

" Oh, what horrid creatures!" cried Lucien, starting back; " if it wasn't for their light color, you might take them for prawns with their heads cut off."

" Yes, if you didn't examine them too closely. I suppose you will be very surprised when I tell you that they are allied to the spider tribe."

" I should never have suspected it. Are they dead, then, for they do not move?"

" Insects belonging to this order are very slow and lazy in their movements. They are found under most kinds of bark; therefore I advise you to take care when searching through it."

" Should I die if I were stung?"

---

* Elytra is derived from a Greek word, ἔλυτρον, a sheath.

" No; but it would cause a very painful swelling, which it would be best to avoid."

" I shall be afraid to meddle with the bark of trees, now."

" Then good-bye to your making a collection of insects. Prudence is a very good quality, but you must not make it an excuse for cowardice."

Upon examining the insects more closely, I saw that one of the scorpions, a female, was carrying three or four young ones on her back. This sight much amused Lucien, especially when he saw the animal begin to move slowly off with them.

" Do you know, Chanito," said l'Encuerado, who had now joined us, which showed that the cooking did not require his undivided attention, " that when the mother of the young scorpions does not supply them with food, they set to and devour her."

" Is that true ?" asked Lucien, with surprise.

" If the little ones do not actually kill their mother, at all events they feed on her dead body," I answered. " You will have plenty of opportunities to verify this fact, for these insects are very plentiful in the *Terre-Tempérée*."

" Ah !" cried Lucien, " I was quite right, then, when I called them horrid creatures."

L'Encuerado, stripping off another piece of bark, exposed to view a salamander, which awkwardly tried to hide itself.

" You may catch it if you like ; there is nothing to be afraid of," said I to Lucien, who had drawn back in fright.

" But it is a scorpion !" he exclaimed.

" You are too frightened to see clearly ; it is a salamander, an amphibious reptile of the frog family. The scorpion has eight feet, while the salamander, which is much more like a lizard, has only four."

" Are they venomous ?" asked Lucien of the Indian.

" No, Chanito; *Indians*" (it was well worth while hearing the contempt with which l'Encuerado pronounced this name) "are afraid of it; once I was afraid of it myself, but your papa has taught me to handle it without the least fear."

And the hunter placed the salamander in the boy's hand, who cried out—

" It is as cold as ice, and all sticky."

" It must be so, as a matter of course; the salamander, like a fish, is a cold-blooded animal. The viscous humor which is secreted by the skin of the salamander is able to protect them for a short time from injury by fire, by means of the same phenomenon by which a hand, previously wetted, can be plunged into melting iron without burning it.* Thus an idea has arisen that these batrachians can exist in the midst of flames. Although these poor animals are deaf, nearly blind, and remarkable for their timidity, poets, much to the amusement of naturalists, have chosen the salamander as an emblem of valor."

Assisted by Sumichrast, I continued the examination of the immense tree, which, being half rotted by the dampness of the soil, supplied us with some very beautiful specimens of various insects.

Suddenly we heard Lucien speaking in supplicating tones; I ran towards him, and found him trying to prevent l'Encuerado, who had got possession of the salamander, from making a trial of its powers of resisting fire.

" All right, Chanito; I will not leave it long on the coals; your papa said that these animals do not mind it a bit."

Lucien would not consent to this cruel experiment, but carried the animal back to the tree on which we had found it.

---

* Thanks to the spheroidal condition of water, discovered by M. Boutigny (of Evreux).

The day was drawing to a close when we returned to the
fire; from the stew-pan an appetizing odor was escaping,
in which one of the couroucous, with a handful of rice, was
boiling, while the other bird was roasting in front. It was
really a capital dinner; first we had some excellent soup, of
which Lucien had two platefuls; then came what was left
of our squirrel, and last of all the roasted couroucou, which
l'Encuerado served up on a bed of water-cresses. We had
an unlimited supply of water; and, although my readers may
smile at what I say, I really believe we drank too much. A

cup of coffee crowned our feast, and then the remains were
left to Gringalet, who licked every thing clean, even to the
very saucepan. Lucien, having finished his meal, lay down
by my side, and was not long before he was fast asleep.

A dismal howling from our four-footed companion woke
us up with a start. We seized our arms. The dog, with
his ears laid back, his tail between his legs, turned his nose
to the wind with an anxious glance, and set up a fresh

"It was really a capital dinner."

howl, which was answered by the shrill prolonged cries of the coyotas, or jackal of Mexico.

"So these miserable brutes think they are going to frighten us?" cried l'Encuerado.

And while we were making up the fire, the Indian rushed off into the darkness.

"Are they wolves, M. Sumichrast?" asked Lucien, anxiously.

"Yes, my boy, but only prairie wolves," he answered.

"Do you think that they will first devour l'Encuerado, and then attack us?"

"You needn't be frightened; courage is not one of their virtues. Unless they were starving, they wouldn't venture near us."

All at once we heard a shot. The whole forest seemed in movement; the cries of the birds resounded through the trees, and the echoes repeated the noise of the report. Gringalet barked loudly, and was again answered by the harsh cry of the coyotas. At length the silence, which for a short time had been disturbed, was once more restored, and the forest resumed its solemn stillness.

CHAPTER VII.

THE CATS'-EYES POMADE.—ARMADILLO.—LUCIEN AND THE
CRUEL FERN.—THE FALLEN MOUNTAIN.—THE WOOD-
PECKER.—THE BASILISK.—L'ENCUERADO'S FRESH IDEA.

GRINGALET, who had been the first to give the alarm,
was also the first to go to sleep again. I could not
help waiting with some degree of anxiety for l'Encuerado's
return. In a quarter of an hour, as the Indian did not arrive, I began to think that, confused by the darkness, he
had missed finding our bivouac. After having called him
two or three times, without receiving any answer, I was
just going to fire off my gun, so that the noise of the report might serve as a guide to him, when I heard the sound
of his guttural cry.

" What on earth has possessed you to chase useless game at this hour of the night ?" I cried, as he came into sight.

" I felt bound to give these screeching animals a lesson, señor; if I hadn't done so, they would have come back to disturb us every night," answered the Indian, gravely.

" Have you killed any of them ?"

" I only managed to wound one. I followed it—"

" At the risk of falling into some pit. You can't see at night—at least, as far as I know."

" Not very well; but that is all your fault," replied l'Encuerado, in a reproachful tone.

" What! my fault ?"

" The *brujos* (sorcerers) have many a time offered me an ointment made of cats' eyes and fat; but they wanted too much for it. You knew much more about it than the sorcerers; and if you would only have told me the way to make the ointment, and how to use it, I should have been able to see at night, long enough ago, which would be quite as useful to you as to me."

This was an old story, and all that I could have said to the Indian would not have convinced him that I could not make him see in the dark.

It was broad daylight when Sumichrast awoke us. The brook, which we could cross at a leap, sometimes rippled over pebbles, and sometimes glided silently over a sandy bottom. The plants which grew on its two banks fraternally intertwined their green branches, and their flowers seemed to exchange their perfumes. From the boughs of the large trees hung gray mosses, which made them look like gigantic old men; the sun gilded their black trunks with its rising beams, and from the tops of the trees the sweet chant of birds rose up towards heaven. Our eyes, which had become accustomed to the comparatively barren places we had traversed the day before, dwelt with delight

upon this lovely and glorious scene ; our hearts rejoiced in
the midst of this calm and luxuriant aspect of nature.   It
was with feelings of regret we got ready to move on again.

"Suppose we weren't to go till the afternoon," said Sumichrast.

"Suppose we don't go till to-morrow," I answered.

These ideas seemed so thoroughly to respond to the wish
of all, that, in a moment, our travelling gear was scattered
again on the ground.   The first thing we did was to take a
bath ; then the thought struck us that we had better wash
our clothes.   Lucien, helped by l'Encuerado, who had nothing to wash for himself, as he wore his leather garment
next to his skin, laughed heartily at seeing us turned into
washerwomen ; still he did not do his part of the work at
all badly.   He then undertook to wash Gringalet, whose
white coat, spotted with black, was sadly in want of cleansing.   Unfortunately, the dog was hardly out of the water
when he began rolling himself in the dust, and, as dirty as
ever, came frisking around his disappointed little master.

We were roaming about in every direction, in the hope
of collecting some insects, when Gringalet pricked up his
ears and showed his teeth.   The rustling of dry leaves attracted our attention to a slope opposite to us, on which an
armadillo was seen.

Generally speaking, these animals only go out for food in
the night.   This one, which we saw in broad daylight, was
about the size of a large rabbit.   Pricking up its ears, it
raised its tapering muzzle so as to snuff closer to the branches.   Its head, which was very small, gave it a very grotesque
appearance.   Suddenly it began scratching up the earth
with its front paws, furnished with formidable claws, and
now and then poked its pointed nose into the hole it had dug.
I had crossed the stream, and was advancing cautiously towards the animal, when I saw it leave off its work, and, bend-

ing down its head uneasily, as quick as lightning it rolled itself up into a ball and glided down the slope. Just at my feet it stopped, and I only had to stoop down in order to pick it up. Gringalet, who then appeared at the top of the slope, was evidently the cause of its sudden flight.

I rejoined my companions, carrying my prisoner, who tried neither to defend itself nor to escape. Lucien examined with curiosity the scales which crossed the back of the armadillo, and its pink transparent skin. I told him that this inoffensive animal, which feeds on insects and roots, belonged to the order Edentata—mammals in which the system of teeth is incomplete.

"But," said he, "I have seen pictures in which armadillos are represented with armor formed of small squares."

"That is another species, which also lives in Mexico," replied Sumichrast.

When we talked about killing the animal, Lucien opposed the idea with great vehemence. He wanted either to carry it away alive or to let it go—both being plans which could not be allowed. Gringalet, however, cut short the discussion by strangling it, l'Encuerado's carelessness having left it in his way. The boy, both angry and distressed, was astonished at the cruelty of his dog, and was going to beat him.

"He has only yielded to instinct," said Sumichrast.

"A fine instinct, truly," replied Lucien, in tears, "to kill a poor beast that never did him any harm!"

"He has saved us the trouble of killing it. Men, and all carnivorous animals, can not live except on the condition of sacrificing other creatures. Didn't you shoot a squirrel yesterday? And you did not refuse your share of those beautiful birds, the plumage of which so delighted you."

"Yes, but I did not strangle the squirrel with my teeth. It's a very different thing."

"For you, very probably; but it was much the same to the squirrel. However, if there's another chance, you shall lend your gun to Gringalet."

Lucien smiled through his tears, and his indignation gradually calmed down. Certainly the result is the same, whether you wring a fowl's neck or shoot it; yet I could never make up my mind to the former operation. Lucien, who was endowed with almost feminine sensibility, was often angry with l'Encuerado, who could scarcely resist the temptation of firing at any thing alive, useful or not, which came within reach of his gun. We had spoken often enough to the Indian on the subject, but he always asserted that if God had allowed man to kill for the purpose of food, He had also ordered him to destroy hurtful animals, as they were the allies of the demon. Unfortunately, horses and dogs excepted, all animals were hurtful in l'Encuerado's eyes.

Gun on shoulder, we made our way up the bed of the stream, often being obliged to cut our path through a thicket of plants. I noticed a fine tree-fern, the leaves of which, not yet developed, assumed the shape of a bishop's crosier. Lucien remarked this.

"You are right," said I, "it is very curious. Do you know Jussieu divided all vegetables into three great orders —*Acotyledons, Monocotyledons*, and *Dicotyledons*. Ferns belong to the first;* they have no visible flowers, and are allied to the sea-weed and mushroom tribe. It is only under the tropics that ferns attain the dimensions of the one you are looking at; in colder regions their height seldom exceeds a few feet. Ferns formed almost the sole vegetation of the primitive world, and we frequently find evidence of some gigantic species which are now extinct."

---

* That is, a plant devoid of *lobes*.

Lucien, being desirous to examine the crosier-shaped stalks, allowed us to get in front of him, then crept under the fern.

As the leaves of this shrub are furnished underneath with long prickles, when he wanted to rejoin us he found himself caught. The more he struggled the worse he became entangled. He cried out to me in a most distressed voice, and not knowing what had happened, I lost no time in going back to him. I found him fighting hard against the thorns which were scratching his face and hands. L'Encuerado and Sumichrast also came to his assistance.

I disentangled the boy as quickly as I could; but already he had several scratches over his face and hands.

"How came you not to think," I said, "that by struggling in this way you would only the more entangle yourself?"

"I saw you all leaving me; I scarcely knew what held me back, and I got quite frightened; but I'm not crying, papa, and yet the fern-prickles scratch terribly."

L'Encuerado turned up his sleeves, and, seizing his *machete*, rushed at the fern.

"Are not you ashamed to attack a child?" he cried. "It's all very fine to display your bishop's crosier and then behave in this way! Try and tear my coat! I know you wouldn't dare to do it! Never mind, though! I'll punish you for your malice."

The poor plant, alas! was soon cut down; thus the growth of years was destroyed in a few minutes.

After an hour's walking, the head of our little column suddenly came in front of a whole mountain-side which had slid from its original position. The sight was a magnificent one; the accumulation of rocks, piled one on the other, had crushed down in their fall the trees that impeded their course. We saw before us an inextricable pile of trunks, monstrous roots, and masses of rock, suspended and apparently ready to fall. The catastrophe must have recently occurred; for here and there a branch was still covered with foliage, and the grass had not as yet carpeted the immense gap. Lucien was so astonished at the wild grandeur of the scene that it actually put an end to his chatter. Without speaking, we joined Sumichrast, who was in advance. That a lagoon must have been filled up by the avalanche of rocks, we saw certain indications. We could hear the rumbling noise of water flowing beneath us. On our left, at the foot of the mountain, extended a wide basin, which, from its regular outline, might well have been made by the hand of man.

Every thing seemed silent and deserted around us, although the bushes that margined the edge of the lagoon must once have sheltered many a guest; now the imposing grandeur of the scene had awed them, or driven them off.

"How could such a great mass as this fall down?" asked Lucien.

"We can only conjecture," replied Sumichrast; "perhaps the stream flowing beneath the base of the rocks had excavated fissures, and thus undermined it."

"The noise must have been terrific," said Lucien.

"Doubtless it was," replied Sumichrast; "and the shock possibly felt for many leagues round."

"Have you ever seen a mountain fall in two like that, M. Sumichrast?"

"Yes; I did five years ago, when I was in company with your father. A whole forest disappeared before our eyes in a land-slip, which also overwhelmed four or five Indian huts. In a year from the present time, the wilderness of bare rocks that we see before us will be again covered with thick vegetation; mosses will grow over these gray-colored rocks, and the stream will have renewed its course. If chance should ever lead us again to this spot, the rich foliage and flowers would almost prevent our recognizing the desolation which now impresses us so much."

I crossed the stream, in order to reach our bivouac by the opposite bank to that which we had hitherto followed. Suddenly a noise, like a mallet striking the trunk of a tree, attracted our attention.

"You told me just now there was no one but ourselves in the forest," cried Lucien.

"Chut!" replied l'Encuerado; "it is nothing but a large woodpecker."

And each of us glided under the bushes and tried to get near the winged workman, who so loudly betrayed his presence. Ten minutes elapsed, but all was silent, and the object of our search appeared to have moved off. In fact, we were about to give up the pursuit, when three blows, struck at regular intervals, resounded near us.

The *Carpintero* (carpenter), for such it is called in Mexico, has very brilliant yellow eyes, red feathers upon the head, while the body is dark-colored streaked with white. It climbs easily up the trunks of trees, resting upon its tail-feathers. At length we observed it, and as we looked, admiring its plumage, it again struck three resounding blows, and ran round the tree as if to inspect the other side.

"The fool!" muttered l'Encuerado; "he thinks he can pierce a tree as thick as my body with three pecks of his beak! He'll soon be eaten."

And he fired at the bird and hit it.

"I say, papa, did the woodpecker really want to pierce this big tree?"

"No, my boy; that is a popular but unfounded idea. The woodpecker strikes the trees in order to frighten the insects that are concealed under the bark; and the action

which l'Encuerado has interpreted in his own way is performed with a view of getting hold of the fugitives."

Sumichrast showed Lucien that the woodpecker, aided
by its wedge-shaped beak, could, in case of need, rip up the
bark under which its prey was to be found; that his tongue,
covered with spines bending backward, is well adapted to
seize the larvæ; and, lastly, that the stiff and elastic feathers of its tail afford it a very useful support in the exercise
of its laborious vocation.

"You often get the better of me in argument," said l'Encuerado; "but it's no use your saying that woodpeckers do
not bore into trees, for I have seen them doing it."

"You are right, up to a certain point," replied Sumichrast; "some species make their nests in dead trees, which
their beaks can with ease penetrate. As for piercing sound
trees, that's quite another question."

While l'Encuerado was preparing the armadillo and the
woodpecker, which we were to have for dinner, we walked
down the course of the stream, the agreeable freshness of
which was very pleasant to us. All at once Lucien pointed
out to me a basilisk sitting on a stone, the rays of the sun
setting off its bright shades—yellow, green, and red. This
member of the Iguana family, which bears no resemblance
to the fabulous basilisk of the Greeks, got up at our approach, puffed out its throat, and shook the membranous
crest on the top of its head. Its bright eye seemed to scan
the horizon; no doubt it caught sight of us, for its flaccid
body stiffened out, and with a rapid bound it sprang into
the stream. The reptile raised its chest in swimming, beating the water with its fore paws as if with oars. We soon
lost sight of it, to Lucien's great sorrow, for he wanted to
obtain a further inspection of it.

Gathering round the fire, we arranged our baggage, ready
to start the next morning. As there was still another hour's

"The dog began to howl desperately."

daylight, Lucien remained with l'Encuerado, and I went with Sumichrast to reconnoitre the route we intended to take.

The sun was setting, and we were slowly approaching our bivouac, when Gringalet's whine met our ears. I hastened forward, for the dog began to howl desperately. I reached the hut quite out of breath. Every thing seemed right, but Lucien and l'Encuerado had disappeared. I looked anxiously into my companion's face.

"No doubt," said Sumichrast, "l'Encuerado has gone to take a stroll, and left the dog asleep."

I raised a call-cry. What was my surprise at hearing it answered from up above us. My son and the Indian were sitting thirty feet from the ground, hidden in the foliage of a gigantic tree. My first impulse was to address l'Encuerado rather angrily.

"Don't flurry him," said Sumichrast; "he'll need all his presence of mind to get the boy down safely."

With an anxiety which may be easily understood, I watched all the movements of the lad, who was every now and then concealed by the leaves.

"Gently," cried l'Encuerado; "put your foot there. Well done! Now lay hold of this branch and slide down. Don't be afraid; I'll not let you go. How pleased and proud your papa will be when he knows how high you have climbed!"

The Indian was wrong; I was neither pleased nor proud. The trunk of the tree was five or six feet in circumference; the first branches sprang at a point no less than seven to ten feet from the ground, and I could not make out how the boy managed to reach them. As for l'Encuerado, or rather the *ape* that went by that name, I knew that no obstacle could stop *him*.

I must, however, confess that I felt all my anger melting

away when I saw the skill and coolness of the young acrobat.   Certainly, Sumichrast appealed to my own reminiscences, and offered to lay me a wager that I had climbed many a poplar without the advantage of such superintendence as l'Encuerado's.   At last the two gymnasts reached the lowest branches, and I breathed more freely.

"Papa," cried the child, "we climbed right to the top, and there found a nest and a squirrel's hiding-place."

"Have you suddenly gone mad?" said I, interrupting him and addressing the Indian.

"Mad!" repeated he, with the most sublime simplicity. "Why?"

"Couldn't you have chosen a tree that was not so tall?"

"Don't you wish Chanito to learn to climb?   At all events, the señora intrusted him to me."

"And so you risk his breaking his bones?"

"I'm not a child," replied the Indian, proudly, standing upright on a branch.

"Enough of these gymnastics!   Come down at once; although God knows how you are going to manage it."

The words were hardly out of my mouth when Lucien reached the ground, suspended by a *lasso* which l'Encuerado had tied under his arms.   The Indian had pulled him up to the lowest branches in the same way.

"You have not acted sensibly," said I to the Indian; "we do not begin to learn to ride by mounting a wild horse. Lucien doesn't know yet how to climb high trees."

"Lucien can climb as well as I can," retorted the culprit; "he has never eaten an orange out of your garden without clambering up to gather it himself."

"That's something new to me," said I, looking hard at my son, who blushed.   "At any rate, orange-trees are very different in size from cotton-woods, so you risked killing him."

"No; I kept tight hold of him. You very well know that if Chanito were likely to come to his death by my fault, I should die first."

"That wouldn't bring the boy to life again. There will be plenty of dangers in our excursion without seeking them out for mere pleasure. I want to bring you all back safe and sound to Orizava; therefore, don't let us have any more of these ascents."

Having uttered this remonstrance, I turned on my heel, for it was no use trying to have the last word with l'Encuerado. I was, however, quite sure that he would not renew the exploit which had displeased me, and that was all I wished.

At supper-time, Gringalet did not show any repugnance to the flesh of the armadillo, the taste of which reminded Lucien of sucking-pig.

"Are armadillos very scarce?" he asked; "they are never sold in the market."

"Just the contrary," replied Sumichrast; "they are very common, and the Indians never fail to feast on them when they can procure them."

"What does the name armadillo mean?"

"It is a Paraguayan word, the meaning of which is, 'encased in armor.' The Aztecs call the animal *ayotochitl*, that is, 'gourd-rabbit'—'rabbit' on account of its ears, and 'gourd' because, when it rolls itself up in a ball, it reminds one of that vegetable."

L'Encuerado had gone to sleep. Lucien soon went into the hut, and I noticed that Sumichrast carefully arranged the leaves which were to form our bed, although he himself lay down anywhere. I was much less inclined for sleep than my companions, and contemplated them all reposing; reflecting on the strange chance which united, under the same shelter, in the midst of the wilderness, persons born

of such distinct races and in such different climates. We
could all surely depend on one another, for in previous
expeditions our mutual friendship had been put to the
proof. Seeing how well Lucien bore the fatigue, I rejoiced
that I had brought him under the protection of such good
guardians. When I entered the hut to seek repose, I disturbed Gringalet, who, before lying down again by his
young master, licked his hand : here was another devoted
friend—" the dog, which combines all man's better qualities," as Charlet observes.

CHAPTER VIII.

WE left our bivouac at daybreak, first ascending and
then descending, sometimes making our way through
thickets and other times through glades; suddenly a flock
of vultures attracted our attention. A hideous spectacle
was now presented to our eyes. A *coyote*—doubtless that
which l'Encuerado had wounded the day before—lay half
devoured on the ground, and more than fifty guests were
coming in turn for their share, and to tear, in turn, a strip
of flesh from the carcass.

"What frightful creatures!" cried Lucien. "I can't think why the nasty smell does not drive them away."

"It is just the reverse; it is the smell which attracts them," I replied. "Even when they are soaring high up in the sky, and scan the horizon with their yellow eyes, their subtle sense of smell enables them to catch the effluvia of the putrefied matter on which they feed."

In some of the towns of Mexico the black vultures are so numerous—living there, as they do, almost tame in the streets—that our young companion was well acquainted with these birds; but he had never been present at one of their joint meals. The sight of one of their bare, black, and wrinkled necks, plunged into the body of the animal, made him almost ill.

"Poh!—what disgusting birds!" he cried.

"You are wrong," I said; "the birds are only obeying the instinct implanted in them. Henceforward you will understand better the name of the 'rapacious order' or 'birds of prey,' which is given by naturalists to vultures, eagles, falcons, and owls. You are aware that the science which describes the habits of birds is called *ornithology*. Cuvier, the great classifier, divides the feathered tribe into six orders—birds of prey, passerines, climbers, gallinaceans, wading, and web-footed birds. In order to prevent confusion, the orders have been subdivided into families, the families into groups, the groups into genera, and the genera into species.

"How are they all to be recognized?"

"By the study of certain special characteristics, which serve as distinguishing marks. Birds of prey, for instance, have curved beaks and claws, legs feathered either to the knee or down to the foot, three toes in front, and one behind; also, the back and inside toe are stronger than the others. The vultures which you are looking at, the only

"A flock of vultures attracted our attention."

6

birds of the order which live in flocks, belong to the *Ca-thartus* genus."*   .

"Look! there are some which keep at a distance. They look as if they were afraid."

"No; they have gorged themselves, and are now digest- ing their meal; unless danger compel them to take flight, they will remain motionless until sunset."

"Will they attack live creatures?"

"Very rarely; for they are dreadful cowards, and, be- sides, do not care much for fresh meat."

We had now left far behind us the miserable crew of carrion-eaters, when Lucien suddenly cried out—

"Oh, papa! look, there's a bleeding tree!"

"It is a *pterocarpus;* that is, a vegetable with mem- branes resembling the wing of a bird. The red sap which is trickling down from its bark is called *dragon's blood*, thus named by the Greeks, who ascribed to it a fabulous origin. The *blood-tree*, for so the Indians designate it, is allied to the asparagus and lily genera, and the gum which exudes from it is a good remedy for dysentery."

L'Encuerado picked off a few dry flakes of this invalua- ble production; and then, dipping his finger into some of the drops which were still liquid, he rubbed it all over Grin- galet's legs and paws, who was thus provided with red top- boots. As a matter of fact, this operation must have had a good effect upon the animal; for this gum, being very rich in tannin, was certain to brace the tissues and muscles; but the first sensation of it seemed to distress the poor beast, who ran along lifting up his legs in a very comical fashion.

"Gringalet walks very much in the same way that l'En-

---

* From the Greek καθαρτίς, "that which purifies." In fact, this bird assists in cleansing the streets in towns where there is no organization for the purpose.

cuerado did the time he put on his beautiful blue slippers," remarked Lucien, in great glee.

"You don't mean to say," said Sumichrast, "that l'Encuerado ever wore blue slippers?"

"Yes; the other day there was a dinner-party, and mamma told him to dress himself as well as he could. He at once ran off to buy a pair of pumps he had seen in a shop, and, just at the moment they were all sitting down to dinner, he made his appearance in his new foot-coverings, and —a cravat!"

"A cravat!" repeated Sumichrast, more surprised than ever.

"Yes, a real cravat; but as he had never before worn any thing on his feet but sandals, he lifted them up when he walked just as Gringalet does now. Mamma advised him to put on his sandals again; but he would not obey her, so he was well punished, for he tripped up and broke a whole pile of plates. It was not until after this misfortune that he could be persuaded to take off his blue pumps; and even then he could not bear to part with them altogether, so he hung them round his neck, and kept on waiting at table, as proud as possible with his grand decoration."

This adventure was only too true, and Sumichrast listened to it with shouts of laughter.

"Why did you hang the shoes round your neck instead of putting them away in a corner?" asked Sumichrast of the Indian.

"I did it to let all the world know that I had bought them, and that they belonged to me," replied l'Encuerado.

Our encampment was established at the entrance of a fresh glade. L'Encuerado had killed five or six small birds; we were, therefore, certain of something for dinner. We had scarcely finished our building operations, when

"Lucien loudly called out to me."

Lucien, who had been prowling about, lifting up stones and looking under stubs in order to find insects, loudly called out to me. When I got up to him, I saw at the bottom of a hole a coral-serpent, measuring about a yard in length. The reptile was coiled up, and remained motionless while we admired its beautiful red skin, divided at intervals with rings of shining black. L'Encuerado promptly cut a forked stick and pinned the animal down to the ground. The prisoner immediately tried to stand up on end; its jaws distended, and its head assumed a menacing aspect. Gringalet barked at it furiously, without, however, daring to go near. The Indian unsheathed his cutlass—the prospect of an unlooked-for addition to dinner quite delighted him.

The flesh of the serpent is a well-known Indian dish. Previous to the conquest of Mexico by the Spaniards, the rattlesnake itself found its place at their highest festivals. Dioscorides* prescribed the flesh of the viper as a tonic, and it formed one of the component parts of *theriaca*, the great panacea of our ancestors, which was one of the principal branches of Venetian commerce. In spite of all these precedents, the dish proposed by l'Encuerado was unanimously rejected.

Having cut off the serpent's head, we all went off to reconnoitre. Going in pursuit of a troop of squirrels, we were led to the edge of the glade without having been able to reach them. A little way in the forest, Sumichrast espied a small russet-colored owl, which suddenly disappeared in a hollow at the foot of an old tree. We all kept quiet for ten minutes, in order to observe the bird's way of hunting. At last it suddenly reappeared, and, standing motionless and upright upon its legs at the entrance of its place of refuge, it looked very like a sentinel on duty in his watch-box.

---

* A celebrated Greek physician in the first century of the Christian era.

Suddenly it started, and slightly bending its body, winked its great yellow eyes several times; then, skimming over the ground with the swiftness of an arrow, it darted into the high grass. It soon made its appearance again, with its feathers erect and flapping its wings. It held in its mouth a poor little mouse, which it carried off into its subterraneous retreat. It was the species of owl called *Athene hypogæa*, which is often met with in the savannahs, and hunts in the day-time as well as in the night.

"What a comical-looking bird!" said Lucien; "and yet I'm half afraid of its brilliant eyes and hooked nose."

"Every one is frightened at him, Chanito," replied l'Encuerado; "and when he settles near a hut at night, and raises his dismal cry, he predicts the early death of some one of those who hear him."

"That can't be," replied Lucien, "for there was an owl in a hole in our garden wall, and papa would never have it disturbed; yet the owl made its cry every night."

"Your father knows how to avert the spell. Besides, the bird that lived in the wall was a common owl."

"Both in Europe and America," interposed Sumichrast, "screech owls, and their kinsmen, the common owls, barn owls, buzzards, and all nocturnal birds of prey, are looked upon by the ignorant as birds of ill omen. Their strange appearance and their mysterious habits give rise to a repugnance which often changes into fear. It is quite wrong to have any dread of them; as a matter of fact, the bird you have just seen is, like all its species, more useful than injurious to man, for it destroys a vast number of small mammals — jerboas, shrew-mice, dormice, and field-mice, which ravage the farmer's crops. You will recollect that the owl, among the ancient Greeks, was the bird of Minerva; with the Aztecs it represents the goddess of evil."

A little way from the spot where we lost sight of the

mouse-eater, there were some enormous holes dug out by the *tuzas*,* the Mexican moles, so dreaded by agriculturists. This animal is about the size of a kitten; it lives in companies, and works underneath the surface of the soil in a way very dangerous to travellers, who suddenly find the ground sink under their feet. L'Encuerado, who was very fond of the flesh of the tuza, which used to be sold in the Indian markets, placed himself in ambush in the hopes of killing one. Five minutes had scarcely elapsed when we heard a gunshot, and the hunter made his appearance with a rather ugly little animal, having a dark-brown coat, short feet, ears and eyes almost imperceptible, a mouth furnished with formidable incisors, and on each side of its jaws a vast pouch filled with earth. Lucien declared that he would never consent to eat of this creature, and promised his share to l'Encuerado.

Our attention was again attracted towards the forest by the cries of five or six *toucans*, and again we set off in chase. These birds are extremely suspicious, and their capricious flight almost baffles pursuit. I succeeded, however, in killing one; the others flew off, raising cries of anger.

"How can they bear the weight of such an enormous beak?" asked Lucien, who had run to pick up the bird, and was struck with admiration at its beautiful green and yellow plumage.

"Nature has made provision for that: the enormous beak, which seems so heavy, is composed of a very light porous substance."

"Then it can not eat any thing hard?"

"No; its flexible beak could not crush any unyielding substance, and it feeds on nothing but soft fruits; and even

---

* *Saccophorus Mexicanus.*

these it breaks up awkwardly. If we could have got near them, you would have seen them plucking berries and tossing them in the air, so as to catch them in their immense jaws."

" What good is its great mouth ?"

" I can't say ; for the naturalists, who have been as much puzzled as you are by this peculiarity, have been unable to explain it."

"Then I am more learned than they are," said l'Encuerado, with a magisterial air.

" Do you know, then, why toucans have such exaggerated beaks ?"

" Because they have been made by a wise Creator," replied the Indian.

" No doubt about that," remarked Sumichrast, smiling ; " but the point is, why they were made so."

" Because their beak, calcined and reduced to powder, is the only efficacious remedy for epilepsy. Toucans are very scarce birds, and if their beaks were no larger than those of other birds of their size, this medicine could never be obtained in sufficient quantities."

L'Encuerado's explanation was perhaps as good as our uncertainty. I remember that the Indians do, in fact, make a great mystery of a powder against epilepsy, and that a toucan's head may often be noticed hanging up to the wall of a hut, as a preservative against St. Vitus' dance.

Instead of resting, Lucien prowled about in every direction, breaking away bark, and lifting stones with all the ardor of a neophyte in entomology. Since meeting with the coral-serpent, he took precautions which gave me confidence ; for it is quite uncertain how a reptile or any other creature may behave when it is disturbed. The child suddenly called out to me ; he had just discovered a nest of *scolopendrœ*, commonly called centipedes, and he was afraid to touch them. The centipedes, surprised at being disturbed, rolled themselves up; their pale blue color somewhat diminishing the repugnance which their appearance generally excites. It was not without some hesitation that Lucien, encouraged by Sumichrast, ventured to place one on the palm of his hand; the insect gradually unrolled its articulations, each of which was provided with two pairs of feet ending in hooks, but its walk was so slow as rather to disappoint the young observer.

" What is the use of having forty-four feet," he cried, " if the centipede can not get on faster than a *carabus*, which only has six ?"

L'Encuerado could alone explain this mystery; but still he kept silence.

" Are these creatures poisonous, M. Sumichrast ?"

" It is said so; but some species—that, for instance, which you are examining—may be handled without danger."

" Here is a little centipede with only twelve legs."

. " It has only just come out of the egg; their rings increase in number as they grow older, and this is one of their peculiarities."

" How hard the rings are! they are almost like armor."

" It is armor, in fact; the *scolopendræ* form a line of demarkation, so to speak, separating insects from crustaceans; centipedes are not very distant relations of lobsters."

" Look, papa! I have just found a chocolate-colored worm, which looks like a centipede."

" That's not a worm; it is an *iulus*, first cousin to the centipede. Don't take it up in your hand, for it will impregnate your fingers with a sickening odor."

We resumed our progress towards our encampment, Lucien and l'Encuerado preceding us. The weather was warm without being suffocating; the slanting rays of the sun were moderated by the foliage, the birds were singing, and to-day, like yesterday, seemed as if it would be one of the least fatiguing in our journey. We were now in the midst of the *Terre-Tempérée,* and were surrounded by white and black oaks. Ceibas, elm, cedars, and *lignum-vitæ* trees only grew here and there; and the mosquitoes, so plentiful in the *Terre-Chaude,* did not trouble us here. The timber, growing widely apart, allowed us to pass easily; we were in a virgin-forest, but were still too high up above the plains to have to struggle against the inextricable net-work of tropical creepers.

The *tuza* made its appearance at our dinner, dressed with rice. Although the appearance of this animal is repulsive, its flesh has an exquisite flavor. I offered a piece of the thigh to Lucien; he found it so nice, that he soon held out his plate—or rather his calabash—for more. Sumichrast told him he was eating some of the mole, though not aware of it: he appeared confused at first, but soon boldly began on his second helping. After the meal, l'Encuerado took from an aloe-fibre bag a needle and bodkin, and set to work to mend Lucien's breeches, torn a day or two before. Two squirrels' skins were scarcely sufficient for the would-be tailor, who lined the knees also with this improvised cloth. Lucien was delighted at this patching, and wanted to try on his mended garment at once. He waddled about, ran, and stooped in every posture, quite fascinated with the rustling noise produced by the dry skins. Gringalet, who had been asleep, suddenly came up to his young master with visible surprise. With his neck stretched out, his eyes glittering, and his ears drooping, ready to retreat in case of need, the dog ventured to take a sniff at l'Encuerado's work, then shook his head energetically and sneezed. After repeating this operation two or three times he seemed to be lost in thought.

"He knows all about it, and can see at once that it is

not badly sewn," said l'Encuerado, with evident satisfaction.

But all of a sudden, after a final and more conscientious examination, the animal began barking furiously, and seizing hold of the patches that had been so industriously sewn in, he tried to tear them away.

"The simpleton fancies the squirrel is still alive!" cried the Indian.

Although driven away at least twenty times, Gringalet kept on returning to the attack, and he assailed the trowsers with so much ardor that a fresh rent was made. Then l'Encuerado became angry, and the dog having been punished, went and crouched down by the fire; but he still continued to show his teeth at the strange lining which seemed so offensive to him.

The sun was setting; its golden rays, quivering among the branches, appeared one by one to get higher and higher until gloom began gradually to pervade the forest. We were assembled around our bivouac, when a rosy tint suddenly illumined the tops of the trees and penetrated through the foliage. As this marvellous effect of light appeared to last a considerable time, we again went into the open glade, so as to be better able to observe it. The sky appeared as if it was all in a blaze; vast glittering jets of light seemed as if darting from the setting sun; a few clouds, tinted with bright red color, flitted across the heavens. The bright gleam became more and more vivid, but without at all dazzling our eyes. A few birds might be heard uttering shrill cries; and the falcons, who were making their way to their aeries, stopped for a moment their rapid flight, and whirled round and round in space with an undecided air.

"The wind will blow tremendously to-morrow," said l'Encuerado; "only once before did I ever see the sky lighted up as it is to-night, and then two days after there was a frightful hurricane, which demolished most of the huts in our village."

"I think we shall get off with nothing but a south wind like that which worried us the day we set off," said Sumichrast.

Wrongly or rightly, I attributed this phenomenon of light to the position of the clouds. The intensity of the light decreased till it was nothing but a glimmer. Night resumed its empire, and there was naught to guide us back to our bivouac but the flame of our fire.

CHAPTER IX.

L'ENCUERADO'S prediction seemed as if it was likely to be realized. About three o'clock in the morning we were awakened by a hoarse roaring; the trees seemed to shiver; sometimes the uproar appeared to grow less and almost to cease, and then broke out again louder than ever. I hastened to warm some coffee; but two or three times the intermittent squalls scattered the burning fagots of our fire, and the hot ashes nearly blinded us. This mishap was owing to the open glade being so near to us, across which the wind rushed furious and unrestrained. Almost before daylight appeared, I led my companions farther under the trees, the state of the atmosphere making me feel very uncomfortable. The lofty tree-tops, roughly shaken by the wind, showered down upon us a perfect hail of twigs and dead leaves. We were almost deafened by the noise of the clashing boughs; sad and silent we proceeded on our way, perceiving no signs of any living creature, and in much trouble how we should obtain our dinners.

Towards mid-day, the wind fell; puffs of heat, which seemed to spring from the ground beneath, almost suffocated us. Lucien did not say a word, but, in spite of my advice, he was constantly lifting his gourd to his lips, a proceeding which could only excite his thirst. Gringalet, instead of frolicking about, as was his custom, followed us closely, drooping his ears and tail. We were, I believe, the only living beings moving under the shade, which now seemed converted into a hot furnace.

Meeting with some rocks, we made up our minds to hurry on, thinking to come upon a stream; a vain hope!—the rocks soon came to an end, and were succeeded by a perfect labyrinth of trees. If there had only been a little grass, we should have set to work to construct our hut; for the dry heat, blown up by the south wind, rendered exertion almost unbearable.

A second time we found ourselves among rocks; but they were so enormous, and so close together, that it was evident we were in the vicinity of a mountain.

"Hiou! hiou! Chanito," cried the Indian, joyously; "forward! forward! we are very nearly at the end of our troubles."

The boy smiled and adopted the swift pace of his guide, while Sumichrast lengthened his strides so as to get in front of me. Following my companions, we soon came upon a dry, barren spot in front of a steep ascent. After we had all taken breath, I gave it as my opinion that we should overcome our fatigue and scale the side of the mountain; but no one showed any inclination to move.

My poor Lucien lay panting on the hard stones, with his mouth dry, his lips bleeding, and his face purple with the heat; he had thought the day's work was over. Nevertheless, as soon as he saw us starting again, up he got and followed us without a word of complaint. I wished to lighten his burden; but he heroically refused, and proportioned his pace to that of l'Encuerado. Gringalet was continually sitting down, and hanging out his tongue to a most enormous length; it was, doubtless, his way of testifying that he moved an amendment against the length of the journey.

"We were quite wrong in finding fault with the shade," said Sumichrast; "for in this unsheltered spot the heat is more insupportable than under the trees. The sun seems to dart into us as if its rays were needles' points."

"Don't drink, Chanito! don't drink!" cried l'Encuerado to Lucien.

The poor little fellow replaced the gourd at his side, and bent on me such a heart-rending look that I caught him up in my arms.

"Let us make a halt," said my friend, who was sheltering himself under a gigantic rock; "I confess that I am deadbeat."

It was a great relief when we were seated down and deprived of our burdens; but, instead of setting to work, according to our usual custom, to collect wood for our fire and to construct our hut, we remained idle, looking at the horizon, without exchanging a single word. At our feet extended, as far as we could see, the tree-tops of an immense forest. We had turned our backs upon the volcano of Orizava; on our right the black summits of the Cordillera stood out against the red sky; the *urubu* vultures were

whirling round and round high up above us—the only
living creatures we had set eyes on since the evening before.

It was now four o'clock; a kind of hot blast beat into
our faces, producing the same sensation as that experienced
in front of a furnace when the door is suddenly opened.
The south wind sprung up again, and squall succeeded
squall—the forest undulating like a liquid surface.

I in vain endeavored to overcome the state of nervous
prostration which had come over me; the terrible wind
which parched and burned us took away all power of will.
Our eyes were inflamed, our lips cracked, and our heads
heavy, and no one cared about eating; all we longed for
was water, and we were obliged to watch Lucien, to prevent him emptying his gourd. He was nibbling a morsel
of *totopo*, which he, like us, could hardly swallow. Sheltered behind the rock, we contemplated with dread the colos-
sal trees round us, which swayed and bent, sprinkling the
ground with their scattered boughs.

The sun set, pale and rayless, as if drowned in the ill-
omened yellow clouds. The wind kept puffing and blowing
at intervals. A few minutes' lull enabled us to collect a
little grass, and then, seated side by side, we watched the
approach of night, dark, desolate, and starless; but the
comparative coolness of the atmosphere gave some little
relief to our exhausted lungs. Lucien went off to sleep;
Sumichrast and l'Encuerado tried to follow his example;
Gringalet seemed afraid to go far away, and crouched down
at our feet. Ere long, I was the only one of the party who
was awake.

What an awful night! About nine o'clock the squalls
ran riot with unexampled violence; if it had not been for
our shelter behind the rock, we should surely have been
swept away. From the forest beneath came a roar like

that of waves beating against a cliff; branches broke off
with an uproar sounding like a series of gun-shots, and the
leaves, driven by the wind, covered us with their *débris*.
Every now and then an inexplicable and increasing hoarse
rumbling filled my mind with anxiety. I listened, holding
my breath with fear; the rumbling seemed to approach,
as if bringing with it new and unknown perils. Then suddenly, prevailing over the tumult, a formidable crash made
itself heard, followed by a shock prolonged by the echoes;
it was the fall of some forest giant, vanquished by the hurricane. Sometimes one might have fancied that a multitude
of men were fighting together in the darkness that no eye
could pierce; there were plainly to be recognized the wild
cries of the conflict and the plaintive moans of the wounded; and then, again, a fresh shock shook the earth, and
deadened the outburst of the mighty lament.

I must confess that at this moment I bitterly regretted
having brought Lucien; I remembered that my friends
had predicted to me all the perils which now threatened us.
While listening to the uproar of the tempest, I felt my resolution give way, and I had serious thoughts of returning to
Orizava the next day.

Towards midnight the storm abated a little, and, giving
way to fatigue, I fell asleep.

I had only just closed my eyes when I suddenly jumped
up again, deafened as if by a hundred claps of thunder joined in one. The darkness was as thick as ever, and the wind
was still more boisterous; the echo of the fallen tree had
scarcely died away before another colossus groaned and
fell. My companions were now all awake.

"What's the matter, M. Sumichrast?" asked Lucien, in a
low tone.

"It is a hurricane, my boy."

"One might fancy that a giant was passing through the

wood, shouting and whistling, and breaking down all the trees as he went along."

"I wish that was all," replied Sumichrast; "but it's something much worse; it is the south wind, the sirocco of the Mexican coast."

"Will it sweep us away, M. Sumichrast?"

"I hope not; thanks to the rock which shields us."

A tree now fell close to us, and covered us with dust. Clingling tightly to one another, every moment brought with it a fresh anxiety. We dared not speak of our feelings, for fear of frightening our young companion, who pressed close up to me. Amidst the universal destruction going on, it only needed a branch driven by the squall to dislodge our shelter, for us to be swept away like chaff before the wind. I had witnessed many a hurricane, but this fearful night exceeded all.

At last daylight appeared; the sun rose gloomily, and exposed the disasters of the terrible night. On every side trees, broken and uprooted, lay prostrate on the ground, or, half suspended by the creepers entangled in their branches, were balanced like the formidable *battering-rams* of the ancients. Lucien was speechless at the sight before his eyes. A sudden cracking noise was heard, and another forest giant slowly bent over, and, describing a rapid curve, crushed its branches against the ground; ten seconds destroyed the work of centuries.

L'Encuerado attempted to go two or three yards beyond our rock; but, surprised by a sudden gust, he had but just time to throw himself prostrate on the ground to prevent being swept away. Something, however, had to be done; it was no use trying to light a fire, and yet, after yesterday's fast and a sleepless night, we felt great need of some comforting beverage. The squalls gradually abated, but were still every now and then violent. Intervals of profound silence succeeded to the uproar of the storm, when the leaves were motionless; then we might have fancied the tempest was over. But suddenly the frightful roar again commenced, and the gale covered the ground with fresh fragments.

We were beginning to take courage a little, when a formidable crash resounded above us; an enormous pine, growing on the mountain a hundred feet over our heads, tottered and then fell, tumbling down the slope with a horrible uproar. Quick as lightning, l'Encuerado seized Lucien, and lay down with him along the foot of the rock; I and my friend immediately followed his example. The fallen giant came crashing down in rapid bounds, smashing every thing in its path, and accompanied in its descent by masses of broken rock. It struck against the block that sheltered us, which gave forth a dull sound, but fortunately resisted the shock; and then the tree, clearing the obstacle with a prodigious bound, continued its impetuous course down to the foot of the mountain. We were nearly crushed by a perfect avalanche of stones which followed in its wake.

I raised myself, not without emotion. The danger had been serious; indeed, the enormous rock to which we owed our safety had slightly swerved. If this accident had occurred in the middle of the night, the fright would have driven us out of our place of shelter, and we should certainly have been destroyed. I first returned thanks to God, and then to l'Encuerado, who, being close to Lucien, had shielded the boy with his own body. The child, who fully comprehended the danger, hung round the Indian's neck.

"I shall tell mamma that you saved my life!" cried he, kissing l'Encuerado.

The latter would have replied, but, affected by the caresses of his young favorite, he could only press him in his arms, while two tears trickled down his dark cheeks.

"His lordship, the wind, is very good to take so much trouble to show us his power," exclaimed the Indian, addressing the wind, in order to hide his emotion; "a grand miracle, indeed! to uproot a pine that was going to die of old age, and to roll it down a mountain-side! Why, I could do the same if I chose, with the help of my *machete*. Oh yes! blow away! and knock down another tree on us, and then you'll thoroughly convince us that the devil is your patron!"

In spite of the serious nature of the occurrence, Gringalet was the only one among us who could hear this speech without a smile; and even the dog rubbed up against the orator's legs, as if to show his approval of all he had said.

The hurricane now subsided; but it was likely enough to redouble its intensity at night, and reason dictated that we should take advantage of the calm for moving onward. L'Encuerado resumed his load, and with a watchful eye led the way up the mountain. I took Lucien by the hand; for there was a danger that some tree which had been shaken by the storm might suddenly fall across our path.

The heat, which continued to inconvenience us, rendered walking a very laborious effort. The lips of our young companion were all cracked, and he spoke with difficulty. We suffered dreadfully from thirst; but it was necessary to bear it patiently, and to be very saving with the small stock of water which still remained in our gourds. Soon we came upon the spot where, an hour before, the tree had stood, the fall of which had so nearly crushed us. A widely gaping hole exposed to our view the broken roots of the colossus, and the earth round them was already dry. We pushed on with much difficulty, exhausted, out of breath, and half famished; for, since the night before, we had eaten nothing but some morsels of maize-cake. Moreover, our eyes were so red and swollen that we were perfectly disfigured.

"Oh, father, I am so tired!" said Lucien to me.

"So we all are, my poor boy; but we must pluck up our spirits again, and keep on walking, for our lives depend on it."

"Father, I am so thirsty! and the water left in my gourd is quite warm."

"It will be better for you not to drink; for a few draughts of water taken when walking increase perspiration, and make the thirst worse, instead of quenching it."

The poor little fellow heaved a sigh, and crept closer to my friend, who advised him to place in his mouth a small pebble, which alleviates thirst by exciting salivation.

In spite of all our exertions, we made little or no advance, and a profuse perspiration added to our exhaustion. Fortunately, every thing seemed to indicate that the tempest was over. L'Encuerado led the way; his manner appeared as if searching for something. At length I saw him throw down his load and plunge into the thicket. Soon he reappeared, with his hands full of a kind of mulberry, the fruit of the sarsaparilla, the acid flavor of which much revived Lucien. We now understood l'Encuerado's peculiar way of walking. He fancied he had noticed a young shoot of this plant, and at first concealed the discovery from us, fearing some deception. I can hardly describe the pleasure that was afforded us by obtaining these berries in such a welcome time. This shrub, with its vine-like and thorny stalk, abounded on the steep slope.

We resumed our march in much better spirits, thanks to this God-send. L'Encuerado filled his cap with them, and walked on bravely, with his head bare. Another half-hour's climbing brought us to the verge of the forest. Suddenly I lost sight of Gringalet. I called him several times, and at last he emerged from a clump of shrubs, with his tail and muzzle wet. Sumichrast rushed in search of the water, and soon cried out to us in a joyous voice—

"A spring! a spring!"

We all tried who could get to it first. Under the foliage of sarsaparilla our companion was kneeling down and catching in his hands a little streamlet of limpid water, which was trickling from between two rocks. With keen enjoyment, he was sprinkling it over his face and arms, an exam-

ple each of us soon imitated. At last I hurried our party away, for the horrible roaring of the hurricane still seemed to din in my ears, and as yet we had no shelter within our reach. After having filled our gourds, we recommenced our climbing, enlivened by l'Encuerado, who kept on congratulating Gringalet upon his discovery, and promising him, as his reward, a whole series of good dinners.

The hour was now approaching at which we feared that

"Sumichrast halted near three gigantic stones."

the hurricane would recommence with redoubled violence; so it became highly necessary to select a spot for our bivouac. Moss and lichens here covered the rocks with a variegated carpet, and, in proportion as we ascended the mountain, the cooler air relieved our lungs. At length our ascent came to an end, and we found ourselves on a plateau dotted over with stunted shrubs, distorted and twisted with the winds and storms. Fresh summits rose in front of us, but they were too far off to cause us any fear. Sumichrast halted near three gigantic stones, placed so as to leave a space between them, in which we could encamp, as if in a fortress.

This spot we selected for our bivouac. The wind still blew in squalls, but the increased clearing of the atmosphere gave us reason to hope that we should have nothing more to fear from the hurricane. We all went in search of fire-wood, and ere long after were enlivened by the gleam of an immense fire.

At sunset, the glittering beams of the sun's very last rays reached our camp. The sky was blue, and the air was fresh, so I abandoned the idea of returning home. Night came on, a fine rain purified the air, and the damp earth breathed forth a wholesome fragrance. Overcome by fatigue, we wrapped ourselves up in our sarapés, and soon fell into a sound sleep.

CHAPTER X.

THE RABBIT.—WILD POTATOES.—A DIFFICULT PATH.—AN
EXTINCT CRATER.—HOAR - FROST.—THE TORRENT.—THE
FAWN.—THE TETTIGONES.—THE DRAGON-FLIES.

THE next day, when I opened my eyes, the sun was
shining brightly in a blue sky. I made up the fire,
and walked off, with my gun on my shoulder, to try and obtain some kind of game, so as to surprise my companions
when they got up. For about a quarter of an hour I
traversed tracts of heath which reminded me of my native
country, when a too confiding rabbit came frisking along
within gunshot, which I knocked over and placed in my
game-bag.

On my return all were up, standing round the fire, and

they hailed me as a conqueror. The terrible trials of the day before seemed to be entirely forgotten; even Lucien had recovered all his liveliness. L'Encuerado took the rabbit, and in an incredible short space of time had it skinned, and placed to broil on the burning coals.

"Well! what do you think of hurricanes?" asked Sumichrast of Lucien, who was watching him cleaning his gun.

"They are most awful! I should never have thought that the wind, which is invisible, could have blown down and broken up trees as big as that one which almost fell upon us."

"Were you much frightened?"

"Rather; and so were you, for you were quite pale."

"The danger was much greater than you imagined. If the uprooted tree had pitched on our rock, it would have upset it, and crushed us beneath."

"Then the wind must be much stronger in forests than in towns?"

"No; for the hurricane of yesterday probably destroyed entire villages. It was one of those tropical storms which happily only break out at long intervals. Many an Indian is at this moment rebuilding his destroyed hut."

Lucien looked very thoughtful, and went and sat down at the foot of a tree. When I passed near him, I saw he had tears in his eyes.

"What's the matter?" I asked.

"I was thinking of mamma and my brothers. M. Sumichrast told me that the tempest must have demolished whole villages; so perhaps our home has met with some misfortune."

"Don't be frightened, my dear boy! Thank God! stone walls can generally stand against wind. Besides, this hurricane can hardly have been felt at Orizava. At all events, your mamma has more reason to be anxious about us, for she knows that we are far from shelter—exposed to all its violence."

I kissed poor Lucien, and comforted him as well as I could, assisted by l'Encuerado, who soon afterwards took him off to look after our roast rabbit.

The *tochtli*, or Mexican rabbit, is different from the European species, although it has the same colored coat and instincts. In fact it is a hare.

"Do you know the family of the animal we are going to have for breakfast?" asked Sumichrast.

"Yes; it is a Rodent."

"Well done; but how did you recognize it to be so?"

"By the absence of canine teeth in its jaws, its large incisors, and its hind legs being longer than its fore legs."

"Come, your memory is good. You should also know that, in Europe, the rabbit, which is nearly allied to the hare, is thought to be a native of Africa. Formerly, the Aztecs used to sacrifice hundreds of these animals to the goddess Centeutl, who is the Ceres of Mexican mythology; and the nobles used to wear cloaks made of the hair of the hare, mixed with cotton. With regard to the larger hare, known farther north as the Jackass rabbit, the Indians generally refuse to eat its flesh, under the pretense that it feeds on dead bodies, a mistake which as yet they have not been persuaded to abandon."

We did justice to our game like guests who have to make up for a forced fast. The meal finished, without further delay our little coterie moved on again. Instead of the abundant and bushy thickets of sarsaparilla, we met with nothing but stunted shrubs. However, as we approached the mountain the vegetation assumed a richer aspect, and the bare rocks no longer protruded through the soil. Here and there, tanagers, with black backs, yellow breasts, and violet-blue throats, fluttered around us; also other variega-

"A labyrinth of rocks brought us out in front of a stony rampart, more than a hundred feet in height."

ted birds of the Passerine family. We were just about to begin climbing the slope, when l'Encuerado, whose piercing eyes seemed to see every thing, exclaimed:

" There are some potatoes !"

Lucien ran towards the Indian, who, with his *machete*, had already cleared away the earth round a small plant with oval-shaped leaves, covered with soft greenish berries. Some wrinkled tubercles were ere long discovered, which we could easily crush between our fingers. This is the origin of the valuable plant for which Europe is indebted to America.

After climbing some time, we came upon a mass of rocks all heaped up in a perfect chaos. Some obstacle or other incessantly obliged us either to jump over or make a circuit so as to get forward. The temperature, however, was refreshing, and rendered our exertions less fatiguing.

The chances of our journey brought us out once more upon the plateau. All the mountain crests we could see were barren, and a profound silence reigned on every side. We stopped to take breath, and the sight that met our eyes impressed us with its stern grandeur. It reminded Sumichrast of the Swiss mountains which he had so often traversed; and some flowers he gathered further recalled his home. While thus occupied, two butterflies fluttered over our heads.

" It is an Alpine species !" eagerly cried my friend.

The locality prevented him from following these capricious insects for any distance: for one moment he leaned over the abyss, bristling up with rocks, and followed, with a longing eye, the two winged flowers which had recalled to him a fleeting image of his fatherland.

A labyrinth of rocks brought us out in front of a stony rampart more than a hundred feet in height, and almost perpendicular. This unexpected obstacle brought us to a

halt. How should we make our way over it? Upon examining the spot, we decided to incline towards the left,
which seemed to us the most accessible road. In parts the
wall diminished in height, but we tried in vain to climb it.
A more successful attempt, however, brought us nearly to
the top, but not without great fatigue, for sometimes the
rock appeared to hang over us. At length, by climbing on
to Sumichrast's shoulders, I managed to reach the flat surface above. I hoisted up Lucien here with the lasso; next I
drew up Gringalet, who was only too pleased to submit to
the operation, and lastly Sumichrast and l'Encuerado. The
terrible obstacle was at last overcome; beyond it the
ground was, comparatively speaking, level, but covered with
stones of a volcanic nature.

We still kept on our way, although it was four o'clock, in
the hope of finding some tree at the foot of which we could
make our bivouac. L'Encuerado put down his load to
climb up a needle-shaped rock, the extraordinary position of
which reminded us of the celebrated leaning tower of Pisa.
When he had reached its top, the Indian called out to us
that he could see a clump of trees. The cold began to inconvenience us and we wanted wood to make our fire, so,
plucking up fresh courage, we continued our journey. The
distance now traversed was inconsiderable; but the ups
and downs and circuits had quite wearied us. Gradually
the rocks decreased in size, and were more widely spread;
a plain slightly depressed in the centre, dotted here and
there with thinly growing thickets, was reached. In the
background there was a clump of firs and a glittering lake,
quite a liquid oasis hidden in a desert.

It now became highly necessary for us to seek shelter,
for our teeth were chattering with the cold. L'Encuerado,
having climbed a tree, cut down the wood that was necessary for the construction of a hut; while Lucien broke all

"Sunset surprised us ere we had finished our labor."

the dry branches off, a task in which I helped him. Sunset
surprised us ere we had finished our labor. The waters of
the lake assumed a dark hue, and the mountain peaks towards the setting sun furrowed the sky with their strangely irregular outlines, and the breeze resounding through the
pine-trees produced a solemn and grave chant, a peculiarity
which has doubtless given to this species of tree the name
of *Pinus religiosus.* As the rays of the sun died away
and the dark shadows covered the sky, the silence became
still more profound. Suddenly the last rays of the luminary vanished; the gathering darkness imbued us with an
emotion which those only can understand who, like us, had
found themselves face to face with some of the grandest
emanations from the Creator's hands.

Lucien, too, was subject to the influence of the twofold
majesty of darkness and solitude; he was speechless, and
looked by turns both at the earth and the sky. The stars
appeared glittering in the blue heaven, and were reflected
on the motionless surface of the neighboring water. Suddenly a luminous ray seemed to dance over the lake, and
then to divide into a shower of sparks. It was the reflection of our fire, to which l'Encuerado had just set a light.

The piercing cold was excessively trying: our *sarapés*
did not seem sufficient to protect us from its influence.
Fortunately we had obtained fuel enough to keep up the
bivouac fire all night. Our meal, although without meat,
was a cheerful one. Each in turn retired to his pine-leaf
couch; and soon I alone remained up, not feeling an inclination for slumber.

What a contrast it was! The night before, at this time,
we were deafened by the uproarious wind, and the forests
echoed with its fearful effects; while we, perfectly helpless,
sheltered behind a trembling stone, could scarcely breathe
the burning air. Twenty-four hours had hardly elapsed,

and a few miles had brought us on to a granite soil where
we felt even unpleasantly cold; it was no longer the uproar, but the silence, which awoke in my mind the rever-
ies of loneliness.

We rose before dawn, perfectly benumbed and hardly able
to move our lips. L'Encuerado stirred up the fire so as to
get the coffee ready. The first ray of light showed the
ground covered with a white shroud of bright hoar-frost.
Lucien had never seen this phenomenon before, and was
never tired of admiring it. Sumichrast explained to him
that the drops of dew, which every morning may be seen
glittering on the grass in hot countries, freeze in situations
of great altitude, and produce those beautiful transparent
globules which, owing to the refraction of light, assume so
beauteous an appearance.

The rays of the sun warmed us but little, so I hastened
our preparations for departure. After skirting the edge of
the lake, we once more found ourselves among rocks. The
summit which we had traversed was doubtless the crater
of some extinct volcano. I took a farewell look at the gigantic semicircle, edged with mountain crests, ere commencing a journey quite as difficult as that of the day before, through the immense stones which had been vomited
forth by the burning mountain. More than once we got
into a *cul-de-sac*, and we sat down utterly discouraged.

For the last time I examined the horizon. We were now
standing on the highest summit of the Cordillera; opposite
us, as far as we could see, rose verdure-clad peaks, which
gradually diminished in height. We were again about to
meet with tropical vegetation, and should ere long reach
the plains and forests of the *Terre-Chaude*. The way
seemed direct and easy; but how many obstacles must be
overcome, how many valleys must be crossed, ere we could
reach our destination!

We descended the slope by a giant staircase, each step of which must have been at least seven or eight feet in height. More than once the lasso was called into use; but all obstacles were at last safely overcome. I can not describe the joy I felt upon once more seeing pine-trees. We sought in vain for any traces of the hurricane; this side of the mountain had evidently not been visited by it.

The slope was now more gradual; our pace became faster, and a few oaks were in sight. A rumbling noise made us stop and listen attentively, but l'Encuerado, who was more expert than we were in making out distant sounds, told us that it was a torrent. Squirrels gambolled on the branches as we passed by, and toucans seemed to tempt us to stop; but we were all anxious to reach the waterfall. Ere long, oaks and birches, and afterwards guava-trees, surrounded us on every side. The ground was now level, and in less than half an hour l'Encuerado conducted us to the edge of an immense ravine, at the bottom of which there was a roaring torrent.

It was not long before the steep bank became less abrupt, and we established our bivouac. While we were cutting down some branches, Sumichrast put his finger to his lips and seized his gun. A slight noise was heard in the thickets, and our companion disappeared. We were listening, holding our breath, when we heard the screech as of an owl; we knew it was a call, so l'Encuerado also glided away through the bushes.

"Why did M. Sumichrast call l'Encuerado?" asked Lucien, in a low voice.

"Probably because he has discovered the trail of some animal."

I had scarcely finished speaking, when a movement in the leaves attracted my attention. A fine fox, with an eager look, and its tail lowered, rushed past me. I fired, but without effect, for it bolted off among the trees, followed by Gringalet. Almost at the same moment, a report told me that l'Encuerado had also seen game.

Lucien was very sorry that I had missed the fox; I only regretted having lost a charge of powder, and also having awkwardly put to flight the quarry which was probably being pursued by my companions. I then continued my work of cutting off the branches, and told Lucien to strike the flint and light the fire. Thanks to l'Encuerado's lessons, he managed his work much better than I had expected.

We heard Sumichrast give a call, to which Lucien answered, and the disappointed hunter joined us.

" What did you fire at ?" he inquired of me.

" At a fox, which I missed ; were you chasing it ?"

" No ; I caught sight of a doe and its fawn, but I could not get near them."

" And where is l'Encuerado ?"

" He wanted to shoot some bird, so as not to come back quite empty-handed."

" Chanito ! Hiou ! Hiou ! Chanito !" we heard shouted in the distance.

" Hallo ! hallo !" answered the boy.

And, soon after, l'Encuerado returned, carrying a fawn on his shoulders.

" Oh ! what a pretty little creature !" cried Lucien; " why didn't you take it alive ?"

" Bullets are the only things that can run as fast as these animals, Chanito."

" What became of the mother ?" asked Sumichrast.

" I was not able to get near her ; but at all events, we have more than enough meat now, both for to-day and to-morrow."

Lucien took possession of the fawn. He had always longed to possess one of **these** animals alive. He duly examined **the** slender legs and tapering muzzle of the poor **creature, whose** fawn-colored back, dotted over with symmetrically arranged spots, would change in color **as it got older.**

" Well, **Master ' Sunbeam,' in what class** will you place **this mammal ?" asked** Sumichrast, addressing Lucien.

" **It is not like any of those I** know."

"Well, **then, you never can have** seen goats, cows, or **sheep. It is a** ruminant, or an animal which has three or **four stomachs. Its lower** jaw is provided with eight incisors, while **the** upper jaw has nothing but a cushion or **gum."**

" **That's right enough," said** Lucien, opening the fawn's mouth.

" In all ruminants, the food, when swallowed, **passes into the first stomach ;** it is then brought up to be **chewed again ; this is called** ' chewing the cud.' You must often **have seen a cow or** a sheep sitting quiet in the sun and **constantly chewing."**

" **Yes,"** replied Lucien, " and l'Encuerado always told me **that they had eaten some bitter** herb."

" **His explanation** is about as correct as that given by the **Mexicans, who say** that an animal which chews the cud is reading the **newspaper.** Another characteristic of these animals is, that their feet are cloven."

" And they have horns !" cried Lucien.

" Not all of them ; for instance, the camel, llama, and **musk-deer,** are exceptions."

It remained for us to decide how our fawn should be **cooked. After a** discussion on the subject, **we left the** point entirely to **l'Encuerado, and I** made my **way down** to the bottom **of the ravine.** Upon lifting up some stones and pieces of bark, I discovered several species of the _Ca-_

rabus family. Lucien caught on a shrub some insects of a very peculiar shape; at the first glance, Sumichrast recognized them as *tettigones*.

"These insects belong to the *Hemeptera* family," said he, "therefore they are allied to the bug and the grasshopper; these insects have neither mandibles* nor jaws; their mouth is a sort of beak, formed of a jointed tube extending along the breast, which you can see very plainly. This order is a very numerous one, and the two species you have just found are peculiar to Mexico."

"Here is one like a fowl, and another like a canoe."

"You are quite right, and you will meet with others which are still more singular looking."

The appearance of these little creatures pleased Lucien very much, and, as he was letting them run about on his hand, he saw them jump off and disappear. He was just going to return to the shrub on which he had caught them, when his attention was attracted by an immense dragon-fly, commonly called in Mexico *the devil's horse*, and in France *demoiselle*. The beautiful insect, after flying round and round, settled on a plant, and was immediately caught in the young hunter's net. The prisoner had greenish eyes, a yellow body, and its wings were dotted over with black and scarlet. It doubled back its tapering body, as if to try and sting the hand which held it, and shook its gauzy wings with a kind of metallic sound. A half-eaten mosquito hung out of its mouth, and, although the dragon-fly was sadly bruised, it continued its meal, much to the amusement of Lucien, who hardly expected to find such tiger-like habits in an insect so elegant in form and so harmless in appearance.

"It is of the order *Neuroptera*," I said to him; "thus

---

* A very hard substance placed immediately under the upper lip, which insects use for cutting and tearing their food.

called because of the veins on its four wings. This insect first lives in the water in the form of a larva, in which state it remains a year—it is very much like the insect you are holding, only, all that can be seen of its wings are small swellings, which grow longer each time the animal changes its skin. This swelling is a sort of sheath to the beautiful gauzy wings which distinguish all the Neuroptera, and the dragon-fly in particular."

"What! does the dragon-fly begin its life by living in water like a fish?"

"Yes, and they are quite as voracious in that state as when they are perfect insects. The larva changes to a grub, and greedily devours water-lizards and young fish; after a certain time, which varies according to the species, it rises to the top of the water by crawling up a reed, and remains perfectly motionless, exposed to the rays of the sun; suddenly, the skin covering the head bursts open, and the dragon-fly, spotted with black, blue, and green, takes flight, and loses no time in darting upon the first insect which comes within its reach."

My lecture was interrupted by the cry of "Hallo! hallo!" from l'Encuerado. It was his substitute for a diuner-bell.

CHAPTER XI.

A BLUE LIZARD.—THE GUAVA-TREE.—A CATARACT.—NEST OF YELLOW SERPENTS. — A VEGETABLE HELMET.—THE KINGFISHER.—HUNTING WATER-FLEAS. — THE TADPOLE. —A COLLECTION OF WATER-BUGS.

THE rice-soup, our every-day fare, was, on this occasion, followed by fawn cutlets broiled on the embers, accompanied by potatoes. This precious tubercle, in its savage state, only reminded us very slightly of its cultivated progeny. The pulp, instead of being floury, is soft, transparent, and almost tasteless. That, however, did not prevent us from eating them, and doing justice to our venison.

While we were smoking a cigar, which was called by Sumichrast, according to circumstances, the calumet of repose, of council, or of digestion, Lucien returned to the shrub on which he had previously found the insects. He collected a great number of these, and also discovered a third species, which was shaped like a triangle, with two horns at its base. He ran to show us these miniature bulls. Afterwards, armed with a long branch by way of a lever, he tried to raise up a decayed root covered with moss. He succeeded to do it, after some trouble, and saw, cowering down among the roots, a beautiful lizard; it had a greenish back, and its mouth and the sides of its body were bright blue; it was a variety which we had never before observed. The little animal, doubtless dazzled by the light, allowed itself to be caught, and then suddenly bending down its head, bit the boy's finger, who at once dropped it. L'Encuerado soon caught the runaway.

"Didn't you know that lizards were harmless?" asked Sumichrast of Lucien.

"That is why they bite, I suppose," replied the boy, shaking his head.

"Yes," said the naturalist, "but you needn't be afraid; its bite is not venomous.

> "'This brute is surely not disposed to strife,
> But you attack it, it'll defend its life.'"

Night came on. A multitude of insects whirled round and round our fire, burning their wings as if they enjoyed it. Lucien wanted to know what attracted so many of these poor creatures to the flame. As he inquired, two or three great beetles suddenly appeared with loud buzzing, and at once precipitated themselves into the burning coals.

"See what comes of giddiness," said Sumichrast. "If since we set out we had walked blindly on without looking

where we went, long ere this we should have found ourselves at the bottom of some ravine."

"But these butterflies and beetles throw themselves into
the fire on purpose," said l'Encuerado, with the inflexible
logic of facts.

"They are not aware that the flame will burn," I replied.

"That's true," murmured the Indian, in a tone of com-
passion.

Fatigue compelled us to give up our relaxation, and we
soon went to sleep in a warm atmosphere, which seemed all
the more pleasant when we remembered our sufferings of
the night before.

Our slumbers were interrupted toward morning by the
frequent cries of a flight of passerines, called "alarum-
birds" (*despertadores*) by the Mexicans. It was hardly
light, and, in spite of l'Encuerado's predictions, it had not
rained. The light of our fire, when we stirred it, soon
drove away our winged friends; but, thanks to their waking us, the first rays of the sun found us all ready to set
out. Just as we were going to start, an unforeseen difficulty
arose—how to cross the ravine and ford the river? L'Encuerado said that it would be necessary to go up-stream; I,
also, agreed with him. Sumichrast, on the contrary, was of
opinion that there was much more chance of the banks becoming less steep if we went in the opposite direction; he
carried the day, and led the way, cutting a passage through
the shrubs with his *machete*.

As we were determined to skirt the edge of the water,
we could not get along without great difficulty. The noise
of the torrent, which seemed to grow louder, attracted us
towards the forest, where the absence of grass and under-
wood enabled us to get on faster. The trees grew farther
and farther apart, and we again came upon brush-wood, ere

long coming out on to a plain, dotted here and there with guava-trees. These trees furnished us with a quantity of green fruit, of which we were all very fond. L'Encuerado availed himself of this unexpected harvest by filling up all the gaps in his basket with them. The wild guava, a sort of myrtle, which grows naturally in the Terre-Tempérée, reaches to a height of several feet. Its fruit, which seldom gets ripe before it is eaten by the birds or larvæ, is luscious, highly scented, and full of pips; they have the reputation of being antifebrile and astringent. When the shrub is cultivated, its appearance changes considerably; its branches grow longer, and are covered with leaves which are silvery on the back, and the fruit they yield are as large as lemons, which they resemble in shape and color.

We all put on our travelling gear again; but when l'Encuerado wanted to place the basket on his back, he found he could not possibly lift it up. I helped him, trying all the time to persuade him to throw away half his stock; but he resolutely refused to follow my advice. When he began to walk, he staggered like a drunken man, and at last fell down beneath his burden, and all the guavas rolled out on to the ground.

Our laughter rather hurt the brave Indian's feelings.

"By Jose-Maria!" he cried, holding up his hands towards heaven, "I am getting old. Oh, what a disgrace, not to be able to carry a handful of guavas! In my youth it would have taken three such loads as those to have made me fall down on my knees like a broken-down horse. Poor old fellow!"

L'Encuerado was certainly exaggerating his former strength; but, at any rate, it cut him to the heart to have to throw away so much of the fruit he had gathered, and our insisting upon his doing so quite crowned his vexation. With a view of consoling him, I reminded him that the guavas would spoil in twenty-four hours, and that his basket held more than we could possibly consume.

Sumichrast was walking about twenty steps in front of us, when suddenly he stopped and drew back. When I got abreast of him, my eyes met an immense ravine, at the bottom of which the torrent was rushing with a loud noise. The water was first calm and sluggish, accumulating in a large basin, then it suddenly burst forth against an immense rock and disappeared, roaring and foaming in two columns, which, after uniting, broke into a thousand little cascades. We all wished to visit the bottom of this ravine, in order to enjoy this wondrous sight in all its grandeur.

Before making our way into the brush-wood we put down our insect-cases and game-bags, for the enterprise required our unimpeded agility. As long as we could cling on to the plants and shrubs, the descent was mere child's play; but we soon found ourselves treading on a reddish ferruginous soil, which some great land-slip had exposed. Sumichrast was the first to venture on this dangerous ground, which gave way under him at his third stride. Our companion rolled over the declivity, instinctively grasping the first branches he could reach; but he let go directly, uttering a piercing cry. Fortunately a shrub kept him from falling into the gulf. I planted my feet as deeply as I could in the crumbling soil, so as to be able to help my friend, who, with his face contracted with pain, raised towards me his right hand, which was already red, swollen, and covered with blisters. The branch he had caught hold of in his fall belonged to a gigantic nettle, called by the Indians *Mala-mujer*, or "bad-woman." This plant only grows on damp banks—"a piece of malice," said l'Encuerado, "adopted in order to play shameful tricks on unsuspecting travellers; towards whom it treacherously stretches out its green stalks and velvety leaves as if offering them assistance."

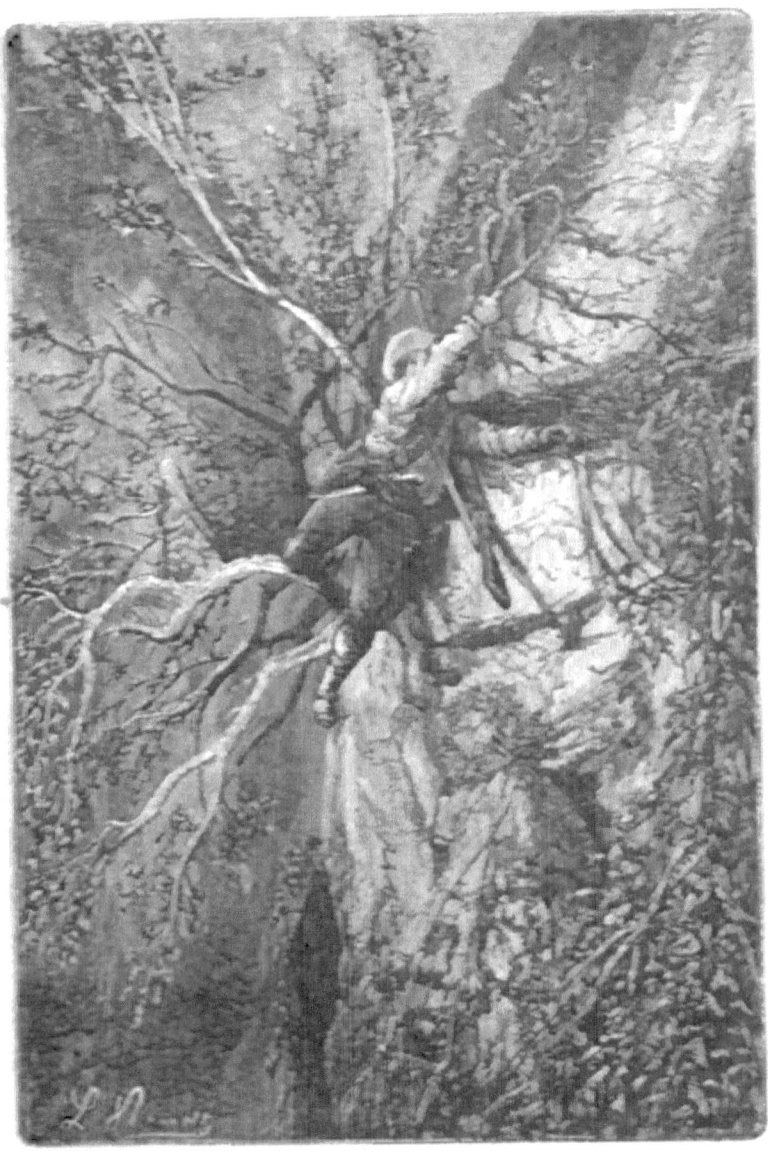

"A shrub kept him from falling into the gulf."

We felt quite grieved at Sumichrast's suffering; for we well knew by experience the intolerable pain which is produced by the sting of this herb. L'Encuerado took Lucien in charge, while I gave my assistance to the injured man. For some distance we moved along without much difficulty, but very soon a whole forest of nettles stood up in front of us. Lucien and Sumichrast sat down, while the Indian and I, by means of our *machetes*, opened out a narrow path; at last we reached again the timber land, so we had now almost got out of our difficulties.

The stalks of the nettles, cut off a few inches above the ground, served to give firmness to our footing. But l'Encuerado, always too confident, tripped up, and his right cheek was brushed by some of their leaves; it only needed this to render him perfectly unrecognizable. Although I pitied him, I could not help smiling at the grimaces produced on his sun-burnt visage by the painful stings. Even Sumichrast, when looking at him, forgot his own sufferings.

Under a cypress, we observed five or six snakes, each about a yard and a half long. One, more courageous than the others, remained under the trees and steadily surveyed our party. Gringalet, furious in the extreme, barked and jumped all round the reptile, which, raising its head from the centre of the coil formed by its body, shot out its tongue. Its skin was of a golden yellow, dotted with green spots, and streaked by two almost imperceptible black lines. L'Encuerado called in the dog; the snake then coiled itself up, slowly turning its head in every direction, as if to select the best direction for retreat. Suddenly it unrolled its whole length, exposing to our view an unfortunate sparrow, which was still breathing. Leaving it unmolested, after a few minutes' delay it seized its victim by the head, by degrees the little feathered innocent disappeared, and the snake remained motionless as though exhausted by the exertion.

"Is it a rattle-snake?" asked Lucien astonished.

"No; it is a common snake—that is, a reptile which is not venomous. This one is called by the Indians the *Yellow-snake*, and, from ignorance, they are in very great dread of them. It is in the habit of climbing trees with great activity, and hunts birds. The statues of the Aztec god of war, the terrible Huitzilipochtli, to whom thousands of men were offered as living sacrifices, had their foreheads bound with a golden snake, and we have every reason to believe that the reptile which we have just seen is that which the Indians thus honored."

A little farther on, Lucien fancied that he saw, stretched out upon the grass, a long white snake. Gringalet, much bolder than usual, seized the reptile in his mouth and brought it to us. But it was nothing but a serpent's skin: I then told the child that all reptiles of this kind change their skin twice a year, and they get out of it as if from a sheath.

We continued our descent, and l'Encuerado, who had taken the lead, suddenly turned back to us with his head covered with an immense vegetable helmet. I at once recognized it to be the flower of a plant I had met with in the neighboring mountains. Nothing could be more splendid than this blossom, which, before it is full-blown, looks like a duck sitting on the water. In a single morning the enormous corolla opens out and changes into a form resembling a helmet surmounted by a crest; the interior of it, lined with yellow velvet, almost dazzles the eyes. The seed of this creeper, the Indian name of which I forget, is flat, and of a heart-like shape, having depicted on one of its faces a Maltese cross.

Even Sumichrast for a moment forgot his injuries while

The Cataract.

examining this wonderful flower, and Lucien, finding a second, very soon covered his head with it; but the poisonous and penetrating odor exhaled from the corolla made him feel sick, so he soon relinquished this novel head-dress.

A few more steps brought us to the bottom of the ravine, and Sumichrast and l'Encuerado set to work to bathe their stings in the cool water; while I and Lucien sat down together on a rock, washed on one side by the stream, and leisurely contemplated the beautiful scene before us.

In front of us was situated an immense mountain, cleft open as if by the hand of some giant, the sides of which were clad with a carpet of verdure of a thousand different shades. At the bottom, as if for the purpose of stopping up the immense fissure, there was an enormous accumulation of gray and dark-tinted rocks, between which appeared, every here and there, the foliage of some tree, enamelled with flowers. From the midst of the mountain, as if from some invisible cavern, sprung out a large sheet of transparent water, which, although calm and almost motionless in appearance, descended in one fall to a rock which projected in the cataract, like the prow of a ship. As if rendered furious by the shock, and seeming to revel in the uproar, the water, converted into foam, bounded over the obstacle, and fell in two columns, separated by the black point of crag; then, springing with impetuous speed, from step to step, down a gigantic staircase, it entered a receptacle hollowed out like a shell, which received the foaming water, from whence it flowed gently into a basin edged with verdure. The torrent, quieted for a time, resumed its course, and striking against impediments, rolled on from fall to fall, and from valley to valley, until it reached the plains, more than three thousand feet beneath.

This cascade recalled to my memory one I had seen about a year before, when exploring the environs of Tuxtla, iu the *Terre-Chaude*—viz., the Fall of Ingénio—one which would be reckoned among the most celebrated in the world, if access to it was not rendered almost impossible by the wilderness.

The sufferings of our two companions were so much alleviated by the application of water that they soon came and sat beside us. I can not describe the proud enjoyment we all felt in this wild spot. We were face to face with this unknown cascade, which we were, perhaps, the first Europeans to contemplate. Behind us the mountain sides seemed to unite and hem in the bed of the torrent. The sun bathed with its rays that portion which was bordered with large trees, among which kingfishers were skimming about. One of these birds came and perched close to us— its breast was white, its wings black on the upper side, and its head-feathers dark green; its stout, thick-set shape, and its short tail, made Lucien remark that it looked like a malformed creature. Always restless, it almost immediately resumed its abrupt flight over the surface of the water, and disappeared among the windings of the ravine.

Lucien pointed out to me an immense willow, the branches of which, drooping over the water, seemed to have at their ends enormous gourd-shaped fruits. I recognized in them the nests of those beautiful yellow birds, spotted with black, which the Mexicans call *calandres*. To convince Lucien of his mistake, l'Encuerado threw a large stone into the tree; the missile fell from branch to branch, and more than a hundred frightened birds flew out from their curious retreats. At first they appeared much alarmed; but when this had subsided, they skimmed over the water, or entered their impregnable habitations.

We made our way down the ravine in hopes of finding a resting-place less rugged, and after a long, winding, tedious course, came upon a sheet of calm water, flowing over a

Fall of Ingénio (from a drawing by the Marquis of Radepoint).

8*

bed of sand. The sun was shining full upon its transparent surface, and, close to the edge, hundreds of flies were whirling about.

" Those are coleopteræ," said Sumichrast to Lucien.

" Why do they turn round and round like that ?" inquired he.

" To find their food, for they are carnivorous, and require a great deal of nourishment. In France they are commonly called *tourniquets*, or *water-fleas.*"

Lucien wanted to catch one, but could not succeed; l'Encuerado and Sumichrast joined in the pursuit. At first I amused myself with watching the useless efforts of my companions; but at last, thinking myself cleverer than they, I squatted down also. There we all four were, with our hands in the water, perfectly motionless, and holding our breath, the better to remain motionless. The insects were all in a close mass, and whirling round like a living mosaic, moving in every direction without separating; but however quickly we raised our hands, we all failed in our efforts.

An hour was spent in this way, and even then we should not have given up the chase if the sun had not ceased to shine on the bank, and the insects had therefore moved beyond our reach, so as to be within its influence. Lucien, vexed at their going away, and l'Encuerado, furious at having been conquered by the agile creatures, commenced throwing stones at them with the hope of wounding one. Even in this they did not succeed, so l'Encuerado satisfied himself by calling them fools, a name which, in his opinion, constituted a gross insult.

About twenty tadpoles, swimming in a puddle of water, were taken by Lucien for fish.

" They are frogs," I said to him.

" Where are their feet, then ?"

" Under the brown skin, which makes them look like fish :

when the time of their metamorphosis arrives, this skin will split all down their back, and a little frog will come out of it. Look at this tadpole I have just caught; you can see the feet through its transparent skin. To-day it is a fish, that is to say, it breathes through gills—those little tufts you see on each side of its head—and perhaps to-morrow it will undergo that metamorphosis which will cause it to breathe through its mouth. The Toltecs, the great nation which preceded the Aztecs in Mexico, counted the frog among their gods."

When putting the tadpole back into the pool, I noticed some whitish insects, which were incessantly rising in jerks to the surface of the water, and diving down again directly. Lucien, astonished at their movements, cried out—

"But, papa, they are walking on their backs!"

"You are quite right; they are hydrocorises, allied to the tettigones, and consequently *hemipteræ*."

The young naturalist was more successful than in his gyrin-hunting, and succeeded in catching two or three of these water-bugs.

"What is the use of their wings?" he inquired.

"Why, to fly with, and to move from place to place."

"Then water-bugs are really able to fly, swim, and walk?"

"Yes; and I'm sure they can see in the dark, too," said l'Encuerado, who, it may be remembered, envied animals this privilege.

"We are certainly justified in thinking so," I answered, smiling, "for they nearly always choose the night for travelling. Take care they don't bite you, for the water-bug bites as hard as its kinsmen of the woods and houses."

A little farther on, Lucien stopped in front of an herbaceous plant, covered from top to bottom with round, flat black insects, speckled with red, and almost resembling mosaic-work. He was very proud of his beautiful discovery, and took hold of two or three of the insects; but feeling their soft bodies give way in his fingers, he threw them down with disgust.

"Oh! what are these horrid creatures?"

"They are wood-bugs," replied Sumichrast; "only they are in the state of *larvæ*, and have no wings."

"What has caused this nasty smell on my fingers?"

"When any one touches these insects, a very strong-smelling yellowish liquid always exudes from them."

Lucien ran off to wash his hands. He rubbed them over and over again, but could not quite get rid of the smell, which seemed to annoy him very much. I concluded from this that in future he would not have many wood-bugs in his collection.

After a long ramble at the bottom of the ravine, we had to return to our starting-point, which was the only side by which we could obtain an exit. We found the cataract perfectly bathed in light. The large upper sheet of water looked like a block of azure-stone, while the spray beneath glittered as if covered with diamonds. Above our heads a rainbow spanned the stream from bank to bank.

I at last succeeded in tearing my companions away from this wondrous scene. We had met with no game, but a great part of our fawn was yet remaining in the basket. Sumichrast was still in pain, and l'Encuerado's face continued much inflamed. We now had to ascend, and we each adopted the greatest precaution while passing the spot where we had seen the serpents. I don't know how we should ever have got up if l'Encuerado had not thought of cutting some branches of dwarf elder for walking-sticks. Above every thing, I wished to keep Lucien from the suffering caused by coming in contact with the *Mala-mujer*, as the Mexicans call it, and it was with a sigh of relief that I saw him safe and sound out of this *cul-de-sac*.

CHAPTER XII.

A RELATION OF GRINGALET.—OUR FOUR-FOOTED GUIDE.—
A REVIEW OF OUR PARTY.—THE ALLIGATOR-TORTOISE.—
THE PHEASANTS.—THE MAGNOLIA.—THE NUTMEG-TREE.
—THE BLUE-PLANT.—THE CATERPILLAR.

AS the sun was setting, our wisest course was to go back
to our bivouac of the evening before, and to postpone
until the next day the discovery of the passage we had
sought in vain. Upon the whole, the sight of the cataract
had amply repaid us for our useless walk.

Our little party, therefore, once more plunged into the
forest, rather at random, though taking care not to go too
far from the stream. Two or three times we seemed to
have reached the spot where we left the bank; but we soon

got into the most inextricable thickets. As the time wore on, I began to think we had passed the place; and, as is often the case in similar circumstances, opinions were divided. A fox, which appeared within gunshot, interrupted our discussion. I fired, and the animal fell. It was a magnificent specimen, and exactly like its European confrere. By a singular chance, at the very moment it was expiring, a crow just above our heads uttered a loud croaking.

"There! the crow is thanking us for having rid him of his enemy, the fox," said Sumichrast to Lucien.

The boy laughed heartily at this joke. In spite of our advice, l'Encuerado would insist upon skinning the animal, whose pelt he wished to preserve. Fortunately, he was very quick at such an operation, and the beautiful fur was soon hanging over his arm, ready to be stretched outside his basket to dry.

"I hope," said Sumichrast to Lucien, "that you have already recognized the fox's relationship."

- "Oh yes! in its color and shape it is like the *cayotte*."

"You are quite right, but the *cayotte* and the fox are both Gringalet's cousins."

"I can scarcely believe that, for Gringalet has short hair, is spotted with black and white, has gray eyes—"

"Those are only secondary characteristics," interrupted Sumichrast. "Gringalet belongs to the carnivorous type, called by naturalists *Digitigrades*."

"Is Gringalet a digitigrade?" asked Lucien, smiling.

"Yes, certainly; that is to say, he walks on his toes, and not on the sole of his feet, exactly like the fox, whose teeth, also, are perfectly similar to those of Gringalet. The principal difference between them is, that the fox has eyes which are formed so as to enable it to see in the dark, a quality which Gringalet does not possess in the same degree."

" Are there such things as wild dogs ?"

" Yes, although the point has been much disputed. But the dog, the faithful companion of man, has been so long domesticated, that little similarity of appearance exists between them. However, the *cayotte*, the fox, and the wolf may be called wild dogs."

We had once more got into the midst of a thicket without discovering the least trace of our resting-place. It became important that we should soon find our starting-point. I noticed that Gringalet, instead of gambolling round us as he generally did, remained behind, pricking up his ears, and appearing excessively knowing.

" What do you think, shall we take Gringalet for our guide ?" said I.

As soon as the animal heard his name mentioned, he rushed towards me, and I patted him.

" Come, tell your dog to lead us to the bivouac," I said to Lucien.

" To the bivouac ! to the bivouac !" cried the boy, patting the animal.

Gringalet really seemed to understand, for he sniffed up the air, and at once went to the front. I soon discovered that he was taking us back by a very circuitous path.

" To the bivouac ! to the bivouac !"

Gradually the noise of the torrent became more distinct, and our guide plunged into the brush-wood. While we were cutting down the branches that stopped up our path, Gringalet waited with his ears pricked up and one foot uplifted. At last we caught sight of the hut, which was greeted with such pleasure and relief as only known by fatigued travellers.

It was not without emotion that I again beheld this spot, to which I had, as I thought, said good-bye forever. The scarcely extinguished embers, and the shelter which we had raised, had quite a home-like appearance. Sumichrast said he felt the same impression, and Lucien declared that his first idea had been that we should find an Indian in the hut.

But what about Gringalet? Had he then really understood us? Those who have made a trial of canine intelligence will not doubt the fact for a moment. The word *bivouac*, having been so often pronounced since we set out, must have struck both the mind and the ears of the animal, so as to have become almost synonymous in his ideas with dinner and rest.

The next day at sunrise we set out, gently ascending the course of the stream. Sumichrast's hand was still in pain, and quite prevented him using his gun. L'Encuerado, though disfigured, had, at least, the free use of his limbs. The inexperienced traveller is incessantly exposed to misfortunes of this kind. Turned out into the midst of various unknown natural objects, he carelessly plucks a leaf, breaks down a branch, or gathers a flower; and in many cases his punishment is prompt and terrible, and the innocent diversion of a second has to be expiated by hours of anguish. In the wild life of the wilderness, dangers become so multiplied, that more courage than is generally supposed is required to face them. Every explorer of unknown scenes must make up his mind to endure hardships. More than one whom I have seen start full of confidence, at the end of three days have returned, wearied, bruised, ill, discouraged, and, in fact, conquered. By degrees, of course, experience comes to the help of those whose moral courage is strong enough to induce them to persevere. They soon learn to recognize at a glance the tree that it is best to avoid, the grass that must not be trodden on, the creeper the touch of which is to be shunned, and the fruit which should not be tasted. At last the requirements of the body are to some extent mastered, and it follows the dictation of the soul without complaint. The long-experienced traveller can scarcely fail to be astonished at the delicate susceptibility of his casing of flesh, which is bruised by blows, torn by thorns, devoured by insects, and yet, day after day, the persevering man continues to face death under its most horrible aspects—poison from venom of serpents, giddiness from sun-stroke, blindness from the power of the moon, want of sleep, hunger, and thirst.

I had just taken a review of our situation when these reflections were suggested to me. Halting, I permitted my comrades to pass me; their appearance, after so many days' travel, I give. First, there was Sumichrast, tall and broadshouldered, his features displaying both mildness and energy; one arm in a sling, his clothes torn to shreds, and his face furrowed by five or six deep scratches; leaning on a stick carried in his left hand, he seemed a little bent; but his vigorous form still told of abundant endurance and determination. Behind him, his gun slung to his cross-belt, came Lucien, slightly stooping, although his step was firm and determined; his face was seamed with scratches, his hands bruised and brown from exposure. As he passed in front of me, he smiled and gave a joyous hurrah, and lifted his cap, beneath which his hair flowed down in golden curls. Gringalet, now reconciled to the squirrels' skins, walked close by his master; truly he looked like standing more work. Lastly, l'Encuerado, his arms and legs bare, and laden with guavas, brought up the rear. The brave Indian tried to raise his straw-hat as he passed by me, his bony visage expanded, and his smile showed a row of white teeth which were worthy of competing with Gringalet's. Well satisfied with my inspection, I shouldered my gun, and resumed the head of the column.

The cliffs of the ravine became gradually more wooded, and the descent was effected without accident. I kept

along the bank looking out for **a ford**. **At last a** bend of
the **stream, where the water flowed** calmly and silently, en-
abled us to do so without difficulty. I then proposed a halt.
Close by us rose some enormous rocks covered with moss,
which, in flood-time, must have been reached by the water;
in front of us was a gentle slope covered with turf.

We were descending the slope when an object, indistinct
**at first, emerged from the edge of the wood, and, appearing
to roll more than run over the** grass, advanced toward us.
It was an enormous tortoise; but a tortoise which might
successfully have raced with the hare. L'Encuerado tried
to stop it, but fell **in his effort. Sumichrast,** quite forgetting
his bad hand, dealt the **animal a blow with** the butt-end of
his gun, the effect of which was slightly to slacken the pace
of the enemy. The Indian, **furious** at his failure, **threw**
down his load, and came running up. Our united efforts
succeeded, about twenty feet from the stream, in throwing
the animal on its back.

Lucien, rather startled at this scene, and at the size of the
tortoise, **then came nearer to** examine it. I kept him at
some distance from the reptile, who was viciously agitating
its enormous feet, armed with formidable claws; while its
mouth, which was like a horny beak, opened and shut men-
acingly.

"**It is a** *galapago*," said l'Encuerado; "it is of no use
for food."

This creature, which is called by the *savants* the *alligator-tortoise*, measured more than a yard from its head to
its **tail.** The latter appendage was almost as long as the
body, **and was** covered with a triple row of scaly crests
fitting **into each other.** The gray, wrinkled, and almost
scaly skin **of the reptile formed rolls** round its neck of a
disgusting appearance—one might almost fancy them **un-**
healthy excrescences. The horrible beast turned towards

us its gaping mouth with a vicious manner. The turtle-fishers much dread the *galapagos*, which, being more agile than the ordinary tortoise, give them sometimes frightful wounds, either with their sharp claws or their horny jaws. Their flesh is declared to be unwholesome.

Just as we were leaving, l'Encuerado wanted to cut off the reptile's head. Sumichrast opposed this useless slaughter, and was inclined to replace the tortoise on its feet. But the Indian refused to assist in this good work, for he asserted that it was equivalent to leaving a rattlesnake alive. Two or three times the animal was very nearly repaying our kindness by a bite; for, as soon as we came near, it managed to twist round on its upper shell. We were about to abandon it to its fate, when suddenly, the slope of the ground helping us, we managed to set it on its feet; as soon as it was turned over, it rushed at Lucien. The enormous rolls round its neck, being all distended, made it carry its head very forward, so, with a single blow of his cutlass, l'Encuerado decapitated the assailant. We were then witnesses to a strange sight, for while Gringalet was furiously attacking the motionless head, the feet, continuing to move, bore along the body, which in a moment disappeared in the lake. Although we had often before seen tortoises survive for a considerable time wounds which were certainly mortal, the strength of the nervous system which was exhibited in this reptile almost staggered us.

"Now, my brave friend, try and swim without your head, and take care not to break your skull against the rocks!" cried the exasperated Indian. "The father saves your life, and then you want to hurt his child! You hardly saw me, or you'd have known that I am pretty well able to bite. Good-bye! and take good care of yourself!"

We may readily see that the Indian was any thing but a generous enemy; but the fact was, the *galapagos* were old enemies, for one had nearly bitten off his hand while he was bathing. The turf-carpeted bank soon led us into the thick forest again. We had been walking for more than an hour through a perfect labyrinth of gigantic trees, and over a bare and yet rich soil—for it is only in the glades that the ground is covered with grass—when l'Encuerado heard the call of a small species of pheasant peculiar to this country.

"Bend towards the left to get near the game," said Sumichrast, in a low voice; "and, whatever you do, don't shake the foliage."

"We're all right now," muttered l'Encuerado; "listen! I'll predict that we shall have a good dinner to-day."

The Indian laid down his load, which Sumichrast and Lucien took charge of, while I followed the former behind the trees. My companion soon went a little in front, and imitated the cry of the bird we were pursuing, so as to make them answer, and thus show us where they were hidden. The imitation was really so perfect that I moved towards it, thinking to find the bird, and of course came upon the Indian lying in ambush. This same mistake had happened to me before with Sumichrast, who imitated the voice of birds almost as well as the Indian. At last his cry produced an answer, and at about a hundred yards from us, on the top of a not very tall oak, were perched three enormous pheasants.

Bent down and crawling behind the trees, I joined l'Encuerado, keeping my eye fixed on the game, which stretched out their necks with an anxious look, and seemed to be listening. Two gun-shots went off at once; one of the birds fell dead at our feet, and the two others flew away. One of these fugitives flew high above the tree-tops, but the other, being wounded, was unable to follow its companion; I darted off in pursuit, making sure of bagging it. The poor bird reached the ground and tried hard to run; I was not more than fifty paces from it, when a tiger-cat, with a black coat, bounded forward, and, seizing it, disappeared before I had time to recover from my surprise. The marauder was abused as a thief and a rogue by l'Encuerado, who had been a witness of this misfortune. Lucien examined the pheasant, which was almost as big as a turkey; but its sombre plumage did not at all answer to the magnificent idea which the boy had formed of this bird. He thought that the head was much too small for the body, and its naked and warty cheeks led him to observe that the pheasant had the appearance of having put on two plasters of tortoise-skin, a remark which was certainly well founded. With regard to the beautiful and many-colored pheasant-species peculiar to Asia and Africa, Mexico possesses none of them, so far, at least, as I know.

About two o'clock in the afternoon, Lucien remarked that the trees grew farther apart, which was a sign that we were approaching an open glade or the foot of a mountain. Sumichrast made the boy walk in front as leader—a reward for the sharpness of his eyes. Proud of this duty, our little guide led us to an opening edged with a rampart of wood at a short distance off.

"Halt!" cried I.

The butts of the guns were dropped upon the ground at this order; our hut was soon constructed, and l'Encuerado immediately afterwards busied himself preparing our meal.

Sumichrast, who, from the state of his hand, was condemned to idleness, remained with the Indian, while I proceeded, in company with Gringalet and Lucien, to reconnoitre the vicinity of our bivouac. Almost immediately, a *yoloxochitl*, a species of magnolia, met our eyes. I called l'Encuerado, who climbed the tree in order to throw us down some of its beautiful sweet-smelling flowers; they are externally of a pinkish-white color, yellow on the inside,

"**A tiger-cat** bounded forward **and** seized the pheasant."

and the petals, before they are full-blown, assume the form of a cross, and afterwards that of a splendid star. The Indian did not fail to remind us that an infusion of the glittering leaves of the *yoloxochitl* is a remedy against diarrhœa, and that its flowers, as their shape indicates, cure palpitation of the heart. A little farther on we recognized a nutmeg-tree, a shrub about ten feet in height, and covered with half-formed fruit. The nutmeg is not cultivated in Mexico, and the tree that produces it is rather rare. The Indians, however, use an enormous quantity of the Molucca nutmegs, either as a remedy or as a condiment—nutmegs, camphor, and asafœtida being the principal Indian remedies. I next pointed out to my young companion a plant named the *blue herb*, the leaves of which stain the water in which they are soaked with a lovely azure tinge. In Mexico a variety of this vegetable is cultivated, in order to extract from it the coloring matter commonly known under the name of *indigo*.

"But how do they manage," asked Lucien, "to obtain from a plant those dark-blue stones that I have seen sold in the market?"

"About the month of March," I answered, "are gathered the fresh leaves of the indigo-plant, which is one of the leguminous family, and pound them in mortars made out of the trunks of trees. The sap which results from these leaves, when subjected to a heavy pressure, is of a greenish tinge, and sometimes even colorless; it does not become blue until after fermentation in the open air. The Indians then boil it in an immense copper, and, the water evaporating, the indigo is left in the form of a soft and gelatinous paste, which is subsequently dried in the sun."

On approaching the foot of the mountain, I found that it would be impossible for us to climb it the next day, the slope being too steep. I sat down on the trunk of a fallen tree, when I detected a very decided smell of roses. Under the bark of a log *esquina* Lucien had discovered five or six beautiful insects of an azure-blue color, with red feet; these insects are very common in the sandy soils of Tehuacan, and are used by the ladies of that district to perfume their linen.   Delighted at this discovery, Lucien continued his search, hoping to find some more specimens which he intended to take to his mother.   He was kneeling down and working energetically, when he pointed out to me an enormous caterpillar. .

It was of an emerald-green color, and had on its back a row of little projections like small trees, symmetrically arranged.   These were of a brilliant red, terminating in shoots the same color as the animal's body.

" What a curious creature !" cried Lucien ; " it looks as if it carried a garden on its back; what use are all these bushes ?"

" It is not known, and it is a curious fact that the butterfly which springs from the caterpillar shows no trace of all this strangely-arranged hair."

" Will a butterfly come from this caterpillar ?"

" Yes, certainly ; all butterflies lay eggs, from which proceed caterpillars, which generally destroy the plants on which they are hatched.   When arrived at maturity, the caterpillar spins a cocoon of silk, more or less fine, in the centre of which it incloses itself.   It is then called a *chrysalis*.   In this cocoon the butterfly is formed, either white or black, yellow or green, and there it remains inactive and imprisoned, like a baby in swaddling-clothes.   In spring it perforates its silken prison, and soon makes its escape a splendid butterfly, subsisting upon the juices of the flowers obtained through its proboscis.   Surely you were not ignorant of all these transformations ?"

" I thought that they only took place in silk-worms."

" Well, now you are undeceived ; all caterpillars and all butterflies are subject to them ; but there are few caterpillars which spin so valuable a cocoon as the silk - worm. Moreover, some bury themselves in the earth ; while others hide in the middle of a leaf, the edges of which they curl round so as to form a kind of bag, in which they are protected from the beaks of birds ; again, some hollow out a shelter in the trunk of a tree, and line their abode with silk more or less fine. Thus, in every case, the chrysalis waits patiently for the time when it will change from a worm into a butterfly, painted with the richest colors."

The subject was really an inexhaustible one, so I deferred the rest of my explanations to another day. Besides, l'Encuerado was loudly calling for us.

CHAPTER XIII.

THE SENSITIVE-PLANT.—GRINGALET AND THE PORCUPINE.—
THE MEXICAN CHAMELEON.—THE KITE AND THE FALCON.
—AN AMPHISBÆNA SNAKE.—A COUNCIL OF TURKEYS.

LUCIEN, seated on the grass, amused himself with touching all the plants within reach of his travelling staff; suddenly he noticed that the branches and leaves of a small shrub shut up when he brushed them with his stick, just like the ribs of a parasol, moved by some invisible spring—it was a *sensitive-plant.*

He called to us to ask for an explanation of this phenomenon, so we assembled round the shrub, which was about three feet high; its leaves finely cut and of a delicate green color, with pink flowers in tufts half hidden among them. The leaves, touched by the stick, shrank up close to the pa-

rent stem, and the oval, slender, and delicate ones, rising on
their stalks, pressed against one another. In about five
minutes the leaves which had been rubbed again spread
out, as if they had recovered from their fright.

It was, however, **only** for a short **time**; for Lucien
amused himself by rubbing his fingers over the leaves,
which immediately doubled up, as if offended by the slight
touch. The Indians call it the "Bashful Plant." A blow
struck on the principal stem is sufficient to make all the
branches close, as if animated by a kind of modest feeling.
When the sun sets, the sensitive plant spontaneously shuts
up its delicate foliage, which does not open again freely until the return of day.

Lucien's first idea, at waking, was to run towards the
shrubs which interested him the day before. They were
covered with dew, and looked as if they were asleep, until
the first rays of the sun fell upon them. Before we started, **the young naturalist again** tested the delicate **sensibility
of the plant,** which Sumichrast told him **was** allied **to the**
tree which produces gum-arabic.

L'Encuerado's **cheek** was less swollen, and Sumichrast
could use his hand, although it still pained him. The
mountain in front of us, which was too steep to climb,
caused us some perplexity.

"Let us slant off to the left, over this moist ground,
carpeted with turf," said Sumichrast, plunging into the
thicket.

About midday, just as l'Encuerado was declaring, in a
grumbling tone, that we ought to have inclined towards the
right, our little troop entered the wood. An undulating
slope led us to a summit not more than twenty yards
across, and **in less than half an hour the** opposite descent
brought us into a delicious glen.

"Hallo! Master 'Sunbeam,'" **cried Sumichrast, while**

helping me to construct our hut, "don't you recollect you are the one to provide the fire?"

"All right," replied Lucien, who seemed to be lost in the contemplation of a dead branch; "I want to get hold of an insect which appears to be making, like us, natural-history collections, for I have just found in its nest a quantity of spiders, flies, and small worms."

"It is one of the *Hymenoptera*," said Sumichrast; "it collects all round its eggs the food the young will eat when they are hatched; the insect is therefore full of fore-thought—a good example for us to imitate."

When the fire was ready, we started off in light marching order to explore the vicinity of our bivouac. Our position was commanded by mountains on all sides, and the glen was scarcely a quarter of a league in length. The pleasant coolness, and the presence of numerous birds, led us to hope that we should meet with a spring, which was all that was needed to convert this remote corner of the world into a perfect paradise. But our exploring only led to the discovery of a greenish pool, sheltered by an enormous rock, and which the dry season would soon evaporate.

Gringalet's barking attracted our attention towards the forest, and I perceived a porcupine on a tree. The animal, sitting up on its hind feet, was looking at us with astonishment. Leaving it undisturbed, it appeared to forget us, and tearing off with its claws a piece of bark, it licked the inner side, which was doubtless covered with insects. Having repeated this operation several times, the animal advanced to the end of a branch, and seizing it with its prehensile tail, let itself down to the ground. Its large black eyes, of unusual mildness, were widely opened, and its nose slit like hares and rabbits. It was just about to stretch itself, when, to our great regret, l'Encuerado shot it; the poor beast fell over **on the ground, and** placing its hand-shaped **paws on the wound, rolled** itself **up into a** ball at the **foot of a tree. Gringalet darted forward to** seize it, **and then** immediately retreated, **howling with** pain; he **came** back to us with his muzzle bristling with the porcupine's quills, which were about two inches **long and finely** pointed. The unfortunate **dog** rubbed his nose against the ground in **order** to get relief, **but, of** course, this only **in**creased his pain. **Lucien** ran to help him, and at last succeeded in extracting **them.**

"Have you lost your senses?" asked l'Encuerado of the dog, while washing the poor beast's nose and mouth. "The idea of trying to bite a *huitztlacuatzin!* Upon my word, I thought **you knew better** than **that.** No doubt it's a good thing to be brave, **but** you must **manage to** be less stupid **when you are** in the forests of the *Terre-Chaude,* unless **you want to be devoured by a tiger, or scratched to pieces by an ant-eater."**

After listening to l'Encuerado's speech, Lucien scolded **him for** firing at the poor animal, and then joined us, **close** to the porcupine, which was dying. It was about the size of a fox, **and its fore** paws were furnished with four **toes** armed with claws. This animal, which is slow of pace and entirely inoffensive, spreads round it a sickening musky odor. It lives on fruit, roots, and insects, and, aided by its prehensile tail, climbs trees with great skill. It but rarely tries to make its escape at the approach of the hunter, who, moreover, utterly despises such worthless game.

L'Encuerado reminded us that we had now been travelling **twelve** days, and that it was the first Sunday in May. **We should have devoted** it to rest if our morning's hunting had been **successful; but,** unless we contented ourselves with a dinner composed only of **rice, we** were obliged to shoot some eatable bird or animal to fill our stew-pot

We heard some doves cooing, and l'Encuerado went off alone in the direction of the sound, for these birds are difficult of approach. Gringalet, notwithstanding our calls, ran after the Indian.

Lucien climbed the rock which hung over the pool, and made signs for me to come to him, saying, in a low voice,

"Papa, come and look at this strange animal."

I also climbed up, and found lying on the top a Mexican chameleon, a kind of round-shaped lizard, with a brown skin dotted over with yellow spots, which seemed to change color in the light. Lucien tried to catch the graceful reptile, which, however, glided between his fingers and disappeared behind the rock.

The Mexican chameleon lives only in the woods and among the rocks. It chiefly delights in the oak forests, where the dark color of its body blends with the hue of the dry leaves, and enables it to lie successfully in ambush for the insects on which it feeds. Sumichrast, who had succeeded in taming a chameleon, told us that the reptile's throat, which was white during the daytime, assumed during the night a dark hue; also, that it liked to be caressed, and became familiar enough to take from his hand the flies which were offered it. The Indians, who hold the animal in great dread when alive, are in the habit of wearing its dried body as an amulet against the "evil eye."

From our lofty observatory we were looking at the beautiful birds which occasionally flew across the plain, when Sumichrast suddenly fired. He had caught sight of a fine magpie, of an ashy-blue color, with its head crowned by a tuft; its throat appeared as if it were bound round with black velvet, a peculiarity which has obtained for it from the Indians the name of the "commander bird." Lucien came down from the rock to go and pick up the game, when an enormous kite darted on the magpie, seized it in

"The kite avoided the shock, and continued to rise in the air."

its sharp claws, and immediately took flight. Sumichrast seized his gun to punish the impudent poacher, but a falcon, about the size of a man's fist, made its appearance, and describing two or three rapid circles, swooped down on the kite. The latter avoided the shock and continued to rise in the air, while its antagonist came almost to the ground, uttering a shriek of rage. Again ascending, with extreme rapidity, by an oblique flight, it a second time overtopped its antagonist, and darted upon it like a flash of lightning. Their wings beat together, and a few feathers came fluttering to the ground. The prey fell from the bird's grasp, followed in its fall by the falcon. The kite, conquered by an enemy about one-fifth of its own size, flew round and round in the air and then disappeared. The conqueror standing about thirty yards from us, eyes glittering and foot firmly planted on its prey, magnificent in anger and daring, Sumichrast abandoned the game to it as a recompense for its courage. The bird, not at all satisfied at being so close to us, buried in the body of its victim its claws —so enormous in comparison to its own size—shook its wings and rose, at first with difficulty, when, its flight becoming more easy as it ascended higher, it carried off its quarry behind the trees.

Lucien, who from the ground beneath had followed all the changes and chances of this combat, soon joined us.

"How was it that that great bird allowed itself to be conquered by such a small adversary?" he asked of Sumichrast.

"Because it was a coward."

"But both have the same plumage, and almost the same shape; I took the small bird to be the young of the other."

"The last is a falcon, and the other is a kite. They belong, in fact, to the same family; but the falcon is noble and courageous, while the kite is perhaps the most coward ly of all birds of prey. Falcons were once used for hunting; for, as you have just seen, they have no fear of attacking adversaries much larger than themselves. Added to this, they are easily tamed."

"But eagles are much stronger than falcons?"

"Eagles are birds of prey which do not at all merit the reputation which poets have endeavored to make for them; although they may be stronger, they exhibit much less bravery than falcons, and only attack animals of small size."

"Yet, surely the eagle is the king of birds; is it not able to look straight at the sun?"

"Yes, thanks to a membrane that shuts down over the pupil of its eye. Among all nations the eagle is the symbol of strength and courage: but still the falcon possesses the latter of these qualities in a much higher degree; it is the falcon which is the real king of birds among ornithologists. The Mexicans, as you know, depict upon their banners an eagle sitting upon a cactus and tearing a serpent."

"Is this intended as an emblem of strength and courage?"

"No, it has another origin. When the Aztecs, who were thought to be natives of Northern America, arrived in Mexico (which then bore the name of Anahuac), they wandered about a long time before they settled. One day, near a lake, they found a cactus growing on a stone, and on the cactus an eagle was sitting. Guided by an oracle, a city was built, which was called Tenochtitlan, and subsequently Mexico."

My historical lecture was interrupted by a distant shot. We had heard nothing of the doves for a long time, and we were expecting to see our companion reappear; but he must have made an enormous curve in pursuing them, to judge from the direction **from which** the report of his gun proceeded. **Fortunately,** from the position of the spot, **there was** not much likelihood of his missing his way : although we had full confidence in his instinct, we feared to **what** extent his ardor might carry him.

We now kept on the look-out, hoping that chance would **throw us in contact with some** game. All at once there **was a movement** to our right in the high grass, and **its waving about pointed** out the presence of some reptile. In **a minute or two we saw** a serpent making its way towards **the pool ; it was the** species which is called by the Indians, as formerly **by the Greeks, the** double-headed serpent. The amphisbæna was about a foot and a half long, and its tail **was swollen at the end,** which gave it a very curious appearance. **Its** skin, covered with large scales, had a bluish metallic glitter. It crawled slowly, and stopped **every instant as if to** bore into the ground, but in reality to **pick up insects or ants.** This singular snake quite **enchanted Lucien,** and Sumichrast told him to fire **his gun at it, so as to be able to study it more closely.** He had no need to repeat **his instructions ;** the young sportsman, who had begun **to handle his weapon** very skillfully, at once placed it to his **shoulder ;** the shot was fired, and the amphisbæna, tumbling **over, disappeared in** the grass. The reptile had been hit, and we all of us clambered down the rock as fast as we could, in the hopes of finding it dead. We sought for it in vain ; the snake had made its escape into some hole, from which it would be in vain to try to dislodge it.

Gringalet now showed himself, soon followed by l'Encuerado. When **he** caught sight of us, the Indian raised a loud **" Hiou ! hiou !"** Waving his hat in the air, he threw upon the **ground some dark** object, which fell heavily on the turf, and then he began dancing. We roared with laughter at his grotesque steps, and Lucien ran towards the

Mistec, who, after his dance, was acting the acrobat on the turf.

"A turkey!" he cried; and an enormous bird, with bronzed plumage, was passed from hand to hand.

"Ah! Ohanito," cried the Indian, "if you had gone with me, you would have seen a whole flock of them! I had chased those miserable doves till I was tired, without even catching a glimpse of them, and was resting at the foot of a tree, when Gringalet pricked up his ears, and running up the opposite slope of the mountain, barked as loudly as if he saw another porcupine. I also made my way there, and heard 'gobbles' resounding in every direction; Master Gringalet had fallen in with a council of turkeys."

"A council of turkeys?" repeated Lucien.

"Yes, Chanito, turkeys hold councils. * They generally travel in flocks and on foot, although they know perfectly well how to fly when they want to cross a stream or to make their escape; and when one of them wants to communicate his opinion to another, he raises a cry, and his companions form a circle round him."

"And what takes place then?"

"The preacher," continued l'Encuerado, without the least idea of irreverence, "lowers his neck and then lifts it up again, raises up the hair-like feathers on his crop, and spreads out his tail like a fan. He then addresses the assembled birds, who strut about with their wings half opened, and answer him with approving gobbles."

The Indian, carried away by his narrative, added gestures to words, strutted about, rounded his arms and lowered his chin upon his breast, in order to imitate the ways of the birds which he was describing.

"But what do they say?" asked Lucien, archly.

"That depends on circumstances," he replied, scratching

his forehead. "The flock just now surprised must have cried out: '**What is** this animal?'—'A dog,' would be the answer **of** the most knowing among them. 'Fly, my friends, fly!' he would cry; 'dogs are always accompanied **by men, and men have** guns.' 'A gun! what's that?'—'A **machine that goes** *boum* **and** kills turkeys.' **Then I make my appearance; they bustle about, fly** away, and spread in every **direction; but my gun had time to go** *boum* **and to** kill this beautiful **bird.**"

I need scarcely say what mirth was excited by this account. While **returning to** our bivouac, Sumichrast told Lucien that the turkey **is a native** of America, and that it **was introduced by the Jesuits into** Europe, where it **flourished well. In a domestic state, the** color of its plumage **altered** to a reddish, a white, and a gray and black **color. But** it never lost the habit of walking about in flocks, and of laying its eggs in thickets, in a shapeless nest, which the young chicks leave the second day after they are hatched. Lastly, the Aztec name of the **turkey—***totole***—is** applied **by the** Indians to simpletons and cowards.

Lucien then told l'Encuerado about the magpie and the amphisbæna.

"**You** killed **a** *maquiz coatl—***a** two-headed serpent!" cried the Indian.

"I only wounded **it, for it** got away; but it had only one head."

"Then you didn't examine it thoroughly; for it would **not** turn round when it crawled away."

"**I did** not notice. I saw it leap up in the air, and that **was all.**"

"Have **you searched** well under the stones? Let us go back; the **skin** of the *maquiz coatl* enables the blind to see. Why did you let it escape?"

"Oh! we shall be sure to find another."

"You can't find them whenever you like; they are very rare," replied the Indian, shaking his head.

While the turkey was roasting under our superintendence, l'Encuerado and Lucien went off to try and find the amphisbæna's hole.

"It looked like an immense pedestal, surmounted by two bronze statues."

CHAPTER XIV.

THE METEOR.—GOD ALMIGHTY'S LANTERNS.—THE SKUNK.
—THE JALAP-PLANT.—AN AERIAL JOURNEY.—THE OR-
CHIDS.—BIVOUAC IN THE MOUTH OF A CAVE.—GRINGA-
LET AND THE BEETLES.—A WHITE ANTS' NEST.

THE sun left us soon afterwards, and we sat talking
by the fire. At last l'Encuerado took away Lucien
towards the rocks, and set up one of those interminable
chants with which his memory was stored. Our fire lighted up with its red gleam the stone on which they were sitting, making it look like an immense pedestal, surmounted
by two bronze statues. Any traveller suddenly entering
the valley would have recoiled in terror before this fantastic apparition; and if any wild beast had been prowling
near us, our gigantic shadows would certainly have made it
keep its distance.

We were just thinking of calling Lucien to come and lie down under the hut, when l'Encuerado shouted out to us. Towards the east, a large luminous disk was shining brilliantly above the mountain peaks. This luminous globe, lengthening out into the shape of an ellipse, appeared to move along.

In fact, it was descending slowly over the wooded crests. Lucien and l'Encuerado kept plying us with questions in reference to it, which we were unable to answer.

"What is it?" cried Sumichrast.

"A meteor!" I exclaimed, struck with a sudden idea.

"If I had my gun ready, I would fire at it, at all events."

"You had better not," said I; "the globe may contain electric fluid, and we might draw it down upon us."

Soon afterwards the meteor passed by us. We threw ourselves down flat on the earth, dreading this unknown visitor. When I ventured to rise, it was some distance away, and yet appeared to be motionless. Rays incessantly quivering sprang from the centre of it; in the middle the light was white, but at the edges it assumed first a yellowish, then a red, and lastly a bluish hue. We were suddenly almost blinded by a flash of intense brilliancy; a formidable explosion, repeated by the echoes, burst upon our ears, and all became silence and obscurity.

While we were returning to our bivouac, Lucien and l'Encuerado pressed us with questions.

"What are meteors?" asked Lucien, eagerly.

"Some scientific men," replied Sumichrast, "look upon them as fragments of planets wandering in space. Getting entangled in our planetary system, they yield to the attraction of our globe, and fall on to its surface in obedience to the law of gravitation."

"But what are they composed of?"

"Generally speaking, of sulphur, chromium, and earth. The phenomenon of 'shooting stars' is connected with that of meteors, and any substance falling on the surface of the earth receives the name of *aerolite.*"

"Do you wish to persuade me that stones rain down from the sky?" cried l'Encuerado.

"Yes, certainly; and if I am not mistaken, it was in your country that the largest known aerolite was found, for it weighed no less than fifty hundred-weights. To-morrow morning we will search for the one we have seen, which must have dropped at the end of the valley."

"Are these stones luminous?" rejoined the Indian.

"No; but they take fire, owing to their rapid flight."

"And whence did the meteor come which passed so close to us?"

"Either from the moon or the stars, or perhaps from the sun."

L'Encuerado half-closed his eyes, and burst out laughing

at what he considered a joke. He laughed, indeed, so heartily, that we could not help joining him.

"Now what do you imagine the sun and moon really are?" asked Lucien.

"God's lanterns," replied the Indian, gravely.

Our young companion was well accustomed to the artless ignorance of his friend, but still he always endeavored to contend against it; so he set to work to teach him something about our planetary system. The dimensions which he attributed to the heavenly bodies seemed to afford great amusement to the Indian. At last, just when the young orator fancied he had convinced his disciple, the latter embraced him, exclaiming:

"What an amusing tale! Oh! how pleased I should be to be able to read such pretty stories as that in a book!"

"Tales, indeed!" cried Lucien, quite indignant.

"Well, the very idea of saying that the earth is a ball, which moves round and round, and that there are stars which are bigger! Many a night have I spent looking at the stars, and I know they are nothing but lanterns, and that's enough!"

"But if you have observed them so carefully," interposed Sumichrast, "you must have observed that they are constantly shifting their places."

"Yes, but that is because the angels don't always light up the same stars, and God has plenty of them in every direction—"

I now interrupted the conversation.

"Come, let us all go to rest!" I cried, cutting short a discussion which I knew, by experience, must end in Lucien and Sumichrast getting the worst of it.

The next morning there was nothing better to do than to go with my companions to look after the aerolite. The ball of fire appeared to have passed just over us, and I fancied that we should be certain to recover some part of it. After an hour of useless wandering, we were compelled to admit that our eyes must have been much mistaken as to distances. L'Encuerado could not help smiling incredulously on hearing the conjectures which I and Sumichrast made; but he was generous enough not to take advantage of the superior astronomical knowledge which he assumed he possessed.

On setting out I again crossed the valley, and then climbing the mountain, I led my companions up to a plateau.

As far as was possible I followed the route I thought the meteor had taken. L'Encuerado was just making his way into the forest when Sumichrast noticed a broken tree, a little to the right. I leaped up on the slope, and soon remarked that the ground, for a space of at least twenty yards, was strewn with black or green stones, which had been in a fused state, and evidently bore the appearance of iron *scoriæ*. There could be no doubt about it; the tree which had been struck had caused the explosion of the meteor, and had broken under the shock.

"These, therefore, are the remains of some of your sky-lanterns," said Lucien to l'Encuerado, who had just picked up some large stones, shining like metal.

The Indian shook his head without answering. The fallen tree, the burned and blackened trunk, the withered and even scorched grass, these strange-looking stones—every thing visibly combined to upset his theory. Each of us added to his load one of the aerolites; then, again returning to the plateau, we plunged into the forest.

One shot that Sumichrast made rendered him happy for the whole day. He had knocked down a green-colored crossbill, of a species still unknown in Europe.

"What a queer bird!" cried Lucien. "How did it manage to eat with its mouth all awry?"

" Its mouth," replied Sumichrast, smiling, " is well adapted to its food. This bird—which we have here met with quite by chance, as it usually frequents mountain-tops—feeds on roots, buds, and pine-cones. Owing to its two mandibles being so strongly made and so curiously arranged it can cut through, as if with a pair of scissors, branches which a bird with a pointed beak could never penetrate."

" God is mindful of all His creatures," muttered l'Encuerado, who was helping to skin the bird. " I had always fancied that these poor creatures were deformed."

Towards midday the chances of our path brought us to the bottom of a narrow valley in the midst of a clump of shrubs; this seemed a fit spot for our bivouac. In the twinkling of an eye, the ground was cleared of brush-wood and our hut constructed. We had scarcely sat down to take breath when a slight rustling in the foliage attracted our attention, and an animal with a bushy tail sprang down from a tree. Gringalet darted at it, but an abominable smell, which almost suffocated us, at once made him retreat. A skunk, which in shape and color somewhat resembles a squirrel, had thus perfectly poisoned our bivouac.

Nothing was left for us but to decamp as quickly as possible, for the stench rendered the place uninhabitable for several days. L'Encuerado could not find enough bad names for abusing the animal, which, however, had only availed itself of the means of defense with which nature has endowed it. Each of us now resumed his burden, sadly enough, I must confess, and not without throwing a disappointed glance at our hut. Sumichrast led the way, and did not stop till we found ourselves perfectly exhausted at the entrance to a deep and narrow gorge. We still felt sickened by the horrible stench produced by the skunk, and, as we did not wish to expose ourselves again to a similar

"Above us, the trees crossed their branches."

misfortune, we took care, before constructing a fresh hut, to search round the shrubs and bushes. A few birds shot on the road rendered it unnecessary for us to hunt any more, as we had an abundance of food, so we all set to work to repair our wardrobes. Our shoes first required our attention, and Sumichrast constituted himself head-cobbler. L'Encuerado's sandals gave him a great advantage over us; for all he required was a sole and a leathern strap, and then he was well shod. But, unfortunately, the delicacy of our skin several times afforded Sumichrast cause for regret that he had not been born an Indian.

L'Encuerado, full of ingenuity, managed to fix some pieces of fox-skin on some old soles, and made for Lucien a pair of buskins as strong as they were inelegant. He promised to make us some like them, and Sumichrast, who succeeded only tolerably well in his cobbling, nominated the Indian "sandal-maker in ordinary and extraordinary to our majesties."

The next morning at daybreak we entered a narrow gorge in which it was impossible for us to walk abreast. The whole morning was spent in travelling along between two stone ramparts, hung with mosses, ferns, and orchids. The moist soil rendered the temperature round us sufficiently cool and agreeable; but the pass was so filled up with the trunks of fallen trees as to render our progress very laborious.

The gorge extended to such a length that I began to be anxious about it, and to fear lest we had entered into a *cul-de-sac*. The perpendicular walls rendered any deviation in our path impossible; above us, the trees crossed their branches and almost hid the sky. No bird enlivened the solitude with its song, and ferns were so abundant that it seemed as if we had lighted upon some corner of the primitive world; as if to render the resemblance more complete, the reptiles scarcely fled at our approach, and obliged us to use the greatest care.

Cutlass in hand, Lucien climbed nimbly over the fallen trees which barred our progress. Ere long our feet sank into a quantity of liquid mud, and I discovered a slender streamlet of limpid water oozing out between two rocks. The pass between the rocks became narrower and narrower, and if a wild beast had then met us we should have had to dispute the path with it. As a rencontre of this kind was by no means impossible, Lucien, to his displeasure, was ordered to follow in rear.

The way now widened a little, and became more clear of impediments, and our little column advanced with rather more rapidity. We walked along silently between these stern and imposing granite walls, with the constant hope of seeing them separate and open out into a valley. Every few yards some fresh turn frustrated our expectations; and if ever any pass deserved the name of the "Devil's Gorge," it was the interminable fissure through which we had been compelled to walk for so long a distance. At various heights there were half-suspended rocks which threatened to fall upon us; for several previously had fallen and now blocked up the path. At last a sudden turn revealed a wide opening; but our joy was of short duration; nothing but a perpendicular precipice lay in front of us.

We looked at one another in consternation; we were prisoners! On our right and left were perpendicular walls more than a hundred feet high, and impossible to climb; before us there was a gulf with a vertical precipice. What was to be done? Sumichrast lighted the pipe of council, while l'Encuerado clung on to the rocks and tried to measure the abyss with his eye.

We were seated near a plant with slender branches and

heart-shaped leaves tinged with red, concealing here and there a flower of a violet blue. I recognized in it the shrub which produces jalap, and is called by the Indians *tolonpatl.* I called Lucien's attention to it, who soon dug up four or five tap-roots of a pear-like shape. Jalap, which has taken its name from the town of Jalapa, whence it was once forwarded to Vera Cruz, grows naturally on all the mountains of the *Terre-Tempérée.* Unfortunately, the Indians destroy the plant by taking away all its turbercles, and the time is not far distant when this drug, so much used in Europe, will, like quinine, become very scarce.

I drew close to the precipice, and perceived l'Encuerado more than twenty feet below me crawling, with all the skill of a monkey, over an almost smooth surface. I ordered him to come up to us again; but he did not seem able to get back, and remained motionless in his dangerous position. Sumichrast hastened to bring me a lasso, which I let down to our daring companion. But instead of ascending, he slid down four or five feet, and placing himself astride on the projecting trunk of a tree, called out to us to let go the lasso; this he tied round a stout branch, and disappeared down the abyss.

It was not long before we saw him again install himself on the tree round which he had rolled the leather strap, when he called out to us that we might descend without any great danger.

"How shall we fasten it?" asked Lucien; "there are no thick branches just at the edge."

"The strap is a long one, and there is a bush not far off with pretty strong branches."

"But then we shall lose the lasso, for none will be left to loosen it."

"Upon my word!" cried Sumichrast, "Master Sunbeam is right."

Then each of us tried to solve the problem, proposing expedients more or less impracticable.

"I've found it out," cried I at last, with quite as much satisfaction as Archimedes when he leaped out of his bath.

Seizing my *machete*, I cut two stakes of a good thickness, which I drove into the ground close to one another, about three yards from the precipice. While Sumichrast with a club was consolidating my work, I cut a stick about a foot long, to the middle of which I firmly tied the lasso. I then placed it crosswise behind the stakes. I considered that when we had let ourselves down to the spot occupied by l'Encuerado, a sharp undulatory shake given to the lasso would be sufficient to disengage the stick. When our preparations were finished, we let down the basket to the man who carried it. Then Sumichrast, who was the heaviest among us, slid down the cord to the tree which grew in so convenient a position. The stakes scarcely yielded at all to his weight. Continuing his descent, my friend soon joined the Indian.

Lucien's impatience was extreme; he was enchanted with this aerial route.

"Now it's your turn," said I, as soon as I had drawn up the lasso.

"Are you going to tie me?" he asked in a disappointed tone.

"How did you suppose you would descend?"

"By holding on to the lasso, like l'Encuerado and M. Sumichrast," answered the boy.

"The grasp of your hands is not firm enough; you must not think of it; I have no wish to risk your neck."

"Oh! dear father! do let me try."

"Certainly not; for if your trial failed, you would not be in a position to try again."

"Then Sumichrast .... slid down the cord to the tree."

Not without some slight vexation Lucien was tied to the lasso, while Gringalet, astonished, barked round us.

"Patience! patience!" I exclaimed to the dog; "it will be your turn next, and then, perhaps, you will not seem so pleased."

I let the lasso slowly down, and the boy was soon safely lodged among the branches of the tree. With care equal to mine, and with still firmer knots, l'Encnerado tied the cord afresh. Then, leaning over the precipice, I heard Sumichrast's voice ordering the Indian to let the improvised cable slowly down. Seeing that the port was safely reached, and relieved of a great care, I began tying Gringalet, who hadn't left off howling since his young master disappeared. In spite of his terror, I launched the dog into the air; he struggled, howled, and nearly evaded l'Encuerado's friendly grasp; the latter, as he again let him down, tried to explain the inutility of his struggles, and the danger of breaking loose. At length, having for the last time examined the stakes and the cross-piece, I also descended. I then shook the lasso, and at once succeeded in disengaging it.

I saw below me Sumichrast and Lucien, seated on a narrow projection, which led by a rocky declivity down to the foot of the mountain. Soon I joined them, followed by the Indian. We had fixed the cross-bar between two stout branches, and for a long time, without loosening the stick, I shook the cord. At last, tired out, and about to leave it, the piece of wood suddenly gave way, and nearly fell on me.

Walking now became very laborious, and it was occasionally difficult to preserve our balance in passing over rocks, sometimes smooth, at others very uneven. Our path lay between perfect hedges of orchids, of which beautiful race Mexico possesses hundreds of species; we stopped at

nearly every step to admire some of these curiously shaped,
brilliantly colored, but often scentless flowers. L'Encuerado pointed out many plants of the lynx flower, called by the
Indians the *serpent-flower*, the fine petals of which are dotted with yellow spots, and marbled with pink, violet, and
white. Farther on, another flower, the tiger-lily, reminded
us, by its color, of the animal from which it takes its name.
Plucking as he went along, Lucien became possessor of
such a bouquet as the richest gardens could not furnish.
Of course he wanted to know the names of all, but he was
obliged to be content with learning that, with the exception
of the vanilla-plant, the brilliant legion of orchids furnishes
nothing utilized in the arts or industrial skill.

We had just reached the foot of the mountain, when an
immense mass of stones obliged us to turn aside. I took
the lead, and an involuntary slip brought me unexpectedly
to a cave. My companions came running up in answer to
my call; I took three or four steps into the entrance, and
immediately made up my mind, from its thorough adapta-
bility, to shelter there for the night. While I, helped by
Lucien, was collecting some wood, l'Encuerado cleared the
ground, and Sumichrast cut down two or three shrubs
which impeded the view. I then ordered the Indian to
light the fire, which would assist us to reconnoitre the entrance to the cavern; which being done, it was necessary
for us to go in search of game for our dinner.

Looking from the plain, I could well judge of the feat
we had accomplished in our descent. Up to the level of
the cave there were shrubs and brush-wood. Higher up,
orchids, with their bright flowers and opal-green leaves;
higher still rose a perpendicular and almost smooth rampart, utterly impassable except through the fissure which
had afforded us egress. Sumichrast guided us through
the thicket, where the frangipanni-plants, covered with

"I then ordered the Indian to light the fire."

their sweet-scented flowers, predominated, announcing our approach into the *Terre-Chaude*, and of a completely altered nature of vegetation. Soon an immense mahogany-tree (*Swietenia mahogoni*), with its thick boughs and dark-green foliage, rose before us; a little farther on a fallen ceiba had crushed four or five shrubs. The ceiba (*Eriodendron anfractuosum*) called *Pochotl* by the Indians, is one of the largest trees known; its fruit, of a pod-like shape, contains a silky down, which possesses a singular property of swelling in the sun. I was pointing out this peculiarity to Lucien, when a formidable buzzing noise met our ears; a whole flock of Hercules beetles had flown out of a bush and struck heavily against the branches of a tree. Lucien caught one and wanted to hold it down on the ground, but the insect got away from him and continued its flight.

"Oh!" cried the boy, "this beetle is stronger than I am!"

"It is not for nothing that it bears the name of *Hercules*," replied Sumichrast, smiling; "as you have just found out, it is as remarkable for its strength as for its size. It is a native of Brazil, and is only occasionally found in Mexico."

"Do they always travel in flocks like this?"

"No; the occurrence is so rare that I shall make a note of it."

"I smell something like snuff," said Lucien, sneezing.

"It proceeds from the beetles," said Sumichrast.

And so powerful was this odor, that it caused Lucien several times to sneeze. This was another fact to note down.

"Papa, do look at them hanging one on to another, and forming something like an immense bunch of grapes. Do they bite with those powerful jaws?"

"They are horns which you mistake for jaws; but their

arrangement quite excuses your error. Look; the upper part of their body is black and polished, and their wing-sheaths are a greenish gray, irregularly dotted with dark spots."

" Here is one which has no horns."

" It is a female."

We were examining with some curiosity all the ways of the insect colony, which was scarcely disturbed by our presence, when Gringalet, who had also taken to sneezing, suddenly set up the most plaintive howl. L'Encuerado had placed on the dog's back three or four beetles, which had buried their claws in his skin. The Indian, surprised at the result of his experiment, hurried to relieve the poor animal, which was rolling on the ground; at last he succeeded in getting hold of him, but he had much difficulty in freeing him from his vindictive assailants. One beetle, indeed, seized hold of the hand of the mischievous wag, whose gri-maces much amused us; as fast as he disengaged one of the insect's claws, the creature—which possessed six—soon found a chance to cling on with others. Annoyed at hav-ing to strive with such a paltry enemy, l'Encuerado at last tore the beetle roughly away, but the blood flowed from his bronze-colored skin. Always too ready for revenge, he threatened to exterminate the whole colony of beetles ; but, smiling at his ill-humor, I forbade his perpetrating such a useless massacre.

" They are nice gentlemen !" he cried; " because they had just heard themselves called *Hercules,* they think they are strong enough to bite the hands of every person they meet ! Stupid fools, with noses longer than their bodies, who fly away when Gringalet barks at them! Bite them ! Bite them !" cried he, setting the dog at them.

But the latter, with his ears drooped and his tail between his legs, refused to obey, and, from this day forward I remarked that the least buzzing from any insect was sufficient to render him uneasy.

Sumichrast, who had caught one of these large beetles, placed a stone upon it which any one would have thought sufficient to have crushed it; but, to Lucien's great admiration, the six-legged Hercules walked off with its burden, almost without an effort. Ere long the beetles one by one resumed their flight, and came buzzing around us, so it became really necessary to beat a retreat, lest we should have our eyes put out by their immense horns; Gringalet followed our example. Lucien sat down so as to laugh at his ease, for l'Encuerado, instead of running away, drew his bill-hook, assuming a threatening attitude to his enemies, and, like one of Homer's heroes, defied them to come near him. At last the whole band of beetles united and suspended themselves to the branch of a ceiba, a tree for which the Hercules beetle shows a marked preference.

But we had in the mean time quite forgotten our dinners, so we set off hunting in various directions. I skirted the edge of the forests, accompanied by Sumichrast and Lucien. We had walked for an hour without finding any thing, when four partridges, with ash-colored breasts, tawny wings, and tufted heads, rose about fifty paces from us, and settled down a little farther on. Having arrived within easy gunshot, I told my son to fire when I did, and two of them (which *savants* call the Sonini partridge) fell dead on the ground. These pretty birds are rarely met with in Mexico, at least in the part where we were.

I now returned towards the bivouac, taking a path through the forest.

"Oh papa, here's a great sponge!" cried Lucien, suddenly.

On our right there was a shapeless, porous, yellowish mass, rising three or four feet above the ground. I saw at once that it was the nest of a termite, or ant, which the Mexicans call *comejen.*

"It is a nest of white ants," I said to my son; "they are insects of the neuropteral order, and allied to the *libellula.*"

"But where are they?"

"You will soon see," I answered.

So, kicking the spongy mass, immediately out came a multitude of insects, which swarmed about in every direction, as if to ascertain the cause of the disturbance. Lucien wanted to examine them closer.

"Take care," I called out to him; "the termites you see are nothing but the inoffensive workers; the soldier ants will soon make their appearance, and if they bite you they will certainly draw blood."

Lucien looked at me, thinking I was joking.

"I am speaking quite seriously," I hastened to add; "termites, like bees and ants, the latter of which they much resemble at first sight, live in communities, and build nests which are often larger than the one you are looking at. This nest, skillfully divided into cells, contains a king, a queen, workmen, and soldiers. The workmen are the clever architects, whose duty it is to build, maintain, and, in case of need, increase the curious edifice which you took for a sponge. The only duty of the soldiers is fighting against enemies that attempt to disturb the peace of the colony."

"But I see thousands of holes; does each termite have a separate chamber?"

"Not exactly; there is first a chamber for the queen, which is the largest; then comes the nursery, afterwards a large compartment, in which the working ants place the eggs which the queen lays night and day."

"How I should like to see all this!"

Being convinced that practical illustration is better than the clearest explanation, I again struck the nest. The workmen, who were beginning to disappear, soon came out again to examine the spot threatened, and in a moment after the surface of the nest appeared to be swarming. I then kept making a noise at one point of the nest only, when the soldier ants soon rushed out, easily recognizable by their enormous heads; finally, I removed a small portion of the outside of the construction, and brought to light a multitude of white specks. These were the eggs, which the workmen hurried to carry farther into the nest. After having caused all this disturbance, I led Lucien away, for the ground was covered with soldier ants, and I was too well aware of the violence of their stings to willingly expose him to them.

"But I haven't seen the queen," cried my young companion.

"She keeps quite in the centre of the building, immured in a cell which she seldom or never leaves, for her bulk is equal to that of twenty or thirty working ants. Sumichrast, who has been a great observer of these insects, asserts that the queen lays about eighty thousand eggs a day. As soon as they are hatched, the young termites are carried off into large compartments, where they are fed until they are old enough to take a part in the labor. During the rainy season, a certain number of white ants are born with four wings, which enables them to proceed to a distance and found other colonies; but these wings are only temporary, and I have often been puzzled by finding immense quantities of them."

"How do the termites manage to build their dwellings?"

"The one we have just examined appears to be formed of earth, kneaded up with a kind of gum which the insect secretes. In the subterranean passages of a termite's nest there are arches which seem to be composed of morsels of wood stuck together by some sticky matter. These insects are omnivorous, and, like ants, take care to lay up abundant stores of provisions."

We were now commencing to climb the mountain, and, raising my eyes aloft, I was glad to see our two companions already seated by the fire.

CHAPTER XV.

LUCIEN had run on in front with the two partridges;
when I arrived at the bivouac, I found an enormous
mole roasting on the fire, and Sumichrast catching with the
utmost care the fat which ran from it.

"How did you kill this animal?" I asked, addressing
my companions; "I did not hear you fire."

"L'Encuerado knocked it down with the butt-end of his
gun, and just at the same moment your two shots brought
us back to the cave."

"Why are you collecting this fat? Is it a prophet of
some new dish in preparation?"

"No; but I intend inspecting the cave, and with this
grease we shall be able to make a lamp, which will be more
than useful."

I approved of Sumichrast's idea, and, as he had discovered a colony of moles, proposed to go after dinner and catch
some of them, so as to increase our supply of light. Besides, I hoped that in this walk we should meet with some
kind of resinous tree, the branches of which might serve as
torches. Lucien could hardly restrain his joy, and wished

to penetrate into the cave without further delay. He scarcely gave himself time enough to eat, and scolded l'Encuerado for being so slow, which was an indirect mode of asking us to hurry.

Having again reached the forest, we searched for a pine or a fir, the branches of which, being full of resin, would have enabled us to show more mercy to the moles. Hearing us mention these two trees, Lucien wanted to know the difference between them.

"They both belong to the Coniferous family," replied Sumichrast; "but firs generally grow upon lofty mountains far inland, while pines abound on sea-coasts, the shifting, sandy soil of which is, after a time, consolidated and fertilized by them."

Sumichrast's explanation still left much wanting; I saw this from Lucien's numerous questions; but without seeing a specimen of each tree it would have been difficult to better describe their peculiar characteristics.

After a long and unsuccessful walk, we halted in front of a guaiac-tree with dark-green foliage, a higher tree than any we had before met with. This fine member of the Rutacean family was covered with pale-blue flowers. It produces a gum used especially by the English in the preparation of tooth-powder; but the hardness of its wood, which would have blunted our weapons, induced me to pass it by. A little farther on, l'Encuerado spied out a *liquid-amber* tree, valuable on account of the balsam that oozes from its branches when cut, which is burned by the Indians as incense. He climbed the knotty trunk of this colossus, and cut off some branches, which Sumichrast split into small pieces, after I had cleared off their leaves. Our work was interrupted by the approach of night, and we made our way to our bivouac, each loaded with a heavy fagot.

As soon as we arrived, Lucien had the satisfaction of trying one of our flambeaux. The branch crackled when lighted, and, as we entered the cavern, five or six bats flew out. I led Lucien by the hand, and very soon he was the only one who could stand upright. Afterwards we entered a vast chamber with a dome-shaped roof, which became lower the farther we penetrated; this was rather a disappointment, as we had fancied there was something more to be seen than a mere cave. A heap of reddish earth in one corner attracted Sumichrast's attention, who examined it to see if he could discover some fossil bones. Standing all together, we must have formed, by the smoky light of our odoriferous torches, rather a fantastic-looking group. More than half an hour elapsed without discovering any results from our digging. L'Encuerado, who had tried to crawl in between the roof and the ground, suddenly raised an exclamation; he had, in fact, all but fallen into a deep pit. In an instant I was laid down flat on my stomach and crawling towards the Indian; Lucien, owing to his size, was able to creep on his hands and feet, and consequently soon got in front of me. We could soon see down into the bottom of the hole; the burning fragments of our torches fell upon a heap of stones at a depth of twelve or fifteen feet. L'Encuerado threw one of the torches into the chasm, and the vague glimmer showed us a yawning opening on the left. Delighted with this discovery, we now beat a retreat, deferring a more thorough exploration until the next day.

The night was dark, and during our absence the fire had almost gone out. Just below us, a tree, the outline of which we could scarcely distinguish, seemed covered with animated sparks. Lucien opened his eyes very widely indeed, not being in the least able to understand this phenomenon, which was produced by thousands of *elaterides*, insects which have on each side of the thorax a yellowish spot which becomes luminous in the dark.

Nothing could be more curious than to see innumerable glittering spots rising, falling, and crossing one another with extraordinary rapidity; one might have fancied it a tree bearing flowers of fire waving about in the breeze. L'Encuerado came up with a specimen, which lighted up his hand with a greenish glimmer. Lucien took possession of it, and the two luminous spots looked to him like two enormous eyes. Suddenly the insect gave a kind of shock to the boy's fingers, who looked at us full of surprise.

"The name of the insect," said Sumichrast, "is derived from a Greek word which signifies elastic; and it has just shown you that it well deserves the family name which has been given to it. Examine for an instant how it is shaped; the angles of its corslet form sharp points; added to this, its sternum also terminates in a point which the insect can insert at will into the cavity which exists under its second pair of legs. The women in the *Terre-Chaude*, by passing a pin through this natural ring, can fix this brilliant insect as an ornament in their hair, without injuring it in the least. Now, then, place it on its back."

"It's pretending to be dead!" cried Lucien.

"Yes; it does that, like many other kinds of insects, in order to deceive an enemy about to seize it."

"Oh, how it jumps!" exclaimed Lucien.

"That is its only means of getting on its feet again, when it has had the misfortune of falling on its back. Look; it pushes the point which terminates its chest against the edge of the hole situated lower down; then it raises its head, piff! paff! you might fancy it was a spring going off. It didn't succeed the first time, but now it is up on its legs, and now you've lost it, for it has flown off!"

Lucien's first impulse was to dart off in pursuit of it, as the route it had taken was shown by its luminous appendages. But it was long past our usual hour for repose, so we all sheltered ourselves as well as we could, and dreamt of our next day's adventures.

Day-break found us all up, and already comforted with a cup of coffee. We had been troubled during the night by mosquitoes; but they were only the harbingers of the legions which are before us. Lucien, full of impatience, could not take his eyes off the entrance of the cave, and followed all our movements with anxiety. A hollow stone which l'Encuerado had found was filled with fat, a morsel of linen served as a wick, and our make-shift lamp soon burned and gave forth light.

As the branches which were to serve as torches were being distributed, I noticed that a yellow and transparent drop had formed at the end of each. This gum, by its odor and color, has given to the tree which produces it the name of *liquid amber.* At last, followed by my companions, I entered the cave; l'Encuerado placed the lamp on the edge of the pit, and the bats which had been disturbed the evening before again commenced their whirling flight.

Preceded by Sumichrast, I ventured down to the bottom of the pit. A narrow passage led from it into a vast chamber, the more distant parts of which we could not discern on account of the darkness. While my friend was exploring, I returned for Lucien. The lamp, thanks to the Indian's skill, was safely let down without extinguishing the light; lastly l'Encuerado himself made his appearance. Passing along the narrow passage, I soon perceived Sumichrast, who looked like some fantastic apparition as he shook his torch over his head, endeavoring to see through the darkness which enveloped us.

The lamp being set down at the entrance of the passage, each of us took a lighted torch, and advanced at a slow pace. Sumichrast and the Indian skirted the wall to the left, while I walked along the wall to the right. Our smoky

torches gave but an imperfect light, and we could scarcely
see beyond three yards in front of us. A little farther on,
the ground was strewn with fallen stones; before ventur-
ing on this dangerous ground, I cast a glance towards my
companions; they were not in sight. I gave them a call—
a formidable clamor resounded through the chamber, and
Lucien crept close to me.

"It is the echo returning to our ears Sumichrast's answer," I hastened to tell him. "They are in another chamber; you call them now!"

The boy, agitated, raised his voice. Immediately the
dark vaults seemed to repeat his words; and the sound increased, as it moved away, as if a thousand persons, placed
at intervals, were repeating some watch-word. A sonorous
"Hiou! hiou!" prevailed over the uproar, and the face of
l'Encuerado appeared on our right before the echo of the
call had died away.

"Come and see a beautiful church!" cried the Indian.
"A church made of diamonds, Chanito!"

We moved towards the entrance by an inclined passage,
down the slope of which we followed l'Encuerado. The
distance between the walls gradually increased, and soon we
found ourselves in a vast hall studded with stalactites; in
it Sumichrast arranged the lighted torches.

The Indian was not far wrong; we might easily have
fancied ourselves in a Gothic cathedral. The wildest dreams
could not picture a stranger, more original, or more fantastic style of architecture. Never did any painter of fairy
scenes imagine any effects more splendid. Hundreds of
columns hung down from the roof and reached the ground
below. It was a really wonderful assemblage of pointed
arches, lace-work, branchery, and gigantic flowers. Here
and there were statues drawn by nature's hand. Lucien
particularly remarked a woman covered with a long veil,

"The wildest dreams could not picture a stranger .... style of architecture."

11

and stretching out over our **heads an** arm which a sculptor's chisel could scarcely have rendered more life-like. **There** were also shapeless mouths, monstrous heads, and animals, appearing as if they had been petrified, in menacing attitudes. The illusion was rendered more or less complete according to the play of the light; and many a strange shape was but caught sight of for a moment, to as rapidly vanish.

While we were moving about the cave, some long needles, hanging from the roof, touched our heads.

"They are stalactites," said I to the astonished Lucien. "The rain-water, filtering through the mountain above, dissolves the calcareous matter it meets with, and produces, when it evaporates, the beautiful concretions you are now looking at."

"Here is a needle coming up from the ground."

"That is a stalagmite; it increases upward, and not downward like the stalactites, through which, besides, a tube passes. Look up at that beautiful needle, with a drop of water glittering at the end of it. That liquid pearl, which has already deposited on the stalactite a thin layer of lime, will fall down on the stalagmite, the top of which is rounded. After a time the two needles will join, adding another column to the grotto, which, in the course of time, will become filled up with them."

"Then do stones proceed from water?" asked Lucien, with a thoughtful air.

"To a certain extent," I replied; "water holds in solution calcareous matter, and, as soon as the liquid evaporates, stone is formed."

"According to this," interposed l'Encuerado, "the pebbles ought to melt in the rivers."

"So they do; but they do not melt so easily as some things—sugar, for instance. Don't you recollect that in the

Rio Blanco the water is almost like milk, and that it leaves a whitish coating on the branches, and even on the leaves with which it comes in contact."

"That's true enough," replied the Indian, who had often wondered at the petrifactions with which the banks of the White River abound.

"But the water that falls down here is quite clear," urged Lucien, holding his torch close to a natural basin.

"But, nevertheless, it contains salts of lime in solution, the same, in fact, as all water, particularly that from wells. And it is for this reason that housekeepers will not use it; for it will not dissolve soap, and hardens the vegetables that are cooked in it."

"Now do *you* understand this?" asked l'Encuerado, addressing Lucien; "I don't."

"Yes, I do, a little."

"Well, you are very fortunate! The other day stones were said to come from the sun or moon, and fly about all covered with fire; now, they are formed by water. Perhaps M. Sumichrast will tell us to-morrow that they come from the wind."

The Indian then walked away, quite indignant; we followed him, smiling at his anger, becoming more and more enchanted by the spectacle which met our eyes. Unfortunately, our torches gave a very insufficient light, and the thick smoke rapidly blackened the arches above us. A great polished stone now impeded our passage, and compelled us to crawl. I took the lead, and, passing through a kind of narrow corridor, made my way into a small chamber. I raised a sudden exclamation; for five or six skulls, symmetrically arranged, seemed to glare at me through their empty orbits.

"Oh father!" cried Lucien, "are we in a cemetery?"

"Yes, my boy; I think this must be a Chichimec burial-

" Five or six skulls .... seemed to glare at me through their empty orbits."

place. This nation, which preceded the Toltecs and Aztecs in Mexico, were in the habit of depositing their dead in caverns."

Sumichrast examined a skull which he had picked up; its white and perfect teeth showed that it must have belonged to a man who died young. A few paces farther on five or six more skulls lay on the surface of the ground; they were inclosed in by fine stalactites, and appeared as if they were grinning at us through the bars of a dungeon.

For more than a thousand years, perhaps, these skulls had reposed in the niches which had evidently been hollowed out on purpose for them. The soil of the grotto had apparently risen at a subsequent period. What revelations as to the ancient history of Mexico might be contained in this cave! Without much difficulty, l'Encuerado broke through the upper calcareous layer, and brought to light some loamy .earth, out of which he procured a small cup of baked clay. I then began digging; my fingers soon touched some hard object; it was a small stone statuette. I had scarcely loosened my discovery from the earth, before Lucien also plunged his arm into the hole and brought out a little fancifully-shaped tortoise, the tail of which had been used as a whistle. Enticed on by these successes, we knelt down so as to break through a wider extent of the calcareous stratum; but our torches began to burn palely, and the close chamber, now filled with a thick smoke, was no longer bearable. Sumichrast complained of humming in his ears, and I also felt uncomfortable; so, much against our inclination, I gave the signal of departure. The lamp was dying out, and was filling the outer chamber with a nasty smell, which gave the finishing-stroke to our unpleasant feelings. L'Encuerado and Lucien were the first to leave the cave; from it I afterwards emerged with Sumichrast, both being quite blinded, when we reached the open air, by the overpowering rays of the sun.

Shouts of laughter resounded on all sides; we had the appearance of negroes, or rather of chimney-sweeps. It was no use thinking about washing ourselves; the contents of our gourds were too precious; and besides, there would not have been water sufficient. As there was water in the cave, l'Encuerado offered to go in and fetch some; but the smoke which escaped from the hole made me feel anxious, so, for the time, I opposed the Indian's re-descending into it.

We were surprised at the time our exploration had lasted; it had taken no less than four hours. Although we had made up our minds to continue our journey on coming out of the cavern, the fatigue we felt, added to a desire to have another look at the subterranean wonders, decided us to put off our departure until the next day.

After resting an hour, we all set off to seek our dinner. I examined with much curiosity the neighborhood of our encampment. The presence of skulls in the cave proved that some Indian tribe had once inhabited this locality; but as the Chichimec (or Chichiquimec, in the chapter-heading) Indians constructed nothing but huts, time had, doubtless, obliterated all trace of their former presence.

I can hardly describe the pleasure I felt in again viewing the woods, the verdure, the insects, the flowers, and enjoying the light of the sun. The interior of a cave, certainly, has the effect of producing melancholy, attributable, no doubt, to the silence and darkness; for the beautiful hall, radiant with stalactites, was but little likely to cause sadness. The effect on Lucien's mind was of a serious character, and he seemed never to be weary of asking questions.

"These natural hollows," said Sumichrast, "often occur in gypsum mountains, but still more frequently in volcanic or calcareous masses. Some, which are as old as the world itself, date from the earliest upheavals of the surface of the globe, when the fused matter which composes the centre of

Crater of Popocatepetl.

the earth **broke through** the scarcely solidified crust, and, rushing **upward, formed the mountain** chains we now see."

" **Then the centre of the earth has been** once in a liquid state?"

" **It is so still, as is shown by volcanoes; but the period of great catastrophes is past.** The molten matter solidified on the surface, as it became cool, and then water made its appearance, and transformed and rendered habitable the thin crust on which we live, the thickness of which is so inconsiderable when compared with the bulk of the globe."

" **What is this molten matter composed** of which is burning under our feet?"

" **The same substances** which we see around us—granite, **porphyry, and basalts, which are** called *igneous* or *Vulcanian rocks*, **as contrasted with the** *Neptunean* **rocks,** such as gypsum or lime, **clay and** sandstone, the agglomeration of which is attributed to water. The science which **deals with these subjects is** called *geology*, a study with **which,** some day, you will be delighted."

" **Then all Vulcanian** rocks can be melted?"

" **Yes, if** they were subject to as great a heat as **that existing in the centre of** the earth, which reaches an intensity at which the imagination recoils. But to return to the subject of caves. Some have been produced by the dissolving **action of water.** Thus, **at** some future date, the spring which we saw gushing **out from the** fallen mountain might **dry** up or alter its direction, and leave for the curiosity of future travellers the sight of **chambers** full of stalactites such as **we** have inspected."

Our geological chat was interrupted by an exclamation **from** l'Encuerado, **who** had just discovered a tree which the Mexicans call "the Tree of St. Ignatius." Its fruit is of a brown color, with a woody husk, something like small melons, which, as they hang on the tree, strike against one another with a sharp sound. L'Encuerado informed Lucien that this fruit is in the habit of bursting suddenly with a loud explosion, and that the flat beans which they contain are much used as medicine.

Sumichrast led the way through the forest, where we were sheltered under the tall trees. After a somewhat long ramble, during which we met with nothing but magpies, I requested l'Encuerado to guide us back to our bivouac. All of a sudden my friend enjoined silence; an opossum,

followed by five young ones, was coming near us on our left. The animal indolently approached a tree of middling size, which it climbed, aided by its prehensile tail. Its progeny crowded busily round the foot of the tree, uttering plaintive cries. The opossum then came down again, and scarcely had it put foot to the ground before its disconsolate family rushed pell-mell into the maternal pouch. Thus loaded, the animal climbed the tree more slowly, and sat

herself quietly on one of the lowest branches. We could
see nothing but the pointed muzzles and black eyes of the
little ones, which seemed as if they were looking down
from the top of a balcony. One of them at last ventured
to emerge, and crawled along the branches; soon the whole
litter followed this example. Sumichrast advised Lucien
to clap his hands, and I ordered l'Encuerado not to fire
at the poor animal. Frightened at the noise, the little ones
hastened to their mother, who set up her thin ears and
showed us a double row of white teeth. One of the stupid
little things, in its haste to reach its asylum, fell down
from the tree. In a moment the opossum had jumped
down close to it, and turned towards ns her threatening
jaws; then, finding all her treasure complete, she disappeared among the brush-wood.

" Why didn't you let me shoot at the *tlacuache?*" asked
l'Encuerado.

" What is the good of killing a poor creature which
would be of no use to us ?"

" You know well enough," replied the Indian, "that this
' poor beast' finds its way into granaries; that it devours
the corn and also fowls, without reckoning the damage
made by them in other ways."

" Yes, that's true enough; but this animal, at least, is innocent of all these misdeeds, for it lives too far from any
town."

This scene had quite delighted Lucien. I acquainted
him with the fact that opossums, kangaroos, and several
other animals of the kind, the females of which are provided with a pouch to shelter the young ones, are, for this reason, called *marsupials.*

The opossum is very common in Mexico. Its long, pointed, and deeply-divided muzzle is armed with fifty-two formidable teeth, although the animal feeds principally on

eggs, insects, and birds.   The young of those species which
are unprovided with the pouch, as soon as they are able to
walk, climb up on their mother's back and intertwine their
tails with hers, which she carries over her back for this
purpose.   This instinct is perhaps more curious than that
which leads them to dart into their mother's protecting
pouch.

Time was getting on; it now became important for us
to reach the spot where the moles were; and l'Encuerado
predicted good sport there without firing off his gun.

CHAPTER XVI.

WHILE making our way through the brush-wood, in
the hopes of putting up some game of a more appetizing nature than the *opossum*, our feet became entangled in the fibrous and creeping branches of the earth-nut,
called by the Indians *tlalcacahuatl*. Although the stems
were still covered with white flowers, l'Encuerado dug up
the soil in which the fruit had buried itself in order to
complete its ripening, and there found a quantity. The
tlalcacahuatl, which is classed by botanists in the leguminous order, produces yellowish, wrinkled pods, each containing three or four kernels, which are eaten after being roasted in their shells; their taste is something like that of a
chestnut. It is now cultivated to some extent in Europe,
and the nut produces an oil which does not readily turn
rancid, and is used in Spain in the manufacture of soap.

Lucien and l'Encuerado were the most pleased at the
discovery, for they were very fond of these earth-nuts,
which, on the days of religious festivals, are sold by heaps
in front of the Mexican churches.

"It is the day but one after Ascension-day," cried the
Indian; "we certainly can not hear Mass, but, at all events,
we can try to please God by eating pea-nuts in His honor."

The sun was beginning to sink, and hunger dictated to us that we should hasten our steps. I therefore led my companions towards the bivouac. We had but just started again, when five or six hares came giddily running almost between our legs. Lucien was skillful enough to shoot one, and Sumichrast knocked down another. L'Encuerado loaded with the game, we proceeded to our hut.

Being now reassured as to our bill-of-fare for dinner by this unexpected windfall, I kept on walking towards the entrance of a glade, the soil of which, being quite burrowed, betrayed the presence of the moles. Each of us lay down under the shade of a tree. Chance led me under a robinia or iron-wood tree, the trunk of which will defy the best-tempered axe. In front of me stood a *tepehuage*, a kind of mahogany-tree, with dark-colored foliage, which will become, some day, the object of considerable trade between Europe and Mexico; the beauty of this red wood, veined with black, renders it highly fitted for the manufacture of furniture.

Gringalet had followed the Indian. I advised Lucien to keep silence, so as to observe the operations of the moles, who would be certain to come out of their burrows as soon as the sun set. In fact, first one, then two, and at last twenty made their appearance; and in less than a quarter of an hour I counted more than a hundred engaged in throwing up the ground, playing about, and fighting, all the time uttering shrill cries. Lucien was much amused as he watched them squatting down on their hinder parts, making grimaces, and gnawing the roots and bark.

A single gunshot would have enabled us to double our store of grease, but it would have been a waste of our powder and shot. In fear of yielding to the temptation, I was thinking of giving the signal for departure, when it became evident that the animals whose games were enlivening us were actuated by a sudden panic. All the moles, which were solemnly seated, nodded to and fro their enormous heads, showing their long yellow incisors, and seemed to sniff the air. Suddenly they all rushed towards their burrows. A *jaquarete* had scattered them by springing in among them. The new-comer, a species of wild-cat, with a coat of the darkest black, left two or three victims dead upon the ground, and then set up a plaintive mewing.

This call soon attracted two young ones, which darted at once on the first mole they came to. Each of them seized hold of one side of their prey, spitting just like cats, and trying to tear it with their formidable claws. The mother was obliged to put a stop to the quarrel by an energetic display of authority, allotting a separate victim to each of her ferocious offspring; then she lay down and yawned several times, while the young ones were tearing to pieces the bodies of their prey. When they had eaten all they required, the mother gluttonously devoured all that was left, without ceasing to watch a third mole, round which the two young carnivora were prowling. Whenever they came near her prey, she gave a growl; and they seemed to know the meaning of this maternal injunction, for they crouched down to the ground, and drew back, lowering their heads, as if from fear. As soon as her repast was finished, the *jaquarete* caught up in her mouth the untouched mole, and made off without noticing us.

" What do you think of these little ogres ?" asked Sumichrast, addressing Lucien.

" How very pretty they are, with their black shiny coats ! They are just like big cats."

" That's very likely, for cats are their first cousins."

" Do *jaquaretes* ever attack men ?"

" No ; but, still, if we had tried to touch her young ones, the mother would perhaps have flown at us."

"To eat us ?" asked Lucien, opening his eyes very widely.

"She would bite and tear us with her claws, or otherwise injure us. But seriously, as a general rule, wild beasts, or *carnivora*, as the *savants* call them, are always formidable, and, whatever may be their size, it is unsafe to provoke them. If one of us, unarmed, had to fight hand to hand with a wild-cat, it is probable that he would receive more injury from the contest than the animal."

Night was now falling fast; but, fortunately, our fire guided us to our resting-place. When we were yet some distance off, we were amused at seeing the Indian prowling round, or gravely sitting down face to face with the dog, with whom, no doubt, he was chatting. Suddenly the dog jumped up, pricking up his ears, and ran out to meet us, while l'Encuerado raised over his head a burning branch to throw a light upon our path.

At day-break we were awakened by the voice of the Indian. The gloomy appearance of the weather threatened us with one of those fine rains which appear to last forever. Sumichrast went off to cut some long switches covered with leaves, one of which light boughs he handed to each of us before he would allow us to enter the cave.

"What are these switches for ?" asked Lucien, in surprise.

"M. Sumichrast wants to catch some bats, Chanito."

"Does he intend to eat them ?"

"Oh no; though I have no doubt they would be very good."

"Their flesh is delicious," interposed Sumichrast; "the wing especially is a tidbit which I can highly recommend."

But my friend could not keep a serious face when he saw Lucien's frightened look; so his joke partly failed in its effect.

L'Encuerado entered the cave on tiptoe. The rest of us,

taking up a position at the entrance, made every preparation
to enrich our collections. Two bats soon fell, beaten
down by our switches. Lucien examined them without
much repugnance, but the shape of their muzzles surprised
him even more than their wings. One of those which he
examined had lips cloven in the middle and doubled back;
the other had a flat nose and still more hideous visage,
and possessed, instead of ears, two enormous holes, at the
bottom of which were situate its black and brilliant eyes.
Added to this, the membrane of its wings was so thin and
transparent that it seemed as if it must tear with the slightest exertion. The poor little animal gradually recovered itself, and showed its delicate and sharp teeth. Sumichrast
took it up, and hung it by the claw at the end of its fore-
arm, in order to show Lucien the way in which these creatures cling to the rough places which form their usual resting-place; but it suddenly let go its hold, and disappeared
in the dark cave open in front of us.

The bat, apparently an imperfectly-formed creature, was
for a long time a puzzle to naturalists. Fontaine makes it
say:

> "I am a bird; look at my wings!
> I am a mouse; the mice forever!"

Savants, also, used to describe it as a bird provided with
hair instead of feathers, and with teeth instead of a bill.
Geoffroy Saint-Hilaire was the first to teach that the wings
of the bat are nothing but the fingers of the animal joined
together by a thin membrane. I had thus another opportunity of proving to Lucien the wisdom of our Creator, and
the simplicity of the means He employs in producing the
infinite variety of beings which people the universe.

"This is the first time," cried l'Encuerado, indignantly,
"that I have heard the devil made use of as a means of be-
stowing praise upon Almighty God."

"Bats have no connection with your devil," said Sumi-chrast; "they are nothing but animals, rather more curi-ously constructed than others."

"Oh! M. Sumichrast, then you can never have examined their wings? The Satan that St. Michael is treading under his feet in the beautiful picture in the convent at Orizava has wings just like the bats. And as to these caverns, every one knows that they are the residences of bad spirits."

"Let us make our way at once into it, then," said Lucien, who in no way shared his friend's superstition.

As on the day before, we descended to its bottom, and, skirting the left-hand wall, entered a wide chamber, in which water fell in a continual shower. We were inconvenienced by the icy drops which ran down our clothes, and I there-fore advised Sumichrast to turn back; but instead of doing so, he pushed on into a winding passage. Before long the roof became so low that Lucien alone could stand upright. I brought up the rear, watching my guides, who kept on as-cending or descending, according to the inequalities of the ground. Sometimes it was necessary to halt, to climb over a rock, or cross a pool of water. At last I saw my compan-ions again resume their upright position; we were now in a hall, so vast that our torches were quite powerless to throw a light up to the roof.

Surrounded by hundreds of bats, flitting round the torches like immense moths, and yet always avoiding them, we had ample opportunity for observing the precision of their flight. At length, stunned by their shrill cries, I again proposed to beat a retreat, but Sumichrast insisted upon continuing our search. He urged that the bats, who went out every night into the open air to seek their food, would not be likely to follow the narrow winding path we had fol-lowed; there must therefore be some other outlet. My friend and l'Encuerado set off in search of it; but I did not

"Our two scouts climbed some enormous heaps of rocks."

dare to venture farther with my boy over the damp and sticky ground. Our two scouts, however, climbed some enormous heaps of rock many feet above us; and we suddenly lost sight them.

The bats still swarmed round us, pushing their familiarity so far as to brush us with their wings. My prudence rather vexed Lucien, who had become very intrepid. After about five minutes, Sumichrast's voice summoned us, and we bent our steps towards the heap of rocks which had been scaled by our companions.

The ascent was difficult, and, in spite of remonstrances, I would not let go Lucien's hand. Fortunately I did not do so, for suddenly he slipped, and, while trying to save him, I dropped my torch; and there we were, perched up on this pile of *débris*, in utter darkness.

"Don't move!" I cried; "you know that we are surrounded by precipices."

"How dark it is! One might fancy that the darkness was solid, and weighed down upon our eyes."

"The fact is, that we are in a darkness in which the light does not penetrate, even by reflection, and, like you, I could readily fancy that I was blindfolded. Call l'Encuerado."

The vaulted roof above us re-echoed the name of the Indian, who immediately replied.

The bats now ceased their flight; but when the light reappeared the uproar began afresh. Lucien related our accident to his friend, who, in his hurry to come to our rescue, fell several times over the rocks. At last he reached us, and, lighting our torches, he guided us over the dangerous ground. When we cleared the fallen rocks, we entered a chamber studded with stalactites, on which Sumichrast's torches threw a light, and the walls of the cave glittered as if they had been covered with crystal stars. From the ground, from the roof, and from the walls, clusters of variegated rays were reflected in every direction, as if emanating from ten thousand diamonds. The beauty of this scene was quite sufficient to dazzle far less enthusiastic spectators than we were. But it was not long before a repulsive, oppressive, thick smoke compelled us to move on, and a few paces through a passage brought us into the centre of an immense hall, lighted by an aperture into the open air.

I joyfully hailed the blue sky, and then closely examining the ground we were treading on, noticed that it was covered with fragments of baked clay. Removing this, it was not long before we came to a layer of damp charcoal. L'Encuerado went outside and cut some branches, which, when pointed at the end, helped us in our digging. After two hours of hard work, we succeeded in laying bare more than a square yard of black and greasy mould.

Thoroughly exhausted, in spite of my curiosity being excited, I was compelled to follow Sumichrast out of the cave in order to breathe the fresh air. A fine rain was falling, and I was so devoted to the idea of my excavation in the cave, that I was very glad to use the state of the weather as a pretext for putting off our departure to the next day.

My companions had hardly recovered their breath before I summoned them back to work. L'Encuerado, as the hole became larger, was quite excited, and soon fancied that he could perceive gold. The fact is, that every Indian believes that all caves and grottoes contain unheard-of treasures, either the work of nature or buried by man, and that these treasures are guarded by some malicious genius, who allows the searchers just to catch a glimpse of the hidden riches, but never permits their being carried away.

" Don't laugh, Tatita," said the Indian to me, with a mysterious air ; " especially just at this moment."

He then went on to tell us that a friend of his, who was tending his flocks on the mountain, ran into the thickets in

" The animal continued to retreat before him, and led him to the month
of a cave."

pursuit of one of his goats. The animal continued to retreat before him, and led him to the mouth of a cave. The Indian, hesitating at first, at length took off all his clothes, so as to be sure that he carried no iron about him, and entered the cavern. But he soon drew back, startled by the sight of fifty broken boxes overflowing with coined money. Instead of profiting by this windfall, and taking possession of the fortune by appropriating some of it which had fallen out on the ground, the stupid fellow returned to his village as quick as he could, and communicated his discovery to his friends. That very evening five of them set out, provided with sacks, intending to convey the treasure to a safe place. They camped in the vicinity of the cave, and the night wore away in drinking to the health of the good genius. As soon as day appeared, they followed their guide. First they ascended, and then they descended; but they never succeeded in finding the spot where all this enormous wealth lay.

"He was not able to find his way back to the spot?" said Lucien, much interested by the story.

"No, Chanito; the cave had become invisible."

"Invisible! but why?"

"Because they had some iron about them!"

"But you have just told us that he stripped off all his clothes?" interposed Sumichrast.

"Ah! but, unfortunately, he kept his flint and steel in his hand."

The afflicted tone in which l'Encuerado pronounced this last phrase drew a smile even from Lucien.

Again we entered the cavern, and picking over with care the layer of charcoal which had already been laid bare, I discovered a small vase of burnt clay, full of ashes. On one of the faces of the urn was depicted a grinning visage, and in the interior was found one of the so-called pilgrim's

scallop-shells with the skull of a bird.   Accustomed as I
was, by long apprenticeship, to such discoveries, I had no
doubt whatever but that a skeleton would soon present itself, and a skull was soon discovered ; then the vertebræ
and tibiæ of a human being.   Next we found some obsidian
arrow-heads ; and, last of all, some small broken clay fig-
ures.   Unfortunately, it was no use thinking about carrying
away all these relics ; so I made up my mind to give up
further labor.   Directly after dinner we busied ourselves in
putting our baggage in order, so as to be ready to start the
next morning at day-break.

CHAPTER XVII.

A FORCED MARCH.—WILD-DUCKS.—VEGETABLE SOAP.—AN
UNWELCOME GUEST.

IT rained all night, and I awoke about seven o'clock in
the morning shivering with cold. It was Ascension-
day, and l'Encuerado, before making up the fire, chanted a
canticle, and, after the manner of Roman Catholics, piously
crossed himself. We were soon comforted with some coffee, and then, each of us resuming his burden, started off
to reach the foot of the mountain. Before plunging into
the forest, I could not help looking back with regret at the
cave we had scarcely explored, and in which so many archæ-
ological curiosities remained .buried. The sun only showed itself at intervals through grayish-looking clouds driven

violently along by the east wind. The state of the earth, moistened by rain which had lasted twenty-four hours, rendered our progression very difficult, for we were traversing a ferruginous soil. Such wretched walking put the finishing-stroke to our ill-humor by smearing and soiling our clothes; for my part, I inwardly anathematized travelling in general, more especially in rainy weather.

Just as we were emerging from this miserable ravine, Gringalet, who had no doubt scented something, suddenly rolled himself upon the ground, frantically. We had proceeded some distance before he rejoined us, covered with a coating of red clay, which gave him as singular an aspect as can well be imagined. The dog ran up and down, bounded about and barked, as if he was making it a business to amuse us. Nor were his efforts without success. We now reached a small plain, in which the sun flooded us with its warm rays. This had the effect of putting us into better humor; for our clothes dried, and with the warmth the feelings of discomfort to which we had been a prey departed.

We were again entering among trees, when l'Encuerado suddenly stopped.

"What is that moving down below there?" he said.

"Some deer," I replied, after looking at them through my glass.

Each of us hurried to hide behind a bush, in hopes that the beautiful animals would come within gunshot. Several times l'Encuerado expressed a wish to move round to the other side of the plain; but I opposed his idea, as the distance was too great. We spent more than an hour in watching the flock browsing, playing about, and licking themselves; but not one of them ventured in our direction. Tired with this inaction, Sumichrast emerged from his hiding-place, and the deer scampered off. Upon the whole, however, this delay had not been altogether useless; for, thanks to the heat of the sun, the ground had become more traversable, and my friend actually hummed a tune as he took the lead.

The time when we ought to have settled our bivouac had long passed, yet we were still on the road. The path we were treading was flat and unpromising, and the water from the cave, with which we had filled our gourds, was so unpleasant in taste that we longed to find a spring. Being unable to get a clear view of the horizon, I directed l'Encuerado to climb to the summit of a lofty tree. The Indian ascended to its topmost branch, and, having surveyed the prospect in every direction, came down far from pleased at having failed to discern what he desired. Fatigue, however, now compelled us to halt.

Our hut was soon constructed, the fire lighted, and the stew-pot filled with water and rice. Not one of us felt inspired with sufficient courage to induce him to go reconnoitring. An hour after sunset we were all sleeping side by side; l'Encuerado had quite forgotten his earth-nuts, and even dropped off to sleep without having been able to finish the chant which he commenced.

I was wakened up by the cries of the tanagers—a beautiful species of bird which lives in flocks. Lucien, like all the rest of us, complained of feeling rather stiff in the joints, resulting, no doubt, from our long journey the day before. On the morrow our little party started with rather a hobbling gait; the presence of the birds seemed to tell us that we were near some stream. Our limbs began gradually to lose their numbness; we were now descending an almost imperceptible slope, and the vegetation assumed a more tropical aspect. As we passed along, I noticed several pepper-plants; and next we came to bushes, round which myriads of *cardinal* birds were flying. Guided by these

beautiful red-plumaged creatures, we suddenly found ourselves on the banks of a stream, running noiselessly over a
bed of white sand.

With as little delay as possible, a fire gave forth its ex-
hilarating flame. Butterflies, dragon-flies, and birds fluttered round the flowering shrubs. There was a perfect
concert of buzzing and twittering, and a gentle breeze agitated the foliage and cooled the air. Nothing seemed
wanting for our comfort but game for our dinner. Fortunately, Providence rarely does things by halves. We
had scarcely sat down to take breath, when a flock of wild-
ducks settled near us. They were at once saluted by a platoon fire, and four victims strewed the ground and water
with their white, brown, and blue feathers.

"These are the first aquatic birds we have met with,"
said Sumichrast; "it will not be long now before we are
among the marshes."

"What birds are wild-ducks related to?" asked Lucien.

"To swans and geese, Master Sunbeam," replied my
friend. "All the individuals of this order, as their name
—*palmipedes*, or web-footed birds—indicates, have their
toes united by a wide membrane. Ducks, many species
of which are found in Mexico, have a flat bill; and their
short legs, placed so far behind, compel them to waddle in
walking, although they can swim with great facility."

"How do they manage to perch on a tree with feet of
that kind?"

"With the exception of the wood-duck, this family never
perch; they pass the day in dabbling in the water, and sleep
upon its surface, or among the reeds."

"Then they must always be wet."

"Not so; nature has covered the feathers of web-footed
birds with an oily substance, which renders their plumage
quite water-proof. Ducks are gregarious, and migrate

"They were at once saluted by a platoon fire."

12*

from one locality to **another, according** to the seasons.
They are so common **on the lagoons** which surround the
city of Mexico, that sportsmen **scarcely** will be troubled
shooting them."

While l'Encuerado was preparing **dinner, I and my com-**
panions walked along the edge of the stream. **Before long**
I **discovered some water-cress—a lucky discovery for trav-**
ellers **who are confined constantly to animal food.** **Lucien**
examined the small white flowers, which have obtained for
all its family the name of *Cruciferæ ;* these vegetables contain an **acrid and** volatile oil, which gives them strong anti-
scorbutic qualities. **The cabbage (Brassica** oleracea), tur-
nip (*B. napus*), radish **(Raphanus** sativus), and mustard
(Sinapis alba), are **of the crucifera order.** **To** this list we
must also add the horse-radish, the colza, the **seed** of which
produces an oil well **adapted for** lighting purposes ; the
crysimum, or hedge-mustard, a popular remedy in France
for coughs; the shepherd's purse, which **the Mexicans use**
as a decoction for washing wounds; and the *Lepidium*
piscidium, employed by the natives of Oceanica for intoxi-
cating fish, so as to catch them more easily.

" **You quite forget the** cochlearia, or scurvy-grass, so use-
ful to sailors as a remedy for scurvy ?" said Sumichrast.

" **You are** right ; but I think I've said enough about the
Cruciferæ for Master Sunbeam to remember."

A few paces farther on, while we were looking for insects
under the leaves of a shrub, Lucien drew back in surprise
at seeing it covered with the pretty little creatures called
tree-frogs (*Hyla viridis*). Instead of flying towards the
water, these reptiles made for the woods. Sumichrast explained to the young naturalist that tree-frogs have sticky
disks on their feet, and by the aid of this mechanism they
could move **about** on leaves and even on smooth surfaces.

"In Europe," he added, " the peasants shut them up in

bottles half full of water, and assert that the animal predicts good or bad weather by either coming up to the top or keeping under the water. The tree-frog, like all its fellows, buries itself in the mud during winter, and remains torpid. This lethargy, which in glacial climates has the effect of preserving it from hunger, must in Mexico have some other cause, for in the latter country it can find food all the year round. The skin of the tree-frog secretes a poisonous matter."

"Come here and look at an apple-tree!" cried Lucien, suddenly.

I hastened to the spot, and found a shrub about thirteen or fourteen feet high, covered with berries of a yellowish color, spotted with red. I recognized what is called in the Antilles the soap-tree. This discovery came just in the nick of time, and Sumichrast helped us in gathering some of the useful fruit which would assist us to give our clothes a thorough wash. Lucien tasted the little apples, which were as transparent as artificial fruit made of pure wax; but he did not like their astringent flavor, and threw them away with every expression of disgust.

A quarter of an hour later, we were all kneeling on the banks of the stream and trying who could perform the greatest amount of washing, the fruit of the soap-tree affording us a plentiful supply of lather. In the *Terre-Tempérée*, a root called *amoli* is a substitute for soap; in the *Terre-Chaude* a bulb named *amolito* is used for the same purpose; lastly, in the Mistec province of Oajaca, the poor find a natural soap in the bark of the *Quillaja saponaria*, a tree belonging to the rose tribe. Even in Europe, a vegetable soap is also found—the soap-wort—a little plant allied to the pinks, and which adorns with its unpretending flowers the edges of ditches, and is employed by housewives for cleaning silk stuffs and reviving their faded colors.

Quite refreshed with our wash, we stretched ourselves close to the camp fire, looking forward to our meal of roast ducks dressed with cresses, rice, and seasoned with allspice. On taking the first mouthful, I made a grimace which was imitated by Sumichrast. The rice had an unbearable aromatic taste. L'Encuerado regarded us with a triumphant look.

"What on earth have you put in the saucepan?" I cried, angrily.

"Don't you think it is nice, Tatita?"

"It's perfectly filthy; you've poisoned us!" But I soon recognized the smell of a kind of coriander with which the Indians occasionally saturate their food. Sumichrast, like me, had not got beyond the first mouthful; but Lucien, who shared to some extent l'Encuerado's weakness for the *culantro*, was having quite a feast. Our bill of fare was thus reduced to a single dish, and I left the broiled duck to my two companions and confined myself to the roast. With an artlessness that approached the sublime, the Indian, thinking that we should prefer the fresh plant to the cooked, the odor of which had been somewhat softened down by the operation, presented us with several stalks. On the whole, however, he was not altogether to blame, for we often ate with pleasure his national style of cookery, and he had full right to be surprised at our repugnance to their favorite *bon bouche*.

Gringalet just tasted the rice, then retired to roll on the twigs of coriander which were lying on the ground, a proceeding which did not much improve his toilet.

The sun was setting, and hundreds of birds were assembling around us. Yellow, blue, green, or red wings were cleaving the air in all directions.

There were finches of a violet-black, with orange-colored breasts and heads, some blue or golden-throated grossbeaks, and birds adorned with a variety of coloring, which the Mexicans call "primroses," while a number of mocking-birds were warbling airs worthy of the nightingale. The sun, lost amidst the golden clouds, bathed the trees and bushes with a soft light. Gradually all became silent and nothing was heard but the murmur of the stream, while birds of prey soared over our heads on their way to the mountains. The eastern sky was now wrapped in shade and the stars twinkled in the dark heavens, while on every bush animated sparks appeared to flit about.

I had been asleep more than two hours, when I was suddenly awakened by Gringalet barking. I jumped up simultaneously with my companions, who were also alarmed by a rustling among the dry leaves. Silence was soon restored, and I fancied, although the dog continued to growl, that it was a false alarm; so I was about to lie down again, when Sumichrast's hand touched me on the shoulder. An enormous serpent was gliding over the ground beside us.

I at once recognized the black sugar-cane snake, which is only formidable on account of its size; the planters are in the habit of attracting it to their fields, to keep them clear of mischievous rodents. L'Encuerado noiselessly left the hut. The snake raised its head, and slowly contracting its rings, and throwing round a bright glance, turned towards us. Sumichrast was just taking aim, when we heard the report of a gun, and our hut was almost in a moment afterwards crushed in by the repeated and furious struggles of the wounded reptile.

There was one moment of utter confusion; I disengaged myself as soon as I could, at the same time protecting the stupefied Lucien, and drawing him away. When I turned round, Sumichrast was approaching l'Encuerado, who, cutlass in hand, was hacking at the serpent, to render it further incapable of mischief.

"I at once recognized the black sugar-cane snake."

At last the fragments of the black snake, blindly tumbling about, became lost in the thicket, and all was again quiet.

"Well," said Sumichrast, "if, instead of being frightened, we had only kept quiet, the snake would not have troubled us, and we should still have had our house to shelter us."

"All's well that ends well," I replied, smiling. L'Encuerado again made up the fire; Lucien complimented the dog on his watchfulness, who thereupon licked his face. This undue familiarity drew upon him a lecture on politeness, the end of which I was too sleepy to bear.

CHAPTER XVIII.

WILD DAHLIAS.—A PAINFUL MISADVENTURE.—THE EUPHOR-
BIA PLANTS.—THE WASHER RACCOON.—SURPRISED BY A
TORRENT. — L'ENCUERADO TURNED HAT-MAKER. — NEW
METHOD FOR DRIVING OUT EVIL SPIRITS.—THE ANHINGÁ.

THE next day, which was the nineteenth since our departure from Orizava, we examined and compared our
compasses, and the course of our journey was changed.
Hitherto we had proceeded in a north-easterly direction,
skirting the provinces of Puebla and Vera Cruz, but still
without leaving the Cordilleras, the numerous valleys and
forests of which are still unexplored. According to my
calculations, and also those of Sumichrast, we were then
abreast with the province of Mexico, and we agreed to move
westward, as if going towards its capital.

" Why are we not to continue to keep straight on ?" asked Lucien.

" Because our journey must have some limit," I replied. "Up to the present time we have only traversed what is called the *Terre-Tempérée;* we shall now soon reach the *Terre-Froide,* and in three or four days we shall again encounter habitations."

" Shall we see any people there ?"

" I hope so; don't you like the idea of it ?"

" I don't object to it; but it will seem so very strange to look again at houses and men."

" Oh dear !" cried Sumichrast; " you have become a perfect little savage."

" Travelling about on foot is so amusing, that I should be glad if the journey lasted a very long time—that is, if I had a chance now and then of kissing mamma."

" Poor Sunbeam !" said Sumichrast; " I can't help thinking of next year when you are at school. You will then often think of your present life."

" Oh papa, if you go out for another excursion during the holidays, I hope you will take me with you, for you see I know how to walk."

" Before we think about another journey, let us first finish the present. You seem to forget that the roughest part of our work is yet before us."

" Do you mean crossing the *Terre-Froide ?*"

" No; we shall only take a glimpse at that; but in the *Terre-Chaude* we may meet with many trials."

" Bah !" said Lucien, kissing me; " the *Terre-Chaude* is almost like home; I shall behave so well, that you will be able to tell mamma that I am quite a man."

The sun was up when I gave the order for starting. Sumichrast went so far as to suggest that, after such a disturbed night, it would be better to spend another day in our charming retreat.

"That's the way," I answered, "in which effeminacy gets
the better of energy, and cowardice of courage! Let us
behave with more boldness, and not be seduced into delay-
ing our journey."

My companion accepted the reproof, and without further
delay our party were *en route*.

The stream pointed out to us the road we were to follow; along the edge of it, sheltered by the bushes and enlivened by the birds which were fluttering about the banks,
we shaped our course. Sumichrast showed us some dahlias
—the flower which would be so perfect if it only possessed
a perfume. It is a perennial in Mexico, whence it has been
imported into Europe, and there grows to a height of about
three feet, producing only single flowers of a pale yellow
color. By means of cultivation, varieties have been obtained with double flowers of a hundred different tints, which
are such ornaments in our gardens. Many a Mexican, who
imports dahlias at a great expense, has not the least idea
that the plant is indigenous to his own soil.

The roots of the dahlia, salted and boiled, are eaten by
the Indians; it is a farinaceous food of a somewhat insipid
taste. Certainly, the wild potato is not much better; and
who can tell whether cultivation, after having enriched our
gardens with its beautiful flowers, may not also furnish our
tables with the bulbs of this plant rendered more succulent
by horticulture.

The course of the stream described numerous windings,
and the desire of keeping on its margin frequently diverted
us from our direct path; at last it doubled round short to
the left, and I bade farewell to it as if to a friend, but,
nevertheless, preserved a hope that its capricious course
would again bring it back in our path.

Our road now commenced to ascend, sometimes crossing glades or groves. Suddenly a wide prairie opened out

before us, and Sumichrast **led the** way through its tall reeds. After a quarter of an hour's walking, our guide be-gan to sneeze; Lucien followed his example, then came l'Encuerado's turn, and at last mine, and ultimately Gringa-let's. These repeated **salvos** were received with shouts **of laughter and** " God bless you," often repeated; but a **sharp** tingling in **the throat and eyes was soon added to the** sneezing.

" I say," **cried my friend,** " what does this joke mean ?"

I looked round me more carefully, and discovered that **we** were surrounded with euphorbia plants.

But this mishap soon became a most serious affair, as the sneezing seemed as if it never **would end, and** our skin, eyes, and mouth commenced to **burn as if in a** fever. On this occasion we **did not care even to construct a** hut or light a fire, but were only **too glad to lie down on the bare cold** ground, and seek in sleep some respite from **our suffer-ings.**

Lucien, although very exhausted, endured his sufferings **with such courage as made** me proud of him. Uncomplain-**ing, he** soon went off **to** sleep; but to myself and compan-ion such **a luxury was refused.**

At length, almost desperate, I woke up the Indian. Our faces had continued to swell, but the Mistec, regarding me with a stupefied look, simply grunted, and turned round to sleep again. However, it became important that we should **have** a fire lit to enable us to prepare our coffee: as for eating, I looked upon it as an impossible matter. With a slowness and awkwardness which I could not overcome, I succeeded in lighting some dry branches, and at length in making the water boil. I then called my companions; they drank the refreshing beverage, without showing any sign that they were conscious of the service I was rendering them, for immediately afterwards they again went to sleep.

It was at least ten o'clock by the sun when Lucien set us the example of rising. Suffering as we were, it was no use to think of resuming our journey; so we made a virtue of necessity, and remained stationary until we felt more fit to endure fatigue.

In the afternoon, Sumichrast and Lucien complained that they were famished, which was an excellent symptom; so we took our guns, and, following in Indian file, ascended the course of the stream.

We met with several pools of water, and then rocks strangely piled on one another, which had slipped down from the mountains above. I climbed the bank, feeling disposed to be content with the first game which presented itself. However, I could see nothing but some toucans, far too wary to get within gunshot of. At last a squirrel presented itself—a poor pittance for five hungry stomachs.

Sumichrast, who had gone on in front, suddenly stopped, and signed to us to be quiet. I glanced down the stream, and, near a hole full of water, I discovered an agouara, or washer raccoon, squatted down, dipping its paws into the water, and rubbing them together energetically. L'Encuerado fired; it gave a bound and fell over. A lizard it was which the animal was washing before devouring—a peculiar and inexplicable habit to which it owes its name. It had a gray coat, and a tapering muzzle like that of an opossum.

The agouara (*Procyon cancrivorus*) is frequently met with in Mexico. It is closely allied to the Bear family, but is much smaller and more active, and is both carnivorous and insectivorous. It climbs trees with ease, and, whenever it takes up its abode near any habitation, makes incessant raids upon poultry. It is tamed without difficulty, and will run to meet its master, and seems to value his caresses; yet, like the squirrel, which it resembles in its vivacity, it will

"Following in Indian file, we ascended the course of the stream."

suddenly bite the hand of any one who feeds it. The flesh of this animal is white, tender, and savory.

L'Encuerado had dug up some dahlia roots, which he baked under the ashes; but either this food was not exactly to our taste, or our still irritated palates could not appreciate its delicacy.

Night came on, and the sky was full of gray clouds violently driven by the wind, although just round us the trees remained quite motionless. It was now too late to construct a hut, and we all stretched ourselves, without other covering than the canopy of heaven, on beds of dry moss.

I woke up perished with cold; not a star appeared in the sky. Of the uneasiness produced by the euphorbia plants, nothing now remained but a sense of weight in the head and a slight inflammation in the throat. I tried to go to sleep again, and fell at length into a kind of painful torpor. I fancied I heard birds of prey crying, and a roaring noise in the recesses of the forest. I got up with a view of driving away this nightmare; but it was not a dream; the day was just breaking, and the birds were welcoming its advent with many a clamorous note. A dull roar, like that of a gale of wind rattling through a forest, resounded louder and louder. I called Sumichrast and l'Encuerado; the latter at once shouted out in horror—

"The torrent!"

Seizing Lucien, I carried him in my arms, while the Indian hastily gathered together all our travelling gear that lay scattered around. With powerful efforts I soon reached the top of the steep bank, followed by my companions and Gringalet. Lucien, suddenly disturbed in his sleep, scarcely had time to know what had happened. A furious uproar perfectly deafened us, and a flood of yellowish water came rushing by; I saw one of our coverings float off on its surface, and almost immediately, as if impelled by some super-

13

human force, the rocks came rolling down, dashing together under the force of the liquid avalanche.

One minute more and it would have been all over with us, or, at the very least, we should have lost all our baggage and weapons, without which our position must have been truly critical. As it was, our hats only had sailed off in company with our covering; this loss much vexed us, for none of us except l'Encuerado could walk with a bare head under the rays of a tropical sun. We should have been somewhat consoled by meeting with a palm-tree; but in the mean time, the Mistec, like all his countrymen, knew well how to meet such an emergency. So we covered our heads with the leaves of the water-lily, often used by the Indian women for a parasol.

We knew by experience the rapidity with which these mountain torrents will overflow. If it had been a month later during the rainy period, of course we should not have exposed ourselves to the peril of camping in the bed of a stream; for we had remarked the evening before that the sky was obscured by gray clouds, and this ought to have put us on our guard.

The furious waves continued to bear down with them, without any effort, immense masses of rock; but the body of the water, which did not increase, showed us that it would ebb as rapidly as it had swollen. L'Encuerado was obliged to content himself with some muddy water for making our coffee; but if we had pretended to preserve all the prejudices of civilized life, adieu to all our idea of traversing Mexico. Besides this, we had a fresh disaster to grieve over; the remainder of the raccoon, which we had kept for our breakfast, had been lost in company with our bag of rice.

We started again, not much enlivened by this series of misfortunes, satisfied with nibbling for breakfast some mor-

"The rocks came rolling down, dashing together under the force of the
liquid avalanche."

sels of *totopo*. **All our indisposition** had now fortunately **vanished,** but we could **not help feeling some** degree of ill-will against both the euphorbias and the torrent. A long march, during which we several times left and rejoined the **course of the stream, brought us close to a** hill at the **foot of which was a vast swamp. I gave the signal for halting.** L'Encuerado **in our march had gathered some reeds, and set** to **work to plait us hats.** Leaving him with Lucien, Sumi-**chrast and I went off in quest of** game. On our return **from** an unproductive **ramble, I** saw that my son was al-ready wearing a funnel-shaped head covering. L'Encuera-do offered me a similar one, which, as my friend remarked, gave me the look of a Chinese. **After** having rested a short **time, I** thought about again looking for game ; but the up-**roar of the torrent seemed** to have frightened away all ani-**mal** life.

This second ramble quite exhausted us, without produc-**ing any** prey but a tanager, far too small to afford food **for so many. L'Encuerado and Lucien, both out in the midst of the swamp, perceived us approaching. The** young **gen**-tleman came running towards us, **holding his** newly-made hat **in his hand ; but, in his haste, he** forgot that the bed of a marsh is almost always slippery, and he fell flat on his face among some aquatic plants. In one leap the Indian was close to him, and soon picked him up ; but, instead of complaining of his fall, Lucien looked up at the Indian with **a** troubled face. The fact was, his hat held some fish he had caught with his insect-net, and at least a third of them **had** disappeared from his disaster.

" **Oh** dear ! oh dear !" cried Sumichrast, who could not help smiling at the piteous face of the young fisherman ; " most decidedly, we are all unfortunate."

This joke was taken in a serious light by l'Encuerado, who smote his forehead as if suddenly struck by some idea.

"It is the genius of the cave!" he cried. "Ah! the scoundrel, after all he owes me, and the precautions I took!"

"What precautions?" asked Lucien, surprised.

"I picked up seven white pebbles, and drew out a beautiful cross."

"What did the cross matter to him?"

"Matter to him! why, Chanito, he knows well that we are Christians, and yet he bewitches us. Wait a bit, I'll match him."

And rearing himself up against the trunk of a tree, standing on his head, with his legs in the air, l'Encuerado kicked about with all the frenzy of one possessed. He fell sometimes to the right, and sometimes to the left, but raised himself after every fall, and resumed his clown-like attitude. Not one of us could keep a serious countenance while looking at his contortions. Lucien laughed till he cried, especially because the Indian, as if on purpose to render the scene more comical, accompanied his gestures with invectives against the genius of the cave and invocations to St. Joseph.

At last I told him to resume his natural position, and to keep quiet.

"Do you really think that I have done it enough?" he asked, addressing me with imperturbable gravity.

"Yes," I replied; "from the way in which you have shaken him, I should say he must have come out either through your mouth or ears."

"Then it's your turn now, Chanito!"

Lucien, delighted at having to execute this feat of skill, tried several times to keep his balance while standing on his head; but overcome by laughter, he was not able, so he fell, to rear himself up again. The more l'Encuerado cried out to him, urging him to persevere, the louder the boy laughed. The brave Indian, who was under the full belief that an

" L'Encuerado .... set to work to plait us hats."

evil spirit must necessarily abandon a body placed upside down, seized the legs of his young master and shook him violently as if he was emptying a sack. Sumichrast at last put an end to this scene by declaring that he was sure the spirit must have taken flight. L'Encuerado then came up to my friend and proposed to assist him into the same position as he had helped Lucien.

" That's enough of it," I cried as soon as laughing allowed me to speak; " M. Sumichrast and I have other means of expelling evil spirits."

L'Encuerado looked at me with wonder, more convinced than ever that my power far exceeded that of the sorcerers of his own country.

We were now close to our fire. Lucien was gravely repeating the words which l'Encuerado had addressed to the demon, when Gringalet commenced howling. L'Encuerado had seized the poor animal by his hind legs, and was violently shaking him, head downward.

" It's all for your good," said the Indian to the dog. " Can't you understand that the evil spirit which you have in your body will be certain to make you commit some folly ?"

Lucien rushed to the assistance of his faithful friend, and at last induced the Mistec to let him go. Not the least convinced of l'Encuerado's kind intentions towards him, Gringalet seemed to bear malice towards the Indian, and for three days was very shy of coming near him.

After this scene the preparations for dinner occupied our attention. If our guns had been more successful, we should have had fat to fry our fish in. While we were deploring our ill-luck, I noticed a flock of birds like ducks flying high up in the air ; they made a wide circle and settled down on the top of a tree. L'Encuerado fired at them, and one fell. It was an *anhinga*, one of the most singular specimens of web-footed birds that can be found anywhere. Represent to yourself an enormous duck with a neck like a swan, a bill straight, tapering, and longer than the head, webbed feet, and widely spreading and well-feathered wings, and then know the *anhinga*. It dives and flies with equal facility, can swim under the water and perch upon trees, the highest of which it chooses for building its nest upon.

The flesh of the anhinga is not valuable, as it is hard and tough. Perhaps a good appetite rendered me indulgent, but I found the flavor very much like that of duck. The fat of this bird, carefully saved, was used for frying our fish. The latter, I must confess, did not seem to us so nice as the dark-colored meat of the anhinga. If it tasted rather fishy, the fish themselves tasted muddy; on the whole, however, our bill-of-fare was a tolerable one.

When night-fall came on, the trees stood out in bold relief against the transparent sky, and l'Encuerado, delighted at thinking that he was now unbewitched, gratified us with one of his unpublished canticles, which materially helped to send us to sleep.

CHAPTER XIX.

THE BLACK IGUANA.—ANOTHER COUNTRY.—REMINISCENCES
OF CHILDHOOD.—THE MIRAGE.—A FIRE IN THE PLAIN.

BY ten o'clock in the morning we had crossed some rising ground, and were passing through a narrow gorge carpeted with ferns. Lucien headed the party, closely followed by l'Encuerado; and led us on to a kind of rocky staircase, down which, in the rainy season, water doubtless ly flowed. This steep path compelled us to halt several times to recover our breath. The branches of the bushes formed an archway over our heads, and their blossoms surrounded us with their rich perfume.

At length a rise in the ground impeded our path, and the heat commenced to inconvenience us. The refraction of light, especially, affected our eyes, and our feet raised perfect clouds of dust. Lucien, who had become quite an enduring walker, throughout kept in front, and often gained ground while we were stopping to take breath. Just as we reached the ridge of the hill, I saw the boy, who was a few yards in advance, suddenly cock his gun and fire. I ran to him, but he disappeared down the slope, crying out to me that he had shot a dragon !

I soon came up, and found the young sportsman standing in front of a magnificent black iguana—*Cyclura acanthura*—which does, in fact, somewhat resemble the supposed appearance of the fabulous animal described by the ancients. Its skin shone with a silvery-gray metallic glitter, more particularly on the dorsal ridge. L'Encuerado joined us when it was dying, when, rubbing his hands, he cried:

"It is a *guachi-chevé;* what a splendid supper we shall have!"

"You have seen them before, then?"

"It is an animal which belongs to my country, Chanito; it abounds in the plains which slope down to the Pacific Ocean. They are beasts which can live without eating; they are sometimes kept for two months with their feet tied and their mouth sewn up."

"The mouth sewn up?"

"Yes, Chanito, so as to prevent them getting lean. When I was your age, during the time of Lent, I used to go iguana hunting with my brothers. We sought them in the shallow marshes which are inundated by water during flood-time. There, in hollow trunks of trees, or in holes made in the mud, we found the black iguanas, and pulled them out by their tails."

"Then they don't bite?"

"Oh yes, they do, and scratch also; so we took care to catch hold of them by the neck, and tie both their feet and their jaws. Sometimes we used to pursue them up the trees; but then, for they don't mind falling twenty or thirty feet, they frequently escaped."

Sumichrast completed this information by telling the young naturalist that the iguana, which is allied to the lizards, is generally a yard in length; and that the female lays thirty to forty eggs, which are much esteemed by the native epicures; also that the green species—*Iguana rhinolopha*—has a flat, thin tail, and swims much better than the black variety, the tail of which, being covered with spines, is not well adapted for progression through water. Thus, meeting with a green iguana almost always indicates the

"I used to go iguana hunting with my brothers."

vicinity of a stream; but the black species is frequently found away from rivers.

Lucien wanted at first to carry his game, but he was overtaxed by its weight and gave it up to l'Encuerado. Another hill was now before us, and the ground became at every step more and more barren, and on which there was little or nothing growing but a few shrubs with a bluish flower. When we had reached the summit of this second ridge, a boundless plain lay spread out before our gaze; we were now on the central plateau of Mexico, in the *Terre-Froide*, eight thousand seven hundred feet above the level of the sea.

What a change there was! The white soil was so light and dry that it was carried away by the breeze, and produced nothing but a few leafless trees. There were also some thorny bushes smothered in sand, and, a little farther on, some gigantic *cacti* astonished us with their strange shapes. The sun, reflected by the red glaring surface, much interfered with our sight, so we directed our steps to the right, where there appeared to be a greater amount of shade.

"Oh, what a wretched country!" cried Lucien. "Can we be still in Mexico?"

"Yes," replied I; "but we are now on the great plateau, almost on a level with the city of Mexico and Puebla."

"Are we going to cross that great plain? I can see neither birds nor beasts on it; in fact, one might almost fancy the very trees were thirsty."

"You are right, for it does not often rain here. Nevertheless, this ground, which at first sight appears so barren, is very fruitful when cultivated. It produces wheat, barley, potatoes, apples, pears, cherries, grapes, peaches, and, in short, all the European fruits, which can only grow in a temperate zone. On this plateau, too, grows the *Maguey agave, Mexicana*, a wonderful plant, which is as useful to the Mexicans as the cocoa-nut tree is to the inhabitants of the lands to which it is indigenous."

L'Encuerado had stooped down under a pepper-tree, and his glance wandered over the scene. The fact was, that we were now about the same height as that at which his own country is situated, and he might easily fancy himself near his native village.

" What are you thinking of?" said I, tapping him on the shoulder.

" Oh Tatita! why did you disturb me? Here I feel myself almost as learned as you, and I could tell you all the names of those flowers which turn their bright faces towards me as if they knew me! It seems as if I had often walked on that plain, and as if I had often seen these trees, bushes, and plants— You are laughing at me, Chanito; it's all very well, but you'll see! Tatita will set me right if I tell you any thing that is not true. Look here, for instance," continued the Indian, rising up and plucking a plant with slender and whitish stems; " this is the *alfileril-lo*, which mothers give their children to cure them of sore throats. Such shrubs are lost here; for their fruit would be useful in my country. Here too, Chanito, is a *mizquitl*, a thorny tree on which we shall be certain to find some gum. Indeed, here are three morsels of it. You may safely suck it; it will not seem very nice at first, but you will soon like it. Oh Tatita! you have really brought me back into my own country."

" We are certainly on the same line, and it is not to be wondered at that you find here the same kind of vegetation as in that in which you spent your childhood."

The Indian was silent, and seemed musing. Sumichrast and I observed him with some curiosity, and Lucien, surprised at his emotion, looked at him anxiously.

"Here is the 'angel-plant,'" resumed l'Encuerado, suddenly. "How pleased my mother used to be when I found one of them."

"What are its good properties?" I asked.

"Oh! it produces beautiful dreams, which seem to lift you to heaven."

The Indian again became pensive, sometimes casting a glance over the vast prospect, and sometimes pulling up pieces of the turf which grew at his feet.

"It only needs a palm-tree to make the landscape quite complete," said he, thoughtfully.

In a minute or so he advanced towards the bushes, and, kneeling down, plucked a tuft of yellow marigold, which are called in this country "the dead man's flower." Afterwards I heard him sobbing.

"Oh Chema! what is the matter?" cried Lucien, running up to his friend.

The Indian raised himself and took the boy in his arms.

"Once I had a mother, brothers, and a country," he said, sadly; "and this flower reminds me that all those are now sleeping in the grave."

"Then you don't love me?" replied Lucien, embracing him.

The only answer l'Encuerado made was pressing the boy so tightly against his breast as to draw from him a slight cry.

This scene quite affected us, and I and my friend, side by side, walked back to the hut deeply sunk in thought.

Hunger soon brought with it more commonplace ideas. The white and juicy flesh of the iguana was quite a feast for us all. Our meal we sat over a longer time than usual; for in conversation we entered upon the subject of our native countries, and the theme appeared inexhaustible. I reminded my friend that, only a few days before, he had shown as much emotion as the Indian on seeing two butter-flies which he fancied belonged to a Swiss species; and I brought forward these feelings to oppose the intention he so often expressed of taking up his abode in the midst of the wilderness, so as to live and die in solitude.

On the great plateau the sun shines rather later than in the lower regions. As the luminary approached the earth, the sky was lighted up with a purple color, and I saw stand-ing out on our left in bold belief the jagged outline of the Cordilleras of l'Encuerado's country. The whitish ground gradually assumed a transparent appearance; our eyes de-ceived us to such an extent that we fancied we saw an im-mense tract of water, above which the trees, appearing as if they were submerged, raised their green heads.

The moon rose, and, far from destroying the mirage, it rendered the illusion still more striking. I resolved to de-scend from the hill in order to convince Lucien how much our vision was deceived.

" There is no mistake about the plain being dry," said he, as we returned to the bivouac, " and yet one might fancy that, as we were mounting the hill, the water was rising be-hind us."

" The layers of the air," I replied, " are unequally warm-ed, and their refraction, which causes the rays of light to deviate in their course, reverses the objects which cover the plain, and, on the other hand, causes them to appear more elevated than they really are."

" So we see water in a place where in reality there is none."

" You don't take the sky into account, which is reflected on the ground beneath us as in a mirror. But the air is becoming cooler, and you will soon see the phenomenon slowly disappear, as if some invisible hand was pushing the mist back towards the horizon."

"The moon rose, ... and rendered the illusion more striking."

While we were looking down over the plateau, and watching the mirage gradually fade away, a distant light suddenly shone out. Loud exclamations hailed the sight of this unknown bivouac; and, fixing our eyes on it, we all formed endless conjectures. We had not expected to meet with any habitation before the next day; and the cry of "land!" on board ship after a long voyage could not have made a stronger impression than the sight of this fire. The air was cool; still l'Encuerado was not allowed to kindle a light, which would perhaps have betrayed us to foes. It was now twenty days since we had met with a human being, and our first feeling, after the instinctive joy at the idea of seeing our fellow-creatures, was, alas! one of distrust.

CHAPTER XX.

THE MORNING AND NIGHT DEW.—THE TERRE-FROIDE.—WA-
TER-SPOUTS AND WHIRLWINDS. — THE BARBARY FIG-
TREES. — THE CACTUS-PLANTS. — THE VIZNAGA. — OUR
HOPES DISAPPOINTED.—DON BENITO COYOTEPEC.

THE sun had not risen when we were up and ready to
start. We shivered with cold, for on the great plateau
which we had now reached, to which the inhabitants of the
lower regions give the name of *Terre-Froide*, the mornings
are frosty. The profound darkness was succeeded by a
dim twilight, afterwards by a fog, which penetrated our
clothing as much as rain.

"There has been no shower," cried Lucien, "and yet we
are all wet."

"It is the dew, Chanito; it is almost as abundant as the night dews in the *Terre-Chaude.*"

"Are not morning and night dews the same thing?"

"Not exactly," I replied; "the morning **dew** is generally of a beneficial nature; but the Mexicans dread the other, which falls after **sunset, and is said** to be productive of fever."

"But from **whence** does all this moisture come?"

"From the air, which always contains a certain quantity, some **of** which it deposits on the ground, on stones and **plants, as** they become cool by radiation."

Just at this moment our attention was attracted by the **first** ray of the sun, which, piercing through a light cloud, shot across the plain like a bright arrow. The horizon, which had been visible, was now obscured by a mist, which gradually rolled towards us. By degrees, however, it drew off, and the trees a short distance away showed their **rounded tops; while** wide breaks **opened** here and **there in the semi-transparent veil, and vanished as** quickly **as they had arisen.**

The **telescope was passed from** hand to hand, and each tried to discover if **there** was a hut where the glimmering fire had been descried the night before. The search was in vain; the reflection of the sun's rays quite dazzled us, and restricted the prospect; but, once in the right course, we might advance without fear of missing our point, and, according to our calculations, we would meet with habitations the next day or the following.

Gringalet's tongue hung out of his mouth; he found the journey over the nitrous soil very irksome, **and** the scanty leaves **of the** mimosa failed to screen **him from** the sun. **What a contrast** it **was to the** pleasant regions we had **hitherto travelled through!**

"Your **country, after** all, is not so nice an one as mine," said Lucien, addressing l'Encuerado.

"My real native country is much more beautiful than that we are now in, Chanito; in the first place, it has mountains and woods, and there it sometimes rains."

"Shall we see any snow fall, now that we are in the *Terre-Froide?*"

"No," replied Sumichrast, smiling; "you will not see any snow before next year, when you will be in France. The winters of the Mexican *Terre-Froide* are like our European springs. It is, however, never warm enough to allow tropical fruit to ripen; but the *Terre-Froide* only deserves its name when it is compared with the *Terre-Chaude* and the *Terre-Tempérée.*"

"It seems to me to have been very badly named, for it is as hot now as the day when the south wind blew so strongly. Gringalet looks as if he was of my opinion, for he lolls his tongue out much more than usual."

"Upon my word!" cried Sumichrast, "Master Sunbeam's remark shows that he is a first-class observer. You are as right as you can be," continued he, placing his hand on the boy's shoulder. "In the plains of the *Terre-Froide* the heat is much more uncomfortable than in the *Terre-Chaude* itself, where an insensible perspiration always mitigates the oppressive rays of the sun. A few days' walking in this atmosphere will do more in bronzing our skins than all the rest of the journey."

My companion suddenly stopped short, and pointed to the horizon with his finger.

"That's smoke," cried Lucien.

"No, Chanito," replied l'Encuerado, "it is a *tornado.*"

Seeing a slender column of dust rising up to the clouds, I had, at first sight, formed the same idea as my son. It was, in fact, nothing but a whirlwind of dust, which disappeared soon afterwards.

"There is no wind," observed Lucien; "how is it that the dust rises so high?"

"The sand rose rapidly, whirling round and round."

" There is every cause for wonder," I replied, " for no *savant* has yet explained the real cause of this phenomenon."

" If we happened to be caught in one of these whirlwinds would it carry us away ?"

" No, Chanito," replied the Indian, " it would be content with throwing us down."

" Then you've had some experience of them ?"

" Yes ; when I used to play with the children in our village, and a *tornado* came within reach, we were always delighted to run through it."

About a hundred paces from us, although there was not the slightest breeze in the air, the sand rose rapidly, whirling round and round. The rotation did not extend over a space of more than a few feet. There was no apparent cause for it, and the phenomenon ceased as unaccountably as it commenced.

Lucien was of course dying with anxiety to run through one of these *tornadoes ;* but all that we saw were quite beyond reach.

" I think," said Sumichrast, addressing me, " when it is thoroughly studied on the great plains of Mexico, we shall be able to explain the cause of this phenomenon. In a general point of view, these whirlwinds are nothing but waterspouts in miniature."

" A water-spout !" asked Lucien ; " what is that ?"

" It is a natural phenomenon very like what you have just witnessed ; but it is of a far more formidable character, for it destroys every thing it comes in contact with ?"

" Did you ever see one, papa ?"

" Only once, at sea. The English steamer on which I had embarked had just left the port of St. Thomas, in the West Indies, and we were still coasting the island ; there was but a slight breeze blowing, the sky was clear, and the water rippled with miniature waves, when, all of a sudden,

a large tract of the sea ahead of us was violently agitated.
An enormous column of water rapidly rose, and formed
something like a dark and terrible-looking column. After
about a quarter of an hour, the fearful phenomenon, which
fortunately had kept on moving before us, remained stationary. The volume, incessantly swelling, assumed a dark-blue
shade, while the column of water, which appeared to feed a
cloud, was of a gray color. A dull roaring noise like that
of distant thunder suddenly occurred. The column broke
in the middle, and the greater portion of the liquid fell into
the sea with a tremendous shock; but the upper portion
sprinkled us with a heavy shower. Half an hour afterwards we were sailing under a cloudless sky and over an
unruffled ocean.

" And what would have happened if the water-spout had
reached the ship ?"

" We should most likely have been swamped."

" How dreadfully frightened you must have been, Tatita !"

" Yes, of course; and I was not the only one who was in
terror; for the officers and sailors watched the course of the
water-spout with evident anxiety."

Chatting in this way, we were now penetrating among
Indian fig-trees— *Cactus opuntia*—commonly called prickly-
pear trees. These plants, covered with yellow flowers,
would, a month later, have been hailed with shouts of joy,
for each of their upper stems would then bear one of those
juicy fruits of which the Creoles are so fond. Lucien stopped in front of two or three of these plants, the dimensions
of which were well calculated to surprise him. Sumichrast
availed himself of this inspection to tell him that the cactus,
a word derived from the Greek, and meaning *thorny*, is a
native of America, and that it grows spontaneously in dry
and sandy soil.

"Everywhere the cactus might be seen assuming twenty different shapes."

"You have forgotten to tell him," added l'Encuerado, "that the tender shoots of the *tunero*, baked under the ashes, will furnish us this evening with a most delicious dish."

A little farther on, the prickly pears were succeeded by another species called the *Cierge* (the *Cactus cereus* of savants). Several of these plants were growing with a single stem, and measured from ten to twelve feet in height, looking like telegraph poles ; others had two or three shoots springing from them, which made them look still more singular. A third species, creeping over the ground, added much to the difficulty of our walking, and obliged us very often to take long strides to avoid them. In spite of all the care we could take, we scratched our limbs several times against their sharp spines.

I again took the lead—for there was not room between the *cierges* to walk abreast—and, climbing up a small hillock, surveyed a wide prospect. Such a complete change could not possibly have taken place in so short a time in any other country. More trees, more shrubs, more bushes ! Everywhere the cactus might be seen assuming twenty different shapes—round, straight, conical, or flattened, and really seeming as if it delighted in assuming appearances so fantastic as almost to defy description. Here and there the *cierges*, standing side by side, seemed to vie with each other in height, sometimes attaining to as much as twenty to thirty feet, while the young shoots resembled a palisade, or one of those impenetrable hedges with which the Indians who live on the plateau surround their dwellings. Farther on, there were vast vegetable masses of a spherical shape, covered with rose-colored, horny, and transparent thorns, which displayed across our path all their huge rotundity, really exhibiting nothing vegetable to the eye but their color. Here and there, too, some creeping species, with their branches full of thorns, formed a perfect thicket ; one might almost have fancied that they were a hundred-headed hydra.

" We might almost imagine we were in a hot-house full of rich-growing plants and golden-colored flowers," said Sumichrast to me.

" Yes," I replied ; " but we must also imagine that we are looking at them through the lens of a microscope. What would a Parisian say if he saw this *viznaga ?*"

The plant I was pointing to was at least six feet in height and three times that in circumference.

" When I was a shepherd," said l'Encuerado, " I led my goats into one of the plains where the *viznagas* grow. With my *machete* I made a cut into one side of the plant, and my goats immediately began to eat the pith with which it was filled. Gradually they hollowed out a hole large enough for two or three of them to enter at once, and this make-shift hut afforded me a first-rate shelter against the rays of the sun and the night breezes."

" Oh !" cried Lucien, with enthusiasm, " if we have to camp in these fields, we must have such a house."

I again examined the landscape round us. There was nothing whatever which betrayed the vicinity of man. Everywhere the *cacti* spread out their variously-shaped flowers, which were nearly all yellowish or pink. Above us was a fiery sky, in which nothing seemed to move but a few vultures; on the ground there were hundreds of lizards in constant motion.

The Indian led the way, followed by Lucien.

" A footpath !" the boy suddenly cried out.

" A mimosa !" exclaimed Sumichrast, whose great height towered over us all.

" A hut !" murmured l'Encuerado, stopping and holding his finger to his lips.

We looked at each other; then, bending our steps to·

wards the spot pointed out by our companion, we each inspected the thatched roof, of which only the top was visible.

With a rapid glance at my weapons I advanced carefully,
followed by Sumichrast. Lucien, l'Encuerado, and Gringalet brought up the rear.

We really felt some degree of emotion; the idea of seeing any human beings but ourselves quite made our hearts
beat; for were we going to meet enemies or friends? This
was the important question to be decided.

The path soon became wider; we were now scarcely two
hundred paces from the hut, and we were astonished not
to hear the barking of dogs, which generally prowl round
au Indian's dwelling. Sumichrast, who was now in front,
came back.

"This silence seems to me a bad omen," he said; "take
care we don't fall into some ambuscade; I don't at all wish
to be robbed, or, worse still, murdered."

Leaving the path to our left, we made our way among
the *cacti.*

"Are we in a savage country?" asked Lucien.

"Possibly, and that is why we have to be so careful," I
answered.

"Do you think any one will hurt us?"

"The mere sight of our weapons might inspire the Indians with a desire of obtaining them; in a spot where every one can do as he likes, there is nothing to prevent them
stripping us and sending us away naked."

"They are not Christians, then?"

"Ah, Chanito, they ought to be," muttered the Indian.

And, taking off his load, we soon lost sight of him among
the under-brush.

Under any other circumstances, Lucien's frightened look,
when he saw us take so many precautions in approaching a

14*

human dwelling, would have amused; but, so far from doing so now, we listened anxiously for the least sound.

At last we heard l'Encuerado's loud and welcome "Hiou!
hiou!" The hut was perfectly empty.

After an hour's rest, passed by the boy in rambling
round it, I gave the word for starting again. The Indian
took the lead, following the still visible traces of a footpath.
The hut, hardly large enough to hold three persons, seemed more like a temporary shelter than a settled dwelling;
l'Encuerado, who was a great authority in such matters,
was of opinion that it was only an offshoot to a larger set-
tlement. After a tolerably long walk, another footpath crossed the one we were following; on its surface we noticed
prints of naked feet—even those of women and children.
But although we carefully examined the horizon, nothing
but the immense white uninterrupted plain bathed in sunshine greeted our vision.

This prospect somewhat damped our ardor. Ever since
the morning, we had been walking on in the hopes of meeting with a human dwelling. We had scarcely eaten any
thing, and hunger and thirst were added to the disappointment we had met with. Lucien proposed to hollow out a
riznaga to sleep in—a project in which he was encouraged
by l'Encuerado's telling him that we might have the luxury
of a window, and could keep off wild beasts by filling up
the entrance with thorny *cierges*. It may readily be understood how much the idea of bivouacking inside a plant
pleased the fancy of our young companion; and perhaps
we should have assisted in realizing his wish, if the barking of a dog had not attracted our attention; so we recommenced our march in better spirits. A rapid descent
brought us near a number of tree-ferns, a change of vegetation which we looked upon as a good omen. L'Encuerado continued to follow the footpath, until he suddenly stop-

ped on a gentle eminence, which overlooked a small green valley with a brook running through it. To my great joy I counted as many as six palm-leaf huts.

The sight refreshed us so marvellously, that we all descended with rapid, long strides. Every now and then either a cock crowing, a turkey gobbling, or a dog barking, came as music to our ears, and I can hardly describe what pleasant feelings these familiar noises produced. As we went on, the bushes on each side of the path screened our view of the huts. The neigh of a horse attracted our attention, and a man, mounted bare-backed, made his appearance about a hundred paces from us.

" Halt !" I cried to my companions.

With my gun hung to my cross-belt, and my hat in hand, I advanced alone towards the rider, who had suddenly reined in his steed.

" Ave Maria !" said I, going up to him.

" Her holy name be blessed !" answered the horseman, raising his cap, from which several locks of white hair escaped.

" Do you speak Spanish, venerable father ?"

" Yes, a little."

" Are you the chief of the village ?"

" What do you want ?"

" We require water and a roof to shelter us."

" You are not alone, I see ; from whom do you come ?"

" We are nothing but travellers wandering through the forests to seek for plants and animals with healing properties."

" But you are armed ?"

" Well, we have a child to protect, and the brutes of the forest are fierce."

" Are you speaking the truth ?"

I then called **Lucien**, who doffed his hat to the old man and saluted him.

" Child, may God bless you !"

" Are we to consider ourselves your guests ?"

" Yes, you are the guests of Coyotepec; come along with me."

Sumichrast and l'Encuerado also approached the horseman, who dismounted and then led the way. The latter conversed with the Indian in the Mistec tongue, an idiom which Lucien alone could understand, he having been taught it by l'Encuerado. From the way in which the old man scanned us, I imagined that l'Encuerado had represented us to him as white sorcerers of no ordinary skill.

Coyotepec—or " Stone Wolf "—might have been about seventy years of age. He was born in this ravine, to which he had given the name of the " *Mountain's Mouth*," though I am ignorant of the reason for the designation. He had been taken, when very young, by one of his uncles to Puebla, but he had soon left the city with the intention of rebuilding the paternal hut, and of knowing nothing of the world beyond his own domain. His six children were all married and lived near him, and the little colony numbered as many as thirty individuals. He was an Indian of the Tlascalan race, as robust and nimble as a man of forty, of middle height, with a brown skin. He wore a hat made of palm-tree straw, and was dressed in a white woollen jacket, fastened in round the waist like a blouse; cotton drawers, scarcely covering his knees, completed his costume.

" What is the nearest town to this?" asked Sumichrast.

" Puebla," was the answer.

" How far off is it ?"

" About eight days' journey."

As the usual day's journey of the Indian is ten leagues a day, the distance must have been about eighty leagues.

The old man could not furnish us with any other geographical information; he had heard the names of Orizava and Tehuacan, but never having visited these towns, he knew nothing of the distance we were from them. For forty years, with the exception of the relations of his sons and daughters-in-law, who paid him a visit annually, we were the first persons who had disturbed his solitude. We availed ourselves of the trunk of a tree to cross the brook, when our guide soon stopped in front of a hut. Four naked children, the eldest of whom might have been ten years old, inspected us with comical curiosity. They had never before seen a white man, and although we were dreadfully bronzed, their surprise was very great. A young woman, whose clothing consisted of a piece of cloth folded round her hips, saluted us in broken Spanish, and bid us welcome. The old man introduced us to his eldest son, named Torribio, a man about forty years of age. His clothing was not quite so primitive as that of his father, but consisted of slashed trowsers ornamented with silver buttons, a cotton shirt, and a felt hat covered with varnished leather. The little colony employed themselves in collecting cochineal, which Torribio carried to Puebla for sale, and this fact accounted for his more civilized costume. At length the old man asked us to come into his hut, round which a large part of his family were assembling. He called his wife, who was a little old woman, dressed in a long cotton gown; then he addressed us, pointing to his children and grandchildren, and said:

"You are my guests; my house is at your disposal, and all my relatives are your servants."

CHAPTER XXI.

BLACK SKINS AND WHITE SKINS.—WE HAVE TO TURN CAR-
PENTERS.—L'ENCUERADO CHANTING AND PREACHING.—
THE PALM-LEAVES.—VEGETABLE BUTTER TREE.

THE dwelling so generously put at our disposal was a
large shed, divided into three rooms by bamboo par-
titions; mats, spread out on the ground, formed our beds,
and the remainder of the furniture consisted of nothing but
two benches. L'Encuerado swept out one of the rooms,
and, collecting some dry palm-leaves, made us a softer resting-place than we had slept on for the last twenty days. A
troop of children—of both sexes, and perfectly naked—
formed a circle round us, and watched our movements with
surprise. I omitted to mention about half a dozen dogs,
who were at first perfectly furious at Gringalet's appearance, but afterwards contented themselves with growling
whenever the intruder came near.

When our baggage had been deposited in the shed, I
went and sat down a few paces from the hut, on a mound
overlooking the brook. Sumichrast soon joined me.
Gradually the sun went down, while the children, previously playing about, went to dip themselves in the beautifully
transparent water. I told Lucien, who was dying to imitate them, to follow their example. He had hardly taken
off his shirt, when the young Indians, who had watched
him undress with evident curiosity, burst out laughing, and
chattered together like so many young paroquets.

" Why do they laugh so when they look at me ?" asked
Lucien of l'Encuerado.

" Of course, because of your white skin; what else
should it be ? They have never seen a human being of that
color before."

" They think it so very ridiculous ?" interposed Sumichrast.

" Yes, rather," replied the Indian; " but you must not
mind it, Chanito ; for, after all, it is not your fault."

We and the young Indians now laughed in concert; and
this incident led on to a long conversation between Sumichrast and me. L'Encuerado, who, we had imagined, envied us our white skins, pitied us, in fact; as no doubt he
would himself have been pitied by Nubians, because he was
only copper-colored.

" Why," said Lucien, who came up to us just as the discussion began, " are not all men the same color ? What is
the reason of it, M. Sumichrast ?"

" It is owing to the influence of the sun, which more or
less colors the pigment of the skin."

" The pigment ?"

" Yes ; a brown matter which exists under the skin, and
gives to it a shade more or less dark."

" Then Europeans have no pigment ?"

" Yes, they have, just like all other races of men ; only
this matter does not affect the whole of their bodies. The
brown spots which cover the face and hands of some people
are produced by the pigment making its way through the
epidermis."

" Then," replied Lucien, " negroes would become white if
they lived in Europe."

" No," I answered, smiling ; " the sun shines in Europe as
well as in America, and however weak its action may be, it
is sufficient to blacken the pigment."

"But if they always lived in the shade ?" cried l'Encuerado.

"It would have to be perfect darkness, a thing which it
is quite impossible to procure."

At this moment our host called us. On a rickety table,
covered with a small cotton cloth, a bowl of thin soup, with
tortilla and tomatoes, was smoking, and we all did full justice to our fare. This dish was followed by a fowl seasoned with pimento sauce and black beans fried in fat ; then
some *camotes* (*Convolvulus batatas*) displayed the bright
colors of their mealy interior, in the midst of a sirup with
which l'Encuerado and Lucien regaled themselves. A
large bowl of coffee put the finishing stroke to our satisfaction. Instead of bread, we ate some freshly made maize-
cakes. Never had any dinner appeared so delicious to us
as this, for we had begun to get rather tired of game,
which had formed our principal food since we left home.

When the meal was over, Lucien ran back to join the
children, who, seated on the bank of the stream, were plait-
ing palm-leaves together. One of them was very successful
in making a grasshopper, and the boys, delighted with the
praises of their guest, vied with one another in their inven-
tions. They presented him with a bull, a fowl, a basket,
and other articles, which were very curious, considering the
material used and the skill of workmanship exhibited.

Lucien, perfectly enchanted with these presents, and finding that our admiration hardly equalled his own, turned to
l'Encuerado, who criticised the articles submitted to him
with an artistic eye :

"Then you, too, know how to weave palm-leaves ?"

"Yes, Chanito, I can make grasshoppers, horses, and even
birds."

"Only fancy ! and yet you have never made any for
me !"

" You are mistaken in that; when you were quite a little child I filled your cradle with them. But as they seem to amuse you, I will teach you to weave them for yourself."

At dark the children disappeared, and our host came to wish us good-night. I told him of the light we had caught a glimpse of the evening before.

" It was Juan," he said.

" And who is Juan ?"

" The eldest of my grandchildren. He is watching a flock of goats in the plain which belong to us."

The voice of the old man woke me next morning, and I got up at the same time as Sumichrast, who was still in a semi-torpid state from having slept so well. Lucien and l'Encuerado, who had risen earlier, had already explored the ravine, led by the youngest of the children; for the elder ones worked, according to their several abilities, at collecting wood or cultivating the fields.

Our first care was to unpack the insects and bird-skins we had collected, and the whole colony now surrounded us and asked us innumerable questions. To our great disappointment, we found we could only retain the most remarkable of our " treasures." Hitherto, the bird-skins had taken the place in the basket of the provisions we had eaten; but, after making an inventory, I came to the conclusion that, when our provisions were renewed, it would be perfectly impossible for l'Encuerado to travel with such an increased load. So we were compelled to reject many of the specimens, though not without regret. Suddenly the idea struck me of questioning Coyotepec about his son's annual journey to Puebla.

" He will start in fifteen days," answered the old man.

" Will he go alone ?"

" No; he takes with him three of our biggest lads and six donkeys."

" And are the donkeys laden ?"

" Yes; but the boys start without any burden."

In an hour's time (an Indian never decides any thing without much consideration) I arranged with my host that he should transport to Puebla two cases in which I could pack my valuables.

Such a piece of good luck made us feel quite jolly; for by this means we were enabled to preserve the whole of our collections, instead of throwing many of them away, as had often before happened.

We were now in want of cases, and Coyotepec had neither saw, hammer, nor nails; but he gave me some rough boards, on which we all set to work.

L'Encuerado and Sumichrast smoothed the planks with the help of two woodman's hatchets, while I cut pegs, all laboring without intermission until the next evening. A little before sunset we had succeeded in making two large and tolerably light boxes, a task which, without proper tools, was more difficult than any one could suppose who had not undertaken it.

Sunday, which was Whitsunday, found us quite amazed at our performance. L'Encuerado had succeeded in weaving some mats to cover the cases, and preserve their contents from the damp. About eleven o'clock our host's family assembled in front of the hut; the women and young girls were dressed in red or blue petticoats, with their shoulders covered with embroidered cotton chemisettes: and the younger boys were clothed in a sort of blouse without sleeves. The grandmother was the last to make her appearance, and she had a necklace of very valuable pearls round her neck. The women wore ornaments made of bits of rough coral, and their fingers were loaded with silver rings.

" We always assemble together on Sunday at the hour

for mass, to say our prayers together," said Coyotepec to me, "and to thank God who covers the trees with fruit, and preserves us in good health."

"We are Christians the same as you," I answered gravely.

Then every one knelt down, and the old man recited the Litanies and a succession of Ave Marias. After this one of the young girls chanted a canticle, assisted by the others, who joined in. The singer had scarcely finished her hymn, when l'Encuerado, perfectly electrified, entreated the audience not to move, and at once struck up one of his favorite chants. He kept us at least half an hour in the burning sun, till, being tired of kneeling, I made signs to him to leave off. But it was lost labor, for my servant pretended not to perceive me, and only multiplied his gestures and cries, repeating the same verse three times running.

"Amen!" at last I cried, in a loud voice, getting up.

Every one followed my example; so, being at last set at liberty, I went away, while the Indians surrounded l'Encuerado to congratulate him.

I had not yet paid a visit to the ravine, which, situated as it was in the midst of the *Terre-Froide*, yielded the same kind of productions as the *Terre-Chaude*. I called Sumichrast and Lucien, and, under the guidance of Torribio, the Indian who every year drove the donkeys to Puebla, we ascended the course of the stream.

Our guide first led us to his hut, surrounded by Bourbon palms. This beautiful tree, belonging to the palm family, has a strange and yet an agreeable appearance. From its very summit long stalks shoot out, at the end of which hangs a wide leaf, which is first folded, and afterwards spreads out like a fan ornamented with points. The Indians cut up these leaves to weave the mats, called *pétates*, which form an article of such extensive commerce in Mexico. They are also used for making baskets, brooms, bellows, and many other household utensils.

Torribio's cabin consisted of but one room, and the fire-hearth was placed outside under a small shed. This primitive abode contained neither chairs, tables, nor benches. Sumichrast was full of admiration at this simplicity, which I considered rather overdone; but my friend compared the life of civilization, in which luxury has created so many wants, with the lot of these men who can dispense with almost every thing, and decidedly came to the conclusion that the latter are much the happier.

On leaving the hut, I noticed to our left a magnificent avocado pear-tree—*Persea gratissima*—the fruit of which yields a pulp called "vegetable butter.' The avocado pear, called by the Indians *ahuacate*, is the same shape as a large pear, with interior of a light-green color and of a buttery nature; its sweet flavor is delicious to every palate. It is either eaten plain, or seasoned with salt, oil, and vinegar.

"The avocado pear-tree, I should think, has no relations among trees!" said Lucien, smiling.

"Yes, certainly it has. It belongs to the Laurel family, and is the only member of it which produces eatable fruit. Its connections, though, occupy an important position in domestic economy. First, there is the bay-tree—*Laurus nobilis*—the leaves of which are indispensable in French cookery; while the berries furnish an oil used in medicine. Next comes the *Laurus camphora*, from the leaves of which camphor is extracted, the crystallized essence which evaporates so easily; then the *Laurus cinnamomum*, the bark of which is called cinnamon; and, lastly, sassafras, the aromatic wood which is said to be a powerful sudorific."

Our guide conducted us across a field of Indian corn or maize. Europe is indebted to America for this valuable gramineous plant. The common bread or *tortilla* of this country, which is a kind of pancake, is made from it. Before the maize is quite ripe, it is eaten boiled or parched;

in fact, generally throughout America, it is used instead of barley or oats for feeding horses and cattle.

As soon as Torribio entered his own plantation, he bent down a few twigs of the *masorcas* without dividing them from the stem.

" Why do you bend those poor plants like that ? Won't they die ?" cried Lucien.

" Yes ; in the first place, because they are annuals, and our guide only hastened their death a few days ; besides, the ears he cut are ripe, and will dry hanging to the stems which have nourished them. This method is as simple as it is expeditious, but could only be put into practice in countries where winter is nothing but a spring."

Behind the maize-field there was a hedge covered with long filaments of a golden-yellow color. These filaments, which were entirely devoid of leaves, grew all over the shrubs almost like a thick cloak.

" What is the name of this wonderful plant ?" asked Lucien.

" It is the *sacatlascale*," answered Torribio.

" It is a sort of dodder," added Sumichrast, " a plant of the Convolvulus family. The European species is destroyed, because it twines round certain vegetables and chokes them. Here, however, the *sacatlascale* is allowed to grow, because some use has been found for it."

" What could be made of these stalks, which are so delicate that they break if I merely touch them ?"

" They are first bruised, and then dried in the sun," replied Torribio. " When they want to dye a black or yellow hue, all they have to do is to boil the paste in iron, or mix it with alum."

While we were climbing the banks of the ravine, Lucien availed himself of such a good opportunity by smearing his hands all over with this bright yellow substance. When

we reached a certain height, we lay down on the grass.
With one glance we could take in the whole of this small
oasis. The stream meandered along, shaded with green
trees; here and there, among clumps of Bourbon palms, we
could discern huts irregularly dotted about. I turned my
eyes towards our host's threshold, and, through my glass,
perceived l'Encuerado, who was still preaching. He had
evidently left off chanting, for his hearers were seated round
him on the ground.

Lucien took possession of the telescope, and I noticed that
Terribio also seemed very anxious to try the instrument.
I told the boy to lend it to him. Our guide, seeing trees
brought so close to him, could not at first account for this
optical effect. I then directed the glass so that he could
see the group of Indians, and I never saw any human face
manifest such complete surprise. The Indian, who appeared perfectly charmed, could not long maintain his gravity.
Every time he succeeded in discovering a hut, he hardly
gave himself time to look at it, but rolled on the ground
bursting with laughter. Two or three times I put out my
hand to take back the telescope, but Torribio hugged it to
his breast, just like a child when any one attempts to take
a plaything away. At last he consented to give it to me,
and I felt really sorry that I had not another glass to offer
him.

Sumichrast led the way round the end of the ravine.
Suddenly the birds, which were warbling on the banks of
the stream, all flew away; a goshawk was hovering above
us in the sky. As it was flying swiftly through the air, it
passed us within gunshot; a shot struck it, and, tumbling
over and over, it fell to the ground about twenty paces from
us. Lucien immediately ran to pick it up.

"It is a falcon!" he cried.

"You are right," replied Sumichrast; "it is the Cayenne goshawk, which is characterized by having a head covered with ash-colored feathers, by a brown body, and black feathers in its tail."

" Will you skin it ?"

" Yes, certainly, Master Sunbeam ; firstly, because this is any thing but a common bird; and, secondly, during the few days we shall stay here, we must endeavor to fill the boxes which we have had so much difficulty in making."

At this moment a finch, with red, brown, and white feathers, settled near us.

" It is the *Pyrrhula telasco*," said my friend, " a species discovered by Lesson, the celebrated ornithologist, in his journey to Lima. Ah ! if I wasn't so economical with the powder—"

" I have some powder," muttered Torribio.

" You have some powder !" I cried; " will you sell us some ?"

" No," answered the Indian, dryly.

" Why not ?" was my rejoinder. " Are you also a sportsman ? Besides, if you are, you will soon be going to Puebla, where you could get a fresh supply."

" I never sell my powder," was the terse response.

" Very well, then, let us say no more about it."

We crossed over the stream by means of a tree which stretched from one bank to the other. Ere the sun ceased to gild the ravine with its rays we found ourselves opposite to the dwelling of the Indian patriarch, which overlooked a hut similar to that of our guide. The sky was a pale blue, and we had a glimpse of the monotonous plain dotted over with the sombre cactus-plant; while just below us figured the fresh oasis, rendered all the more charming by the contrast. The birds warbled in the shrubs, and one by one flew away in order to return to the trees, among the branches of which they had perhaps first crept out of the paternal

nest.   A warm breeze was blowing when we got up to return to the village.

"I have some powder!" exclaimed the Indian, abruptly.

"Yes, very likely, but I also know that you don't wish to
sell any."

"No, I don't."

The powder is surely mine, I thought to myself; and, after walking about twenty paces, I again took up the subject.

"Even if your powder was very good, I wouldn't buy it
of you; I know men like you mean what they say; nevertheless, if you like, I will make an exchange."

"What could you give me?" replied Torribio, with affected indifference; "I don't want any of your birds, and
my gun is quite as good as yours, if not better."

"That's true enough, therefore say no more about it."

And I continued to follow my guide, who walked slowly
on.   He soon turned round again.

"The magic glass," said he, with a great effort.

"Come! now we've got to the point," murmured Sumichrast.

"It is a bargain, if your powder is good," said I.

"Will you really give the glass to me?" cried the Indian,
his eyes lighting up with joy.

"I am always a man of my word," I replied.

Torribio hurried on so fast that Lucien was obliged to
run in order to keep up with us.   After crossing the stream,
our guide conducted us to his hut, and showed us four cases
of American powder which was quite sound, and more than
five or six pounds of assorted shot.

I was overjoyed at this discovery; but I maintained an
indifference quite equal to that of our guide, who was squatting down on the ground with his chin resting between his
knees.

"Here is the telescope," I said.

His features remained perfectly motionless, but his eyes sparkled and his hand trembled slightly as he seized the object of his longing. I showed him how to use and clean the instrument; then, loaded with the boxes, which were so precious to me, and followed by my companions, I returned to Coyotepec's dwelling.

"Why didn't Torribio say at once that he was willing to exchange his powder for the telescope?" asked Lucien.

"The reason is, because an Indian always tries to conceal his wishes and passions."

"But why didn't you offer him the instrument directly?"

"If I had shown too much eagerness, very probably he would have refused to make an exchange, and the Indian seldom retracts what he has once said."

Of course, l'Encuerado, always the most extravagant in its use, was perfectly delighted to see our stock of ammunition trebled.

We had scarcely finished our dinner, when we heard the sound of a guitar: the Mistec, after having preached, had succeeded in convincing his congregation that a dance was the proper method of winding up the day. The space in front of the patriarch's dwelling having been swept, and two crackling fires lighted, ere long the women made their appearance, in what they considered full dress, and their hair loaded with flowers. The national air of the *Jarabe* was played, and the dancers trod the measure with energy. Lucien, who had joined the crowd, wanted to teach the polka and waltz to the Indian children. Sumichrast stood by, laughing most heartily; but his merriment increased on seeing l'Encuerado's gambols, for never before had such wonderful capers been cut. He sang, strummed on his guitar, and danced—often doing all three at the same time. About ten o'clock, Lucien retired to rest. The fatigues of the day, in spite of the noise of the guitar and the songs, soon sent him to sleep.

At a proper hour I desired every one to go home. They kissed my hands, some even embraced me, and obeyed; so silence once more reigned in the little valley. Before my going to sleep, l'Encuerado was already snoring, with his head on Gringalet's back.

CHAPTER XXII.

MEXICAN OAK-APPLES.—A STREAM LOST IN AN ABYSS.—
THE WILD NASTURTIUM.—SPORTSMEN DECEIVED BY CHIL-
DREN.—THE GRAVE-DIGGING BEETLES.—THE COCHINEAL
INSECT.—MEXICAN WINE. — GOOD-BYE TO OUR INDIAN
HOSTS.

A S soon as it was light, I awoke Sumichrast and Lucien.
L'Encuerado was sleeping so soundly, after his ex-
ploits of the night before, that we hesitated to disturb him.
I intended to hunt for insects all day, so as to fill up the
vacant spaces in the specimen-boxes that Torribio was to
take to Puebla; so we bent our steps towards the bottom
of the valley. As the inhabitants were still asleep in their
huts, Gringalet passed safely all his sleeping brother-dogs
with his tail boldly cocked.

The winding path brought us out into an extensive hollow covered with verdure. In a hundred paces more, we reached some pyramid-shaped rocks, which were bound together by the gigantic roots of a tree with scanty foliage. The water glided noiselessly through the stones, and disappeared under a low arch shaded by gladiolas, covered with blossoms.

Lucien, who was leaning over the opening, wanted to know what became of the water.

"Perhaps it is absorbed by sand underneath; perhaps it will reappear in the valleys, where the surface sinks to its level," I answered.

"Do streams often go under the ground like this?"

"Yes; particularly in Mexico, where these subterranean passages are numerous. Near Chiquihuita, about five leagues from the road which leads to Vera Cruz and Cordova, a large river vanishes into a cave, which is more than three miles in length."

"Oh, how I should like to see such a large grotto!"

"Your wish shall be gratified, provided we do not lose our way in the *Terre-Chaude.*"

Sumichrast had only a few minutes left us, when we heard a report, and he reappeared carrying a magnificent bird, whose red plumage had a purple metallic lustre.

"We have never met with this fine fellow before," said Lucien.

"It is the most brilliant of all the American passerines," I replied—"the *Ampelis pompadora;* but its splendid attire lasts only for a very short time. In a few days its bright-colored feathers fall off, and are replaced by a sombre, dull-looking coat. This moulting, which is common to many birds, has more than once led ornithologists into error, who have described, as a new species, a bird which a new dress has prevented them from recognizing."

" The water .... disappeared under a low arch."

The neighborhood of the *sumidero* furnished us with a dozen birds of different species; among others, several tanagers peculiar to America, and a pair of pretty light-brown cuckoos, with fan-shaped tails, which are merely birds of passage in this locality.

"When you are speaking of a bird, why do you often say it belongs to Brazil, Guiana, or Peru, when you actually find it in Mexico?" asked Lucien.

"Because, at certain seasons of the year, many kinds of birds migrate," answered my friend; "and they are often found at an immense distance from the country where they breed. This beautiful blackbird, for instance, is never seen in Mexico except in the spring, which has caused it to be called here the *primavera.*"

"Look, papa, at these beautiful yellow flowers; they cover the trunk of this tree so completely that it appears as if they grew on it."

"They are the flowers of the *tropæolum*, or wild nasturtium. This plant has been cultivated in Europe, where its seed is eaten preserved in vinegar, and its flowers are used to season salads."

"Then the Mexicans do not know its value, for I have never seen it on their tables."

"You are right; but still I should have thought that the piquant taste of the flowers of the *tropæolum* would have just suited them. Perhaps they find it too insipid after having been accustomed to chewing capsicums."

"You have the seasoning, and I have the salad!" suddenly cried my friend.

And he showed us a handful of an herb called purslane.

This plant, which grows in abundance in damp ground, has red flowers, which close every evening and open again in the morning. I gathered the fleshy leaves, while Sumichrast, who had found a plant covered with seeds, show-

ed Lucien the circular hole on the seed which has given to
the plant its family name (*Portulacæ*).

Some maize-cakes and a salad formed our frugal breakfast, which was discussed on the edge of the stream.   Lucien especially seemed to enjoy it, for I was indeed obliged
to check him, the appetizing flavor of the salad had so
sharpened his appetite.

When we had finished our meal, Sumichrast tried to
climb the steep bank; but the ground gave way under his
feet, and two or three times he fell.   I left Lucien to manage for himself, for his falls were not likely to be dangerous.   As he was much less heavy than we were, he succeeded in reaching the level of the plain first, and with
very little trouble, when he amused himself by laughing
disrespectfully at our efforts.

"You had better take care of your ears," cried my friend,
addressing Lucien; "if I could reach you I would use them
to hang on by."

In vain we tried to find a more accessible path.   At last,
getting rid of my gun and game-bag, I accomplished the
ascent.

"That's all very well!" exclaimed Sumichrast, fatigued
and cramped with his exertions; "but how am I to reach
you, now that I have two guns and two bags to carry?"

"Wait a bit!" cried Lucien; and, running down the
slope, he soon disappeared.

I heard him cutting at something with his *machete;*
soon after he came up again, carrying a long stem of cane.

"Now we'll try and fish up M. Sumichrast," said he.

Sitting down on the bank, I held out the rod to my companion, who at once seized it, and, thus supported, gradually managed to bring up all our hunting-gear, and ultimately
himself, when, instead of pulling "Master Sunbeam's" ears,
he gave him a kiss as a reward for his ingenious idea.

"Four children appeared."

About two hundred paces farther on the verdant ravine came to an end, and we were surrounded by cactus-plants. Lucien employed himself hunting **lizards, and** Gringalet seemed to think he was proving his intelligence by running in front of the boy, so as to frighten **away all the game.** The young **hunter succeeded, however, in** catching **a green** saurian—an *anolis*—which, being more courageous than lizards **generally are, tried to bite the** hand that **held it** prisoner, **and angrily puffed up its crest,** which is variegated like **a butterfly's** wing.

Suddenly Gringalet barked uneasily; then we heard **a** shrill whistle, and immediately afterwards the cry of a ca-**yote.** I called in the dog, and, with **my finger** on the trig-**ger of** my gun, cautiously advanced, telling Lucien to keep **at my** side. We walked so noiselessly that we surprised **two or** three adders which were coiled **up** in the sun. The screech of an owl **now** struck on our **ears.** I exchanged a look of surprise with my companion; **this was neither** the time nor **place for** a bird of this kind. A fresh yelping **and** barking **then** resounded; but this time **it was so** near **to us** that **we halted.** Gringalet dashed on before us, and **four** **children appeared, repulsing the dog** with cactus-leaves in their hands, **which they used as** shields.

"Well!" cried Sumichrast, "here we have the cayote, the owl, and the dog, which have so puzzled us."

My companion was not wrong: the young Indians were carrying provisions to their elder brother, who was taking care of a flock of goats. In order to enliven their journey, they amused themselves by imitating the cries of different animals, and they did it with so much accuracy that we had been completely duped.

About three o'clock, my friend, who was anxious to pre-pare the birds he had shot, left us to return to Coyotepec's dwelling. **I continued walking, accompanied by Lucien,** but soon stopped to look at the dead body of a mouse which grave-digging beetles were burying.

These insects, five in number, were excavating the ground under the small rodent, in order to bury it. These industrious insects had undertaken a work which would employ them more than twenty-four hours; two of the beetles were lifting up one side of the carcass, while the others scratched away the sand underneath.

"Why are they trying to bury that mouse?" asked Lucien.

"They are providing for their young. They will deposit their eggs beneath the dead animal, and the larvæ, after they are hatched, will feed on it."

I disturbed the active creatures, which, unfortunately for them, belonged to a rare species. Their antennæ, which are club-shaped, terminated abruptly in a kind of button, and their elytra, which are a brilliant black, are crossed by a belt of yellow color. In vain I turned over the ground and the prey, but I could only find four of them.

On a path leading to a glen, we noticed some cicindelas. Lucien began chasing them, but the agility of his enemies soon baffled him.

"How malicious these flies are!" he cried; "I can't succeed in catching one of them."

"They are not flies, but coleoptera, allied to the Carabus family. Give me your net."

Lucien was anxious to obtain one of them, and at length was successful. He was delighted with the beautiful metallic color of their brown elytra, dotted over with yellow spots; but the insect, after having bitten him, escaped.

"What jaws they have!" he said, shaking his fingers; "it's a good thing those creatures are very small. Do cicindelas live in woods?"

"They prefer dry, sandy places, and can run and fly very

swiftly. This insect has an uncommonly voracious appetite; look at this one, which has just seized an immense fly, and is trying to tear it in pieces."

The capricious flight of a stag-beetle led us to the edge of the ravine; and, continuing to follow a zigzag path shaded with shrubs, we came out in front of a hut. On the threshold there was a young woman spinning a piece of cotton cloth, whom I recognized as one of the dancers of the night before. The loom which held the weft was fastened at one end to the trunk of a tree, the other being wound round the waist of the weaver. Lucien examined it with great curiosity; and when he saw the weaver change the color of her threads, he understood how the Indian women covered the bottoms of their petticoats with those extraordinary patterns which their fancy produces.

Within a short distance of the hut there were some nopal cactus-plants.

"Look at these plants," said I, addressing Lucien; "the sight of them would probably affect l'Encuerado to tears, for they are principally cultivated in his native land. The numerous brown spots which you can see on their stalks are hemipterous insects, commonly called cochineal. They have no wings, and feed entirely on this cactus, sucking out its sap with their proboscis. The male only is capable of movement; the female is doomed to die where she is born. At a certain time these little insects lay thousands of eggs, and their bodies become covered with a cottony moss, which is intended as a shelter for their young. The cochineal is gathered when, to use the Indian expression, it is ripe, by scraping the plant with a long flexible knife, and all the creatures, still alive, are plunged into boiling water. They are taken out as soon as they are dead, and dried in the sun. Afterwards, packed up in goat-skin bags, they are sent to Europe, where they are used for dyeing and for making the carmine which gives to some kinds of sweet-meats their bright pink color."

A little farther on, I found myself facing a *maguey*— *Agave Mexicana*—a sort of aloe, from which *pulque* is extracted. The maguey only blooms once every twenty-five or thirty years, and the stalk, which is to support the clusters of flowers, grows, in the space of two months, to a height of about sixteen to twenty feet. The stalk bears at its summit no less than four or five thousand blossoms, and the plant expends all its strength in producing them, for it dies soon after.

In the plantations on the plains of Apam, where the maguey is largely cultivated, they prevent its flowering. As soon as the conical bud appears from which the stalk is about to spring, it is cut off, and a cylindrical cavity is hollowed out with a large spoon to the depth of from five to eight inches. The sap collects in this hole, and it is taken out two or three times a day with a long bent gourd, which the Indians use as a siphon. It has been calculated that in twenty-four hours a strong plant should supply about three quarts of a sweet liquor called *Agua miel*, which is without odor, and has an acidulated sweet taste.

The *Agua miel* is collected in ox-skins, placed like troughs on four stakes, where the liquor ferments; in about seventy-two hours it is ready for delivery to those that use it, among whom must be placed many Europeans. A maguey plant is serviceable in producing sap for two or three months.

Pulque is an intoxicating beverage, the flavor of which varies according to the degree of fermentation; it might be compared to good cider or perry, and is said to fatten those who habitually drink it.

I reached Coyotepec's dwelling just as the sun had set. Sumichrast was finishing his work, and l'Encuerado, coming from a heap of dry palm-leaves, presented to me a splendid broad-brimmed hat, which he had just made.

The next day and the day after were spent in hunting after specimens, and our boxes were soon filled up and packed. I explained to Torribio, who was to start at day-break, how to handle the cases, and then intrusted to him letters which were to announce our early return. Lucien had written to his dear mother and his sister Hortense, and he had to open his letter at least twenty times to add postscripts, often dictated by l'Encuerado.

In the evening we bade adieu to our kind hosts, for we were to start early. Thanks to them, we had renewed our stock of salt, rice, coffee, sugar, and maize-cake. In default of black pepper, we took with us some red capsicums; but the most precious of our acquisitions was the powder and shot I had received in exchange for the telescope.

On the next morning I learned that Torribio was already on his way towards Puebla. He had started about mid-

night, so as to avoid crossing the plain during the heat of
the day. I now hastened our own departure. We were
in possession of good hats, but our garments, which had
been mended with some soft leather, gave us the appearance
of mendicants; this, however, did not trouble us much.
My shoes, and also Sumichrast's, had been strongly, if not
elegantly, repaired, and were quite as good as new; Lucien, too, now possessed a pair of spare sandals.

The inhabitants of the little colony ranged along our path,
and, overwhelming us with good wishes, bid us another
adieu. I pressed all the hands that were held out to me,
and then, guided by the band of children, who still surrounded the young traveller, we commenced to ascend the
path which had led us down into this hospitable little oasis.
When I reached the summit of the hill, I waved my hat as
a last salutation to Coyotepec; l'Encuerado fired off his gun
as a farewell, and we plunged into the labyrinth of cactuses,
taking a straight course towards the east.

CHAPTER XXIII.

THREE days of difficult travelling brought us into the
midst of the *Terre-Tempérée*. Thus we had traversed
the whole breadth of the Cordillera, at one time shivering
on their summits, at another perspiring, as we penetrated
narrow and deep-sunk valleys, just as the chances of our
journey led us. Every now and then we caught a sight of
the pointed cone of the volcano of Orizava, which assisted
us in taking our bearings. At last, four days after taking
leave of Coyotepec, we established our bivouac at the foot
of a mountain, close to a clear and icy stream.

While l'Eucuerado was making the fire, Lucien discovered under a stone an enormous black and hairy spider, with feet armed with double-hooked claws.

"Isn't this a tarantula, M. Sumichrast?"

"No, my boy, it is a bird-catching spider—so called because it is said to attack the humming-birds' nests and destroy the young ones."

"May I catch it?"

"Not with your fingers; its bite is dangerous."

"One might easily fancy it was watching us, from the expression of those two big eyes near its mouth."

"There is no doubt that it is looking at us; just menace it with this little stick, and you'll soon see it assume the defensive."

The enormous spider raised its front feet, and two black and polished horns issued from its mouth. After a moment's hesitation, it suddenly darted at the end of the stick, which Lucien let go in fright.

Ten or twelve paces farther on, the young naturalist discovered another spider, and plied me with numerous questions about it. I could only give him a few general facts as to this curious class of animals.

"But, I say, papa, there must be a great many different species of spiders, for I see some at every step—green, black, and yellow."

"There are so many species that all of them are not yet known; indeed, I believe that the Mexican spiders have not hitherto been described. It is necessary to study them on the spot, for their soft bodies change their shape in drying, and the proper means of preserving them are not within the reach of an ordinary traveller."

In passing along, I broke through some threads of a light web stretching between two bushes. The proprietor of the web—a gray spider—immediately made its appearance, and set hurriedly to work to repair the involuntary damage I had committed.

"Where does the thread come from?" asked Lucien; "it is so thin that I can scarcely see it."

"From four reservoirs situated at the lower part of the spider's abdomen, and filled with a gummy matter which becomes solid as soon as it is exposed to the air.· These reservoirs are pierced with about a thousand holes, from each of which proceeds a thread invisible to the naked eye, for it takes a thousand of them to form the thread the spider is now spinning."

"How sorry I am now that I hadn't collected more of these curious insects! Some we have met with were very curious."

"In the first place," I replied, "spiders are not insects; they have both heart and lungs, but insects breathe through air-pipes.* Added to this, insects have antennæ, and undergo metamorphoses, which is not the case with the spider. You must recollect, too, that the spider is akin to the scorpion."

"Yes; but scorpions don't know how to spin."

"Well, all spiders do not possess this art. One of the species you were looking at just now lives on plants, and would be much embarrassed if it happened to fall into the web of its spinning sister; added to which, it would run no small risk of being devoured."

"Will spiders eat one another?"

"Without the least scruple, and scorpions do the same. It is, in fact, a family vice."

"I am not at all astonished, then, that the whole family are so ugly."

---

* The air-pipes are two vessels, one on each side, extending the whole length of the body, provided with branches and ramifications. They serve for the reception and distribution of the air.

"If they were ever so beautiful, it would make no difference in their evil disposition. They have, however, some good qualities; such, for instance, as patience and resolution. The poor spider, now, that we are looking at, is working desperately to catch a prey which is constantly escaping. Sometimes it is the wind which destroys the web so industriously woven; sometimes a great beetle plunges heavily through the net. Nevertheless, the spider is not the least discouraged; he again sets his snare, and, while he is quietly watching for the game necessary for his subsistence, it too often happens that he is himself carried off in the beak of some bird."

Lucien and I now went among the trees in quest of something substantial for our dinner. The first thing we met with was a kind of marten, which looked viciously at us, and greeted us with a shrill cry. Gringalet darted off in pursuit of the animal, and followed it until it reached its hole. This animal, like the European marten, from which it differs only in size, often establishes itself in barns and granaries, where at night it amuses itself with the noisiest gambols. In the environs of the Mexican towns, many a house, invaded by these martens, is abandoned by its owner, because it is thought to be haunted by ghosts.

"Look out for yourselves!" cried l'Encuerado, suddenly.

A mephitic weasel or skunk, an animal which somewhat resembles a polecat, came running by. Gringalet, tired of waiting for the marten, crossed the trail of the beast, and set off after it, in spite of our calls. The skunk suddenly stopped and scratched up the earth with its sharp claws; then it voided a liquid of such a fetid odor that the dog was compelled to beat a retreat.

L'Encuerado, with his finger on the trigger of his gun, started again, and led us along noiselessly. He suddenly stooped down to listen.

"An animal came tumbling down about ten paces from us."

"It is a *quimichpatlan*," said he to me, in a low voice.

"A flying squirrel," I repeated to Sumichrast.

Lucien was about to speak; but I pointed to the Indian, who, half-hidden behind a dead trunk, was carefully examining the top of an ebony-tree. At this moment l'Encuerado placed his gun to his shoulder and **fired**. **He** had taken good aim—an **animal** came tumbling down about **ten paces** from us, **spreading out, in its convulsive** movements, the membrane which **joined its legs** together and covered it almost like a cloak.

Lucien took possession of the "flying squirrel," and, as they always go in pairs, my two companions went in pursuit of the other, which they soon succeeded in killing.

"Are we going to eat these animals?" asked Lucien.

"Why shouldn't we?" I rejoined. "They are squirrels; and, even supposing that they were rats, as the Indians assert, their flesh should be none the less savory."

"**Can these** animals fly for **any** length of time?" **asked Lucien.**

"**As a matter of** fact, they do not fly at all; but **the** membrane **which** unites their limbs acts like a parachute **in** keeping them up in **the air,** and materially assists them in some of their prodigious leaps."

"Can they run as fast as squirrels?"

"Nothing like it; they do not, indeed, often come down **to** the ground; but their activity on trees renders them not unworthy of their family."

"**I** thought," observed Lucien, "that bats were the only mammals that could fly."

"There is also the flying *phalanger*," observed my friend; "an animal of the marsupial order, which is a native of Australia, and somewhat resembles the opossum. It is said that, **when it** catches sight of a **man, it hangs itself** up by the **tail,** and does not **dare** to move; but I think this story will do to go along with l'Encuerado's about the glass-spider."

The Indian started off straight to the bivouac, and I led my companions by the side of the stream, admiring as we passed some magnificent trees. One of these was covered with brown fruit, with whitish insides, which had a rather nice acidulated taste. I hastened to pick half a dozen of them, knowing what a treat they would be to my servant.

As we went on, the banks of the stream gradually became lower, and ere long a lake, deliciously shaded by cypresses, poplars, oaks, and ebony-trees, opened to our view.

I sat down upon a rock, with Sumichrast and Lucien by my side, and from whence my eye could wander all over the blue and transparent water. We kept silent, being charmed with the smiling grandeur of this retired corner of the world. Birds came flying by, and, settling down close to us, warbled for an instant—then again took flight, after having given us time to admire the rich colors of their plumage. The motionless water was covered by long-legged insects with transparent wings, which seemed to skim over the polished surface as if impelled by some invisible agency. Sometimes an azure and purple attired dragon-fly flitted by, and all the insects fled at its approach, like sparrows before a hawk. A brilliantly-colored butterfly dashed against the voracious insect, and a furious combat took place between them; but the dragon-fly, which was eventually the conqueror, was in turn vanquished by a bird.

We were just moving off, when the deep water seemed to be agitated, and, although on the surface the flies and gnats continued their evolutions, the fish in hasty flight disappeared, and communicated their terror even to the water-snakes. A tortoise, however, seemed to deem it unnecessary to retreat, only drawing its head and feet under its shell.

"The sun was just setting."

Almost immediately an animal swam vigorously up to the reptile, and, having stopped to smell at it, continued its course.

"Are there such things as opossum-fishes?" asked Lucien, surprised.

"It is an otter," said I, in a low voice.

And quickly descending the rock, I followed Sumichrast to the water's edge, at a spot where the animal appeared inclined to land. We waited for an hour without any result.

My friend proposed to go and take a hurried dinner, and then return to our post near the rock. In a few minutes we had joined l'Encuerado, for, unknown to us, our bivouac was established about four gunshots from the lake. The Indian jumped with joy on hearing of the appearance of what he called a "water-dog."

"You may set me down as a fool," said he to Gringalet, caressing him, "if by to-morrow morning I don't give you one of your brother's legs for breakfast."

"Are otters really relations of Gringalet?" asked Lucien of me.

"Yes; according to Cuvier, they are digitigrades. Added to this, the otter may be tamed and trained to bring fish out of the water, which it is very skillful in catching, for it eats scarcely any thing else."

The sun was just setting, and behind us the dark outlines of the trees stood out against the orange-colored sky, while hundreds of birds were warbling and twittering around. A dark shade spread over the horizon, and all was solemn silence. Ere long the sky was glittering with stars, and the moon rose slowly above the trees. Its pale light penetrated the foliage, giving to the masses of leaves those fantastic shapes which make one dream of a supernatural world. As the moon advanced higher, it diffused more and more light over the scenery, and few spectacles could be more splendid than such a tropical night as this.

The report of a gun suddenly cut short my reverie, and l'Encuerado's shout of "Hiou! hiou!" summoned us to him. While I hurried Lucien along as fast as I could, I heard some loud shouting, which almost smothered the furious barking of the dog, and then saw my friend Sumichrast grasping the throat of an animal which Gringalet was worrying. Alongside, l'Encuerado was lying on the ground, pressing his right arm, and uttering cries of pain. He had been bitten by the wounded otter which he had attempted to catch hold of.

This was not the time to blame him, so I led l'Encuerado to the bivouac, where I was reassured by an examination of the bite, which I had at first feared was serious. After dressing the injured part, the Indian seemed much relieved.

My friend—after Lucien had examined its broad muzzle and wide nostrils, its smooth, black coat, and its feet, webbed like ducks—skinned the game, and put it at once upon the spit. When the meat was cooked to a nicety, I covered it over to protect it from insects, and then proposed retiring, for I foresaw that the Indian would be unable to carry his load the next day, and that either Sumichrast's patience or mine would be taxed in taking his place; for we did not intend to prolong our stay by the stream. Sleep surprised us ere this weighty question was solved.

" L'Encuerado was pressing his arm, and uttering cries of pain."

CHAPTER XXIV.

"HOW is your arm now, l'Encuerado?" I asked, finding the Indian up when I awoke.

"Pretty well, Tatita; but I find I mustn't move it much. If I do, it feels as if the blackguard water-dog was still holding me."

I again dressed the wound, the Indian continuing to hurl fresh abuse at the otter. I made him keep quiet, and prepared the coffee. Sumichrast and Lucien then rose, and we decided to start—the rainy season, which was approaching, rendering haste necessary.

L'Encuerado, in spite of our remonstrances, insisted on shouldering the load; but, on raising the burden, he found he was unable, so I shouldered the load.

At last, after no end of exertion on my part and Sumichrast's—for we alternately bore it—three leagues were traversed. We then halted at the foot of a hill, among ebony, mahogany, and oak trees.

L'Encuerado took charge of the camp, while I, with my friend and Lucien, climbed a neighboring hill. The trees which crowned its summit were limes—*Tilia sylvestris*—here the type of what bear the same name, and which are so plentiful in Europe, where they have been so changed by cultivation that they scarcely appear to belong to the same species as their brethren in the virgin forests. The wood of the lime is valued by the Indians for making various odds and ends, which are sold by thousands in Mexico. In Europe, the bark of this tree is used for well-ropes, and the charcoal made from its wood is preferred to any other for the manufacture of gunpowder. Few trees are more useful, and its beautiful green foliage makes it highly ornamental in a garden.

Our attention was attracted to a familiar noise—the cooing of doves. I moved gently under the trees, and soon put to flight several fine specimens, of a dark, ashy-blue color, with a black band across the tail-feathers, which were of a pearl-gray. I killed a couple of them; and Sumichrast, who was better placed, knocked down three others. They were quite sufficient for our dinners. They were the first of this family that we had killed, and Lucien in vain tried to make out what he called their relationship.

"They are neither passerines," said he, "nor palmipedes. Climbers, too, have differently-made feet."

"Your doubts are very natural," interposed my friend; "even ornithologists are very undecided on this point.

Nevertheless they class pigeons among the gallinaceæ, looking upon them as a link between this order and the passerines."

" Why don't they **make an order for them by themselves ?**"

" Bravo, **Master Sunbeam ! your idea is an excellent one,** but **it has been already** proposed ; several naturalists **reckon an order of *columbidæ*. But** you ought to know **that pigeons· inhabit the** whole **surface of** the globe, and **that they** are white, blue, red, green, and brown ; and sometimes all these shades blend together, and add their brilliancy to the pleasing shape of the bird. The pigeon or dove, which is adopted as the emblem of mildness and innocence, is readily tamed ; its flight is rather heavy, but lasting ; and, in Belgium chiefly, **it is** used as a bearer of letters, by conveying the bird to a long distance from its home, to which its instinct always leads it to return."

Lucien seemed very thoughtful.

"I wish I had known that before," **he said ;** " we might **have brought** a pigeon or two with us, and then poor mamma would have had news **of us before now."**

Sumichrast, who had taken upon himself the office **of** head-cook, vacant owing to l'Encuerado's wound, returned to the bivouac laden with our game. I skirted the wood in company with Lucien, who was the first to discover a West Indian cherry-tree—*Malpighia glabra*. The red fleshy **and** acid fruit was much to our taste ; so the boy climbed **the** tree in order to get plenty, rejoicing in the idea of giving **his friends an agreeable** surprise. When he had finished, **we went to** examine a dead tree. A piece of bark, **quickly** pulled off, discovered a quantity of those insects commonly called earwigs.

" Do you notice, papa, those white specks one of the **earwigs** is covering with its body ?"

"It is a female sitting on her eggs ; but look at this !"

"Eight, ten, twelve little ones ! How pretty they are ! One might well fancy that they were being led by the big earwig, which keeps turning round to them. There ! now she has stopped, and the little ones are crawling all round her."

I could hardly get Lucien away from his interesting study ; but the hissing of a snake which I turned out from under a stone soon brought the boy to me. I caught hold of the reptile, which rolled itself with some force round my arm. The boy, quite speechless with surprise, looked anxiously at me.

"Oh father !" exclaimed he in terror, running towards me.

"Don't be alarmed ; this reptile has no fangs, and it is so small I can handle it quite safely."

"But it will hurt you with its sting."

"It has no sting ; there is no danger to be feared from its tongue. Here, you take hold of it."

The boy hesitated at first, but gradually growing bolder, allowed the snake to wind round his arm. When close by the fire, he held it out to l'Encuerado, who shrank back ; for he fully believed all reptiles to be venomous. Lucien in vain urged him to handle it.

"I shan't mind touching it," he said, "when you have told me the words you say to make yourself invulnerable."

"I am no more invulnerable than you are," replied Lucien, smiling. "This snake is quite harmless, and I should never touch one without taking papa's advice, even if it exactly resembled this."

"And you didn't repeat any words ?"

"No ; papa had it in his hands, and it coiled round his arm."

"I understand, then," murmured the Indian ; "it is the serpent that is charmed."

Gringalet, quite as mistrustful as l'Encuerado, ran off directly he saw the reptile move. I told Lucien to let the snake go, and the Indian unsheathed his cutlass; but I would not allow him to injure the poor creature.

Our new cook was perfect master of his art. He supplied us with some excellent maize broth, roasted pigeons, and then a rice-cake—certainly rather shapeless, but of a delicious flavor. The cherries completed this regal bill of fare, and the "calumet of peace" was associated with a cup of coffee. At nightfall, Sumichrast, avoiding Lucien's questions, went slyly to rest, an example I was not slow in following—the weight of the basket having fatigued me more than my pride allowed me to confess.

The next day the rising sun found us already on the road. L'Encuerado's wound was less painful, and did not prevent his using his gun. Had it not been for my express prohibition, he would have resumed his burden. When we reached the summit of the hill, he led us among the trees, and, commencing a descent, our little party did not stop till we had reached the bottom of a dark and damp glen, close to a greenish pool. After utilizing our halt by filling our gourds and killing an armadillo, we hurried to get away from a spot where the air seemed poisoned with pestilential miasma. Having again ascended the slope, I advanced through a grove of firs, encouraging my friend with the load, who was archly challenged to a race by Lucien.

"That's not at all generous," said I to him; "if Sumichrast did not carry the basket sometimes, what would become of us?"

"I'm only sorry that I am not strong enough to help you," replied the boy. "I only tease M. Sumichrast because I know it amuses him, and makes him forget his burden, when he walks more easily."

"You never were more correct!" responded my friend.

"I certainly fancied you were indulging your own humor without thinking about me."

A fresh ascent quite exhausted us, and Sumichrast vowed that he must relinquish the basket until the next day. I then took it; but in a very little time I was compelled to take the same resolution as my friend, so we settled down to bivouac.

While my companions were engaged in the cooking, I walked a little way on the plateau. I had not gone above two or three hundred yards before I called to the others to join me; for the *Terre-Chaude* was stretched out at my feet.

Departing day at last cast its mysterious veil over the tracts we were about to traverse. Just before it became quite dark, a snow-clad corner of the volcano of Orizava was seen in the distance. I lifted up Lucien, and, kissing him, pointed it out, thinking on the dear ones who were behind the mountain, counting the days till we returned. Gringalet barked, as if claiming a caress for himself, and, guided by the dog, we reached our bivouac to enjoy a well-deserved repose.

"The *Terra-Chaude* was stretched out at my feet."

CHAPTER XXV.

A GROUND-SQUIRREL.—A MOUSE'S NEST.—HUMMING-BIRDS
AND THEIR YOUNG ONES.—THE LOCUST-TREE.—MEXICAN
WOLVES AND THEIR RETREAT.

I WAS suddenly awakened by the report of a gun just
as the day was breaking. L'Encuerado showed me an
enormous squirrel, with a gray back and white belly—a species which never climbs, and is, for this reason, called by
Indians *amotli* (ground-squirrel). This animal, which lives
in a burrow, has all the grace and vivacity of its kind, but
it can never be domesticated. It generally goes about in
numerous bands, and, when near cultivation, will commit in
a single night great destruction; the farmers, consequently,
wage against it a war of extermination.

Just as we were setting out, l'Encuerado, whose arm was

visibly healing up, again took charge of the basket. I allowed him to carry it, on the condition he should tell me as soon as he felt tired. I went in front, leading Lucien by the hand, and the rocky slope was descended without accident. The oaks were small and scattered, and left us an easy passage over ground covered with dry leaves, which rustled under our feet.

"We might almost fancy we were in Europe," said Sumichrast, suddenly halting.

"Yes," I replied; "it seems as if the yellow leaves had already felt the autumnal winds."

"There's a dead tree," said my friend; "I feel sure, if we examine its bark, we shall find some insects of our own country."

My friend's hopes were not realized, and the only result of his search was to disturb the rest of two mice with slender muzzles. One of them escaped, while the other tried its best to protect a litter of five little ones, buried in some fine vegetable débris. Lucien examined the young ones with interest, and after replacing the bark, as far as possible, in its original position, rejoined us outside the wood. A descent so rapid that we could scarcely keep our balance brought us among a quantity of bushes covered with double thorns, which Lucien very justly compared to bulls' horns in miniature. At last the ground became more level, and, directing our course to the right, we turned into a plain, surrounded by woods.

"Both trees and plants seem larger here than on the mountains," said Lucien.

"You are quite right," answered Sumichrast; "the vegetation in the *Terre-Chaude* is more vigorous than that of the *Terre-Tempérée*. As you advance farther into it, you will be able to judge."

"Did you see that great insect that flew buzzing past us?"

" Yes, Master Sunbeam ; but it was a humming-bird, not an insect."

" A humming-bird !" cried the boy, at once unfolding his butterfly-net.

And off he went in pursuit of the fugitive. The agile bird made a thousand turns, and always kept out of reach of the young sportsman, who at last stopped suddenly in front of a shrub. When I joined him, he was contemplating three little nests, fixed in forked branches, and covered outside with green and yellow lichens.

" There's the bird !" said Lucien, in a low voice.

I lifted up the little naturalist ; two hen-birds flew off, and at the bottom of each nest he could see a couple of eggs of a greenish color, and about the size of a pea.

" If you hold me a little closer, papa, I can take the eggs."

" What would be the good, my boy ? Look at them as long as you like, but don't deprive the little birds of what is most dear to them."

" There's one bird which has not moved," observed Lucien.

" Then, no doubt, its little ones are hatched."

" The whole of its body seems to glitter ; it looks as if it was blue, green, and gold color. It sees me, and is moving. Now it is perched upon the tree ! Only look, papa ! there are two young ones in the bottom of the nest."

I put Lucien down on the ground, so that he might go to l'Encuerado, who was calling him. The Indian had found a humming-bird's nest fixed on a branch, which he had cut off and was bringing us. The elegant little structure was a perfect marvel of architectural skill, lined inside with the silky down of some plant. Two young birds, still unfledged, and scarcely as big as nuts, opened their beaks as if to ask for food. I directed l'Encuerado to replace the branch on the tree from whence he had cut it, and to fasten it so that

it could not fall down. I followed him, to make sure he
did it rightly. As soon as we came near the shrub, the
mother fluttered all round the Indian, and at last settled
down, panting, on her young brood.

"You're a brave bird!" cried the Indian, "and I ask
your pardon for having carried away your house. Don't
be afraid, my name is l'Encuerado, and you may safely trust
in me. Don't tremble! I would sooner be hurt myself
than cause you the least harm. There, now you are all
firmly fixed again, and you may live in peace. Your little
ones can tell you that I have not teased them; I only wanted to show them to Chanito. Good-bye, Señor *Huitzitzi-
lin!* you are a brave bird, and it's I, l'Encuerado, who tells
you so!"

And the Indian went away, saluting the valiant mother
with so many waves of his hat that the poor bird must
have thought her last hour had come.

"What do these beautiful little birds feed upon, M. Sumichrast?"

"On the juices of flowers and small insects. Look!
there is one hovering, and its wings are moving too fast
for us to see them. Don't stir! I see a branch so covered
with blue flowers that it can hardly fail to attract the bird.
Now it is settled above one of the corollas, and plunges its
head into it without ceasing to beat with its wings. Its
cloven tongue soon sucks out the honey concealed in the
flower, and its little ones will greet it when it gets back
with open beaks to receive their share of the spoil."

"They are funny birds, those," said l'Encuerado to Lucien. "In three months—that is, in October—they will go
to sleep, and will not wake up till April."

"Is that true, father?"

"I rather fancy that they migrate."

"Now don't teach Chanito wrongly," said l'Encuerado,

"And the Indian went away, saluting."

repeating a common phrase of mine; "the *huitzitzilins* do not migrate; they go to sleep."

"This fact has been so often related to me by Indians living in the woods," said my friend, "that I feel almost disposed to believe it."

"Don't they say the same of the bats and swallows? and yet we know they change their habitat."

"Yes; but with regard to humming-birds, they assert that they have seen them asleep. At all events, it is certain that they disappear in the winter."

The clucking of a bird of the gallinaceous order, called the hocco—*Crax alector*—interrupted our discussion, and my two companions carefully proceeded towards a dark-foliaged tree, a little outside the edge of the forest. The clucking suddenly ceased; we heard the report of a gun, and I saw three of them fly away into the forest. L'Encuerado was climbing a tree when I came up, for the bird he had shot had lodged among the branches.

"Do you see the long pods which hang on that tree?" cried Lucien.

"It is a locust-tree covered with fruit," said my friend; "it is a relation of the bean and the pea."

"Are the pods eatable?" asked the child, as one fell at his feet.

"You may taste the dark pulp which surrounds the seeds—it is slightly sweet; but don't eat too much, for it is used in Europe as a medicine."

L'Encuerado dropped at our feet the great bird which Sumichrast had killed. It was larger in size than a fowl, with a crest upon its head. Its cry—a sort of clucking of which its Spanish name gives an idea—tells the traveller its whereabout, although it is ready enough in making its escape.

L'Encuerado returned to the bivouac, and Sumichrast

led us along the edge of a ravine, obstructed by bushes and shaded by large trees.

We had been quietly on the watch for a minute or two, when three young wolves, of the species called by the Indians *coyotes*, came running by, one after the other. They were soon followed by a fourth, and then the mother herself appeared. She glared at us with her fiery eyes, and then raised a dull, yelping noise, which brought her young ones to her.

"Upon my word!" exclaimed Sumichrast, "does this wretch intend to give us a present to her children?"

I stuck my *machete* into the ground, so as to have it at hand; and the brute lay down on the ground, as if ready to spring.

"Now then, my fine lady, come and meddle with us if you dare!" muttered my friend, imitating l'Encuerado's tone.

The *coyote* uttered a shrill cry, and almost immediately a sixth came and stood by her.

"Don't fire till I tell you," said I to Lucien, who seemed as bold as possible.

"You take the dog-wolf," cried Sumichrast to me; "but we won't provoke the contest."

Seeing us evince no fear, the brutes suddenly made off. Sumichrast descended to the bottom of the ravine, and then called me. I noticed among the high grass the entrance of a burrow strewed with whitened bones. Two yards farther on I saw the head of one of the animals, with eyes glittering like a cat's, glaring out of the entrance of another burrow. I threw a stone at the beast, which, far from showing any fear, curled up its lips and showed us a very perfect set of teeth.

As it was by no means our intention to make war upon wolves, I returned to the plain with Lucien, who had shown

"I threw a stone at the beast."

no ordinary coolness. I was glad of it, for my great wish was to inure him to danger, and I feared the Indian's misadventure with the otter might have had a bad influence.

"Didn't those wolves frighten you?" asked my friend of the boy.

"A little—especially their eyes, which seemed to dart fire."

"And what should you have done if they had sprung at us?"

"I should have aimed at them as straight as I could; but wolves are much braver than I thought."

"They were anxious to protect their young ones, and their den being so near made them all the bolder."

When l'Encuerado heard that we had *coyotes* near us, he made up a second fire for the night. The eastern sky was beginning to grow pale, and as we were supping we saw the paroquets in couples flying over our heads towards the forest. Humming-birds were flitting in every direction, and flocks of other passerines flew from one bush to another. When they offered to perch near our bivouac, l'Encuerado requested them in polite terms to settle a little farther away, and, on their refusal, urged his request by throwing a stone at them, which but rarely failed in its purpose. The sun set, and the mountains stood out in black relief against the pink sky.

The moon now rose, and I can hardly describe the marvellous effects of light produced by its rays on the sierras. L'Encuerado had made a second fire, and had taken Gringalet aside to insist upon his not roaming beyond the ground illuminated by its flame, telling him that the *coyotes*, which would doubtless pass the night in prowling round our bivouac, were very fond of dogs' flesh. As if to add weight to this prudent advice, a prolonged howling was now heard, which the dog felt obliged to respond to in his most doleful notes.

17

"Oh !" cried Sumichrast, " are those beasts going to join in the concert made by the grasshoppers and mosquitoes ?"

Lucien, who had gone to sleep, started up.

" Where's my parrot ?" he cried.

" Sleep quietly, Chanito !" replied the Indian. " It is roasted, and we shall eat it to-morrow morning at breakfast."

This reply and Lucien's disappointed face much amused us. L'Encuerado's fault was too much zeal: not knowing that Sumichrast was going to skin the bird, he had sacrificed it. In order to repair his error, he promised Lucien hundreds of parrots of every color; so he went to sleep and dreamed of forests full of birds of the most brilliant plumage.

CHAPTER XXVI.

GRINGALET'S barking, the yelping of the coyotes, the
heat, the song of the grasshoppers, and the sting of
the mosquitoes, all combined to disturb our rest. About
five o'clock the sun rose radiant, and was greeted by the
cardinals, trogons, and parrots. Lucien was aroused by all
these fresh sounds, and his eyes rested for some time on the
wall·of verdure which seemed to bar the entrance of the
forest. A cloud of variegated butterflies drew his attention
for an instant; but he was soon absorbed in contemplating
the humming-birds with their emerald, purple, and azure
plumage.

L'Encuerado, whose arm was now completely healed, had again taken possession of the load, and Sumichrast commenced cutting the creepers in order to open a path. I relieved him every now and then in this hard work, and Lucien availed himself of the moments when we stopped for breath to have a cut at the great vegetable screen which nature places at the entrance of virgin forests, as if to show that there is within it an unknown world to conquer. Unfortunately, the small height of the boy rendered his work useless; but he at least evinced a desire to take his part of the labor. At last the thick wall of vegetable growth was passed, and we found ourselves in a semi-obscurity, caused by the shade of gigantic trees.

" Are we now in a virgin forest?" asked Lucien.

" No, for we are only just entering it," I replied.

" But the ground is so bare; there are no more creepers, and the trees look as if they were arranged in lines."

" What did you expect to meet with?"

" Plants all entangled together, birds, monkeys, and tigers."

" Your ideal menagerie will, perhaps, make its appearance subsequently. As for the entangled plants, if the whole forest was full of them, it would be absolutely impenetrable. The soil is bare because the trees are so bushy that no rays of the sun can penetrate, and many plants wither and die in the shade; but whenever we come upon a glade, you will find the earth covered with grass and shrubs."

" Then the forests of the *Terre-Tempérée* are more beautiful than those of the *Terre-Chaude?*"

" You judge too hastily," replied Sumichrast; " wait till our path leads along the edge of some stream."

" All right," muttered the boy, shaking his head and turning towards his friend; " the woods we have gone through are much more pleasant. It is so silent, and the boughs are so high that we might fancy we were in a church."

The boy's remark was far from incorrect. The dark arches of the intersecting branches, the black soil formed by the accumulated vegetable *débris* of perhaps five or six thousand years, the dim obscurity scarcely penetrated by the sunlight making its way through the dark foliage—all combined to imbue the mind with a kind of vague melancholy. The limited prospect and the profound silence (for birds rarely venture into this forest-ocean) also tend to fill the soul with gloomy thoughts, and prove that health of mind as well as of body depends upon light.

A furnace-like heat compelled us to keep silence, and tree succeeded tree with sad monotony. The moist soil gave way under our feet, and retained the traces of our footsteps. At a giddy height above our heads the dark foliage of the spreading branches entirely obscured the sky. Every now and then I gave a few words of encouragement to Lucien, who was walking behind me quite overcome with the heat; especially, I recommended him not to drink, in the first place, because the water must be economized, and next because it would only stimulate his thirst.

" Then we shall never drink any more," said the boy.

" Oh yes! Chanito," rejoined the Indian, " when we form our bivouac, I shall make plenty of coffee, and if you sip it, in a quarter of an hour your thirst will be quenched."

" Then I hope we shall soon reach our bivouac," said Lucien, mournfully.

If I had consulted my own feelings, I should now have given the word to halt; but reason and experience enabled me to resist the desire. It would really be better for Lucien to suffer for a short time than for us to lose several hours, especially if we failed to find the stream we were seeking. It was necessary to cross without delay the inhospitable forest which we had entered, instead of waiting until hunger and thirst imperiously cried—Onward! when perhaps we might be too exhausted to move.

The ground became undulating, and I hastened forward, thinking to meet with what we wished for, when a glade, which enabled us to catch a glimpse of the sun, enlivened us a little. Here there was some grass, and a few shrubs and creepers. I called Lucien to show him what to us was a new plant, the *Bromelia pinguin* of botanists.

Its ripe pink fruit was symmetrically placed in a circle of green leaves. Lucien, kneeling down, tried to pluck them.

"Pull one from the middle, Chanito," cried l'Encuerado; "that's the only way to get them."

The boy seized the centre berry, which came out, and, like the stones of an arch when the key-stone is taken out, all the cones fell. Under their thick husk there was a white, acid, melting pulp, well adapted to quench the thirst; but I recommended Lucien not to eat more than two or three of them. A second clump, a little farther on, enabled us to gather a good stock of them. Providence could not have placed in our path a more valuable plant, for the hundreds of cones which we had gathered would enable us to brave the necessities of thirst for two or three days. We now walked on at a quicker pace, and Lucien, a little refreshed, kept his place courageously by my side.

"Well!" said I, "you must confess now that virgin forests may have something good in them. How do you like the *timbirichis?*"

"They are excellent; what family do they belong to?"

"They are akin to the pine-apples, and therefore belong to the *bromelaceæ.*"

"But the pine-apple is a large fruit, which grows simply on its stalk."

" Yes, so it appears; but in reality it is formed by an assemblage of berries all joined together. The strawberry, which belongs to the rose family, is similarly formed, and few people would believe, when they swallow a single strawberry, that they have eaten thirty or forty fruits."

For an hour we scarcely exchanged a word, but walked silently on, soaked with perspiration, and scarcely able to breathe the heated air.

" I think there is a glade," murmured Lucien, pointing to the left.

" So there is; forward! forward!"

Five minutes after we reached an open spot bathed in sunshine amidst a thicket of tree-ferns and high grass. The trees, placed more widely apart, were covered with gigantic creepers drooping to the ground. Here we again heard the note of the hocco.

While I was clearing the ground, Sumichrast and l'Encuerado took up a position amidst the bushes. I gave some water to Gringalet, whose tongue hung out, for he had possibly suffered most, as he would not eat the fruit which afforded us relief.

Two shots were fired shortly afterwards; but the sportsmen soon returned with such a disappointed air that I felt sure they had been unsuccessful.

I made a joke of the matter, and pretended that the dry maize-cakes were better than the fattest turkey. I spoke with such apparent seriousness that my companions began to get animated, and a sharp controversy gave a zest to our frugal meal. I asserted, too, that the tepid water in our gourds surpassed in flavor the product of the coolest spring, and that the acid *timbirichi* was the best of fruits. Gradually, however, I gave way, and at bed-time pretended to be quite converted. I had amused our party, and that was all I wanted.

The night passed without any incident save the continued attacks of mosquitoes, and the unfortunate Gringalet pressing close to us to avoid the cruel stings of the blood-thirsty insects which much annoyed him.

At sunrise I gave the word to start, and all day long we met with no glade to give variety to our path. I could not help admiring Lucien, who, although suffering from heat, fatigue, and thirst, uttered not one complaint, but only looked at me with a sad face. Two or three times I tried to enliven him; the poor little fellow then shook his troublesome burden and smiled back so painfully that I was quite affected. L'Encuerado, overwhelmed by his basket, puffed noisily, and declared every now and then that he could sniff the river and the smell of the crocodiles. This nonsense enlivened our march a little; but soon, dull and silent, we resumed our sluggish pace. At last fatigue compelled us to halt, when Lucien and l'Encuerado went off to sleep, quite forgetting their suppers. I proposed to Sumichrast to regain as soon as we could the mountain path.

" Let us keep on one day more," said my friend; " we have still four bottles of water left, and even if we give Lucien and Gringalet the largest share, it will serve us for another twenty-four hours."

The next day, just as we were starting, l'Encuerado killed a hocco. The fire was soon lighted, and the game washed down with a mouthful of brandy, which somewhat restored our energy. About midday, when the heat was most intense, the aspect of the ground altered, the trees became wider apart, and our strength seemed to redouble.

" Now, Master Sunbeam !" cried Sumichrast, " lengthen your strides a little, if you please; don't you hear the murmur of a stream ?"

" Three days you've been telling me this story, so that now both Gringalet and I are skeptical."

"How will you behave when you cross the savannahs?"

"Just as at present. I would walk without drinking, so as not to excite my thirst," replied the child archly, who had failed to be convinced by our reasoning.

"Oh, come! I thought you were too ill for irony. Never mind, I can bear witness that you have behaved like a man. What do your legs say?"

"That they would be very willing to rest."

"You would like to find yourself at Orizava?"

"I should rather see a stream, an alligator, and a puma."

"You are most unreasonable. I should be contented with the stream."

"Don't you find that the mosquitoes in the *Terre-Chaude* bite much sharper than those in the *Terre-Tempérée?*" asked the boy, addressing l'Encuerado.

"No, Chanito; they are all alike, for they belong to the same family, as your papa says."

"Then they must be more numerous here, for every instant one receives a fresh pinch."

"You must not complain yet, Chanito; you'll see what it will be when we reach the stream."

"How will it be then?"

"We shall not be able to open our mouths without swallowing some of these blood-suckers. But, Chanito, do you know what these mosquitoes are?"

"Yes, papa told me yesterday that they were *diptera*, and relations of the gadflys. Their proboscis is a kind of sheath inclosing six lancets, by the help of which they pierce our skin and suck our blood."

"But where do these hungry wretches come from?"

"From the water, where the insect lays its eggs. You know those little worms which are constantly moving up and down in pools; they are the larvæ of the mosquito."

"The mosquito, that terrible scourge of the *Terre-Tem-*

pirée and the *Terre-Chaude*, renders these regions inaccessible to the inhabitants of the **Terre-Froide**. They can not get accustomed to their bites, which cover their bodies with large red pustules, causing fever and want of sleep, and giving the victims the appearance of having just recovered from small-pox."

Again we walked on without talking, for the heat dried up our throats. Suddenly some singular cries reached our ears.

"The clucking of an oscillated turkey!" cried Sumichrast.

L'Encuerado laid down his burden, and my two companions started off in search of the birds. They joined us again in about a quarter of an hour, each carrying a fowl with metallic-colored plumage dotted over with spots, almost as large as a common turkey. It belongs to the gallinaceous order, and is only found amidst the forests of the New World, particularly in Honduras.

"Well!" cried Sumichrast, "we have plenty to eat now; but this is a bird which is found at a long distance from streams, and warns us to economize the contents of our gourds."

Five hundred paces farther on we saw some stones covered with moss, and an enormous upright rock like a tower. We saluted the colossus without stopping to examine it, and lengthened our strides, although the ups and downs in our path gradually became more numerous. Gringalet every instant raised his nose to sniff the air, and the hope of at last emerging from the forest drew us forward with increased ardor, impelled, as we were, by the desire of at last finding the longed-for stream. Lucien actually mustered up a run, while his cheeks flushed and his eyes glistened with anticipation.

"Here are grass and flowers! Forward! forward!" cried Sumichrast.

" Forward !" Lucien re-echoed.

The great trees, which were now farther apart, allowed the rays of the sun to penetrate the foliage, and the creepers drooped down in flowery festoons. The convolvuluses, the ferns, and the parasites, all entangled together, compelled us to use our knives. A somewhat steep ascent, anxiously scaled, led us up to a plateau. In front of us stretched a prairie dotted over with thickets, and bordered with forests of palm-trees, laurels, magnolias, and mahogany-trees, from which sounded the songs of various birds, mingled with the harsh cry of parrots.

Panting, weary, and perfectly soaked with perspiration, I proposed to bivouac on the plateau. Indeed, the sun was setting, and we had only just time to collect the wood we required for the fire. This task finished, I went and sat down with Lucien on the highest point we could find. The mountains of the *Terre-Tempérée* showed against the horizon, although we were already at least fifteen leagues from them. We long looked down on the tree-tops of the forest we had just crossed, and the uniformity of the dark-green foliage had a most gloomy aspect ; and, while close round us there were a number of birds fluttering about the trees, none of the feathered tribe ventured into the solitudes we had so lately traversed.

" I can not catch a sight of either rivulet or stream," said Lucien.

" Courage !" replied Sumichrast, who had seated himself by us. " The birds which are flying round us can not live without drinking, and their large number shows that there is plenty of water near."

"Hiou ! hiou ! Chanito."

"Obé ! obé !" replied Lucien, darting to the place whence he heard the familiar cry.

The two friends went down the hill together, l'Encuerado carrying his enormous gourd.

" Can he have discovered water?" said I to my companion, and I approached the fire where the game was roasting under the inspection of Gringalet. Sumichrast remained to look after the cooking of the birds, and I overtook Lucien and the Indian just at the moment when they were bending over a plant with scarlet-red leaves, which grew encircling the stem of a magnolia. About a glassful of limpid fluid flowed from it into the calabash.

" Can we get water from this shrub by merely pressing it?" asked Lucien, with surprise.

" All that is needed is to bend it," I replied. " It treasures up the precious dew between its leaves, and l'Encuerado and I should have died of thirst in one of our expeditions if it had not been for this plant."

" Why doesn't it grow in every forest?" asked Lucien.

" Certainly, if it grew everywhere, one of the greatest obstacles to travelling in the wilderness would be removed."

" And what's the name of this plant?"

" The Creoles call it the ' Easter flower;' it is one of the *bromelaceæ*."

" Does it produce any fruit good to eat?"

" No, but in case of extreme necessity its large red leaves would appease hunger."

We reascended the hill, when an uproar proceeding from the edge of the forest reached our ears. L'Encuerado smiled, showing us the double range of his white teeth.

" See down there," he said to Lucien, pointing to a corner of the wood, away from which all the birds seemed to be flying.

There was a whole tribe of monkeys frolicking about among the creepers.

" Let us go and look at them more closely," said Lucien.

" It is too late now, Chanito; they have just been drink-

"There was a whole tribe of monkeys frolicking about."

ing, and will soon go to sleep; but we shall eat some of them to-morrow—and now our supper is waiting for us."

We finished our meal, and when the sun was setting we saw the paroquets fly by in couples, and humming-birds flitting about among the bushes; suddenly a formidable roaring made us all tremble.

"Oh! what is that dreadful noise?" cried Lucien.

"A tiger!" said l'Encuerado, whose eyes glittered with excitement.

"Not a tiger, but a jaguar (*Leopardus onca*)," said I; "the former animal is found only in the Old World."

The king of the American forests again saluted the setting sun. Gringalet, with his tail between his legs, came crouching down close to us; a second fire was lighted, and we lay down to sleep with the indifference which familiarity gives even in regard to the very greatest dangers.

CHAPTER XXVII.

L'ENCUERADO AND THE PARROTS. — GRINGALET MEETS A
FRIEND.—THE COUGAR, OR AMERICAN LION.—A STREAM.
—OUR "PALM-TREE VILLA."—TURTLES' EGGS.—THE TAN-
TALUS.—HERONS AND FLAMINGOES.

THE parrots that we heard chattering were quite sufficient to wake us up in the morning. The sun rose
red and angry; a perfect concert soon greeted its appearance. The hoccos set up their sonorous clucking, and birds
of every kind came fluttering round us. Lucien, now reconciled to the virgin forests, was never tired of admiring the
varieties of trees, shrubs, or bushes, and the infinite number
of the winged inhabitants which enliven them. We slowly
descended into the plain; even now the heat was too much
for us, and long marches would soon be impossible. A

flock of cardinals, with crested heads, flew around us and settled on a magnolia, which then looked as if it was covered with purple flowers. Farther on, some paroquets, no bigger than sparrows, greeted us with their varied cries. L'Encuerado, after tossing his head several times, and shrugging his shoulders, at last stopped, and could not refrain from answering them.

"Come and carry it yourselves!" he cried; "come and carry it yourselves, and prove that you are stronger than a man!"

"What are you asking the birds to do?" demanded Lucien.

"They are making fun of my load, Chanito; a set of lazy fellows, who all of them together would not be able to move it!"

Sumichrast made his way into the forest, cutting away the creepers with his *machete* in order to clear a passage. In less than an hour we had crossed five or six glades. Suddenly I noticed that Gringalet had disappeared. I called him, and a distant barking answered me.

"Can he have met with a stream?" said Sumichrast.

I advanced in the direction in which I had heard the voice of our four-footed companion, and suddenly came upon him baying furiously at a young cougar, which Sumichrast ran towards, but the animal fled into the wood.

"Where did you turn out this fellow, Gringalet?" asked l'Encuerado, quite seriously. "Don't trust too much to his friendship, for it might be the worse for you; lions seldom fondle any thing without hurting it."

"Was it a lion?" asked Lucien.

"Yes," I answered; "but an American lion, or cougar, known by *savants* as the *Felis puma.*"

"How I should like to have seen it! Had it a mane?"

"No; the puma is without one."

We were crossing another glade, when Gringalet suddenly rushed between our legs. On looking back, I saw the puma slyly following us.

"Well, upon my word!" said Sumichrast; "does this fellow want to prove that a cougar will attack a man?"

L'Encuerado, who had put down his load, was already aiming at the animal.

"Don't shoot!" I cried, authoritatively.

The puma did not advance any farther, but glared at us with its yellow eyes, its tail lashing its sides with a measured movement, while it displayed a formidable row of tusks. Suddenly it stretched itself along the ground, as if about to play. Lucien was now able to examine leisurely the beautiful tawny color of its coat. It surveyed us with such a quiet, gentle aspect, that it seemed as if it belonged to our party, even pushing its confidence so far as to begin its toilet by first licking its paws, and then rubbing them over its muzzle.

I gave the word for continuing our journey. L'Encuerado obeyed very reluctantly. After this rencontre I placed Lucien, who congratulated himself upon having had such a near view of the beautiful animal, in the middle of the party.

"If we don't eat the lion, it will eat us," said the Indian. "If we had only wounded it, it would have gone and told all its companions that it was any thing but prudent to go too close to our fire."

"Well, if it comes near us again, I give you leave to shoot it."

"You do? it's a bargain!" cried L'Encuerado. "Stop a minute, Tata Sumichrast; cock your gun, Chanito; you shall have the first shot."

We stood together in a group, and I looked in vain for the cougar.

"I looked in vain for the cougar."

"The rascal has got in front of us," added the Indian. "We'll astonish him in a moment. Come this way, Chanito, but don't run or turn round. Do you see that tree that stands in front of us?. Not so far that way—that one we were just going to pass under. Look at the wonderful fruit it has on it!"

"It is the puma!" exclaimed the boy.

"That's pleasant!" muttered Sumichrast. "Then there are two pumas."

"No, no, Tata Sumichrast, it is the same one. Aim between its eyes, Chanito; fire!"

There were two reports almost at the same moment, and the animal tumbled down upon the ground without uttering a cry.

"Don't be too quick, Chanito," continued the Indian; "this is not a water-dog; always reload your gun, whether the enemy be dead or not, before you trust yourself within its reach."

Gringalet ventured to bark round the beast, and I kept in readiness to shoot, while my companions cautiously advanced. The cougar had been struck in the forehead, and no longer breathed. It was about three feet in length, and its hair, which was slightly waved on some parts of its body, showed it was a young one. The Indian raised the animal's enormous head.

"Come," he said, "you deserve to die like a warrior. You are the first of your race which ever ventured so close to my gun. Was it Chanito you wanted to devour?"

"I think it much more probable that it wanted Gringalet; what a pity it is that we can't tame these beautiful cats!"

"Cats!" repeated Lucien.

"Yes, to be sure; the great African lion itself is nothing but the largest and strongest of all the cat tribe. Didn't you know that?"

"I thought the lion was a beast by itself; but, at all events, it is the king of mammals?"

"It is rightly thought to be the strongest of all the carnivora: its head, which it carries upright, and its beautiful mane, give it a majestic appearance. With regard to its reputation for generosity, I scarcely know what it is founded on; I fancy that the famous lion of Androcles had just enjoyed a plentiful meal when it spared the life of its benefactor."

It was no use to think of skinning our victim, for the flies were already swarming on the dead body, although it was still warm. L'Encuerado wished to attribute to Lucien the honor of killing the puma; but the boy, although he had always longed to achieve such a feat, said at once that he had missed his aim.

I stopped in front of a tree (*hymenæa*) belonging to the leguminous family, the pods of which contain a sweet pulp, and from its trunk oozes out a resin, which is much sought after by the Indians, who use it as a cure for stomach-ache. A little farther on, a mango-tree tempted l'Encuerado, who, like all his countrymen, was fond of its fruit. I disliked the nauseous smell and taste of them, which reminds me of turpentine, although in some countries, where care is taken in their cultivation, they are said to be delicious.

Sumichrast, who was our guide, had to open a passage for us through a perfect net-work of purple-flowered creepers. I helped him in his work, and when we had overcome this obstacle, we found ourselves in a small plain, in the middle of which rose a clump of palm-trees. Gringalet ran off to the right, and soon returned with his muzzle all wet. Lucien, who was in front of us, first reached what was a wide, deep, and slowly-flowing stream. At this sight, l'Encuerado turned three somersets in succession, and struck up a chant; our manifestations of delight, if less noisy than his, were, at all events, no less sincere.

" L'Encnerado turned three somersets."

A gentle breeze was **blowing,** while the air was cool and soft ; so that, **forgetful of the past, and** sanguine for the future, **we built** our bivouac. **While at** work, our eyes were **attracted on** every side **by the insects** and birds, whose **splendid colors** literally **enamelled the** trees in which every **shade of green blended harmoniously.** It would be **difficult** to describe the wild grandeur of the scene around us. **We** might have fancied we were in one of those marvellous **gardens** which Arabian story-tellers delight in depicting. The **roaring** of some wild beast reminded us that our fire was nearly out. At last **I set** the example of going to rest. We intended to pass three or four days in this spot, as it **was so favorable to our** pursuits.

" Nobody can **accuse us of being too fond** of rest," said my **friend ; " this is** the 20th of April ; therefore we have now **been** travelling uninterruptedly forty days."

The next day at dawn I set off with Sumichrast on an **exploring expedition, leaving Lucien still** fast asleep. We **returned, about eleven o'clock, with a** dozen birds, among **which we had a** greenish-yellow woodpecker, with a bright red tuft on **its head ; also** a *Cuculus vetula,* a species of cuckoo, which feeds on lizards and young serpents.

During our absence, l'Encuerado had cut down three palm-trees and hollowed out the lower part of the trunks, in order to collect their sweet sap. He also wove a sort of **palisade** of creepers round several thick stakes, in which we could sleep without fear of surprise. In a hole near the **top of one** of the palm-trees, Lucien spied out a parrot's **nest, and had** taken possession of two young birds, red, green, and yellow **in** color, which seemed to adapt themselves **wonderfully to** the attentions lavished upon them by the boy.

" What are you going to do with these poor orphans ?" I asked.

"I am going to take them home to my brother and sister. L'Encuerado says that they would perch on the edge of his load."

"How shall you feed them?"

"With fruit, and sometimes with meat. M. Sumichrast said yesterday that they would eat any thing that was given to them. I have already named them 'Verdet' and 'Janet.'"

"They will be sure to get within reach of Gringalet; are you sure that he will leave them alone?"

"L'Encuerado has already given him a lecture about it."

"Still I am very much afraid that 'Verdet' and 'Janet' will come to an untimely end."

While we were resting, Lucien and his friend went off to examine a caoutchouc-tree. The boy came back much disappointed.

"Your India-rubber-tree isn't worth much," said he to Sumichrast, showing him a thick white liquid, which he had just collected.

"And pray why not?"

"Because India-rubber ought to be black and dry."

"It will acquire these qualities as it grows older. The India-rubber oozes from the tree in the form of a milky liquid, like that with which you are now smearing your fingers.

About three o'clock, when the sun was shining perpendicularly down upon us, I conducted my companions through the thickets, in order to explore the course of the river. Very soon we were obliged to cut our way with our *machetes*, and several reptiles made off before our approach. Gradually, as we advanced, the bank became covered with swamp ivy, bignonias, and cedar-trees, till we at last came out on a sandy shore, where five or six turtles were apparently asleep. In spite of all our exertions, the creatures reached the stream. L'Encuerado discovered two little heaps of sand, one of which was still unfinished, and contained twenty eggs about as big as **chestnuts,** and covered with **a whitish** skin. **A** little farther on, Lucien **caught a small red turtle, the size of a crown-piece.** On hearing from l'Encuerado that it **would** live several **days** without eating, he made **up his mind to take it home with** him, and gave **it** the **name of " Rougette."**

Gringalet began growling; **a deer had** just shown its graceful **form among** the **branches.** We all concealed ourselves as well as we **could, and when the** beautiful animal came down to the water Sumichrast shot it dead. I left l'Encuerado **to** help **the** sportsman **in** skinning our prize, **and went** on with Lucien. The stream gradually became wider, and we suddenly found ourselves fronting an immense **flooded plain, above** which flocks **of** wild ducks were **circling.**

I sat down on the ground in order to admire the lake **and its banks, edged with royal palm-trees, the foliage of which, though dark at** the base, **is a** beautiful green at the summit. The appearance of a water-eagle, with its grayish-white head, disturbed the aquatic fowls; as if by enchantment, some of them hid among the rushes, but the bird of prey passed over without taking any notice of such game, which it doubtless considered unworthy of itself. A tantalus settled down at about twenty paces from us, and plunged into the stream and remained motionless.

" Oh papa! what a curious bird! it looks as if it had a bald head."

" You are quite right; it is the bird that the Indians call *galambao.*"

" It's almost as tall as I am !"

" Don't you see that it is mounted upon long legs like stilts?" replied I, laughing. " It is a relation of the stork."

" This is the first bird of that kind we have met with."

" These long-legged birds, or waders as they are called, are scarcely ever found except in marshes, or on the banks of large rivers. They can always be recognized by their legs, which are of an enormous length, and devoid of feathers below the knee—a conformation which enables them to capture their prey in shallow water."

" Is this tantalus going to fish ?"

" I should imagine so, for birds of its order have no other means of obtaining food."

" One might almost fancy that it was asleep, with its great bill drooping down over its chest."

" Woe be to the fish that is of your opinion. There ! did you remark its sudden movement ? It plunges its head down into the water like a flash of lightning ; and now you can see it holds its prey in its beak. Now it is spreading its short black-edged wings in order to take flight, and divide among its young brood the products of its labors. Do you see that beautiful large bird with a tuft on its forehead ? That is the *Ardea agami*, a wader of the heron genus. But look, there is a flock of egretts (*Egretta alba*), clothed in their plumage as white as the ermine. They fly about in flocks, but separate for their fishing. These birds have rather a grave and sad air, and utter now and then a wild and plaintive cry."

We stopped to watch these waders gloomily standing in the water, until we heard l'Encuerado's " Hiou ! hiou !" informing us that our companions were approaching the bivouac. I took Lucien through the forest, replying to his numerous questions about the Grallatores, when we heard the chattering and clatter produced by a band of monkeys. About twenty wild turkeys, doubtless frightened by the noise, rushed between our legs. I let the poor fugitives go, for we had already more victuals than we could con-

sume. Lucien wondered at the number of animated beings which surrounded us, all the more surprising when
compared with the gloomy solitude we had just passed
through.

"In the *Terre-Chaude*," said I, "the water-side is always fertile, for the inhabitants both of the prairies and the
forests meet there."

"Why don't the Mexicans live in such a varied and
beautiful country as the *Terre-Chaude?*"

"Because a dragon guards the entrance to these countries
where nature lavishes its choicest gifts."

"A dragon?"

"Yes; the yellow fever. A terrible malady which cor-
rupts the blood, and selects the most robust frames for its
victims. The negro only can labor under this burning sun;
where even an Indian is overcome by the marsh fever."

"Are we liable to catch these fevers?"

"We should be in danger if we staid here till the rainy season."

"How that tree is loaded with fruit!' said Lucien, interrupting me.

"They are the Mexican medlars. To-morrow we will come and gather some of them. Five or six different species of their genus grow in these virgin forests. These beautiful trees produce various fruit, which is more or less in request. That which has attracted your attention—the *Sapota achras*—is especially well known. It is considered the most wholesome of all the tropical fruits; and from the trunk of the tree oozes out the white gum called *chicle*, which the inhabitants of the *Terre-Chaude* and the *Terre-Tempérée* are so fond of chewing."

The night overtook us just as we were discussing a haunch of venison roasted by l'Encuerado. A distant roaring told us that we were surrounded by wild beasts; but we had every confidence in our two fires and the screen which l'Encuerado had constructed; so we went quietly to sleep, although we were awakened several times by a renewal of their frightful uproar.

CHAPTER XXVIII.

WE were all stirring by sunrise. After throwing away
the remains of yesterday's meat, one night in this
climate being enough to putrefy it, l'Encuerado arranged
some fishing-lines along the stream, and our little party set
off, struggling against the heat, the mosquitoes, and the
horse-flies.

The Indian, following the flight of a purple-feathered
bird, led us close to an immense ant-hill. The little colony
seemed very busy; but I hurried Lucien away, fearing he
might be bitten by them.

"The ants are relations of the termites, are they not, M.
Sumichrast?"

"No, Master Sunbeam; the ants are relations of the bees, and, consequently, belong to the order of *Hymenoptera*. There are male, female, and neuter or working ants. The males and females are born with wings; but after the females have laid their eggs, they drop off these appendages, and assist the workers engaged in constructing the habitation, taking care of the young ones, and collecting the provisions required for the colony."

"Look here! one might fancy that the very grass was walking along."

"It is the ants which have stripped a tree of its leaves, in order to hoard them up in their store-houses—a useless precaution, for these insects become torpid during the winter months."

Lucien approached the moving column, which was divided into two lines going contrary ways; one of them advancing loaded with vegetable remains, and the other going back with empty mandibles. Nothing could be more interesting than to see thousands of these little creatures walking along in perfect order, eagerly carrying or dragging a load five or six times greater than themselves. Lucien followed them. The column entered the forest, and crawled up a tree, the lower limbs of which were already stripped of their leaves, causing it to look as if it were dead. The ants climbed nearer and nearer to the top, and the summit was visibly losing its foliage.

"How long will they take to carry away all the leaves off that great tree?" asked Lucien.

"They will have finished their work by this evening," I answered.

Gringalet, who with generous confidence was lying down a few steps behind us, and had not seen his enemies creeping slyly over him, got up and began howling.

"Will you never be prudent?" cried l'Encuerado.

"It stood up on its hind legs."

18*

"Any one must be as simple as a new-born infant to squat on an ant-hill. This is the second time you have done it."

Here the advice-giver was suddenly interrupted; he made a face, lifted up one of his legs, and walked away with long strides; then he sat down on the ground in order to catch the ants which had secreted themselves under his leathern shirt. I could not help laughing at him.

"Look here, Gringalet's skin is all over lumps!" said Lucien, stroking the animal.

"They are caused by parasitic insects," said Sumichrast, "called ticks. In future we must clear Gringalet every evening of these inconvenient visitors."

"But they won't come off."

"Pull them suddenly; their mouth is a kind of disk armed with two hooks, which, if once buried in an animal's skin, are difficult to extract."

"How hideous they look with their little legs placed close to their heads; here is one which is quite round, like a pea."

"It is because it has begun its meal."

"Does the tick only attack dogs?"

"The dog has his own peculiar species; other kinds lodge under birds' feathers, and some birds have two or three sorts of parasites. There is one belonging to the turkey, to the peacock, to the sparrow, to the vulture, to the magpie, etc. I don't think there is a bird or animal which does not, like Gringalet, possess its own peculiar parasite."

We had started off again, and another glade led us towards a field extensively ploughed up by moles.

Sumichrast led the way, and conducted us towards the lake I had mentioned to him the day before. L'Encuerado caught hold of my arm to call my attention to an enormous animal moving about in the midst of the foliage.

The animal came down slowly, and we could only see it indistinctly. At last it reached the lower branches. It was an ant-eater (*Myrmecophaga jubātā*). It remained motionless for an instant, moving its enormous muzzle, and darting out its flat tongue, which, being covered with a slimy coating, enabled it to catch up the ants with facility. At length the " bear," as it is called by the Indians, slid down the trunk, hanging on to it with its enormous claws, its prehensile tail strongly clinging to the sides of the tree.

At the sight of this shapeless beast, only fifty paces from us, Lucien rushed to me in terror. Sumichrast had just cocked his gun, and the noise made the ant-eater turn tail and prepare to run off, when it found itself face to face with l'Encuerado. It stood up on its hind legs, with its snout in the air, and then stretched out its arms ready to strike any one who was imprudent enough to come within reach of them. Nothing could be more strange than the appearance of the animal in this defensive position. Suddenly a shot was fired, and the ant-eater crossed its fore legs and fell down dead. L'Encuerado had once been nearly throttled by an ant-eater, and hence it would have been of no use for me to have attempted to prevent his shooting it.

" Do not come near, Tata Sumichrast," cried the Indian; " these beasts die very hard, and I still bear the marks of their claws on my skin. Let me just tickle him up with the point of my *machete*."

" You need not have been afraid," said Sumichrast; "its ugliness is no proof that it is vicious. It will not attack human beings, and only makes use of its strength to defend itself. It is of the order Edentala, and akin to the armadilloes."

" Does it eat any thing but ants?" asked Lucien.

" Ants and other insects. It climbs trees, and its bushy

"The bank to the right was covered with cranes, and that to the left with spoonbills."

tail distinguishes it from its brothers, **the** little ant-eater (*M. dydactyla*), which seldom visits **the ground, and** eats **more** insects than ants, and the tamandua (*Tamandua tetradactyla*)."

" But how many ants does it take to satisfy it ?"

"**Thousands;** and **it would die of** hunger if it had **to** take **them one by one;** but, thanks to the length **of its** tongue, **it is enabled to pick** up hundreds at a time."

" What a very peculiar meal !"

" Didn't you know that some Indians are ant-eaters? In the *Terre-Froide*, for instance, dishes are made of red ants' eggs, and there is one species which secretes a sweet liquid, of which children are very fond."

On the shore of the lake a fresh surprise awaited us. The bank to the right was covered with cranes, and that to **the** left with spoonbills, with delicate pink plumage, one of **which Lucien** shot.

" **Oh, what** beautiful birds !" said he.

"**What a** curious beak !" he further exclaimed, **examin**ing his victim, which Gringalet had just brought him.

" Yes, that is why this bird is called a spoonbill."

" Is it good to eat ?"

" It is rather tough ; but when any one is hungry—"

Sumichrast put his finger to his lips to enjoin silence; two smaller waders made their appearance and settled close to us.

" Now, Master Sunbeam," said Sumichrast, " fire at the bird to the left, while I aim at the one to the right. Those are egrets, and your sister will like some of their beautiful feathers **to** put in her hat. Now, then—one, two—fire !"

The two shots sounded almost at the same moment, and **the** birds fell over on to the ground. This double report **put to** flight **all** the spoonbills and **cranes,** and the lake was soon perfectly deserted.

We now took the road leading to the "Palm-tree Villa," and l'Encuerado went on before us to take up his fishing-lines.

The heat became perfectly overpowering, and Sumichrast fell asleep. About half-past three, I went off with Lucien towards that portion of the forest close by the stream, with the intention of collecting insects. First one object and then another tempted us into the interior, till the oblique rays of the sun admonished us to turn back. But imagine my dismay when, by neglect not to notch the tree-trunks as I passed them, I discovered I did not know in what direction our camp lay.

"Are we lost?" asked the boy, in an anxious tone.

"We have gone too far," said I to the lad; "and perhaps we shall not be able to get back to the 'Palm-tree Villa' this evening. I am going to fire off my gun to attract l'Encuerado's attention."

The report resounded. I listened with an anxiety which increased when I perceived that I had only three cartridges left, and Lucien only retained two charges.

"You had better shoot now," said I to the lad, "so that l'Encuerado may understand that we are signalling to him."

I again listened almost breathlessly, but in vain.

"We must rest here without our supper," said I, with a gayety I was far from feeling; "if we go on walking, we might lose ourselves."

After cutting some fagots and making a fire in a semi-circle round a tree I lay down, with my dear companion beside me; and, though I tried hard to conceal it, I could not but feel the gloomiest forebodings.

About midnight the breeze calmed down, and I closed my eyes that I might the better hear the slightest noise. Several times I thought I caught the faintest vibrations of a dull sound; but I ultimately attributed these noises to

"The head and bright eyes of a superb jaguar appeared about fifty
paces from us."

my over-excited imagination. Suddenly a terrible roar re-
echoed through the forest and woke up Lucien.

"What is the matter? Is it Chéma?"

"No, my boy; it is a jaguar."

"Will it come near us?"

"I hope not, but go **on with its nocturnal hunting; any-
how, behind the fire we have** nothing to fear."

I put **Lucien** back against the tree and cocked my gun,
when the head and bright eyes of a superb jaguar appeared
about fifty paces from us.

CHAPTER XXIX.

A NOCTURNAL VISITOR.—THE FALL OF A TREE.—A FEAR-
FUL NIGHT.—THE MONKEYS.—MASTER JOB.—ALL RIGHT
AT LAST.

AFTER looking at us for a moment, the animal crept
cunningly round us, alternately appearing and disappearing behind the trees. I hastened to make up the fire,
and then sat down near Lucien, who, gun in hand, was
bravely watching the enemy.

"Whatever you do, don't fire," I said.

"If I did, would the animal spring upon us?"

"He would far more likely retreat; but we shall want
our ammunition to-morrow."

For an hour the animal kept prowling round, every now
and then bounding off. At last it came and sat down
about twenty paces from the fire, then stretched itself on
the ground and rolled about as if in play; but if we made
the slightest movement it immediately got up, and, laying
back its ears, showed its formidable teeth. Suddenly a
noise as if of breaking branches was heard, followed by reports like those of guns; then came a horrible roar. Lucien, frightened, rushed into my arms.

"What!" said I to him; "don't you remember the noise
made by the fall of a tree?"

"Oh papa! I have heard nothing like it since the day of
the hurricane."

"We now came upon some creeping plants."

"That is quite true; but it is an incident to which you will soon be accustomed, for the first storm will probably overthrow many of these formidable giants. The tiger is frightened too, for he has made off, you see. Try and go to sleep, my dear boy, for to-morrow we may perhaps have to walk a long way."

I leaned my head against that of the child, who soon dropped asleep. The forest had resumed its majestic silence, which was only disturbed by the distant fall of another and another colossus.

My anxiety was extreme, and though I knew our friends would range every way in quest of us, we might so readily wander in opposite directions, as we had no ammunition to signal with should they come near.

Towards morning, exhausted with fatigue, I fell asleep, and dreamt, in my feverishness, that we were nearly at the end of our journey, and close to Orizava, in sight of home. A slender thread of light announcing the dawn of day awoke us, and we arose.

The clearness of day now broke upon us. For a quarter of an hour I kept my ear to the earth, listening in the hopes of hearing some signal.

Again and again I cocked my gun with the intention of firing, and as regularly I laid it down, when I reflected I might only be throwing away my ammunition.

At length I took observations of the bearings of the ground, and followed, as far as possible, our trail of the day before.

In this operation we fortunately came upon a pool of water, at which we quenched our thirst; but though our hunger was excessive, and game plentiful, we dared not discharge at it a single shot.

We hastened forward, and came upon some creeping plants, indications that we were approaching a glade.

Some birds were singing in the branches as we hurried on, but I had made up my mind to shoot the first one large enough to make a meal for my brave little companion and self.

In spite of my efforts, I could not succeed in hiding my grave presentiments; but my son's prattle, which was even gayer than usual, quite justified the name of "Sunbeam" given him by Sumichrast.

"Don't be so serious," said he to me, suddenly; "you need not be distressed about me. I have already guessed that we are lost; but I am with you, and I am not a bit afraid but that we shall soon find our way again."

The poor child had not the least suspicion of the danger. Every moment, too, tears came into my eyes, and I felt my courage getting weaker; I made a strong effort to dispel my thoughts, and vowed that I would strive on with faith and energy to the last hour.

"L'Encuerado will be sure to find us," said Lucien, with such an air of conviction that I could not help sharing his confidence.

"Yes," I answered; "Sumichrast and l'Encuerado will find us or die in the attempt. It can not be possible—" I had not courage to finish my sentence.

We commenced our march again with increased energy.

"Look out!" cried Lucien, suddenly; "it seems to me as if some one were moving the branches close by."

"It is a monkey," said I; and off I went in pursuit of the animal, which, leaping from branch to branch, seemed to set us at defiance. Suddenly it uttered a guttural cry, and was answered by twenty more. I hid behind a tree, and told Lucien to keep silent. Two or three times the active creatures moved farther away, but at last they came so close that I could fire safely. I never, I think, took more pains with my aim; the gun went off, and the band scat-

"The monkey . . . . slid down, and fell dead at our feet."

tered in every direction in a most precipitous flight. The monkey I had aimed at seemed only wounded, when, as I was going to fire a second time, it slid down and fell dead at our feet; its young one, which we had not at first perceived, was sitting upon a limb about ten feet from the ground, uttering low, and almost inaudible, plaintive cries.

In a quarter of an hour the animal was skinned and hung in front of a large fire. While I was superintending the cookery, the young one moaned incessantly, and my companion tried every persuasion to coax it down. Urged by Lucien, I ascended the tree, and tried to catch hold of the motherless little creature. No doubt it was paralyzed by fear, for it only showed its teeth, and allowed me to place it on my shoulder. It clung to my hair and wound its tail round my neck, as I descended, and I was in fear every moment of feeling one of my ears bitten. Nothing of the sort happened, for the poor brute's teeth chattered with fear; I placed it close to the fire, where it immediately resumed its lamentations. Then, by means of a flexible creeper, I secured it round the middle of the body and tied it to a bush.

When we had satisfied our appetite on the dark and tough monkey's flesh, I proposed to Lucien a fresh start.

"Shall we take our little captive with us?" he asked.

"Yes, certainly. It will be a resource for our supper, in case we do not fall in with our friends."

"Oh no," cried the boy; "let us at least put off killing it till to-morrow."

I hastened my pace, carrying on my shoulder our new companion, whom we at once dubbed "Master Job."

I examined more carefully than ever the ground and the bark of the trees, seeking for any thing which might direct our course. With a sickly feeling at my heart, I saw the

sun approach the horizon. The boy, quite broken down
with fatigue, looked at me, with his eyes full of tears. At
last I halted, and the dear little fellow stretched himself beside me and fell asleep.

While listening with ear and eye alike on the watch, I
fancied I heard the distant report of a gun. I jumped up
—was it the fall of a tree? or was it a signal from one of
our companions? I seized my gun, but I hesitated before
expending my last cartridge but one. At length I pressed
the trigger, and I listened anxiously as the sound of my
shot died away, alas! without echo. Lucien did not move.

"Jump up! jump up!" I cried; for a dull barking moved
the air. Suddenly I fired my last barrel; then, with eyes
shut, mouth open, and nostrils dilated, I listened intently,
almost forgetting to breathe. Minutes—they seemed ages
—elapsed without any thing more interrupting the silence.
Lucien looked at me with a scared face; I pressed my
weapon to me in despair at having expended my last
charge, when a gunshot was heard ringing out clear and
close.

"It is l'Encuerado!" cried Lucien.

"Yes, my boy," I said, almost frantic.

"Reply to your friend!" I exclaimed; "one of the bar-
rels of your gun is still loaded."

Lucien fired, and was answered almost immediately.

"Call out, so as to guide them," said I to the boy; "for
we have no more powder left."

"Ohé, ohé, ohé!" called Lucien.

"Iliou, hiou, hiou!" replied a still distant voice.

At the same moment Gringalet rushed to us as swiftly
as an arrow, and jumped upon his young master. After
having overwhelmed us with caresses, the dog made off
again, and ten minutes later the Indian made his appearance, and, running to the boy, clasped him in his arms, and

rolled with him on the ground in the excess of his wild emotion. I, too, heartily greeted Sumichrast, but was almost too affected to speak.

All my companion's efforts to discover our trail had been ineffectual; and Gringalet himself, when put to the task, had hunted in vain round the thickets. The fact was, they looked for us on the right, while we had gone to the left; for Sumichrast could not bring his mind to the idea that we had turned our backs to the stream.

L'Encuerado, after cooking, spread out on the spot his stock of provisions, to which every one did justice. Master Job was lodged safely under the shelter of a large branch, and deep sleep took possession of the whole party.

.CHAPTER XXX.

THE next day found us at work building our raft, and
l'Encuerado went off with Lucien in quest of some
flexible creepers, to be used for binding together the various
portions of it. When our companions joined us, Sumichrast was squaring out the last trunks. Lucien, laden
with creepers wound all round his body, carried besides, at
the end of his stick, the carcass of a horned snake—*Atropos
Mexicanus*—which has scales standing erect behind its
eyebrows, like little horns, which have obtained for it its
Indian name of *mazacoatl*. The reptile was nearly two feet
long, and of a grayish color, and gaped with formidable

jaws, more than usually dilated by the blows, I suppose, which l'Encuerado had given it.

Sumichrast, with infinite precaution, showed to his pupil the tubular fangs, by means of which serpents inoculate the terrible venom with which some of them have been endowed by nature.

"When the reptile bites," said my friend, "its two fangs press on a small bladder at their base, and the poison is thus injected into the wound."

Our naturalist rendered his explanation still clearer by pressing on one of the fangs, from the end of which oozed out an almost imperceptible drop of liquid.

"How is it that the serpent does not poison itself?" asked Lucien.

"In the first place, it does not chew its prey; and, secondly, its venom is only dangerous when it penetrates direct into the blood; and a man, if there is no scratch in his mouth or in the digestive tube, can swallow the poison with impunity, although a very small quantity introduced into his veins would cause immediate death."

After our meal, which consisted of turtle and some palm cabbage, which in flavor resembles an artichoke, I set the example of commencing work. In less than two hours the materials for the raft had been carried to the edge of the stream, and the frail bark which was to carry us down to the plains was constructed and afloat. A little before sunset, l'Encuerado, provided with a long pole for a boat-hook, pushed it out on the water to ascertain its powers of buoyancy; and the trial having been judged satisfactory, the raft was moored, and we all lay down in front of our "Villa" to enjoy a siesta.

At last, when every thing was arranged for the voyage, l'Encuerado, naked down to his waist, went behind as pilot. We gave a farewell salute to the "Villa," by a loud hurrah,

which seemed to frighten our menagerie, and with a last
look at the forest in which I had spent so many miserable
hours the mooring was cut, and the raft floated slowly and
silently down the current.

The raft soon drifted into a lagoon, covered with waders
and web-footed birds, which scarcely moved as we passed
them, and some time was lost before we could regain the
course of the stream. At length, guided by the palm-trees,
our skiff glided between two banks bordered by trees, the
high tops of which sheltered us with their shade.

Every thing was calm around us, and we remained silent,
awed by the majesty of nature. The stream flowed on in
one single sheet; creepers hanging from the tree-tops drooped down into the water; while kingfishers skimmed from
one shore to the other, and humming-birds, with their varied and shining plumage, fluttered about the flowers.
Every now and then a low-hanging tree impeded our passage, and we had to bend down on the raft to avoid being
struck by such obstacles. A mass of under-wood often hid
the interior of the woods from our view; but here and
there a break in the foliage allowed us a glimpse into its
depths. Ebony-trees, cotton-wood, pepper-trees, and palms,
were intermixed with tree-ferns, magnolias, white oaks, and
willows. Here and there, too, a sunbeam marked out a vast
circle of light upon the dark water, and myriads of aquatic
insects, gnats, dragon-flies, and butterflies sported in the air
or swam over the glittering surface.

After a time, the state of inaction to which we were
doomed, aggravated by the stings of mosquitoes and large
green-eyed flies, became a perfect torture.

" Those are horse-flies," said Sumichrast to Lucien ; " they
are very fond of blood, and are a misery to all kinds of
mammals from one end of America to the other."

" Their bite is more painful than that of the mosquitoes,"

"In front of us opened a glade, bordered by tall palm-trees."

answered the boy, from whose hand a drop of blood was trickling.

"That is because their proboscis is **armed with lancets** which are sharp enough to pierce the hides of bulls and horses."

During this voyage, **Lucien** amused himself by teaching the two parrots to repeat the names of his brother and sister; but **the** birds, **with** one foot held up and their heads bent down, although they paid great attention to the words repeated by the boy, as yet did not profit much by the lesson.

In the course **of our** voyage we were constantly losing trace of the **current in** some vast lagoon, and had often a long search till we found it. **In one** of these searches, I caught sight of such a picturesque bay that I proposed a **halt.** In front of us opened a tolerably deep glade, border-**ed by** tall palm-trees. L'Encuerado pushed the raft to land over the aquatic plants, and I jumped ashore to moor our craft.

A fallen tree tempted us into the forest, and on **the** damp ground Lucien caught sight of a magnificent rattle-snake, seemingly torpid. Sumichrast discharged his gun at the reptile, which reared itself up, and then fell down dead. A noise immediately resounded in several directions, and two or three snakes of the same family appear-ed, one of them followed by three young ones. The snake killed by my friend measured more than a yard in length. Its skin was speckled with black, brown, and gray spots, and its flat, triangular head had a very repulsive look. Lu-cien, with a blow from his *machete*, cut off the rattles which give to the reptile its name. These horny append-ages, of which there were seven, were given to l'Encuerado, who, like all his fellow-countrymen, believed them to be **endued with** miraculous **virtues—among** others, that of

tuning guitars and preventing the strings from breaking.

A shot fired by the Indian led us back to the bivouac;
our companion had just killed an ocelot, called by the Indians *ocotchotli*.

"You see this animal, Chanito?" cried l'Encuerado, who
was stroking its black and brown spotted fur; "well, its
tongue is poisonous. When it kills a stag or peccary, it
buries its prey under some leaves, then climbs the nearest
tree, and howls until it attracts all the carnivorous animals
near. When they have feasted, it comes down and devours
what is left."

"But why does it call the animals?" I asked.

"Didn't I tell you its tongue is poisonous? If it ate
first, the venom would be communicated to the food, and
the animals that feasted on the remains would die."

This fable narrated by Hernandez, and still told by the
Indians, must have originated in some as yet unobserved
habit of the *ocotchotli*.

After dinner, when Lucien was going towards his pets to give them some fruit, he saw **an unfortunate** tortoise between **Master** Job's paws. The monkey was turning it over, smelling at it, and then depositing it **on the ground,** persistently poking his fingers into its shell, a proceeding which by no means tended to enliven the melancholy animal. According to l'Encuerado's advice, Lucien **stuck up** some branches near the water, and put the tortoise into this miniature inclosure.

Night came on, and Lucien was still teaching the birds to **say** "Hortense" and "Emile." To our great astonishment, **Gringalet went** and stretched **himself** close to Master **Job, who, without** hesitation, commenced freeing him from the vermin **which** were lodged **among his** hair; then the **two** friends went to sleep side by side. About nine o'clock, **when I was** making up the fire before going to rest myself, **Janet** opened one **of** her eyes and chattered **a** short sentence; **but** l'Encuerado was much too fast asleep **to answer** her.

CHAPTER XXXI.

THE HUNTERS HUNTED. — ESCAPE FROM PECCARIES. — A
JAGUAR-HUNT. — AN IBIS. — THE CAYMANS. — THE WILD
BULLS.

AFTER we had finished our breakfast next morning,
we embarked our baggage and menagerie, and prepared to depart. I was just going on board the raft when
a noise attracted our attention to the forest, and two peccaries rushed past us, pursuing one another. L'Encuerado,
taken by surprise, shot at one of the animals without killing it, and we all gave chase. Hardly had we gone a hundred paces, when the Indian, who was in front of us, turned right about, shouting out, "To the raft! to the raft!"

A noise like the gallop of a troop of horses seemed to

"A band of peccaries was pursuing us."

shake the ground. A band of peccaries was pursuing us; and as my two companions halted to fire, I succeeded in gaining the raft, on which I placed Lucien. The peccaries, about a hundred in number, rushed on in a furious crowd. Sumichrast, who was closely pressed by them, leaped upon the frail bark, almost capsizing it, while l'Encuerado ran along the shore.

" Cut the mooring and push off !" he cried out to me as he disappeared in the jungle.

Some of the peccaries rushed after the Indian ; the others, chasing and hustling one another, deafened us with their gruntings. I cut the mooring-line ; and, seizing hold of the boat-hook, directed the raft towards the right bank, whence the uproar seemed to proceed.

" Hiou ! hiou ! Chanito !"

" Ohé ! ohé !" I answered.

I was just going to spring off, when the Indian came in sight, followed by Gringalet, and plunged into the water, holding his gun above his head.

L'Encuerado, instead of coming to us on the raft, turned towards a peccary which in its eagerness had fallen into the water and was endeavoring to reach the bank. He seized it by an ear and dragged it towards the raft, assist‹ ed by Gringalet, who swam, barking, behind, and biting it when opportunity offered.

" Fire your gun at this poor wretch's head," called l'En-cuerado to Sumichrast.

This was no sooner said than done, and l'Encuerado leap-ed on board, dragging his victim after him.

The peccaries collected on the shore continued to utter loud grunts of rage ; but we were beyond their reach, for the raft was soon carried past them by the current.

" Are peccaries carnivorous ?" asked Lucien.

" Yes, indeed, Chanito. If one of us had been knocked

down by the band, there wouldn't be much left now but bones."

"Isn't the peccary a wild boar, M. Sumichrast?"

"It is a pachyderm—consequently, a relation of the pig," answered my friend. "The wild boar is solitary, while the peccaries always go in flocks; this makes them formidable enemies in spite of their small size.

"What, small! this one is larger than Gringalet!"

"The wild boar is twice as big. A characteristic of the peccary is, that its tail is rudimentary, and the bristles spotted with black and white; moreover, only its legs are eatable."

L'Encuerado went round the edge of the lake in order to trace the course of the stream. We lost more than an hour in false channels, and the raft ran aground in a shallow.

When the sun had set, and all the birds were flying over us to their retreats, we landed to bivouac for the night.

A deep-toned roaring sound awoke me up with a start; the first thing I saw was Lucien, with his gun in his hand, crouching down close to Sumichrast. On the shore, about sixty yards from us, I saw a long tawny form, and two shining eyes. A second roar told me the name of our nocturnal visitor, whose voice I fancied I had heard in a dream.

"And where is l'Encuerado?" I asked my companion.

"He is crawling away to the other side."

A shot cut these words short; the animal gave another roar, and rushed into the jungle. We heard a noise like a scuffle, and then the jaguar again came in sight; it ran round and round, roaring with rage. A final bound brought it to within twenty paces of our camp fire, when it fell never to rise again.

"Hiou! hiou! Chanito."

This sound took a weight off **my mind, for I** could not
but feel alarmed for the safety **of l'Encuerado.**

"Ohé! ohé!" was responded.

Gringalet, who was let loose, ran towards the enormous
creature, and barked at it from a safe distance. The Indian
came up, with his gun upon his shoulder.

"The beast is justly mine, isn't it, Tatita, and I am still
the tiger-hunter?"

"Yes," I replied; "but let the tigers alone, if they will
allow you, and let us go to rest."

We were all going to lie down, when the roar of a tiger
again shook the air.

"Hallo!" cried my friend; "is your beast come to life
again?"

"No, Tatita Sumichrast; but my tiger is a tigress, and
her mate is come to see after her."

I told the Indian not to move.

"Let him do as he likes," said my companion; "he will
only disobey you."

Half an hour elapsed; all was profound silence, and we
could hear the slightest rustling of the leaves. Suddenly
there was the report of a gun, and, five minutes afterwards,
we greeted with "bravos" the triumphant "Hiou! hiou!"
of the Indian, who, streaming with water, came to dry himself at the fire.

"I was obliged to ford the stream," he said; "but his
lordship has got the ball between his two eyes this time."

"You are a brave fellow," responded Sumichrast, shaking hands with him.

"Now I shall sleep quietly," the Indian whispered to
Lucien.

Master Job, Gringalet, Janet, and Verdet, all had their
eyes wide open when I awoke at day-break. Lucien rose
just as I was starting for the water's edge and accompanied me.

An elegant bird with a long curved bill came and settled down on the bank; the boy remarked the beautiful bronze-colored plumage of the wader. I informed him it was an ibis.

"The Egyptian bird which devours serpents?"

"One of its kinsfolk," I replied; "the ibis feeds, generally speaking, on worms, mollusks, and even on sea-weed or aquatic plants. It may, perhaps, sometimes eat water-snakes; but as to feeding exclusively on reptiles, or destroying them systematically, that's quite another story."

We now reached the bivouac, and found my companions up, and l'Encuerado in a state of high excitement over his exploit.

Having drunk our coffee, we all turned up our sleeves, and set to work to skin our magnificent prizes. This difficult operation employed us all the morning, and was scarcely finished when I carried our baggage on board the raft, which was soon pushed off from the bank.

Our way lay through walls of the densest foliage, which often met overhead, while such was the awful stillness of the solitude, that we felt oppressed, and only spoke in a low voice.

The hour for rest had long passed, and yet no one proposed to land. The fact was, we wished some more animated resting-place; and though l'Encuerado, with his pole, shoved us onward with energy, the numerous bends hindered our progress, and it seemed as if night would surprise us still afloat. At last the palm-trees became more crowded, and the stream emerged from the forest, to cross a prairie; here the raft was moored under a canopy of creepers.

Our first care was to stretch the tigers' skins on the heated ground, and, while I was helping l'Encuerado, Sumichrast and Lucien went off in quest of our dinners. The fire had

"The banks of the river were covered with alligators."

been for some time burning, when **we** heard a distant gun-shot.

Sumichrast returned laden with **a** green iguana, and Lucien was dragging by a string a little alligator about thirty inches long.

" Look, **M. L'Encuerado !**" **cried the** boy ; " here is **an alligator** or **cayman, a relation of** the lizards, and **an enemy of man. This ugly young beast** has only baby-teeth, **so can not bite much. It** feeds on fish, otters, calves, and many **other animals. It** is an amphibious being, M. L'Encuerado, **a creature that lays** eggs like fowls, but buries them in the **sand, where the** sun has to hatch them ; it is a brute, too, which is so fond of man that it eats him whenever it has a chance.

" Take care it does not bite you," said I to the boy ; " how **did you** manage to catch it ?"

"**I pursued** it, thinking it was a big lizard ; M. Sumichrast called out to me not to handle it, and then tied this creeper round **its neck.**"

" You don't intend **to take it** away with you, I hope ?"

" No ; it is an ill-tempered creature, and is always anxious to use its teeth. I shall just show it to Master Job, and then let it go."

Neither Job nor his companions seemed flattered by this introduction, and the boy was disappointed when he deposited it at the water's edge ; for, instead of plunging in, as he expected, it made a semicircle, and ran off towards the forest.

" Don't young alligators know how to swim ?" he asked.

" Yes, Chanito ; but they do not **go** into the water till they are old enough to defend themselves against the big males, which would devour them."

The sun had scarcely risen, when I saw on the shore, at about ten paces from us, three monsters luxuriously stretched out. One of them, from sixteen to twenty feet long, with a brown and rough body, opened its enormous jaws and showed us its frightful teeth. I took Lucien by the hand to lead him nearer to the reptiles, the better to inspect them.   .

"I like tigers better than these creatures," said he; "certainly their roaring is frightful to listen to, but they are by no means so hideous."

"Look along there, M. Sumichrast!" cried Lucien, when we had again taken to our raft; "there are eyes floating on the water!"

"You are not mistaken; they are crocodile's eyes."

The child nestled up to me, and I encouraged him; but these dark eyes appearing in every direction, and following every movement of the raft, troubled him beyond expression.

The banks of the river were covered with alligators, with their mouths wide agape. Some of them glided down into the water and came near us, but the majority remained motionless, not caring to exert themselves. Lucien's fear began to calm down. He had so wished to see plenty of alligators; now he complained that there were too many.

"Look at that one," said Sumichrast, "climbing up that spit of land. He turns round with difficulty, and looks as if he scarcely had the use of his limbs. The fact is, that his body has no proper joints, and only moves in one piece. The best way, therefore, to escape from an alligator is to run up and down, making the turns short and rapid."

The stream had hitherto flowed almost on a level with its banks, now the latter became gradually higher, and we floated along under an arch of foliage. L'Encuerado happened to raise himself to point out to Lucien a tree covered with parrots, between whom and the Indian there immediately commenced a lively chatter. Diverted by this

" The Indian and his branch descended with a splash into the river."

amusing **conversation, none of us** perceived an enormous **branch, which** just **grazed** our heads but **upset our entertainer.** When he emerged from the water, instead of swimming towards us, l'Encuerado made his way to the bank, and began, with cutlass in hand, to hew and hack at the tree which had been the cause of his accident.

" If you're going to cut down that colossus," cried my friend, " we had better encamp here, for it's eight days' work at least."

"Only wait ten minutes more, at most, Tatita Sumichrast. It shall never be said that this great booby broke my head and then laughed at me, to the heart's delight of the parrots, who no doubt were the instigators of such conduct."

L'Encuerado, by the notches he had cut in the tree, could easily climb up to the lowest branch ; but in his haste he slipped and fell a second time into the water.

In **a** twinkling the Indian was up astride again on his branch, jabbering like an ape, and slashing his knife into it, when of a sudden it gave a loud crack, and he and it descended with a splash into the river. At this noise the parrots sent up a wild scream and flew off, while the branch floated past us to the ocean. Our companion climbed up again on the raft, and laughed so heartily at his defeat of the tree and the fright he had caused to the parrots, that Lucien soon joined in his gayety. He was, however, thoroughly exhausted, so lay down, when he slept the peaceful sleep of a child which has tired itself out with a fit of passion.

For two hours I managed the raft, and then l'Encuerado, awaking, resumed his post in silence. Suddenly there was **a** heavy tramping on the ground, the boughs moved, and the head of a wild bull appeared among the creepers. The animal surveyed us for a moment with its fierce eyes, and **then made off, bellowing** hoarsely.

The sight of this new denizen of the forest confirmed the omens as we had already read them, and soon, accordingly, there burst upon our view an immense savannah. We were just about to pass the last shrub on the bank of the river, when l'Encuerado suddenly brought the boat to a stand-still. I stood up and saw a herd of wild cattle moving rapidly down to that portion of the stream which we were about to pass.

"Look out!" cried Sumichrast; "this is better worth seeing than the crocodiles."

L'Encuerado landed, and, crossing the prairie, called us. I found him close to an enormous willow-tree. Without loss of time, Lucien, Sumichrast, and I climbed up among the branches, taking Gringalet with us; but the Indian preferred posting himself in a more isolated position.

"We shall have roast fillet of beef to-night," cried he, executing among the branches such a series of gambols that I feared he would finish by falling.

The cattle approached. The ground trembled under their feet, and we were deafened by their bellowing. One of them, a magnificent bull, with a black coat sprinkled with white spots, took the lead. The drove, which first trotted on, and then stopped to browse, followed its imperious-looking chief; the caymans, as if awakened by the uproar, assembled at the opening of the savannah, and numerous watchful eyes were to be seen on the surface of the water.

The wild drove halted at about fifty paces from the stream; the black and white bull advanced alone and, first leisurely taking a drink, plunged into the water; he reached the opposite bank, where he halted and turned right about. Then the entire drove, above which was hovering a cloud of horse-flies, dashed at full gallop into the stream to join their guide. Although the drove must have consisted of

"The entire drove . . . . dashed at full gallop into the stream."

hundreds, in less than a quarter of an hour there were not
left more than five or six on our side, and these seemed
afraid to cross. Suddenly a gun was fired, and one of the
animals came rushing past our tree with a jet of blood
flowing from his chest. Suddenly he stopped, groaned, and
sank down upon the ground. I cast a glance at l'Encuerado, who descended to the lowest branch, continuing his
gymnastic exercises. The young bulls on our side, frightened by the report of the gun, at last made up their minds
to cross; one of them, however, stopping to drink, was
seized by a crocodile, and gradually drawn under the water. A second disappeared in the middle of the stream;
and a third, after a fearful struggle, reached the bank.
The whole drove, goaded on by the horse-flies, then resumed their furious course, and were soon lost in the distance.

These cattle range the prairies in droves of sometimes
forty thousand, and were originally imported by the Spaniards.

CHAPTER XXXII.

THE next morning l'Encuerado started alone on the
raft; for we had resolved to cross the savannah on foot,
and thus escape, for an hour or two, the insects which took
advantage of our forced immobility in order to bleed us at
their leisure.

Flocks of black vultures hovered high up in the sky,
bending their course towards a spot not very far from the
river bed. Our curiosity led us in that direction, and in a

large hole, with perpendicular sides, about twelve yards wide, we saw several hundreds of these bare-necked gentry fighting over the carcass of a buffalo. We were retiring in disgust, when the vultures, who had not seemed the least alarmed at our presence, suddenly manifested fear, and, abandoning their prey, stood around in evident concern. A new guest had made its appearance in the sky, and soared round and round above us. It settled down heavily, and folded its black and white wings; the new-comer was the *Sarcoramphus papa* of the *savants*—a bird akin to the condor.

This king of the vultures, as the Indians call it, had a black tail, and white plumage on its back. Its neck was adorned with a ruff of pearl-gray feathers, and the top of its head was streaked in symmetrical lines with a dark down; on its yellow beak there was a fleshy protuberance, the utility of which ornithologists seek in vain to explain. The magnificent **bird** darted round **it a** domineering look, and, **advancing towards the prey,** began to feed. New **guests were incessantly arriving, but** they all kept their distance.

At last the *sarcoramphus* flew away, and immediately the vultures rushed *en masse* on the carcass, which soon disappeared under the crowd of beaks.

We now made for the raft, but the distance was greater than we had calculated; and, before going on board, it was highly necessary to free ourselves of the hundreds of *ticks* which we had collected in the savannah. These insects are black, and as small as fleas, and gather in masses at the extremities of plants, ready to attach themselves to any animal that brushes against them. They then bury their claws in the flesh, and greedily suck the blood. It is a tedious job to pick off one by one these troublesome parasites, **which cause** an almost unbearable itching.

About five o'clock in the evening, the raft came to shore in a bay shaded by palm-trees. L'Encuerado hastened to stretch out his tigers' skins, and, as night was at hand, we contented ourselves with the remains of a tortoise. The Indian, who had walked but little, cocked his gun and strolled along the edge of the river. In about a quarter of an hour he returned, looking pale and excited.

"Have you been bitten by a serpent?" I cried.

"No, Tatita," he replied, quite out of breath; "something worse than that! I have seen *it?*"

"What?" I exclaimed.

"A ghost!" said the Indian in a low tone, crossing himself.

"Pluck up your spirits," said I to the Indian; "if you have, we'll kill it to-morrow."

"You can't kill *it*, Tatita."

"With ordinary bullets, no; but those which Sumichrast knows how to prepare will soon settle him."

My curiosity was raised; for this ghost was an animal called a tapir, which the Indians believe possessed of supernatural powers; and, as I had never met with one, I was anxious that we should come across it.

"And didn't you aim at it?" cried my friend.

"No; I ran away," replied the fearless tiger-hunter.

Thus l'Encuerado, whom the evening before we had seen braving tigers, crocodiles, and wild cattle, now trembled at the mere idea of facing an inoffensive animal, which was only a relation of the peccaries, with a snout terminated by a non-prehensile proboscis, yet to which his imagination attributed certain demoniac qualities. He that night utterly refused to go to rest; at the least rustling of the leaves he expected to see the ghost appear. Instead of directly opposing his error—which I knew would be of no use—I endeavored to convince him that my power far surpassed that of the object of his dread.

"The reeds were pushed aside."

"If it wasn't for that," I urged on him, "do you think I would permit Lucien to sleep in so dangerous a neighborhood?"

Sumichrast gave the Indian two bullets, and solemnly told him that with these projectiles he would surely kill the object of his dread if he aimed straight. L'Encuerado gradually recovered his self-possession; the idea of slaying in one of its most formidable shapes the cause of his superstition excited his self-esteem, and he went to sleep, and no doubt dreamt of his next day's exploit.

At day-break we walked down to the confluence of the two rivers; in front of us stretched a broad prairie covered with thick grass. If the tapir had not quenched its thirst in the night, it would be sure to reappear; therefore Lucien and Sumichrast turned to the left close by the stream, while I and my servant crouched down behind the trunk of a tree at the entrance of the forest.

We remained in this position for more than an hour, when suddenly the reeds were pushed aside, and two of the looked-for pachyderms came out together on the greensward.

L'Encuerado kept on crossing himself without intermission.

"Fire," said I, in a low voice, "and aim straight at the forehead."

The gun went off, and the tapirs decamped; but one of them fell on the ground before it could enter the water; it was dead ere we reached it.

"You have killed the object of your dread," said Lucien, who ran up to examine the curious animal.

"Yes, Chanito, thanks to the enchanted bullets."

L'Encuerado having positively refused to touch the tapir, Sumichrast undertook to cut it up, as we much wished to taste its flesh. All our efforts to induce the Indian to do

likewise were fruitless, and his ingenious mind found a re-
tort to all our arguments. The flesh of the animal reminded us a little of that of the peccary, although it was less
highly flavored.

About midday the tigers' skins were taken up, and the
raft was soon floating over the combined streams. We had
at first thought of proceeding in this way as far as the
Gulf of Mexico; but the season was now too far advanced

to admit of such an excursion. We at length made up our
minds that the next day we should abandon our raft, and
return by the shortest route to our starting-point.

At dawn of day our bivouac was enlivened by hundreds
of birds. L'Encuerado cut the mooring line of the raft,
and let it float down the stream, thanking it at the same
time for the services it had rendered us, and wishing it
prosperity in its lonely voyage to the ocean.

As I stood watching the frail bark gliding away, two

"The deer sank down under the weight of a puma."

herons perched upon it, and it soon glided out of sight laden with its winged passengers.

We were all ready to start; the "Tapir River," as Lucien had named it, we bid adieu to with three hurrahs, and our little party set off, following Sumichrast, who carried Master Job perched on his shoulder.

Our way lay in part through a prairie, where the heat was overpowering, and in part through palm-tree woods, infested with mosquitoes. At last, overcome by fatigue, we felt compelled to halt and bivouac for the night.

As we were arranging our bivouac next night, l'Encuerado saw a crayfish, and set off with Lucien to try and catch some of them. I and Sumichrast started on the trail of some deer we had seen bounding past. We had scarcely gone more than five hundred yards before we climbed a hill beyond which a savannah was spread out before us as far as the eye could reach, the high grass of which looked almost like ripe wheat.

Sumichrast, who had halted, summoned me by an imitation of the cry of an owl. I hastily and noiselessly joined him, when he pointed out to me, among the trees, a deer quietly browsing, which would no doubt pass within gunshot. I stood watching by my friend, following with anxiety all the movements of the graceful animal, for twice it threw up its head and showed some vague uneasiness. Sumichrast, fearing that it was about to make off, was getting ready to fire, when the deer gave a bound and sank down under the weight of a puma, which had sprung upon it. I fired at the carnivore, which the ferocious brute responded to by a loud roar, then, dragging its prey a distance of about fifty yards, it suddenly made off. The venison of the deer, and more than thirty small crayfish caught by Lucien and his friend, were a godsend to our larder, and amply made up for the short commons of previous occasions.

We watched the sun go down from the top of the hill, and descried on the horizon the bluish line of the Cordillera, with the volcano of Orizava towering up towards the west. Henceforth this mountain was to be our guide while crossing the immense savannah, an undertaking which filled me with dread.

"Shall we cross that great plain?" asked Lucien.

"Yes, Master Sunbeam, it is the shortest way to Orizava."

"How many hours shall we be in doing it?"

"Hours? We shall be three or four days at least."

At this moment a storm, which we saw impending, burst over us, and we hurried pell-mell to our hut. For four hours the heavens continued to pour down, amidst thunder and lightning, a perfect deluge, and we were all, in spite of our shelter, soaked to the skin. The clouds broke up, and a few stars shone out; about midnight the clear sky regained its azure tint, while the moon dimly lighted up the landscape. L'Encuerado, who slept through it, now woke up to help us to rekindle the fire and get ready a cup of coffee; after enjoying which, and changing our clothes, we all retired to rest.

In the morning we held a council to deliberate about the route, and, after some debate, we agreed to l'Encuerado's proposal, and decisively resolved to cross the savannah direct.

It would have been madness to travel, so heavily laden as we were, under the rays of a vertical sun; so I proposed not to start till the evening, and that henceforth we should travel by night, a plan which quite rejoiced Lucien.

After the baggage had been equally divided, and every thing that was useless thrown away, I counted the maize-cakes, our only food, and found we had enough victuals for several days, besides crayfish, and the flesh of an armadillo.

"While the moon dimly lighted up the landscape."

We filled our gourds up to the necks with water and corked them tightly, then lay down in the shade to gain strength for our next stage.

About four o'clock l'Encuerado called us to dinner, and by sunset we started, home-bound, each with his allotted burden over his shoulder. Sumichrast, with Lucien following, led the way.

" Well, Master Sunbeam, you are nearly as much lost in the stalks here as you were in the forest. Are your boots well greased ? We shall have many days of hard walking."

" Where are all the wild cattle and horses ?"

" Not far off, I hope ! first, because they would guide us to the ponds and the streams where they drink; and, secondly, we may need them to furnish us with food."

" Then shall we find nothing to shoot here ?"

" Nothing at all where the grass is so high as this; animals seldom venture into the midst of these solitudes."

" And the birds ?"

" They are never to be seen unless the grass grows close to the ground, excepting birds of prey; and they, perhaps, are hovering over us now, hoping we may become food for them."

For more than five hours we kept on without stopping. I then proposed a halt. By lying down on the grass we at once found a soft bed, and Lucien and the rest of us soon went to sleep. Before daylight l'Encuerado awoke us, when, after taking our bearings, he undertook to be our guide. As the first sunbeam appeared, we halted to form our camp and erect our tent. We cleared a large space, and a hole in the ground served as a fire-place. Our crayfish remained perfectly fresh, and while l'Encuerado was broiling them, I and Sumichrast watched the direction of the flames, as it was highly important for our safety that the savannah should not be set on fire. The meal dispatched, and the fire extinguished, we squatted down under the shadow of the grass, and resigned ourselves to sleep.

I woke about midday, nearly roasted by the sun, which had now replaced the shade. Calling my companions, so that they might change their position, a new arrangement of our covering gave us more shelter, and soon once more all were asleep; but in the short intervening time Lucien began to repeat to the parrots the names of Hortense and Emile.

At midnight, l'Encuerado shouldered his load and took the lead. The second night passed like the first, and we travelled at least eight leagues.

Our third night was interrupted by five or six halts, but we plodded on till dawn. At the first gleam of light, I examined the horizon; there was nothing but bluish-looking mountains to the right, and in every other direction only the gloomy and deserted plain. On this day we had to be satisfied with maize-cakes; but the hope of at length reaching the woods cheered every one.

"One night more," said l'Encuerado and Sumichrast, "and then we shall have rest and abundance."

The fourth day's march was much more wearisome, especially to poor Lucien, who, still uncomplaining, yet commenced to limp dreadfully.

The day broke, and I again examined the horizon, but could see nothing except the sky and grass.

"I am afraid we are not going the right way," I said to l'Encuerado. "God grant we have not been walking at random for these three days."

The Indian stood up on his basket, and carefully examined the outline of the mountains.

"We are in the right path," said he, positively; "the savannah is very wide, that is all."

" Lucien began to repeat to the parrots the names of Hortense and Emile."

L'Encuerado's assurances only half convinced me. Lucien's feet were so covered with blisters that he could scarcely put them to the ground. Unexpectedly I discovered that he was weeping silently; so I took him up in my arms, when he soon fell asleep.

In this emergency, l'Encuerado, with the straps and poles of our tent, managed to make a kind of litter, upon which we placed the boy. Sumichrast helped me to carry him, and though we had to stop hundreds of times to rest

our arms, still we accomplished several leagues. The day had scarcely begun to dawn, when I again examined the horizon; alas! nothing was changed, and the only things I saw were flocks of black vultures, which are not generally regarded as a happy omen.

Owing to an accident by which our reserve gourd was burst and the contents spilt, we were tormented by thirst, and the only food we had to eat only half restored our rapidly-failing strength. In another day all our maize-cakes

21

would be exhausted, and the rice was of no use without water. Fatigue gradually dispelled these gloomy thoughts, and we fell asleep.

I awoke about four o'clock in the afternoon, and was dismayed to find that l'Encuerado had deserted us, accompanied by Gringalet.

Having passed a whole night in useless waiting, hoping for his reappearing, we resolved to pursue our journey. So we put all the baggage into one heap, and set Janet and Verdet at liberty, leaving them the sack of rice, which we could not carry. Then, loaded with our guns and gourds —alas! almost empty—we prepared to start on our journey without having the courage to undeceive Lucien, who thought we were going to meet his friend.

At last, having examined the horizon carefully, I placed Master Job on my shoulder, and, led by Sumichrast, Lucien being borne between us, we pursued our course.

CHAPTER XXXIII.

THIRST.—L'ENCUERADO'S RETURN.—THE DESCRIPTION OF
HIS JOURNEY.—JANET, VERDET, AND ROUGETTE.—HUNT-
ING WILD HORSES.—OUR LAST ADVENTURE.—THE RE-
TURN.

THE undertaking was beyond our strength. Panting
and suffocated with heat, and tormented by thirst, we
were compelled to desist.

Lucien's feet pained him dreadfully, but the brave little
fellow kept constantly saying, "I should be all right if I
could only have a good drink."

My friend several times gave him his gourd to wet his
tongue from, but it was only temporary relief. Night came
on, and we began to prepare for our almost hopeless march.
A mouthful of brandy gave us a little artificial strength.

So even before sunset, I mounted Lucien on my shoulder, and we recommenced our journey.

Twenty times I was forced to take breath, and twenty times I struggled on again; but happily the grass became shorter, which was a good omen, and hope revived.

Sumichrast now lifted up Lucien, and walked on with a determined step. I took up Master Job, and followed closely in his rear. We heard a dull noise, and stopped to listen. It was the report of a gun, and by-and-by we heard a horse galloping, and then a well-known bark.

"That's Gringalet," said Lucien.

"Hiou! hiou! hiou! Chanito!"

Our emotion scarcely allowed us to answer; the Indian sprang from his horse, and, running towards the child, pressed him to his heart, and then, stretching out his arms, fell senseless to the ground. I rushed towards him and opened his gourd—it was full! With the help of Sumichrast I poured a few drops of brandy between his teeth. He gradually regained his senses, and looked at us in surprise. He was exhausted from hunger and fatigue.

"If I had eaten or drunk," he said, simply, "I should have wanted to go to sleep, and then what would have become of you? But my hunger and thirst spurred me on, so that I have not lost a moment."

"My good fellow!" I answered, "you ought to have taken something to restore your strength; for if it had failed, what would have become of us?"

L'Encuerado did not hear me; he had just fallen into a deep sleep, and we soon followed his example. When we awoke, l'Encuerado mounted the steed he had brought, and, taking Lucien up in front, led us back to the baggage.

"Why did you start without letting us know?" asked Sumichrast.

" Because you would have prevented me from following

" We had to cross some muddy marshes."

out my plan. **I was convinced** there were woods and flocks
not far ahead of us, and as I feared **not** the sun for myself,
I started as soon as you were all fast asleep, having forti-
fied myself for the journey with a drop of the cognac. I
often longed, as I proceeded, to lie down and rest, but then
I thought of Chanito, and ran **on** faster than ever. With-
out knowing **why, I stumbled, and I** think I must have fall-
en **asleep. When I opened my eyes the sun** was set, and
Gringalet **was licking me with his tongue.** I got up, sta-
pefied **as I** was, and ran forward, **without** halting, to the
verge of a wood. I dashed in among **the** trees, and in less
than **a** quarter of an hour I came upon a great lake, and
horses and buffaloes running wild. My strength, however,
began to fail, and it took me more than four hours to catch
this mustang," continued the Indian, looking down on his
steed, "but I soon made him know his master was on his
back."

Having returned to our bivouac to recover our treasures,
we resolved to start immediately, as the sky was obscured
by clouds.

Next day l'Encnerado **set to work** to provide us all with
horses. Having prepared **a lasso,** the agile Indian darted
off at full gallop towards a drove which were grazing some
distance off; and by night had captured five of their number. Two days, however, were spent in breaking our
mounts and rendering them docile; but as our stores were
visibly diminishing, and we were considerably freshened
up, it became highly necessary for us to start.

Next morning our little cavalcade crossed the plains and
woods almost **at** a gallop. The blue mountains in front
looked higher and higher, and the outlines of the volcano
grew more defined.

The second day of **our** march we had to cross some muddy marshes, in which **our** horses mired **up** to their bellies.

On reaching firm ground again, we hoped to perceive a human dwelling, but the trees restricted our view.

At last, in the afternoon of the third day, just as we were endeavoring to go round two wild bulls engaged in a combat, a horseman came out in front of us, halted for a moment as if in indecision, and then turned short round and rode off, after having fired his gun at us.

We hurried on our horses, making sure of soon coming upon a *hacienda*, when we heard another gunshot, and a

bullet whistled by our ears. The Indian rode swiftly towards the would-be murderer, but he went off at full gallop. In spite of my cries, the Indian fired at him, and horse and man rolled upon the ground.

The fool had mistaken us for horse-stealers; and the Indian, after soundly thrashing him, at my entreaty let him off.

When night came, we were at the foot of the mountains; so all we had to do was to join the main road from Vera

Cruz to Mexico. Our horses were **now set at** liberty, af-
ter having been overwhelmed with compliments and polite
speeches by l'Encuerado. The brave animals at first ap-
peared undecided which way to go, and remained without
moving, keeping **their** noses to the wind. At **last one** of
them neighed **and darted off, when the** rest followed **at** the
top of their speed.

We were now scarcely twelve leagues from Orizava, and
almost painfully impatient to reach **it.** Woods, mountains,
valleys were crossed with a kind of feverish haste, **and** the
approach of night alone forced us to bivouac.

At about three o'clock in the morning, Lucien began to
reproach us for our laziness.

Wood-cutters now passed, who saluted me by name, and
one guided **us for** more than a league, astonished **at** l'Encuerado's tales. He left us at the foot of a mountain, the
last **we** had to cross, the steep acclivity of which somewhat
damped **our ardor.**

Lucien was the first to arrive on the plateau. A few
steps farther, **and the town** of Orizava lay stretched in
peaceful repose **at our feet.**

As the young traveller contemplated the town in which
was his home, involuntary tears moistened his cheeks; **he
stretched out** his arms towards it and sobbed.

All **of us,** however, shared his **emotion to** some extent.
Now that we were safe, we rejoiced that I had undertaken
this expedition. I thanked God for **His** manifest protection, and, for the last time, gave the word to start.

As we descended the mountain, the town became more
distinctly visible. **L'Encuerado** could name the churches
and **streets; at** last Lucien discovered his home, which was
easily recognizable by the magnificent orange-tree. **In**
order to satisfy the boy's impatience, we made our way

through a steep ravine. Our little party reached the valley just as the bells were ringing for vesper prayers.

The sun was setting, and we were wrapped in obscurity;
Indians kept crossing our path at every step, and the lamps
were here and there shining out through the dark. The
Rio Bianco barred our passage; but large stones, placed
at intervals in the river, enabled us to cross it almost dry-
shod. Then Gringalet suddenly barked, and darted off
like an arrow.

Twenty minutes after, we entered Orizava by some of
the side streets, to prevent a crowd following at our heels.
When we were about fifty paces from our house, Lucien
and l'Encuerado darted off at a racing pace; they found
all the inmates of our home assembled on the threshold.
Gringalet had announced our arrival.

When I entered the court-yard, Lucien and his mother
were sobbing in one another's arms; Emile, Hortense, and
Amelie were grouped round the basket, on which Janet
and Verdet were sitting. I noticed, standing in a corner,
the cases which had been intrusted to Torribio.

L'Encuerado came and leaned against the door of the
room, twisting the broad brim of his hat quite out of
shape.

"If it had not been for him," I said to my wife, "we
should have died!"

The brave Indian stooped and kissed the hands of his
mistress.

My children, who had gone out for a few minutes, now
burst into the room; they had ransacked the basket, and
were disputing for poor Rougette, who was placed in the
fountain in the garden. Janet and Verdet, perched on the
back of a chair, stammered the names of Hortense and
Emile, as well as could be hoped. The two children became pale with pleasure and surprise.

Just at this moment, Master Job, introduced by Gringa-let, came and sat down on the carpet, and allowed the children to caress him.

It was delightful to sit down to table surrounded by all the beings dearest to my heart. L'Encuerado kept praising Lucien, who continued exciting his mother's emotion by relating to her the principal incidents of our journey.

"I am sure, mamma, that you will let me go with papa another time," said Lucien. "Our collection is not finished yet, and it must be completed sooner or later."

The young naturalist might be recognized in this question, for the collector is ever insatiable.

His poor mother shook her head, and embraced her boy without replying. But her silence seemed to show that she would not willingly expose her son to the perils of a fresh journey.